VISIONS

LAURA N. ANILE

This edition published by GlassHouse Publishing 2015

A Cataloguing-in-Publication entry is available from the National Library of Australia.

Print ISBN: 9780992279011
Ebook ISBN: 9780992279028

For my family whose unwavering support made this book possible.

Thank you for believing in me.

"The most beautiful thing we can experience is the mysterious. It is the source of all true art and science. He to whom this emotion is a stranger, who can no longer pause to wonder and stand rapt in awe, is as good as dead: his eyes are closed."

Albert Einstein

PROLOGUE

THE CHILD BEGAN SCREAMING, a scream that made your blood run cold. Her mother instantly tried to placate her, eventually smothering her mouth when those attempts failed. That only intensified the screaming, agitating the girl more.

The gunman flew into a rage, demanding the girl be silenced before *he* silenced her. His hand twitched in fury. *Could he honestly harm a child?* I wondered, as fear crashed over me. The interminable screaming shrilled through the bank as the girl thrashed in her mother's arms. My skin tingled, the air electrified with trepidation.

The gunman pointed the weapon directly at the child, narrowing his eyes. A growl erupted from his throat as his feeble control shattered and his finger pulled back the trigger.

There was no time left to decide, to think. There was only time to act.

Instinctively, I jumped in front of the young girl as I heard the deafening crack of the gun being fired.

I jumped so violently that I awoke, drenched in sweat.

1

AN UNWELCOME GIFT

I COULDN'T BE DREAMING, my eyes were open. But somehow what I was seeing was not the living room in my apartment, where I was sitting. I rubbed my eyes, trying to refocus. What on earth was going on? I could still hear the television, just a quiet humming in the background. All of the recent late hours at the office were clearly beginning to take their toll.

It was night, the darkness cloaking someone standing in the shadows. I started to recognize the setting; it was the rooftop of my apartment building. I was disappointed in myself, if I was daydreaming so vividly (which I hoped I was doing, as opposed to potentially losing my mind), couldn't I have come up with something a little more interesting? Walking along the Ponte Vecchio in Florence, visiting the Eiffel Tower in Paris or sitting on the London Eye perhaps? My rooftop wasn't exactly a place I longed to visit.

I pinched my eyes shut, but the image refused to fade. A shiver crawled up my spine. All of my internal alarm bells were ringing—loudly. Something wasn't right. Keeping my eyes closed, I rubbed my temples and took a deep breath. Seeing something that wasn't there was more disconcerting with my eyes open.

The image became clearer, like I was suddenly thrust forward. I couldn't escape it, held hostage inside my own mind. My heart was racing, along with my thoughts. Tensing, I tried to work out what my fragmented mind had mysteriously conjured.

Who was that in front of me? From his stature and physique, I could tell it was a man, but his back was turned. I caught a glimpse of his face as he staggered, a half-empty bottle in his hand. I recognized him as my neighbor from across the hall. Jeremy didn't appear to be much older than me, I pegged him to be in his late twenties. Until about a month ago, he'd lived with his girlfriend, Becca. From what I could tell—the walls were thin and she never lowered her voice when she was worked up—she'd moved out a few weeks after he'd lost his job. Apparently, she didn't like that they no longer ate in expensive restaurants or went clubbing, claiming he wasn't 'fun' anymore. Becca was a lot younger than Jeremy and being supportive was evidently not her strong suit.

He'd looked so defeated when I'd occasionally passed him in the hall. I wanted to tell him that it was only a rough patch, and things would look up. But we'd only ever exchanged pleasantries and I didn't want to pry, nor did I want to let on that I'd overheard their arguments. So I'd said nothing.

Why on earth was I visualizing Jeremy on the roof?

I pondered whether it was because I was subconsciously feeling guilty. *I should try to talk to him.*

The image propelled me forward once more, making me dizzy. From this angle, I could see the moisture on Jeremy's cheeks glistening in the moonlight. He took another swig from his bottle and pulled his phone out of his back pocket. Instead of making a call, he put on some music, turning the volume all the way up then setting the phone on the ledge in front of him. The song had a strong beat and soon he began to sway to the music. But his balance wasn't what it should've been, and he was stumbling more than dancing.

My drunken neighbor throwing a party-of-one on the roof. Not exactly riveting. I tried to break free of my mental prison. I rubbed my eyelids, consciously channeling all of my thoughts into a mental picture of my living room. A sense of satisfaction washed over me as the rooftop image became hazy around the edges. My mind was my trophy, I valued it above all else. *I am still in control,* I assured myself, with focused concentration. *My mental faculties are intact.* My head throbbed from the war raging inside but finally the nebulous image began to fade.

Breathing a sigh of relief, my eyelids fluttered open before my heart skipped a beat and I was precipitously pulled back into the vision before me.

Jeremy had climbed up onto the ledge. *Was he thinking about jumping?* This strange hallucination felt so real that I was nervous about him standing in such a precarious position, with no barrier to protect him from falling.

No, Jeremy, it's not worth it! I mentally screamed, all thoughts of my living room gone.

With a tenuous grip on the bottle, he threw both of his arms up into the air and shouted, "I'm king of the world!" Laughing, he took another drink and snorted, "Yeah, right."

Gazing behind him, he shifted his feet in an attempt to climb down, having achieved his childish goal of re-enacting the famous scene from *Titanic.* I mentally chastised him for such reckless behavior. My palms were sweaty and my heart beat erratically. I needed to get a grip on reality.

Shaking my head, I consciously slowed my breathing and tried once more to concentrate on my living room to break the spell I was under. No more wine for me.

It felt like it happened in the space of a heartbeat.

A bird swooped down towards his head. Although it never actually touched him, he was startled and lost his grip on the bottle. His natural instinct to reach for it caused him to lose his already tenuous footing. The look of sudden realization and depth of terror in his eyes pierced my soul. Desperately trying to regain his balance, he flapped his arms wildly. I couldn't help but notice the irony that he resembled a bird trying to take flight, except, of course, he couldn't fly.

Subconsciously I had leaned forward, wanting to reach for him, but as I outstretched my hand, he disappeared. With a scream of horror I realized he'd fallen from the ledge. Startled, I snapped out of the vision as my eyes refocused on my living room. Panting, I wiped the tears streaming down my cheeks. *What had just happened?*

I looked around me, regaining my bearings. I struggled to think of a logical explanation for why my mind was playing tricks on me. The only cause I could think of was the evening's mixture of wine and spicy food, compounded by a lack of sleep. Yes, that had to be it. No lasting damage. But why such a strange hallucination?

Was my subconscious trying to tell me to pay more attention to Jeremy? That he was perhaps more vulnerable than I'd realized?

If this was somehow an inexplicable result of repressed concern or guilt, I wanted to assuage it quickly. I looked at the clock. It was nearly 9:00 P.M. *Not too late to go and check up on him,* I thought. I'd invite him over this weekend.

I went across the hall and knocked on the door of apartment 302. No answer. Perhaps he'd gone out or gone to bed early. I shouldn't disturb him. But I knocked again automatically, as if some unknown magnetic force were pulling me towards the door. I could tell the light was on inside from the faint glow under the door. I knocked three more times. No answer.

My heart thumped heavily in my chest and gooseflesh covered my arms. I told myself that I was being ridiculous, but that same gravitational pull that kept me at the door started pulling me towards the stairs to the roof. I shook my head, like that would somehow shake the ominous feeling I had. I trotted back to my apartment, only to stand frozen with my hand on the doorknob, fighting the urge to turn my feet back around. *What am I doing?* I scolded myself.

I went in and let the door shut behind me. I made it halfway to the kitchen before a chill crawled across my skin, making every nerve-ending tingle. Images of Jeremy on the roof assaulted me and turned my stomach in knots. *This is ridiculous.* But even as I thought the words, I turned and grabbed the cardigan lying on the back of the couch.

As I climbed the stairs thinking about how creepy it would be up there in the dark, I assured myself that I only needed to take one quick look—and no one needed to know that I'd completely lost my mind. My heart rate quickened with each step, the echo in the stairwell reminiscent of a steady drum beat accenting the feeling of foreboding. More than once, I considered turning back, but my feet kept moving upwards, obediently marching to the drum. I justified the absurdity of the endeavor with the knowledge that unless I checked, I wouldn't be able to get it out of my mind. And what I wanted to do more than anything was to forget all about the events of the evening, go to bed and never order anything from *Spicy Joe's* again.

The door to the roof loomed in front of me, mocking, daring. The stairwell fell eerily silent. I tensed as I grabbed the handle, almost expecting to hear the crash of cymbals. Squaring my shoulders, I slowly opened the door, holding it ajar with my foot as I peered around it. One quick peek to confirm that I was totally insane and I was out of there. I couldn't see anything in the darkness and with a sigh of relief I turned to exit. As I did, I caught sight of a faint reflection. I stopped and squinted my eyes to try and make it out.

Holy crap, there was something there. *Someone* there.

My mind started racing. It could be a psycho serial killer peeping into the building across the street for all I knew. I certainly didn't want to make his day by gift-wrapping myself on a darkened roof, just like all those horror movies when the blond cheerleader runs *away* from the exit and you think she's so stupid she doesn't deserve to live. But despite the fact that I wanted to run as fast as I could, my feet remained frozen. *What if. . . ?* I could barely even think the words. What if it really *was* Jeremy? I was reluctant to go forward to investigate; if I let go of the door I might as well put on the cheerleading uniform and hold up a neon sign flashing VULNERABLE AND ALONE—COME AND GET ME. I shuddered at the thought.

As I was deliberating my options, the man staggered, revealing a glimpse of his profile in the soft light reflected from the neighboring building. Seeing the bottle in his right hand, I gasped and a shiver ran down my spine. This was exactly the scene from my hallucination. *Exactly.* How was that *possible?* I swallowed. Possible or not, Jeremy was here.

I pinched my arm to make sure I was awake, then shook my head at how silly that was. I was here and I couldn't ignore the fact that Jeremy shouldn't be alone. The darkness of the night enveloped him, the enfolding shadows seeming to reflect his inner turmoil. Despite not knowing him very well, I could tell he was kind and gentle, and right now, he needed a friend. I took a deep breath and removed my foot from behind the door. It slammed shut with a thud of finality, echoing through the chilled night air. Jeremy jumped, whipping his head around to identify the source of the intrusion.

"Is that you, Jeremy?" I called out, trying to sound casual, but the high pitch of my voice betrayed me.

"Huh?" Jeremy sounded surprised, and nervous, like a child who was interrupted doing something that they didn't want anyone to see. He squinted, and I could see him reaching for my name. "Um . . . Annabelle?"

Close enough. "Yes, it's me." I tried to sound cheerful.

"Wotcha doin' up here?" he slurred.

"I . . . ah . . . sometimes come up here to look at the stars and think." A flimsy excuse, since a blanket of fog prevented any stargazing, but it was the best I had. I moved forward to stand next to him and could see him more clearly in the pale light. His thick dark hair was disheveled, and his usually well-kept facial stubble had grown longer. His tall frame towered over me but I noticed his hazel eyes were bloodshot.

"I've never seen you up here beshore." He furrowed his brow. "Before," he corrected himself, enunciating the word carefully and looking proud that he'd managed it.

I wrapped my cardigan more tightly around me. I hated lying. "Ah, it's been a while since I've had anything really bothering me. I only come up here when I need answers."

He stood up straighter and nodded in understanding. I smiled to myself, impressed that I'd lied so convincingly given the circumstances. If Jeremy had known me at all, he'd know that this would be the last place I'd come, at night in the dark, unless I was carrying an Uzi and had five armed guards surrounding me.

"What's bothering you?" he asked, his eyes softening.

Panic seized me, I hadn't pre-empted the question. What was I going to say, that what was bothering me was the fact that I'd somehow ended up on the roof at night to find a neighbor I'd already mysteriously seen fall—potentially to his death—all from the comfort of my living room? Not even I could believe it, so how could he?

I stuck with a watered down version of the truth, leaving out all the crazy. He probably wouldn't remember any of this tomorrow anyway. I just had to distract him long enough to make sure he *had* a tomorrow.

"It's hard to explain. Have you ever felt like without warning your life was abruptly spinning out of control? Like you'd ended up somewhere without having any idea how you'd gotten there?

Like you were on your way to Buckingham Palace and you ended up at the witch's house in *Hansel and Gretel* instead?"

Hansel and Gretel? Seriously? *He wasn't going to want to abandon his pity party to talk to an idiot who spoke about fairy tales!* I scolded myself. The next thing I'd tell him was that I was upset because I'd lost my shoe at midnight and my carriage had turned into a pumpkin. Sheesh. If I was going to sound like an imbecile, I might as well have told him the truth. Nope. On second thought, I planned to never say that aloud. *Ever.* If anyone at my law firm heard that, they'd have me committed.

He looked at me for a long moment, appraising me. I squirmed under the intensity of his gaze. He'd probably *want* to jump just to get away from the crazy neighbor in a minute. I needed a save. I decided to say something he could actually relate to.

"So, mind if I crash the party? At least no one will complain about the music. But no re-enacting *Titanic* while I'm here. We know what happened to Leonardo at the end of the movie." I laughed nervously, fidgeting with my hair.

He raised his eyebrows and looked down at the phone in his hand. It was then that it occurred to me that I'd interrupted him about to put on the music. The only sounds on the roof came from the rustling of the wind and the distant noise of the traffic below. He looked at me curiously, cocking his head to one side.

Okay, that was weird. I've just told him what he was about *to do. How do I explain that? Think.*

I laughed again, and it sounded awkward even to my ears. I rushed on, trying to mask my embarrassment. "I mean, isn't that what all you guys do? If it's not re-enacting that scene from *Titanic*, it's the one from *A Few Good Men* with Jack Nicholson telling Tom Cruise, 'You can't handle the truth.'" I paused, acknowledging my Jack Nicholson impersonation had just bombed and this was going from bad to worse. Flushed, my nervous rambling kicked into overdrive. "And since we're on a rooftop, the *Titanic* scene seemed the more obvious choice. You know, the ledge, the height, the scenery." *Shut up, shut up, shut up.*

The intensity of his gaze unnerved me. The momentary silence was disrupted by my continued babbling. Surprisingly, the silence was more unsettling than my maundering.

"So, before I rudely interrupted, were you celebrating or commiserating?" Maybe I could get *him* to talk.

He deflected the question. "Not celebrating. Just needed some air." He spoke slowly—obviously the lingering affect of the alcohol—but his speech was surprisingly improved. "Why is your life spinning out of control?"

Oh, no you don't, buddy. Clever, but no cigar. I wasn't here to spill my secrets. And clearly, neither was he. I gave him a mischievous smile. "I'll tell you mine, if you tell me yours."

A half-smile touched his lips. I took that as my cue, hoping he'd be more receptive to my eagerness to get off the roof. "I'll tell you what. How about instead of swapping sob stories in the cold, we go back downstairs. You can come and hang out at my apartment if you like—we can watch some bad reality TV. That always makes me feel better about my own life," I joked. Ordinarily I'd never let a guy I didn't know into my apartment, but my instincts told me I'd be safe with Jeremy. "And call me Isy."

He paused only a moment before answering. "Sounds good to me. You can call me Jez." This time when he smiled, it reached his eyes.

2

ABNORMAL IS THE NEW BLACK

WHEN I FINALLY got to bed that night, sleep evaded me. A million thoughts were running through my mind.

A mere hallucination I could deal with. Worrisome, yes, but it was explainable and—pending the embargo on *Spicy Joe's* in the future—avoidable. *But how could a hallucination possibly come to fruition?* There was no scientific explanation I could think of. After fitfully tossing and turning, I finally chalked it up to some kind of weird coincidence or intuition. If I told my friends about this, they would surely think I was mad. I decided this was something best kept to myself. Seeing things that weren't there was my definition of *crazy*, and if that was what was happening to me, then I'd at least try to keep up the pretense that it wasn't.

I was honestly glad that I was able to help Jeremy. Now I just had to force myself to stop questioning the how or why. Despite my inquisitive nature, this was one time I didn't want to probe too deeply, in fear of inadvertently opening up a Pandora's box of the mystical variety. I convinced myself that the most sensible thing to do would be to forget it. I would keep a closer eye on Jeremy to make sure he was okay, but I reassured myself that I was only being neighborly.

I was finally able to drift off about an hour before my alarm went off. The radio vanquished the peaceful silence and I groaned at the idea of having to drag myself out of bed. I had a busy day ahead. Today was the day that the Federal Trade Commission's Bureau of Competition ruled whether the merger I'd been working on for weeks would be cleared to proceed.

I had been at Barkley Robinson Wade, one of San Francisco's largest and most prestigious law firms, for three years, specializing in antitrust and competition law. Working at Barkleys definitely had its perks, a firm with those kinds of resources could afford to be generous. We had kitchen staff who prepared dinner when we were working back late (which was often) and everything we wanted at our fingertips, including butlers to bring our coffee during video conference calls. Of course, that came at a price.

Working a sixty-hour week was the norm and working well into the night was certainly not uncommon. Lawyers do not have a reputation of being the most easygoing group of people. We were trained to be critical, objective, skeptical and mistrusting, with only the highest standards. Anything less than perfection was unacceptable.

You could put a brilliant fifty-page document together with only one small error in it, and that one small error would be the only thing that a well-trained lawyer would focus on. This impossible standard led to high levels of stress, and in turn, intolerance for the same small errors of others. Despite all of that, there was a certain pride that came from being with a prestigious firm that was known for its high standards and recruitment of only the best and brightest.

My goal was to make senior associate and my supervising partner had indicated that I would be favorably considered in the next round of promotions. Determined to prove myself, I'd been taking on additional work and putting in more hours than ever.

I arrived at my office on the thirty-seventh floor at 7:30 A.M., turned on my laptop and went to the kitchen to make coffee and scan the business papers, my morning ritual. I inhaled the heavenly aroma of freshly brewed coffee that pervaded the air, hugging the cup with my hands.

Robert, who had an office three down from mine, walked in. "Morning, Isy. Good luck with the ruling today."

"Thanks, Rob. There's an article in the *Wall Street Journal* about a new infrastructure project you'll be interested in—check it out. You coming to drinks tonight?"

"Thanks, Isy, I'll take a look. And I'll try to make it tonight."

I drank the rest of my coffee in two gulps, hoping the caffeine would kick in soon to offset the lack of sleep. The rest of the morning and most of the afternoon passed in a flash. When you were expected to bill for every six minutes of time, it was amazing how quickly the day passed.

At 4:30 P.M., Harrison Jarvis, the partner I reported to, stuck his head in my office. A smile as rare as an eclipse warmed his expression, indicating the news must be good. Despite his ordinarily serious demeanor, Harrison was one of my favorite partners at the firm and I was thankful that I worked closely with him. Tall and fit with salt and pepper hair, he was a tenacious man in his early forties who sported a no-nonsense approach. Harrison was truly brilliant, and internationally recognized as such, but was one of those few lawyers who were humble about it.

"Good news, Harrison?" I asked.

"I just got off the phone—we've been cleared. The client is thrilled. Drinks tonight at seven o'clock. Thanks for all your work on this, Isy. I'm very pleased."

"That's great news. I learned a lot working on this matter with you, Harrison. Thank you for the opportunity. I'll see you at drinks." I was beaming. This would definitely help in my bid to make senior associate.

I turned back to my laptop and immediately opened an email to shoot off to a couple of friends, giving them the update. Just as I started typing the words *GREAT NEWS*, my vision blurred. I blinked and rubbed my eyes, but my vision was mottled with red and green dots. *Not enough sleep*, I thought. I closed my eyes for a minute until it passed, then finished my email and went back to work. I had a few loose ends to tie now that the merger had been approved.

I didn't realize the time when Harrison was at my door again. "Isy, are you coming? It's quarter past seven."

"Already? I'll just be five minutes. I'll meet you down there."

Fifteen minutes later, I was sitting at the table in the bar, toasting our win with Harrison and talking about his last vacation in England. Chatter from the throng of people thrummed through the bar, the room percolating with a bustling energy.

"I'd love to get back to Europe," I confessed in a wishful tone. "It's been ages since I was there. Where exactly did you go?"

Harrison was telling me about his visit to Stonehenge and Bath when the red and green dots reappeared. I closed my eyes for just a second, not wanting Harrison to think I was disinterested in his travel tales. The haze subsided and my eyes refocused. But now I wasn't looking at Harrison, I was looking at traffic lights.

You have got *to be kidding me.*

Not again, not *now*. Once was a coincidence, but twice was a very, very big problem. This was a pivotal moment in my career and I deserved it. I'd worked hard for it. Paying attention to Harrison was not a lot to ask. I squeezed my eyes shut but the unbidden image refused to evanesce. I opened them—traffic lights. I closed them again—traffic lights. *This cannot be happening.*

I considered excusing myself to go to the restroom, but being blinded was hardly conducive to walking. A cold sweat broke over my skin. *Crap, crap, crap.*

I viewed the scene before me, an imprisoned spectator. I watched as a pedestrian crossing light turned green and noticed the sidewalk was made of cobblestones. A man in a blue shirt carrying a pink shopping bag stepped out onto the road. *Thrilling*, I thought.

I squeezed my eyes shut again, deciding it was better than looking like a mannequin staring vacantly into space. I felt a tightening in my left arm and panic coursed through me. I was having a serious medical problem—a heart attack perhaps? An aneurism? Stroke? Oh God, I was too young for this. As my left arm began to shake, I was both terrified and relieved: terrified I could be having a stroke and relieved that the problem was a medical one.

I flashed back to the movie *Phenomenon*, where a medical problem explained everything that happened to John Travolta's character. I couldn't believe I hadn't thought of that last night! Presuming I could get to the hospital in time, everything would be okay. Then I remembered the medical problem in the movie was an *inoperable brain tumor* and the relief was gone, replaced by pure terror. Suddenly I was glad I wasn't alone. The pinching in my arm became more severe, I would probably pass out soon. Harrison would know what to do. Crippled with anxiety, I gave in to the hallucination. Maybe if I stopped trying to fight it, it would pass quickly.

I watched as the man took two steps out onto the road. A horrible thud made me jump as the man first hit the windshield of a small black car and then bounced off like a pinball and slammed into the pavement. A scream pierced my ears and I flinched in horror.

My eyes refocused on the surroundings in the bar. I turned to see that Harrison had his hand on my arm and was shaking it, obviously trying to get my attention.

I looked at him blankly and blinked. Understanding dawned about the squeezing sensation in my arm. *Dear Lord, how long had he been doing that?*

"Isy? Isy? What's wrong?"

I was struck mute. I had no idea what was wrong with me, what was happening to me.

"Isy? Can you hear me?" He lifted his hand in front of my eyes and waved it up and down, discerning if I was responsive.

Dear Lord, how long had he been doing that? This was bad. This was very, very bad. Although I didn't know how dire my physical or mental health was, I did know there was an immediate problem facing me: potentially losing everything I'd worked for. Forget about a promotion; at this point, Harrison was probably thinking about my medical insurance. A shudder went through me with the thought that a hospital could be exactly where I was headed.

But not today.

"Sorry, Harrison. I'm okay," I apologized quickly. This was the only problem I was equipped to deal with right now. *Think.* How could I explain a mental episode? "I . . . I'm just getting a migraine. I had a stabbing pain start from behind my eyes and it made my vision blurry. I should probably get home to bed before it starts again."

Okay, that sounded believable—it was half true anyway—but I wasn't sure how long I'd been mute for.

Harrison looked at me with concern, but with less panic. "Oh, I see. I didn't know what had happened to you—it was like you were catatonic all of a sudden. It's probably all of the late nights we've been working. You need some sleep. Go home now."

"Thanks, Harrison, and sorry again that I missed some of your story. I want to hear the rest later. Good night."

He nodded. "See you tomorrow."

I got up to leave, hiding the twitching of my lips. Only in a law firm do you have a *catatonic episode* and do they still expect you to show up to work in the morning.

I went straight to bed when I got home, rubbing my head in an attempt to erase the problem like scribble on a chalkboard. There was no denying that I needed a brain scan but I wasn't sure I was ready to have my worst fears proven. But what if it happened again when I was presenting to my colleagues, sitting with a client, or in front of the Commission? What about if I were crossing the road or, worse still, driving?

This last thought brought me quickly back to what I had seen. What was that? This was different to last night. Last night I'd seen something I'd recognized, *someone* I had recognized. Tonight I could identify neither the place nor the person. I'd only seen the man from behind, I hadn't even seen his face. The place was a mystery: a location with cobblestone streets. I tried to shake off the unease settling in my stomach. Maybe I was worrying too much. Perhaps the unsolicited cinematography had been brought on by the stories that Harrison had been telling me of Europe. Yes, that would make sense. Weren't we just speaking of Europe and hadn't I just told him how much I longed to visit there again?

My mind was obviously playing tricks on me again, a game I didn't want to play. I felt like I'd been spun around with a repressive blindfold entrapping me like a noose, stealing my vision and disorientating me. This was nothing like the previous evening, there was no possible way this could come to fruition. I was thousands of miles away from Europe—a very respectable safety buffer. I deliberately slowed my breathing, consoling myself with the knowledge that it was impossible for that scene to play out in front of me. I'd overreacted and this was purely another hallucination. Why I would visualize something so horrible was beyond me, but that would be something for a doctor to work out, since clearly I was in need of one.

Where were the hallucinations coming from? My thoughts came full-circle. Dear God, maybe I *did* have an aneurism or tumor.

I pushed down the resurgence of panic. *Phenomenon* was just a movie, I couldn't let it rattle me. As terrifying as the thought of having a potentially life-threatening condition was, I took 421comfort in the knowledge that it would at least explain what was happening to me. It would make sense. And it was treatable (or so I reassured myself). I would make a doctor's appointment first thing in the morning.

Everything would be okay.

It had to be.

* * *

I detailed my symptoms to my doctor who prescribed a mild sedative—for what he described as 'anxiety'—and referred me to a specialist. Three doctors later, a battery of tests—including a CT scan that revealed I was claustrophobic—and weeks of anxious waiting resulted in being no closer to figuring out what on earth was wrong with me.

The upside was that I was definitely tumor-free. The downside was that two of the three doctors recommended I see a psychiatrist. After taking blood tests to confirm that I wasn't on any drugs, they told me there were no *physical* causes to explain my vision impairment. This is how they phrased it, with a strong emphasis on the word *physical*, as if to infer the cause was undoubtedly *mental*.

They didn't tell me anything that I hadn't already considered myself. Still, sitting on the other side of their desk, I couldn't help but sink into my chair a little.

After the episode in the bar, I had been having the same recurring nightmare nearly every night for a month. The same man in the same blue shirt carrying the same pink shopping bag, crossing the same street with the same black car running the same red light. The same terrible thud. I awoke each night screaming, drenched in sweat.

I tried the sedatives my doctor had prescribed to knock me out and keep the nightmares at bay. They worked like a charm for the first three nights, but by the fourth night, the nightmares broke through their fortress with unrelenting assault. I persisted with the pills for two more nights in sheer desperation, but all they achieved was to leave me with an unshakeable drowsiness in the morning. Eventually, I was so exhausted from the lack of sleep that I could barely function during the day.

Harrison had started eyeing me with a look of concern. If this continued for much longer, it wouldn't be long before he started allocating his important matters to someone else on the team. If he lost his faith in me, my promotion would be jeopardized. I couldn't believe the timing of it. If I were going to lose my mind, did it have to be *now*? Couldn't it have been *after* I got my promotion? I started to wonder if this had all been brought on from stress. Maybe this was a sign that I needed to take some time off.

Then I remembered Jeremy. Whatever had happened that night, I did indeed find him on the roof, exactly where I'd seen him. Was it possible that that hadn't just been a coincidence?

Jeremy dropped by at least once a week now. There was something about him that I found endearing and we had become good friends since that fateful day on the roof. I could tell he was feeling better because, as the weeks passed, his humor rippled to the surface and his care-free personality began to shine through.

He'd had a few job opportunities and I soon realized he was very skilled in his field. He decided to contract until he found the right position and a role as a computer software engineer looked very promising. He'd had two interviews already and was preparing to complete his psychometric testing. I broke out the champagne on his last visit, toasting to his brilliance in spite of his protests. An empty bottle later, he wanted to toast me. But the last thing I felt like doing was toasting my slow demise.

On more than one occasion I wanted to tell him what was happening to me, but I couldn't find the words. I didn't want him to look at me the way the doctors had—right before they referred me to a psychiatrist. I couldn't blame them, it was a natural assumption. Logic dictates that where there's smoke, there's fire . . . Would Jeremy think the same?

I started thinking again about taking some time off. I hadn't planned to take a vacation before my promotion, focusing only on proving myself and my dedication to the firm. Now that I was worried my work would start slipping, being away for a couple of weeks wasn't the worst idea.

My best friend lived in Florence and I'd wanted to visit her for a while. This seemed like the perfect time. Thanks to my singular focus on being promoted, I'd accrued a lot of vacation time, but if I wanted to go too suddenly, Harrison would get suspicious that Florence was code for mental breakdown. I needed a cover story to explain the sudden departure.

I broached the subject when I ventured into Harrison's office to get approval on some documents I'd prepared. His office was immaculate, in spite of the dozens of folders that cocooned him.

He was scribbling furiously in a file, his lips pursed as the pen scratched across the paper, branding it with red ink that besieged the printed text.

"Hi, Harrison. Here are the documents you requested for sign off. Is there anything else I can assist you with at the moment?" Always better to offer something before making a request.

"Just leave them on the table and I'll take a look this afternoon."

He dismissed me without a glance and I hovered awkwardly, debating whether I should wait until he was in a better mood. I shifted my feet, resigned to leave, when he tore his eyes away from the file and eyed me with raised eyebrows. "How are you feeling today?"

It was now or never.

"Great, thanks, Harrison. It's amazing what a good night's sleep can do," I lied. I gave him a wide smile like I didn't have a care in the world, trying to ignore the heat that was crawling across my cheeks like little red flags. "I just got an email from a friend of mine who lives in Florence. She's getting married. She was going to fly home and have a barefoot ceremony on the beach, but now they've decided to save the expense and get married there—after all, it's Florence!"

My voice rose in excitement and I hoped I wasn't overdoing it. This was much more personal information than I'd normally give Harrison, particularly when he looked like he was in the middle of something. He cocked his head and wrinkled his forehead, appraising me. The illusory heat of the glaring spotlight conjured in my imagination further heated my burning cheeks.

I willed my limbs not to twitch under his scrutiny. Mustering my confidence, I continued. "Of course, I'd *love* to be there, but it's just so last minute . . ." I let my voice trail off. There were always so many brides getting married in Florence that I was sure I would come across one during my time there and be able to snap a photo or two of her for evidence. This would have seemed slightly paranoid to me a few years ago, but my lawyer training had taught me to always be prepared and cover all bases. *Show me the evidence.* Harrison's mantra rang in my head, like the bell that trained Pavlov's dog. Except instead of salivating, this bell triggered the instinctive response to plan ahead and prepare for the worst-case scenario.

"When exactly is it?" he asked, clearly aware where this was going.

"Um . . . in three and a half weeks. She managed to secure the date that someone else canceled, otherwise she would've been waiting for months. They decided to be spontaneous."

He raised his brows. I was sure he was going to tell me to forget it. Then to my surprise, he turned to his calendar and reviewed the work schedule.

"Actually, Isy, that might work out well. If you go for two weeks and come back by June tenth when Project Aurora starts, I could probably work around your absence. You've got a lot of vacation time that you haven't taken, and now is probably a good time for you to also get some rest." The pointed look he gave me proved he'd definitely noticed the change in my behavior of late. His statement held more than the words he voiced aloud. The unspoken warning was evident in his eyes: *Whatever the problem is, it better not return with you.*

"Harrison, are you sure?" I didn't wait for a response in case he reconsidered. "I mean, that would be so fantastic, and my friend will be absolutely thrilled! I will call the travel agent today!"

I'd already checked online that morning to check flight availability. All I had to do was finalize my booking. Although my story was a lie—yet another example of my downward spiral—the part about wanting to visit my best friend in Florence was true. Julia and I had known each other nearly our whole lives. She was the one person in the world in whom I felt I could confide this secret without fear of repercussions. And she *did* get married, only it was about two years ago and it was in San Francisco. I had photos of her wedding that I could use, but my hair had been a lot longer at the time and you would notice the difference. Plus, the backdrop looked nothing like Florence. Details I'd work out later.

For now, all I needed to know was that I was getting away. Already I felt lighter, like the change in time zone and routine would somehow rewire my brain.

Florence, here I come.

3

FLORENCE

THE PLANE TRIP to Florence was unbearably long, although I managed a couple of hours sleep without any nightmares. When I awoke, the same images continued to play through my mind unabated, causing a cold sweat to break over my skin. A thought that I'd locked away, refusing to acknowledge, drummed against my skull. Florence was supposed to be my reprieve, my sanctuary. Now, heading to my destination, I could no longer ignore the fact that I was about to arrive in a city brimming with cobblestone streets. Something as innocuous as Florence's streets somehow had the power to chill me to the bone. I wrapped the blanket more tightly around myself, trying to smother the fear that I was a pawn on a chessboard being moved by unseen forces. *Jules will know what to do,* I reassured myself.

Needing to occupy my thoughts, I focused on trying to conjugate verbs in Italian. The last time I'd been in Italy was about seven years ago, when I'd traveled with Julia during summer break at college. Jules was in an art program, following her passion to be a painter. We had spent a month in Florence during that trip, studying Italian at a local school. But with seven years of non-practice, I'd unfortunately forgotten most of it. I pulled my Italian dictionary out of my bag and began my quiet refresher course, pleased that the knowledge was still buried there, squirreled away.

Julia was fluent in the language. She'd returned four years after our trip; with her love of art, Florence was like Heaven to her. It was then that she'd met Gianni, the handsome Italian plumber. Their love story read like a romance novel. Julia decided to stay and now worked as a local tour guide, visiting the museums and enjoying her art on a daily basis, and occasionally selling her paintings.

Julia and I had been best friends since kindergarten. Despite the distance, we had maintained our friendship, although I had found it more difficult to share my innermost thoughts over the phone. I was relieved I would be able to speak with her in person and share some of my anxiety over recent events. Jules was the friend who knew me best, who never judged me and was always able to offer a new perspective that I hadn't considered on any situation or problem. Just talking things through with her offered comfort; she was better than any psychiatrist.

Finally, after what seemed an eternity, the plane began its decent into Florence. After so many hours of traveling, I was exhausted. The plane landed around midday, Italian time.

I went through customs and flashed the hideous mug shot on my passport. The customs officer gave me a quick glance as he eyed the passport. With my combination of dark brown hair, blue eyes and fair skin, I could pass for a number of nationalities. I cringed under his scrutiny, knowing the picture was far from flattering. But after sleeping on a plane, the hideous photo was probably complimentary compared to my current appearance.

Julia, on the other hand, always appeared camera-ready. She had beautiful olive skin, green eyes and dark curly hair. She often passed for a local—until, of course, they heard her American accent.

She was waiting for me at the gate when I came through customs, waving eagerly and smiling widely. Going through customs here was not as long a process as it was entering America, and I passed through quickly without any problems.

"Isy! Isy!" Julia screamed, waving me over in her direction. Not that Florence airport was very large.

"Jules!" I exclaimed with equal enthusiasm.

She threw her arms around me at once, squeezing me tightly. I had last seen Jules at her wedding in San Francisco, but no matter how much time passed, when we saw each other it was like it was only yesterday.

"It is *so* good to see you! It's about time you came to Italy to see me! I mean, really, how many times does a girl get married?" she teased as she winked at me, aware of the impromptu-wedding excuse I'd given at work.

I smiled. "I don't know—two, three times max?" I returned her teasing tone, shrugging my shoulders. "Probably depends on the number of breakdowns I have." I had only told her that I'd been having a few personal issues, but promised I'd explain everything to her when I arrived in Italy.

Concern instantly clouded her expression. "You know, you've had me very worried about you. I expect you to tell me everything. Immediately."

"I will—but can I unpack first?" I gave her a reassuring smile.

"Let's hurry then." She pulled me along towards the taxi stand to the right side of the airport.

Julia lived in the center of Florence, just a few minutes walk from the Duomo, Ponte Vecchio, Piazza della Signoria—well known for the replica statue of Michelangelo's David—and the Uffizi, the home of much of Florence's renaissance art. It was ideal.

We jumped into the cab. "Via Ghibellina, numero cinquanta-quattro," she instructed the driver. He nodded and pulled out onto the road.

The twenty-minute ride in from the airport was an experience in itself. I'd forgotten how crazy the Italian drivers were, and the pedestrians alike. In the center of Florence, the sidewalks that hugged some of the narrow streets were smaller than the width of a welcome mat and a single person could barely walk comfortably on it. As a result, many of the pedestrians and cyclists—of which there were many—often used the road. The same road that was already narrow for a single car.

The cab driver was impatient, honking his horn and giving many well-known Italian gestures to anyone who got in his way. Changing lanes on the wider roads encircling the city center involved no turn signals or mirror checks. You definitely needed courage to drive here. Normal road rules didn't apply. The only rule seemed to be: move it or lose it.

As we passed the Duomo, the most famous church in Florence, our driver lost what little patience he had left. Tour groups flocked to the Duomo like seagulls, and it was bursting with pedestrians, horse carriages, cars, motorini and cyclists. What little room left on the street was taken by the pigeons. Our driver expertly maneuvered the car through the crowded street circling the Duomo and—with a take-no-prisoners approach—promptly hit the gas, roaring the engine in warning to the pedestrians swarming the road.

A male tourist who'd just crossed the street jolted his head in the direction of the engine's roar. His eyes widened before he started frantically gesturing to the other side of the road, waving his arms in gesture to stop. I quickly turned my head to see who he was gesturing to and saw the rest of his family walking idly, about to enter the road from a side street. I would've glanced back at the man, but we were already past him and long gone.

In the next instant, the cab was turning onto Via Ghibellina. People were scrambling out of the way, but an older couple was foolishly stubborn and ignored the car speeding around the corner. The driver braked hard and moved an inch to the right, just narrowly missing them by that very inch.

The street whirled by in a blur before the cab abruptly pulled up in front of Julia's apartment building. That is, he moved the cab as close as possible to the parked cars to try and allow any approaching vehicles to get past him. There was absolutely no available parking on the street, every inch of space next to the curb was taken. I wasn't sure how the drivers managed to parallel park with no space between their vehicle and the cars directly in front and behind. It had to be an art form.

I was reaching into my bag for my wallet when Julia handed the driver the twenty-five euro fare.

"Jules!" I exclaimed in protest. She merely smiled back at me.

She lived on the third floor. Big suitcase. No elevator. I hadn't factored that in when I'd packed.

"I'd forgotten about your aversion to packing light," she teased as she eyed my suitcase. "You grab one end, I'll grab the other."

I was panting by the time we reached her apartment, but Julia looked like she could do the trip all over again without breaking a sweat. She plonked the bag down in the second bedroom and gave me a quick tour of the apartment.

There was a large living room to the left of the entrance, with a tiny hallway leading to a small bathroom and a large bedroom. The apartment had very tall ceilings and the walls in the living room were covered with prints of Julia's favorite artworks and her own paintings.

Two large glass doors gave the impression of a balcony, although there was only railing behind them, acting as a barrier to the large drop below. The glass doors flooded the room with sunlight that danced along the walls and illuminated the bright and beautiful paintings.

To the right side of the entrance was the second bedroom. The high ceiling allowed for a loft, and the space upstairs was full of Julia's arts and crafts. Next to the second bedroom was the kitchen with a large table in the middle of the room. Julia liked to host dinner parties and I could imagine the table filled with animated guests, talking loudly and gesturing with their hands as Italians often do. There were two more large glass doors in the kitchen, this time leading out to a balcony filled with plants, two beautiful iron chairs and a small round table.

The apartment was more spacious than I'd expected and considered quite large for the center of Florence. I was happy for her that they were doing well.

"Gianni said to give his apologies. He wanted to come to the airport to greet you," Jules explained. "But personally, I'm glad I have you alone, so you can spill. I'll make us lunch while you get settled. Make yourself at home, Is. La mia casa è la tua casa."

* * *

After I had unpacked and showered, and we'd both had lunch, Julia sipped the tea she had just made and reached her hand over to touch my arm. "So, tell me what's been happening, Is. I'm certainly not complaining that you *finally* took some time off work to come and visit me, but I wish it were under better circumstances. I hate to see you upset. Tell me what's going on."

Where should I begin? With Jules, I didn't have to worry about choosing my words carefully, or her judging me. Knowing I could finally air all of my thoughts, they came out in a rush. The words spilled from me like a dam bursting, the deluge threatening to inundate her. Uneasily shocked, her eyes were filled with concentration as she focused on letting it all sink in.

"What do you think it all *means*, Jules? I mean, the thing with Jeremy, at least I was able to help. But this other *thing*"—I didn't know what to call it, calling it a *vision* just seemed like I should be wearing a scarf on my head and holding a crystal ball—"it's just so weird, I don't know how to make sense of it. It's like the more I try to ignore it, the more frequent the nightmares become. I don't recognize the person, and I don't know exactly where it is, so what *is* it? I just don't get it. I feel like I've got a jigsaw puzzle in front of me and I'm missing half the pieces. I'm so confused. Do you think it could be real? And if so, how is this happening to me, and why? Maybe the Jeremy thing was a fluke and there is no Blue Shirt Guy, maybe I'm just losing it. There's no evidence he actually exists."

Jules wore the same look of concentration on her face as she was thinking it through. The muscles in my jaw loosened. I felt so incredibly relieved to be talking about it so openly with someone who would not judge me and who could hopefully offer me a new perspective, one I desperately needed.

She started slowly. "Well, first of all, let me say that I don't think there's anything wrong with you. And there's no way that what happened with Jeremy was just some fluke. You saved him, Isy, because you saw what you saw. That is *amazing*—think about that for a minute.

"I know you like everything to be logical and to fit neatly into your little box, but sometimes things don't fit. You have to keep an open mind. The best things in life are sometimes those that come to us from outside the box. I think this is a gift, Is. Where it comes from, I don't know. What it means exactly, I'm not sure. But I think you should go with it, instead of fighting it. Your eyes are clearly open—you know what I mean—I think now you just need to open your *mind*."

Jules always believed in the power of the universe and all of that kind of thing. She was probably the first one to buy *The Secret* and every book just like it.

I raised a brow. After flying halfway across the world, she'd better have something better than that up her sleeve. My mind was currently a whirlpool of unbidden images, thoughts, doubts and apprehension. I struggled to sort through the dumping ground it felt like some unknown hacker had turned it into, and I needed more than fridge-magnet sayings to help me wade through the clutter and find myself again.

Jules pushed a plate of cannoli towards me. "I mean, this nightmare you're having—you first saw it the same way that you say you saw that Jeremy guy, right?"

I nodded, the mouthful of cannoli keeping my mouth busy, which I suspected was her intention.

"So then, it would make sense that it is a glimpse of something real, of something that could happen, the same way that the Jeremy vision was." I cringed at the word *vision*, but she ignored me and went on. "You saw it for a reason, so this mystery guy must exist. I think you're meant to save him." She seemed pleased with her conclusion and I didn't need a premonition to realize that she *wanted* him to exist.

I heard Harrison's voice ringing in my head. *Show me the evidence . . .*

"But Jules," I protested, "I have no idea who this person is, or where he is—how could I possibly help even if you think I'm supposed to?"

"You say that you saw cobblestone streets? That the place looked old-worldly?" she clarified.

"Aha," I mumbled through another bite of cannoli.

"Like, say, somewhere like *Florence*?" She pronounced the word slowly, sounding out each syllable like I was a three-year-old. "Have you noticed any cobblestone streets here by any chance?" I detected the slightest look of smugness on her face.

I put the cannoli down, letting the pent-up irritation spill from my lips. "Really, where?" I snapped. Taking a deep breath, I tried again, this time without the sarcasm. Jules was only trying to help and lashing out at her wouldn't achieve anything. "It hasn't escaped my notice, Jules. The thought definitely crossed my mind but I didn't want to think about it. I mean, I was coming here for an escape. The whole purpose of this trip was to help find solutions, not more problems. I didn't want to think about the fact that I might be running *towards* the problem instead of escaping it. Not to mention the fact that the nightmares started *before* I ever planned to come here. I couldn't bear to even begin to think about what that could mean. The whole thing is completely freaking me out."

She leaned across the table and took my hand. "This is a lot to work through. It would freak anyone out. Let's just try to focus on one thing at a time, then maybe it won't feel so overwhelming."

I wasn't sure if her sympathy was making me feel better or worse, so I stuffed those emotions down with the rest of my cannoli. Looked like even if I lost my remaining sanity in Florence, I'd be gaining a couple extra pounds to take home with me. Not exactly the trade-off I'd been hoping for.

I pushed the plate away. I wasn't ready to concede defeat yet. I told myself that Jules could still pull the elusive rabbit out of the hat and provide the answers I was looking for. And after I found Blue Shirt Guy, maybe everything would go back to normal. Maybe I could heed Harrison's warning and leave it all behind here.

I was definitely ready for some hat pulling. I looked at her expectantly, holding my breath.

"Okay, so we agree that this street corner must be in Florence. The difficult part will be figuring out *which* street corner. Although I dare say that you won't have to look for it too hard, I'm sure that you will come across it when you are meant to. It's probably close by somewhere. Can you remember any other details about the street—a building or sign perhaps?" She leaned forward, her eyes shining brightly. Jules seemed to think that my nightmare was her very own *Da.Vinci Code* to solve.

"Sorry, no, Jules, and I unfortunately don't have the 1-800-dial-a-psychic number on me to find out."

"Isy! Really, you can't have that kind of attitude. I'm willing to bet that's why the nightmares started—to make sure you pay attention and learn more about the surroundings. I know this is a lot to process, but I think you're looking at it the wrong way. I'd love to have this kind of gift—it's just so interesting! Seriously, how can you continue to go to that firm every day and look at all that legal stuff"—she rolled her eyes as she said that last part—"when you have a much more important gift?"

"Hey, I've worked very hard to get where I am at 'that firm,' thank you very much! I'm certainly not about to just throw it all away because one thing came true." Jules opened her mouth to interrupt, but I raised a finger to cut her off. "And besides, as romantic an idea as you make it sound, I'm not an oracle. And even then, it certainly wouldn't pay the bills, you know."

A smile ghosted across her lips. "Always the logical one, aren't you?"

"Well if I let you get your way, you'd probably have me walking around with a magic-eight ball in one hand and an oversized magnifying glass in the other," I teased.

"Touché," she said, still smiling. I'd been there when she'd bought the magic-eight ball at a market years ago. "Baby steps. We'll just take this as it comes, one step at a time. And we'll figure it out together. You're not alone, Is. I'm here with you. Me and the magic-eight ball I will have gift wrapped for you later, Madam Scarfhead."

I laughed, releasing some of the built-up tension. Jules knew me so well. The rabbit was yet to appear, but I was exactly where I needed to be. I breathed a sigh of relief—and hope.

4

PAGING PRINCE CHARMING

THE NEXT DAY Julia had to work in the afternoon. I decided to take a walk and reacquaint myself with some of my favorite places in Florence. That was the true beauty of the city, you could easily walk everywhere and take in all of the main sights. The first time I visited, I remembered feeling like I was walking around in a living postcard. It's just that pretty. And that compact.

I started at the Duomo, walking past my old school, La Scuola di Leonardo da Vinci, on Via Dell'Oriuolo. I continued towards the Ponte Vecchio and window-shopped in the jewelry stores along the bridge. The lookout at the bridge's center was overflowing with couples posing for photos, turning this way and that to get the perfect angle of the scenery behind them. A cacophony of voices in an array of different languages sailed the breeze, filling my ears with its unique melody.

The scintillating afternoon sun was unrelenting and I decided to head over to my favorite piazza in Florence, Piazza della Signoria, to seek refuge in the shade and watch the world go by. The Palazzo Vecchio had been the home of the Medici family who once ruled the city. It continues to dominate the landscape, shading the square. Watching over the entry to this magnificent fortress stands a replica of Michelangelo's statue of David. It's every bit as beautiful as it was intended to be. In the middle of the square sits the fountain of Neptune, with the constant flow of tourists in front taking their pictures. The piazza is constantly bubbling with life and it's the perfect place to sit and watch it all unfold.

I was trying to take Julia's advice and just take everything as it comes. Pushing my troubles to the back of my mind, I sat in the shade in front of David on the steps encircling the Loggia della Signoria and appreciated the beauty that enveloped me. Hundreds of people passed by, many of them tourists, all with their own stories to tell. Some of the couples held hands and seemed to thrive on the romance of the city, while others walked together in brooding silence. Children chased after pigeons, weaving through the many street vendors who were trying to unload their gadgets, scarfs, knockoff purses and other goods.

Eventually my mind started replaying the conversation I'd had with Julia. What if Blue Shirt Guy *did* exist? What if it was like the incident with Jeremy and I was supposed to help him?

Before my mind could race ahead thinking about all of these questions, I reminded myself that today was supposed to be a 'no-worrying' day. I pulled a book out of my bag, seizing the opportunity to finally finish it. I enjoyed reading but hardly ever got a chance to read for pleasure, since most evenings were spent reading legal documents or keeping up with the ever-changing regulatory landscape. Before I got lost in *A Thousand Splendid Suns*, an incredible story set in Afghanistan which reminded me of all the bigger problems in the world, I snuck a peek at the book the girl sitting beside me was reading.

Unsurprisingly, it was a vampire book, and the girl appeared to be completely engrossed in it. I scoffed, wondering how women could be so taken in by these versions of the supposed modern-day Cinderella story—where the prince was actually a blood-thirsty vampire. Women wanted to believe they could tame the beast, a concept as old and antiquated as fairy tales themselves. I knew why women wanted to embrace the illusion—after all, with his super-human strength, power and immortality, this knight in shining armor could protect his Cinderella from all danger and would never die and leave her. The reality that most people couldn't seem to be monogamous and loyal to each other in *one* human lifetime, let alone over millennia, was apparently irrelevant to the fantasy.

I'd had many discussions with Jules about this, since *Twilight* was her favorite book and she'd pestered me until I read it. She'd argued that it was a story about overcoming overwhelming challenges to find true love and figuring out what you were willing to sacrifice in order to hold on to that love. A love she'd claimed held true intimacy in every look, every touch, every word.

Although I didn't often admit it to Jules, I *wanted* to believe in the possibility of Prince Charming (and had secretly seen the appeal of Edward), but the realist in me knew that fairy tales didn't exist.

There was no more chance of finding that Prince than

there was of vampires actually existing. The constant threat of being attacked by other vampires—which seemed to be a common denominator in the genre and confused me further as to why women glorified the idea of a relationship with the walking dead—was at least one thing I could relate to: the fact that even in these fairy tales, everything came at a price. Nothing was perfect, nothing was free—it just depended on how much you wanted it and how much you were willing to give to have it.

Despite how much I tried to avoid thinking about my own problems, this last thought brought me straight back. *Everything comes at a price.*

I'd been given a chance to help Jeremy—that was definitely worth a price. And I had—up until this point at least—a blossoming career that had definitely come with hard work and sacrifice. I'd paid for that by giving up a lot of my personal life.

Was there another price required to balance all of the good fortune I had in my life? Was this the price that the universe wanted in turn? That I should help others? There were certainly a lot of people better off than me, so what was their price then? Why was this happening to *me?*

It occurred to me that all of Jules's ranting over the years had finally engraved themselves into my head. I was starting to believe in all that hoo-ha about the power of the universe. It wasn't that I was a complete non-believer, I just didn't run out and buy every book on universal power, fate, karma, or whatever else you wanted to call it. I had focused on what I could touch, feel and see.

I laughed inwardly as I repeated that last thought in my mind—what I could *see.* If I wouldn't believe anything that wasn't directly in front of my eyes, was this a way of making me see, of making me *believe?*

I took a deep breath. Baby steps, I told myself. Baby steps. I didn't have to figure everything out today. I didn't need to stand in court and present an argument, all I needed was patience. Unfortunately for me, the latter was what I hadn't mastered as well.

* * *

I had planned to meet Jules in front of La Rinascente, a department store in Piazza della Republica, at 6:00 P.M. I stood in the shade of the building, people-watching and dwindling down the last few minutes before she arrived. The piazza was bulging with locals and tourists, the stream of chatter carrying across the wind like an undulating ribbon dancing through the air.

A fire performer in the middle of the square captured my attention for a few moments before I locked eyes with a guy in the crowd. Even though a sea of people watching the performer enveloped him, he was staring intently in my direction. The moment his piercing gaze caught mine, I felt a lightning bolt jolt my body and heighten every sensation. I was suddenly very self-conscious, straightening up and running a hand through my long hair. I couldn't see anything below his shoulders but from the sculptured features that were visible, it was obvious that the guy could grace a billboard for Calvin Klein. But it was more than that that had my heart racing. I was inexplicably drawn to him. I couldn't explain it. I desperately wanted to know who he was.

His gaze continued to hold mine, like a fly caught in a web. A blush slowly crawled across my cheeks. *Please, please come over,* I thought. The distraction of a vacation romance sounded exactly like what the doctor ordered! The thought of a drop-dead-gorgeous Italian guy—*this* drop-dead-gorgeous Italian guy—made me tingle with anticipation. This guy definitely looked like he knew how to make a woman feel like a woman . . . For just a little while, I could let myself be enraptured by Calvin and let all of my troubles melt away. Somewhere inside me, salacious thoughts awakened a part of me that I barely remembered existed. I'd been so focused on my career of late, I hadn't had time for romance or dating. But the normal rules didn't apply on vacation.

I telepathically tried to will him to cross the distance between us. Indecision briefly crossed his features before a smile played on his lips and danced in his eyes. He edged sideways and looked around him as if mapping his path out of the crowd.

My heart skipped a beat and I smoothed my hair in place. Just as I was beginning to think that serendipity was smiling sweetly down on me like a welcome friend, Lady Luck turned on me quicker than a bad oyster. Everything seemed to coalesce to conspire against me. The street performer finished his act and the crowd immediately dispersed, some people moving forward to put money in his case and others making a run for it before they could be guilted into making a donation. The crowd engulfed Calvin and I lost sight of him. I was so focused on locating him again that I didn't notice the swarm of tourists making a beeline across the piazza. Their guide chose that moment to position the group right where I was standing—leaning up against the side of the department store—to give them instructions and some tidbit of information. They swallowed me up, buried under a blanket of flashing cameras and maps. I edged my way across the wall of the building, trying to extricate myself so that Calvin could find me—*if* he was looking.

Just when I thought I was home free, an old woman begging for money approached me with her cup held out for change. She was undoubtedly targeting the large tourist group, which I *thought* I'd just escaped. I was trapped. There was no way I'd find him now. When Lady Luck turns on you, she goes all the way. Right now, she was mocking me.

One last desperate scan of the people around me revealed no sign of him. My shoulders slumped.

"Signora," the woman pleaded, looking weak and frail, "per favore, aiutami." I'd been warned that some of the beggars on the streets of Florence weren't legitimately impoverished, but standing right in front of her, I couldn't ignore her.

As I was scrambling to pull out my wallet—still hoping to get away quickly—she suddenly leaned in and looked at me more closely, the way you would do a double-take and stare if you're not sure if you recognize someone. Her eyes were piercing and I shrank back from her. It was like she was trying to look into the depths of my soul. I tried to look away, but she leaned in closer and held my gaze with mesmerizing force. I edged back as far as I could, trying to keep some distance between us, but she continued to close the gap. I was blocked.

"Hmm . . . sì, sì," she whispered softly, like she was speaking to herself. "Sei una donna con quattro occhi—due per vedere e due per vedere *la verita*. Un vero regalo. Ma lei lo sa? Non sono sicuro." She shook her head.

She was freaking me out so much that I reached into my bag and pulled out a handful of coins, having no idea how much was there. I threw the money into the cup she was holding and wriggled around her to free myself.

I bolted.

I scanned my surrounds again, hoping for a miracle, but I instinctively knew that he was gone. Lady Luck was surely laughing, reminding me that what she giveth, she can quickly taketh away. Dejected, I spotted a gelateria a few yards away. Still shaken from my encounter with the old woman, I walked straight in, knowing that she wouldn't follow me in there. I bought myself a nocciola gelato and waited for Jules inside. Only after she sent me a text message confirming that she was at our meeting spot did I feel confident in leaving my safe harbor and venturing back.

"Jules!" The relief was evident in my voice as I approached the corner.

"Isy, are you okay? You look white as a ghost."

"I'm fine, I just had this"—I paused as I quickly surveyed the area to make sure I couldn't see her—"really creepy old lady come up and stare into my eyes." I frowned, realizing that description didn't relay the true weirdness of it. Jules obviously thought the same because she looked at me like I was a big baby making a big deal out of nothing.

"Really? Thank goodness there were witnesses, or who knows what could have happened! I mean, an old lady was *looking* at you—what has this world come to?" Her voice was thick with sarcasm and amusement.

"Ha ha. Yeah, funny, Jules. No, seriously, it was weird. She told me that—" I broke off in mid sentence and gasped. My eyes followed two girls who had just exited the sliding doors to La Rinascente.

"She told you what? Why are you behaving so strangely? What are you looking at?" Her eyes followed in the direction I was looking.

"The bag that girl is carrying—it's pink."

She looked over. "And? It's the La Rinascente bag. She obviously bought something. Seriously, Isy, you're starting to worry me a little."

"Jules, it's *pink.* It looks exactly like the bag from my . . . the bag that Blue Shirt Guy was carrying."

"Oh! That's brilliant—it's a clue! Maybe that street corner isn't too far from here. Maybe it's a sign!" Her speech was picking up speed as her excitement grew. "Maybe we should hang here for a while and watch the people leaving the store. Maybe Blue Shirt is here!"

I shook my head. "Jules, I don't think it works like that. I mean, what are the chances? There's no way I'd get that lucky." I started to tell her about Calvin, but just like my tale of the old woman, the story would sound pathetically uneventful to her so I stopped myself. What would I say? *A hot guy was looking at me . . .*

And? she'd ask.

And nothing. End of story. No Pulitzer prizes there.

I couldn't convince her that staking out the department store would be futile. And since some misguided part of me reluctantly held onto the hope that Calvin could still meander past, I didn't argue too vociferously. An hour and a half passed before Jules was willing to divert her eyes from the store entry as she spoke.

"Okay, maybe he's not here today after all. The store will be closing soon anyway. We've still got two weeks. Let's go to dinner. I told Gianni to meet us at Il Teatro on Via Ghibellina at eight o'clock, just near home. You'll love it—great food and good service. Let's go." She gently grabbed my arm to pull me along before turning to me like she'd forgotten something. "Hey, you never told me what that woman said that had you so freaked before. You were really pale."

"Oh, yeah. It was *so* weird, but it was probably just a coincidence so I shouldn't have let it freak me out. I overreacted. And you know my Italian's a little shaky, so I may have misunderstood."

"What'd she say?"

"She looked deep into my eyes like she saw something, and then, kinda to herself, she whispered something about me having four eyes: two to see and two to see 'the truth.'" I paused, distracted by Jules's reaction. She'd stopped mid-step, her mouth gaping open.

"Why are *you* freaking out now? It was a woman asking for change. Don't they say weird stuff like that to people all the time, trying to get them to give them money?" I asked.

"I've never heard anything like that before. They usually just ask for money. Did she say anything else?" Jules sounded intrigued.

"Um, she seemed to ask herself a question and then answered it."

Jules's eyes were wide. "What'd she ask?"

"I think she said, 'But does she know? I don't think so' and shook her head. It was at that point that I did a runner. She was really freaking me out, the way she stared."

"Well, I owe you an apology, Isy," Jules offered, "for making fun earlier. No wonder you were white. It's not every day that a stranger stops to tell you that you have a second sight."

The color that had returned to my face quickly drained again. "Let's not say anything about this to Gianni, okay? And I mean, *anything* about this whole thing. I don't want him to think I'm weird. Promise me."

"Isy, he's married to *me*—like he'd think *you're* weird. But okay, I promise."

The next few days consisted of a semi routine. I'd walk around the city during the day and meet Julia in the evening in front of La Rinascente. We'd get gelati and watch the people coming out of the store for an hour or so. This was Julia's idea, but I didn't protest. I was starting to watch just as carefully as she was. But night after night, day after day, there was no sign of the elusive Blue Shirt.

After a week passed, I was starting to wonder whether I'd ever find such a needle in a haystack. It seemed unlikely. Still, my eyes darted to every pink bag and blue shirt that I saw.

5

NEEDLE IN THE HAYSTACK

AT THE BEGINNING of my second week in Florence, I started my morning at Piazza di Santa Croce, a beautiful church distinguished by the Star of David adorning the top of the building. Pausing on the steps, I lifted my sunglasses to the top of my head and soaked in the atmosphere. Laughter sang across the square and reverberated through the bustling crowd. Absently, I noticed the tension I usually carried in my shoulders was gone. After a week of being immersed in the beauty of Florence, enjoying *la bella vita*, spending time with Jules and sleeping in, I'd finally managed to hit pause on the incessant stream of panicked thoughts that had mercilessly tormented me since the day I'd seen Jeremy on the roof.

Jules had finally convinced me that there was nothing I needed to do. If I was meant to help Blue Shirt, our paths would cross. If it was indeed a *premonition* of sorts, it was pointless trying to analyze the mechanics of it. Jules quashed the fear of a brain tumor, citing the evidence of the scans I'd already had. If I had a clean bill of health and my sanity was intact, if this was actually *real*, it couldn't be explained. It just was. Jules's words.

It just was.

Much easier to accept as a bystander, I'd told her.

I wasn't as confident and I decided that if I didn't find him, it could be that the nightmares had been triggered by residual stress over the Jeremy episode. Either way, the practical side of me knew that my vacation days were dwindling and I wanted to enjoy the time I had left here.

Taking Jules's advice, I'd put it out of my mind.

"You can't think your way out of it. All you need is a little faith and patience," she'd told me.

I raised my brows.

"I realize that's a stretch for you, Ms. Facts and Evidence. You want control, and you think facts and figures give you that. But this time, you can't use your head. You have to use your heart."

I didn't tell Jules the reason I'd agreed with her, but I saw the logic in her words. If the nightmares had been triggered by stress, it was a result of me overthinking it. They wouldn't cease until I stopped concentrating on it. And if I did find Blue Shirt, I'd have to cross that bridge when I got to it. I couldn't let it consume me.

I gazed across the piazza, unequivocal pleasure visible on the faces of those around me. *Life is good*, they seemed to whisper.

And it would be even better with coffee, I thought.

I sauntered over to Oibò, a bar at the far end of the piazza on Via dei Benci, and luxuriated in the tantalizing aroma of the freshly ground coffee beans. After swallowing the last of my brioche and steaming macchiato, I slipped on my sunglasses and ventured back into the summer heat, making my way across to the Duomo. The humidity was stifling and the shaded side of the street offered some relief from the blazing sun. My phone beeped and I pulled it out to look at the message. It was from Julia.

NEED 2 MEET U @ 6.15 INSTEAD OF 6 2NITE. C U THEN :)

If I hadn't been looking down, I may have spotted the pink bag sooner. When it caught my eye, I was about ten steps from the corner of Via Giuseppe Verdi and Via Ghibellina. As was the norm, as soon as I saw the bag, I instantly scanned upwards to see who was carrying it and, more importantly, what they were wearing.

I stopped dead in my tracks. I could only see his back, but it was definitely a man, wearing jeans and a dark blue shirt. Oh my Lord—*it was Blue Shirt*! Not a myth, not a hallucination. He existed—and here he was!

I scanned the surroundings. Blue Shirt was standing at the crossing next to the farmacia, while the pedestrian light was red. A wave of panic hit me. I looked across the road and saw the bar, Caffe Michelangiolo. Although I hadn't recalled the bar earlier, now that I was looking at it, I recognized it from the vision. This was the same corner. This was the man. This was the crossing.

There was only one thing missing from the scene—a small black car. I wasn't going to wait to find out. I couldn't see the traffic on Via Ghibellina from where I was standing, but I knew the light was going to turn green in a second and he was going to step out onto the road. I leaped forward and ran the few steps to close the distance between us. In those two seconds, my mind raced—how would I get his attention to stop him?

I reached him just as the light turned green. As his left foot stepped down from the curb, I grabbed his right arm and yanked it back—hard. Not exactly subtle. His head spun around instinctively and he looked aggravated by the unwanted touch—well, rough handling, really. His left fist was clenched, presumably ready to defend himself if necessary, but his eyes softened when he realized it was a woman tugging at his arm.

At that exact moment, a little black car flew past us, the loud roar of its engine echoing in my ears. For such a narrow road, it was traveling way too fast and pulling attention from everyone on the street. The parked cars near the corner of the intersection had previously obscured it from view, the black car only coming into sight as it swerved around a motorino that had stopped at the crossing before flooring it through the red light.

"Sorry," I apologized, as I quickly released his arm, my eyes still trailing after the black car. "It's just that that car didn't look like it was going to stop." I realized I was speaking English and repeated the same thing in Italian. "Scusa, mi dispiace, ma non imaginavo che quella macchina si fermasse."

I turned to look at him. Like me, his eyes had darted to the road when he heard the roar of the engine. He'd seen the car race past as it had accelerated in an attempt to get through the light.

"How did you just— I didn't see the— How did you see— Way too fast." He shook his head as he struggled to regain his composure.

For a second, I merely gaped at him, shock rendering me mute. Blue Shirt wasn't only familiar because of the guest-starring role he'd had in my visions—I'd seen him elsewhere. I'd seen him in the piazza when his gaze had caught mine. I openly stared at the Calvin Klein model, too stunned to stop. This stranger I'd felt inexplicably connected to and couldn't understand why . . . until now.

His gaze found mine and I witnessed the same recognition I'd just experienced register in those mysterious eyes. Now that I was closer, I couldn't help but notice they were a depthless blue, like the sky at twilight. Time stood still while we just stared at each other, our eyes locked. Electricity seemed to crackle in the air between us.

Finally, I found my voice and broke the silence. "Are you okay?" I asked. He clearly spoke English.

A smile slowly spread across his face, illuminating his features. "Yes, yes, thanks to you, that is. I was focused on the street ahead and I guess I wasn't paying enough attention."

I, on the other hand, was possibly paying *too* much attention—to him. He had short black hair, a square jaw and flawless complexion, the gift of height, and definitely the physique of a Calvin Klein model. I pegged him as around mid-thirties.

"That's okay. It was nothing at all." *Don't drool, don't drool.*

"Are you kidding? I think you may have just saved my life. If you hadn't grabbed me, there's a chance I would've been road kill. I owe you a . . . well, I don't know how to repay someone for that, but I definitely owe you something."

His accent was distinctively American. I thought about the irony of traveling across the world and having Blue Shirt turn out to be *American*.

"Seriously, it was nothing. Where in the States are you from?" I asked, curious.

"San Francisco. I've been traveling around Europe—heading home next week. Rome's our last stop. What about you?"

My heart skipped a beat. He wasn't just American, he was from *San Francisco*. What were the odds? Meeting an incredibly good-looking guy in Florence who was heading home to San Francisco next week? Could fate be this completely wonderful to me? Could Lady Luck—now my dear, sweet friend—have been steering me here all along? Could my self-inflicted romantic dry spell be about to come to an end? This was the kind of guy for whom all rules were broken. And I'd gladly break mine. Would this be a story to tell our grandchildren, *or what*?

Whoa, where did *that* thought come from? These visions were doing more than just affecting my sight. I had to pull myself back down to earth before he noticed my tongue hanging out of my mouth.

"Um, San Francisco, too, actually. Bay Area."

His eyes widened. "Really? That's incredible! A strange woman saves me in Florence and she's practically my neighbor."

Was it just me, or was even his voice sexy?

Of course, I had noticed his use of the word *strange* and hoped it referred to me being a stranger and not *bizarre*.

"Yeah," I agreed. And then the worst thing happened. I let out a nervous laugh. Only it didn't sound like laughter, it sounded more like a pig squealing—and then I snorted.

Ugh! Kill me now. How *embarrassing*. The horror was painted all over my face.

He must have still been too overcome with gratitude to run and escape the snorter. Instead, he smiled and I forgot my name.

"Look, would you let me buy you a coffee or something at

least? I know it doesn't exactly make up for saving me or anything, but I'd like to say thank you properly at least."

My stomach did a flip. Get a coffee with Blue Shirt, now permanently renamed Calvin? Absolutely! Was the sky blue? The Pope Catholic? Would my grandchildren love this story? Darn it, too far ahead, too far ahead. I had to pull myself together before I got overly excited and ruined it.

The realist in me warned that it was just a coffee with someone who was merely being polite and nothing more. The normally-caged romantic in me, though, had broken free and gotten so excited by the idea of this fateful meeting that it was twisting my stomach in knots at the mental image of kissing him. There was something about him. I'd felt it the second our eyes locked in the piazza. It felt like we were destined to meet.

Hold it together, Isy, I scolded myself. *Be normal.*

"It's really not necessary, but I can't say no to coffee. It's just so good here," I responded, accepting his kind invitation with a returning smile. I'd just had coffee about ten minutes ago but I wasn't about to tell him that. There was no such thing as too much coffee in Italy, anyway.

His face lit up and his eyes radiated warmth.

Why, hello . . .

"Which direction are you heading in?" he asked. "I've been stopping for coffee at a bar called Gilli in Piazza della Republica that's really good, but we can go somewhere closer if you prefer? Everywhere is good anyway."

"I know the place. I was on my way to the Duomo, so that would suit me perfectly." I tried to contain my enthusiasm, it sounded like I was practically singing the words.

"Great. Ladies first," he said as he gestured for me to walk ahead on the narrow sidewalk. Then he stepped out onto the road to walk beside me. The action was so gentlemanly, it endeared me to him. *Chivalry is not dead*, I thought.

"So how long have you been in Florence?" he asked, making conversation. His tone was casual, but a note of curiosity crept into his voice. I had a feeling he was confirming in his own mind that it was me he'd seen a few days ago in the piazza. I wondered whether he'd mention it.

"Just a week. I've come to visit a friend who lives here. It's a relatively quick visit. I've got one more week before I fly home."

"Must be a good friend to come all this way."

"My best friend actually. I feel guilty that I haven't come to visit her more often. I've let work get in the way. Now that I'm here, I realize just how much I miss seeing her every day." My tone turned solemn. I hated the idea of only having one more week with Jules. She had a way of making everything seem better.

"Sounds like you're very close. It must be very difficult being so far away," he empathized. I nodded. I couldn't believe how easy it was to talk to him, how natural and comfortable it felt. "So what do you do that keeps you so busy—for work, I mean."

I hesitated. Sometimes when I told people I was a lawyer, they gave me *the look*—the dubious look that indicated they thought lawyers were ambulance-chasing bloodsuckers who loved to feed off others' misery. There were so many misconceptions about lawyers: heartless, arrogant, overconfident, unfaltering composure, swimming in money from the day we finished law school. The truth was that a lot of lawyers were swarming in insecurities, always striving to be the best. We were just better at masking it, and many often overcompensated with arrogance. I wanted him to get to know me a little better before he jumped to any conclusions.

"Let's just say that my job is to make sure that companies act in the best interests of the public. It's a corporate job, I won't bore you with the details. What about you?" It was a slight slant on the truth, but not exactly a lie, either.

"Actually, that sounds interesting. Tell me about it. Is it a government job?" he probed.

Darn it, now I was going to look like an idiot for not just telling him in the first place. I sighed as I gave up the charade.

"No, but I do work a lot with the FTC—the Federal Trade Commission—which is focused on preserving the interests of consumers. I'm a corporate lawyer"—I paused to observe his reaction; a look of surprise—"but don't hold it against me," I joked.

"Really? I never would've guessed. You don't look like a lawyer." He sounded like he meant that as a compliment, which really meant it was an insult.

"So what's a lawyer supposed to look like then?" I responded with a slight edge to my tone. It was an automatic reflex. My romantic self was going to be shoved back in the cage more quickly than I'd anticipated. One stereotype that was indisputable: our pride.

I'd heard all the lawyer jokes before—especially from Jules—and I normally wouldn't respond with much more than an eye-roll so long as there wasn't any malicious intent. It hadn't bothered me when other people had said worse—much worse. With him, though, any insults cut me deeper than they should.

He must have heard the offense in my voice, as he immediately put his hands up in a surrender position, palms forward. "I was going to say someone who's had their personality extracted, but it wouldn't be nice to tease my hero of the day," he said, winking. "I suppose I imagine lawyers to look more like librarians—or angry sharks. But I see that some lawyers are actually vibrant, caring, lovely women—I mean, *heroes*," he corrected, hitting me again with that big, warm smile.

His obvious attempt to butter me up surprisingly worked. I blamed my relaxed vacation mode. "We're the mutant lawyers who are actually part human. Sometimes we save the human pedestrians, and sometimes we push them in front of the speeding vehicles. Luckily, it was your day today."

"Phew." He pretended to wipe the sweat from his face.

"Don't worry, I'm not going to sue for defamation." I quipped.

He chuckled. "Well at least I know where to go if I ever do need a lawyer."

I shook my head. "I'm a corporate lawyer, so I can't help you if you rob a bank or something. You'd be on your own and in big trouble. Unless, of course, you don't get caught."

"So your advice really is: just don't get caught. I bet you charge hundreds for that, too." The corner of his mouth quirked, the amusement dancing on his lips.

"Only if we *like* you, otherwise it's thousands. Let's just say that whatever you stole would now belong to us." I gave him a wink.

We reached the end of Via Ghibellina and turned right into Via dei Proconsolo. As we crossed over the street, he stuck his head out to make sure there was no oncoming traffic and gently placed his hand at the middle of my back to guide me across the road. His touch was so gentle, I could barely feel it.

"So is your best friend a lawyer, too?" he asked once we'd reached the other side of the street. Again, he gave me the sidewalk and walked on the road beside me.

"No, she's an artist—which is why she loves living in Florence so much. She says she's already died and gone to Heaven."

He nodded. "Life is all about passion. So is being a lawyer your passion then?"

The question took me off guard. No one had ever asked me that before. Wasn't it kind of a weird question to ask someone you'd just met? And shouldn't the answer automatically be yes? After all, it was what I'd decided to do with my life, what I'd made so many sacrifices for.

He looked over at me and must have seen the consideration in my expression. "That wasn't a trick question." He hopped up on the sidewalk behind me as a car approached, giving me a few more moments to consider my answer. He looked at me expectantly as he fell back in step beside me.

"I guess I've never really thought about it that way before. I've chosen a path and set goals for myself, in order to keep moving forward. But if I stop to think about it, I guess I'm not really sure what my 'passion' is. That's quite sad really . . ." I let my voice trail off as I pondered it. "Hey, how did you manage to turn that around so I just went from being successful to sad in about thirty seconds? You haven't told me what *your* job is. Let me guess: a psychoanalyst?" I teased.

He laughed and the sound of it was rich and sultry.

"Let me tell you, after picking on me all this time, it had better be *good*, or you're about to cop it," I mocked, a glint in my eye.

"Hmm, I think I should keep it a mystery then," he responded in a playful tone.

"You can't do that—you'd force me to sue for pain and suffering. The suspense is killing me."

He laughed again at my expression and the sound sent shivers of pleasure through me. "Let's just say that my passion is helping people."

He was as evasive as I had been. "Okay—so I suppose I have to guess now. Not any kind of analyst or counselor then?" It seemed to fit him so well.

"Nope. Care to try again?" He was clearly enjoying the suspense.

"I need another hint. I mean, even a drug dealer could *claim* that he was helping people."

"Ah, the suspicious lawyer. How about this—one could argue that I *am* a drug dealer, of sorts." He raised his eyebrows at me, trying to be mysterious.

"Pharmacist?" I guessed.

He shook his head. "Nope."

"Pharmaceutical sales rep?"

"Nope."

"Actual drug dealer?"

He chuckled, then put his hands up again in the same surrender position with his palms forward. "Nope. I'm legal, ma'am."

Who else dealt with prescription drugs, I mused. "Doctor?"

"Hole in one. Well, actually, hole in four."

Seriously? This handsome stranger with a smile to kill was also funny, chivalrous and intelligent—with just a little mischievousness thrown in for good measure—*and* his passion was helping poor little sick children? Something had to be wrong with him, no one could be that perfect. Or perhaps that *was* what was wrong with him. He was that perfect. He was probably looking for a perfect woman to make him a set. Some Barbie doll who would go swimming at the beach and, with one tiny flick of her head, still have perfect hair.

"Well, you can't blame me," I responded, "I mean, you don't really *look* like a doctor."

He chuckled again. "I suppose I had that one coming."

We were on Via Speziali Corso now, close to the piazza we were heading towards. I was amazed at how quickly the time passed. Once again, I was struck by how comfortable and effortless it was talking with him. I was beginning to feel like I'd known him forever, while at the same time feeling like there were a million things I wanted to know about him.

"So what brought you to Florence? You said 'our last stop is Rome'—who are you traveling with?" I presumed it was a friend since he'd been walking on his own. If he was traveling with a girl, surely they'd be together.

He paused, seeming to hesitate for a moment. "My fiancée. We both wanted to see Italy, and you can't come to Italy and not come to Florence, right?"

My heart sank. My imaginary grandchildren just died, shot dead. The vacation romance was also hit by the firing squad, slaughtered without mercy. Lady Luck was definitely off the Christmas list. I was annoyed at myself for not suspecting this sooner. Dr. Ken had to have a perfect Mrs. Barbie. It made sense. They probably had the Dream House and all the accessories, too.

I managed to keep my tone nonchalant. "Where is she now?" I asked, curiosity getting the better of me.

"Shopping." He looked down and held out the bag he was carrying as evidence. "I was a little shopped-out, so I told her I'd meet her in a couple of hours. What time is it?" He glanced at his watch. "Ah, it's been nearly two hours already. That went quickly. If you don't mind, I'll send her a text and tell her to come and meet us at the bar when she's ready."

You can't be serious, I thought. The only thing worse than knowing Dr. Ken has his perfect Barbie, is being forced to *meet* Barbie and witness her perfection firsthand. Although I had to admit that I was curious, I couldn't bear seeing her slide her hand into his, looking adoringly into each other's eyes. Evidence of the shattered illusion. No thanks. I'd been dreaming about him for weeks—okay, I'd only seen the back of his head up until now, but still—I certainly didn't need another reason to keep dreaming about him. My work here was done. It wasn't going to turn out the way I would have liked, but at least I had this puzzle solved. It was time to leave. Save myself the pain of wanting something I couldn't have.

But how on earth could I suddenly exit? Wouldn't that be too obvious, too embarrassing? *I'm sorry, I didn't realize you had a fiancée. Goodbye.* That's really subtle.

I suddenly felt very uncomfortable. He must have asked me something because he was looking at me like he was waiting for a response. I had no idea what he'd said. I'd been too busy trying to plan an exit strategy and had come up empty. Time to panic.

". . . Of course, if you'd rather not . . ." He was still looking at me expectantly.

Rather not *what?* I wondered.

I sighed and gave up trying to pretend that I'd been listening. "I'm sorry, I missed that. Rather not what?"

"Join us for dinner later, if you're free."

Oh, how sweet and thoughtful. Of course, I'd rather gnaw off my arm and eat that.

"What a kind invitation, but I really shouldn't intrude"—he shook his head, no doubt about to assure me that I wasn't intruding, so I continued quickly—"and I actually have plans tonight. But thank you. That's very kind."

He opened his mouth to say something else and I feared that it would be to extend the invitation to another time. I cut him off before it got messy. "I'm sorry I was distracted. When you asked the time earlier, I realized I'm running late. Julia—that's my friend—is going to kill me. She's only got a short break from work and I was supposed to meet her for an early lunch. I'd better run."

He furrowed his brow, his smile temporarily gone. I needed to make a quick exit before any holes in my story appeared.

"It was a pleasure meeting you . . . um?" Had he mentioned his name? I couldn't think of it, I still only thought of him as Calvin.

"Oh! How rude of me, I didn't introduce myself." He extended his hand to me. "Matthew, Matthew Austin."

I took it. "Isabel Cartier, but everyone calls me Isy. It was a pleasure to meet you, Matthew."

"My friends call me Matt. And the pleasure was all mine, Isy. I feel terrible that I can't at least invite you to dinner to say thank you again for today." He genuinely looked disappointed.

I shook my head. "No need. I didn't do anything. Enjoy the rest of your stay in Italy, Matt—and buon viaggio." I took a step in the direction of the nearest side street. I was starting to feel rather annoyed as it all dawned on me. If he had a fiancée, what had all the staring in the piazza been? Or had I just been imagining it? He was inviting me to dinner *with* his fiancée, so he couldn't have any dishonorable intentions. *God, had he been looking at something* behind *me in the piazza?* I repressed a groan. I suddenly felt like an idiot; now I couldn't even trust my instincts about when a guy was flirting with me.

"You, too. It seems that we'll be going home about the same time. Perhaps we'll see each other there?" It sounded like he was looking for confirmation.

Not a chance. "Yeah, maybe," I answered, without committing myself. I gave a little wave as I took another step back and turned. "At least I know where to go if I ever need a doctor," I said over my shoulder.

"Well, you can find me at . . ."

The rest of his response was swallowed by the sound of hooves clicking against the cobblestones as a horse and carriage approached. The horse sneezed, even he seemed indignant. I made sure I walked away briskly, like I was in the terrible hurry I said I was in, and I was already down the little side street before he could finish his sentence.

Lady Luck, my ass.

6

BURST OF COLOR

AT QUARTER PAST SIX, I met Jules in front of La Rinascente as per our routine. She was already waiting when I got there, leaning against the wall of the building opposite, watching the entrance.

"Hi, Jules," I greeted her. "You're earlier than I thought. How about we go for a walk tonight? Or go and sit in Piazza della Signoria? I just came from there—there's a street performer who's hilarious. He sneaks up behind the people walking between Palazzo Vecchio and the Uffizi and imitates them. Their reaction when they finally notice him is really funny. He's got a big crowd watching."

"But, Isy," Julia protested, looking confused, "don't you want to stay and watch the people coming out of La Rinascente?"

"Nah, no point. Nothing to see here, let's move it along," I teased as I placed my palms on her back and pushed her forward.

She threw me a look over her shoulder, her eyebrows pulled

together in confusion. "What are you talking about, Is? What do you mean there's no point? What about Blue Shirt?"

"Blue Shirt is Matthew Austin. Puzzle solved," I said as calmly as I could. Jules was about to become hysterical enough for the both of us.

I wasn't disappointed. Her eyes widened so much that I thought her eyeballs might actually pop out. She stopped breathing for a moment, then drew in a huge gasp of air. When she finally found her voice, she could barely get the words out.

"Wwwhat? *What*?" is all she could initially manage.

"I met him earlier today," I explained. "Happened exactly the way I had seen it. Turns out that the corner wasn't that far, like you thought. I was walking behind when I spotted him and I managed to catch his arm just in time. It was at the corner of Via Giuseppe Verdi and Via Ghibellina. Funny, huh?"

Julia's mouth was still on the floor. "Oh . . . my . . . God," she gasped.

"I know. Guess I'm two for two." I shrugged. I was trying to downplay it, but I didn't know who I was trying to convince more: myself or Jules.

"You *are* two for two!" Her enthusiasm momentarily dimmed as she appraised me, narrowing her eyes. "Are you completely freaking out right now? You're acting strangely casual—*too* casual, in fact. Not at all what I expected."

"Well, there's no point freaking out. So far whatever is happening to me seems to be helping people, so at least something positive has come out of it. And I know I'm not losing my mind. It really *did* happen." This sentiment didn't necessarily reflect the rising tension and confusion boiling inside me, but I did take some solace in the fact that my cognitive ability was no longer in disrepute—whatever was happening was real, not imaginary. Take that, doctors! I'm not insane! Unfortunately, I couldn't smugly tell them this, since my story would still *sound* delusional to their ears.

"That's a good attitude to have." Jules seemed impressed, but she didn't hide the surprise in her tone. "Now—you have to tell me *everything*. Don't leave anything out. What did he say? What did you say? How did he react? What happened afterward? Did you find out more about him? What was he like? Is he a local? What—"

I cut her off before she could fire off any more questions. She was bouncing up and down like an excited four-year-old in line to see Santa. "Calm down, Jules. I'll tell you—but give me a *chance*. One question at a time, okay? Sheesh, you're hyper."

She smiled, then pretended to zip up her mouth and looked at me patiently.

"Let's go grab a coffee where we can sit and I'll give you all the details. How about Oibò? That is, if you can wait that long," I said, laughing.

She pouted her lips. "It's a tough ask, but okay."

We headed to Piazza di Santa Croce. When we got to the bar, we took the booth to the right. It was the only booth and offered more privacy—exactly what I was looking for given the story I was about to tell.

She sat quietly as I spoke, and even though I could see the questions burning her lips, she waited for me to finish before she fired them off at me. After a moment of silence, the tirade began.

"So he asked you to coffee, *and* dinner, and you didn't agree to either? And he also wanted to organize to see you back in San Francisco, and again, you didn't give him the chance? But you really got along well, and he was funny and cute and thoughtful . . . Isy, what did you do in a previous life that you think you have to punish yourself for?" She seemed almost irritated.

"Ah, Jules, did you conveniently miss the part about how he has a fiancée?" I asked her sarcastically.

"Ah, Isy," she said, returning my sarcastic tone, "did *you* miss the part where you are still allowed to have friends? For goodness sakes, Isy, why does it always have to be all or nothing with you?" she asked, frustrated.

"Because I don't think you can be friends with someone you're attracted to," I snapped. "And I really didn't feel like meeting his fiancée. Why do you care so much anyway? I did what I had to—I stopped him from becoming road kill. When exactly did I tell you that I had a premonition of us becoming lifelong friends?" I wasn't in the mood to be scolded.

She heard the petulant tone in my voice and softened hers a little. Her eyes were sympathetic. "I'm only telling you this because you know I love you and I want the best for you. You are so preoccupied with trying to protect yourself from getting hurt—or even having feelings for someone if you don't think it will be reciprocated in the immediate future—that you don't let anyone in. Sometimes opportunity knocks and you slam the door." She reached out and put her hand on my arm. "I just want you to give people a chance. Especially this one, because I think there's a reason you two met, regardless of whether that reason is romantic or not."

"Well, I think that reason has something to do with the fact that he still has two usable legs—just a hunch," I retaliated.

"Of course there's that. But Isy, have you considered why you see the people you do? There'd be thousands of people who have traffic accidents every day, but you didn't see any of them.

"Have you noticed that the two people you've helped so far—Jeremy and Matthew—you seem to have a bond, a connection with them? They're people who touch your soul in some way. You don't just help *them*, they help *you*."

"That sounds like a romantic notion, Jules, but I don't see how Matt has helped me. Unless you think I'm going to suddenly need a doctor in the near future." This idea immediately sent panic waves coursing through me. Maybe I was like John Travolta's character in *Phenomenon* after all . . . it just hadn't shown up on the scans yet.

Jules snapped me back from the minefield I'd just delved head first into. "You are super paranoid," she scoffed, rolling her eyes. "How many times do I have to tell you that I don't think you're dying? Geez, you're pessimistic sometimes. You always go straight to the worst-case scenario. What I meant is that I think Matt has a message for you—about finding your passion and following your dreams. Not settling for what you think you're supposed to do, what you think is expected of you. Just because you're good at something, Is, doesn't mean that that's the thing that will make you happy. Sometimes the best things in life are the things that require the biggest risks. You need to figure out what your real passion is—and just go for it."

I repressed a groan. Jules had such an idealist view of the world. "I can't jump out of bed everyday and dance my way to work with a marching band in tow. Not everything is rainbows and kittens, you know."

She tsked me. "And not everything is black and white, Is. I thought you were starting to see that now."

That much was true. I was frustrated that I had no idea how any of this worked, that there wasn't a manual to consult. I was intrigued by the idea that Jeremy and Matt had helped me. Ruminating on this revelation, I knew it rang true. Jeremy and I had become good friends since that fateful day. Without Jules back home, I was starting to rely on seeing him to brighten my day. He always had a kind word and a smile for me.

Matt's questions had affected me more than they should have. They'd actually gotten me thinking about the path I was on and where I was headed. There was something missing from my life, I'd known it for a while. My friends thought I was missing out on romance, but I'd always been the type of person who was self-sufficient. I wanted to be complete on my own before finding someone to share my life with.

I'd put that feeling of yearning down to the fact that I hadn't yet reached my goal of becoming a senior associate. Now I started to think that maybe it was something else. I had a feeling that figuring out what was missing was going to be even more difficult than finding it.

"Not everyone is like you, you know. We don't all just pick up a paintbrush at age four and find our 'zen'"—I air-quoted the word, emphasizing my skepticism—"And besides, I don't have time for hobbies. I'm on the precipice of reaching my goals in my career right now. I have to stay focused."

"I never said it was easy. Look at me, I work as a tour guide to pay the bills because my art doesn't always sell. But I still chose something that keeps me around art. Something that I enjoy, too. But I, of all people, know that it's anything but easy. And as for your career—you've had blinders on for so long, I'm not even sure you've stopped to think about what you're racing towards anymore. There are many aspects to life, Is, and I'm afraid you're missing out on a lot of it."

She paused for a second and leaned forward. "Speaking of which, I don't think you should just write Matt off, either. I think you *should* get in touch with him. You *should* be friends. It doesn't have to be all or nothing—not with work, and not with people. It's about balance, and keeping the door open to be able to let good things in." She leaned back in her seat. "I'm sorry, that's the end of my sermon for the day. Go in peace, my child," she whispered, making the sign of the peace with her right hand.

I rolled my eyes. "I wouldn't expect anything less from you. You always have a strong opinion and you're never afraid to share it. It's one of the things I love about you," I told her, and then threw in, "Even though it's also one of the things that sometimes annoys me the most about you."

She smiled innocently and shrugged. "So—Matt?"

"What about him? I can't contact him. I didn't wait to hear how, remember?" I reminded her.

"Have you ever heard of a little thing called the Internet? I'm sure we can find him," she announced confidently.

"His name isn't exactly uncommon, you know. It may be more difficult than you think. Plus, what, I'm going to tell him that I stalked him online and tracked him down? I don't think so!"

"You wouldn't be stalking him—he obviously wants to see you. Honestly, Isy, if you make me, I will create an email address in your name and *I'll* email him," she threatened.

"You wouldn't dare." I glared at her. "Not if you value your life," I warned with fire in my eyes.

She held up her hand, backing down. "Easy there, Rocky. But you definitely should. We'll google him as soon as we get home. At the very least, I want to find out more about him and see a photo or something. Then it's over to you—I mean, I can only lead a horse to water. Come on, Black Beauty, let's go."

Julia was right, it was easier than I thought to find him. The stalker woman brought up his bio, which conveniently displayed his photo. She was drooling all over it.

She had her laptop on the kitchen table, while I stubbornly sat on the opposite side of the room with my arms crossed, trying not to look as interested as I actually was.

"Stop pouting. What, you're not even curious?" she challenged, momentarily tearing her gaze away from the screen to stare me down.

I didn't respond.

"Oh, that's interesting . . ." She knew the curiosity would kill me. Evil woman.

"What is?" I finally asked, relenting.

"He's a cosmetic surgeon. Says here that he's—"

I cut her off. "What? A cosmetic surgeon? You have *got* to be kidding me! All that hoo-ha about how his passion is helping people and how does he help? By giving women who are paranoid about their bodies bigger breasts or smaller thighs! Pleeeease!"

How quick I'd been to think he was so perfect. I couldn't believe he had the gall to make fun of *my* profession feeding off the pain of others. Ha!

"Isy, before you start calling him Dr. Evil or something, let me finish. I was trying to explain that it says in his bio that he specializes in skin restoration, particularly for burn victims. The big, bad, evil cosmetic surgeon is actually a saint. Come look at this."

Burn victims? He helped burn victims? Guilt immediately washed over me for being so harsh. I took this in with a mix of awe and disappointment. Awe because it was such a noble and worthwhile thing to do—and he really *did* help people—and disappointment because it only endeared him to me more. I needed to see his flaws to bring me back to reality, not see his angel wings. I sighed.

Jules noticed my slumped shoulders. "What's wrong? What could you possibly have against that?"

"It's just that he's *so* perfect. I think I preferred the big, bad, evil, breast-enlarging cosmetic surgeon," I confessed.

"You should feel really good about yourself, Is. You helped someone who helps so many people. Even if the accident hadn't killed him, he could've injured his hands and not been able to operate. You were meant to save him. And in a way, now you're a part of it—all the people in the future who he helps, it's because you helped him today. Smile, you deserve it."

It was a nice thought. I couldn't take so much credit, though; all I'd done was pull on his arm. An arm that no doubt performed miracles.

"I'm glad," is all I voiced aloud.

* * *

The rest of my time with Julia passed much too quickly. I couldn't bear to leave, I felt like I needed more time with her. I was just starting to really relax, to feel free.

I hadn't had any more visions since my encounter with Matt. Despite my fears, I hadn't continued to dream of him, either. I finally felt a sense of peace, resolution.

But I had other questions I still needed to answer. I wanted more time with my friend—the one who understood me better than I sometimes understood myself.

I had been quiet the last two days of my time in Florence, solemn at the thought of leaving. Jules had noticed, but hadn't said anything. I knew how disappointed she was, too.

The night before I left, she knocked on the door to my room as I was packing.

"Isy, can I come in? I want to give you something," she told me.

"Sure, come in, Jules. What is it?"

She entered carrying something in her hands. A cylinder.

"I was up last night so I could paint this for you," she explained as she opened the lid and pulled out the canvas.

"Jules, you shouldn't have, you already have so much to do. It's me who should be giving you gifts to thank you for all of your help, not to mention your hospitality." I suddenly felt guilty that I hadn't thought to get her a present. I wished I had.

"It's no big deal, Isy. I felt inspired so I painted it. I wanted you to have a reminder of your visit here. Maybe I'm being selfish because I want you to come back again soon."

She unrolled the canvas and let me see her masterpiece. It was beautiful, an abstract piece alive with color.

"Wow, it's amazing," I breathed. "I'm going to have it framed as soon as I get home and hang it in the living room," I promised. "Thank you so much. I absolutely love it." It was one of those rare pieces that could brighten a room and also your spirits.

She beamed at me. "I'm glad. Now let me explain it to you. Abstract art is subjective of course, but this painting has a story: *your* story. I made it abstract so only you and I would know exactly what it represents," she explained. She seemed to be proud of herself for keeping it our secret.

She pointed to a patch of blue and pink in the bottom left corner. "This part represents Matt—all we knew of him in the beginning." Her warm smile was almost as big and bright as the painting.

Then she pointed to a swirl of black in the bottom right corner and a wing-shaped outline in between the black and blue patches. "And this represents the black car, with the wing being you who swooped in to save him. The warm colors over here," she explained, gesturing to deep yellows, orange and red across the top of the painting, "represent his personality, the things we know about him now: his passion, his humor, his caring nature. This swirl of white in the middle is the unknown—the path that follows. Find out what's in that space, Isy."

She paused as she watched my eyes rest on each section of the painting.

"I wanted you to have this because I don't want you to forget about him. Even if this next path splits in two and they never collide again, you should still remember. Remember that these beautiful colors continue to flourish," she said as she pointed to the top section of the painting, "because of this wing. That old woman was right: you have a gift and it's a blessing. What could be more worthwhile in life than that?"

I stepped forward and threw my arms around her, Jules gently holding the canvas to the side.

"Thank you, Jules. I could never have done this without you. You know, I think this top section represents *you*, too. I will miss you so, so much. But I'll look at this everyday and think of you, I promise."

I had tears in my eyes as I boarded the plane the next day, but it wasn't until I took my seat and buckled the seatbelt that I let the tears flow. I carried the cylinder with me on board for safekeeping. Before I'd left, I'd asked Jules to sign it for me. I told her that an original Julia Davanti would be worth millions one day, but I'd never part with it.

As the plane took off and left Florence airport, my heart felt heavy from having to say goodbye. But it also felt oddly lighter, having found some of the answers I'd been looking for, and the patience to handle not yet conquering the entire puzzle. I whispered—too quietly for anyone to hear—*Goodbye Florence, and thank you.*

7

SHADOWS

I WAS NOT looking forward to my first day back at work. I was still on European time, so when the alarm went off that morning, I wanted to cry. But more than that, I wasn't ready to face Harrison and all of his questions about my trip—and the non-existent wedding I attended.

I wasn't ready to flip open a copy of the *FTC Act* and turn all of my concentration back to the legal world.

But it was Monday.

Monday.

Ugh.

I got to work early so I could sneak into my office and not have to greet everyone on the way. I reluctantly booted up my laptop, knowing I would have a zillion emails awaiting me and it would take all morning—maybe all day—to get through them all.

My heart wasn't in it. My mind was still in Florence.

I opened up my email and waited for the flood. They started pouring in and I watched the counter of unread emails go up . . . and up . . . and up. I groaned as it passed three hundred and fifty.

As I was about to get up and go make a cup of coffee to help me face the backlog of emails screaming for attention, I spotted one from Jules. Thank goodness, a pleasant email to start the morning—just what I needed.

Buongiorno Isy!

Hope your first day back is a good one. Try to relax – I know you, you'll try to make up for two lost weeks by staying at work till midnight every night – DON'T!

I'm so happy that you came to Florence. It was great having you here. I miss you soooo much. And I'm glad I was able to share the experience with you – can you believe that it actually happened?! It did!!

Since I know you'll go straight back into work mode, I wanted to send you an email to remind you of the incredible experience you had here – and no doubt the journey that will continue for you. Be open to it. Remember I am here anytime that you need to talk. I am on the edge of my seat waiting to hear what happens next! Make sure you keep me in the loop!

Now I know how you feel about a certain someone you met here – but I stand by what I told you. I don't think that you should forget about him. Since I know you'll try... well, it's up to you. But I hope you will contact him. Remember that he wanted you to. The events of the past couple of weeks should prove to you that some things happen for a reason. And you can never have too many friends, right?

Dr. Matthew Austin
matthew.austin@saintfrancismemorial.org
Tel: (415) 555 0125

Miss you already
Jules xx

Ugh. She'd copied in a photo of him underneath—were there no bounds to her persistence? Right now, Dr. Matthew Austin was the last person I wanted to think about. I was finding it difficult enough to concentrate as it was, and I certainly didn't need any further distraction. Especially a distraction that had my heart racing at the mere mention of his name. The photo flipped my stomach.

I could kill Jules. She went from easing me into my day to throwing my restrained mind into overdrive. Suddenly I could feel the gentle touch of his hand on my back . . .

"Welcome back, Isy." Harrison was at my door, interrupting my reverie. "Are you okay? You don't look well. You look really flushed, and upset, like someone just ran over your cat."

Oh great, thanks, Jules. Harrison was supposed to see me refreshed, and now he had that same worried expression on his face from before I'd gone away.

"Oh, hi, Harrison!" I greeted too enthusiastically. "No, I'm great! Maybe just a little jet-lagged. The trip was fantastic! The wedding was absolutely beautiful—the bride was stunning, the weather was gorgeous, the food was divine, the music was lovely, the ceremony was amazing, the groom was—"

Harrison cut me off. "I get it. Everything was 'amazing.' I'm glad you enjoyed yourself." He scrutinized me for a moment before he continued. "So, you're feeling better then?"

"Absolutely!" Again, too enthusiastic. Not much got past Harrison. Even I wouldn't believe it.

"Hmm . . . okay then." At this point, I think it was easier for him to accept my answer than bother to ask too many questions. He only needed to know that I was ready to work and give one hundred per cent. My personal life wasn't of *that* much interest to him.

"I'll let you get through your email," he continued slowly. "This afternoon I want you to come and see me about a matter I want you to get involved in—section five. It's going to court, so we'll be working with the litigation team on this one. It's an important case and I'll need all hands on deck. Are you ready to roll up your sleeves? It will require one hundred and ten per cent."

As I thought, he was only interested in my ability to perform—and perform very well. Section five of the *FTC Act* referred to unfair and deceptive acts or practices. If it was going to court, it was definitely a substantial matter for our client, with public perception as important as any legal ramifications.

Was I ready to not have a life outside of work and only live and breathe this matter? *Absolutely not.*

"Absolutely, that sounds great, Harrison. Thanks for including me. Who is the client?" I inquired with an eager tone. I was a lawyer, I knew how to feign interest. Harrison wasn't really asking—say no and I might as well pack up my office.

"Parkmores," he informed me.

This *was* big. Parkmores, a large pharmaceutical company, was the firm's largest client, bringing in roughly thirty-five million dollars per year. Given the size of the account, the client justifiably expected only the highest level of service and, of course, only the best outcomes.

If I did well on this, it would raise my profile in the firm. If I didn't do well, they'd probably move my office to a closet somewhere. It was an all-or-nothing type deal. It meant that my phone had to be on twenty-four/seven. Nothing short of death would be an excuse not to deliver.

"I'll come and see you this afternoon," I promised, smiling.

Harrison nodded and left my office.

I turned back to my laptop. Jules's email was still on the screen. I hit delete.

* * *

I got home at eleven o'clock that evening, totally exhausted. I had flown in on Sunday morning. One day at home hadn't exactly been enough to get over the jet lag.

There was a note on the door.

> Sorry I missed you yesterday, I was away for the weekend. Come and see me.
> Jez

How sweet. I didn't know when I was going to get the chance, though. It looked like I'd be stuck at the office all week.

I went inside my apartment, put my bag down and collapsed on the bed. I felt like I hadn't slept in a month, but I was overtired and couldn't sleep. So I took a sleeping pill and let myself slip into sweet unconsciousness.

This routine continued all week. And each morning I awoke to the sound of my alarm, having been dead to the world, in deep, dreamless sleep.

On Thursday, there had been another email from Jules, which I also deleted. All it read was:

Dr. Matthew Austin
matthew.austin@saintfrancismemorial.org
Tel: (415) 555 0125

Because I love you
Jules xx

She gets points for persistence.

Jeremy had also been persistent, leaving three more notes on my door during the week.

Tuesday:

Came by but missed you. Come see me
when you get home.

Wednesday:

Have muffins. Don't make me eat them all.

Friday:

Are you still alive? Don't make me beg,
I know where you live :)

Poor Jeremy. I wished I had been eating muffins and chatting about Florence with him. But I'd been chained to my desk at the office instead.

Thankfully, I only had a couple hours of work to do on Saturday from home and then the rest of the weekend would be free. Although I was planning to sleep for most of it.

When I got home on Friday night, I wrote Jeremy a note and slipped it under the door.

> *Jez – sorry, alive but barely. Late nights at the office. Will be home tomorrow. Any chance of a muffin? ☺*
> *Isy*

I went inside and, as per usual, collapsed on my bed. No need for sleeping pills, I was already half asleep before my head hit the pillow.

* * *

I could see a darkened sidewalk, which looked like a tunnel. It was daylight, but the stretch of sidewalk was blackened by the overhead scaffolding and the barriers positioned next to the road.

A shadow moved inside the darkness, coming towards me. As it inched closer, the hazy figure of a man in a dark suit came into view. There was a loud noise and the man's head jerked upwards.

I was jolted awake by the noise, which turned out to be the banging at the door. I looked at the clock, wondering what time it was. One o'clock in the afternoon. I couldn't believe that I'd slept through until the afternoon, without even waking.

The knocking continued. I pulled on a robe and went to the door, combing my bed hair with my fingers and pulling it back into a ponytail. I peered through the peephole. God bless him, it was Jeremy.

I opened the door with a huge smile, no doubt looking a fright.

"Oh shite, did I wake you?" he asked, looking down at his watch, confused. He was holding a basket.

"Just catching up on some sleep. I was having a really bizarre dream. But I had to get up anyway, so it's good you came. What do you have in there?" I asked, leaning forward to try and peek into the basket.

"Goodies for the half dead," he teased. "I figured that you wouldn't have had a chance to stock up on groceries since you've been back, so I took the liberty of bringing you lunch and a couple of bare essentials. May I come in?" he asked, giving me one of his big, warm smiles that could melt hearts.

"Sorry, Jez, of course! Anyone who brings me goodies is always welcome," I said as I gestured for him to enter. "La mia casa è la tua casa." As soon as it was out of my mouth, I immediately thought of Jules. "This is really sweet of you."

Jeremy placed the basket on the table. "It's nothing."

"No, seriously, Jez, you're the best. Thanks, I love you." As soon as *those* words were out of my mouth, I instantly regretted them. It's something I would say to Jules all the time, without a thought. Of course, we knew that it was never meant in a romantic sense. But would Jeremy know that?

Now I worried that my casual use of the word *love* may make things awkward between us. He'd reacted when I said it—a slight pause. I panicked, fearing he would run screaming from the room. Then I saw the smile slowly spread across his face. *Oh dear Lord, no. Please don't let me hurt Jez.* Suddenly, *I* wanted to run screaming from the room.

". . . bro." I tacked it on after the pause, then bumped my shoulder to his. Embarrassment instantly colored my cheeks. *What an idiot.* Bro? Since when had I used that term—ever? *I love you . . . bro.* That had to be up there with my Hansel and Gretel humiliation from the roof.

A look of confusion replaced his smile.

"Sorry, I sound like I've had a few, huh!" I screeched, and immediately followed up with two short hiccup laughs, made worse by the huge snort in between.

Great work, Isy, I thought. *Make sure he'd never* want *you to mean it seriously.* I would've been consumed by my own embarrassment if I weren't so worried about hurting Jeremy.

He looked at me, the mess I was in my robe with bed hair and probably mascara under my eyes—Dear Lord, I just remembered I hadn't bothered to take off my makeup last night—and smiled.

"You really are tired, huh?"

"And starving! So, what's in the goodie basket?" I asked, more relaxed now that the awkwardness seemed to have passed. I tried to discreetly run my fingers under my eyes in a pitiful attempt to wipe away any mascara residue. But I had a feeling the whole clown-face look was already burned into his retinas.

"Well, I have muffins, as per your order. And I also have some focaccias for lunch, some apples, milk and bread—and, of course, chocolate." He smiled, pleased with his assortment.

"Jez, thank you! That is really, really thoughtful of you. And you're absolutely right—the cupboards are bare, except for some canned goods and cereal boxes. This is absolutely perfect. Will you have lunch with me?"

"Well, not to be presumptuous or anything, but I brought enough for two. And . . . I also took the liberty of bringing over a couple of movies"—he paused, looking away for a brief second before adding—"if you have time, that is."

I looked at the DVD covers. *Notting Hill* and *Jumping Jack Flash*. The first was a total chick flick he'd obviously chosen for me. The second was an old movie with Whoopi Goldberg that I'd seen a million times as a teenager. I liked the fact it was a reversal of the normal 'boy saves girl' theme. Did he know it was one of my favorite movies? Had I told him? That would be sweet if he'd remembered.

"You brought *Jumping Jack Flash*? That's one of my favorites."

"I know. You mentioned it once, ages ago." He pulled something else out of the basket. "I forgot to mention the popcorn."

"I am going to write to the Pope—you should be considered for sainthood."

He bowed, crooning, "Here to serve, my lady." Then he added, "But you realize that to be considered for sainthood, you first have to be dead."

I cringed, remembering that fateful day on the roof. I couldn't imagine life without him now. "Then you'll have to settle for my undying gratitude. I'll grab the plates. You sit down. The least I can do is serve *you*."

He sat down and gestured for the napkin to be put in his lap, winking. "So is the food good here?"

I giggled. He always made me smile, no matter what condition he found me in.

I poured him a drink, excusing myself while I ran to change and make myself presentable. I cringed when I saw the horrifying reflection in the mirror, complete with bird-nest hair and panda eyes. I looked like I'd been on the losing end of a catfight—which had taken place during a tornado. The fact he hadn't ridiculed me or tweeted a photo of me captioned, *'When animals attack'* was a testament to his kindness. When I returned, I found him looking at the photos stuck to my fridge.

"That's Jules, my girlfriend in Florence," I explained, noting the photo that had caught his attention. It had been taken on a girl's night out, both of us smiling widely with a cocktail in one hand and an arm around each other.

"You look amazing here," he said.

My lips twitched in amusement. He was obviously surprised that I cleaned up okay when I actually bothered to dress up—or get dressed, period, given how I'd answered the door. It wasn't just the fetching look I'd treated him to today, he usually only ever saw me at home in the evenings or on weekends, generally in my track pants or some other equally attractive clothing.

"Don't sound so surprised. I am presentable most of the time—remember I work in a corporate office. But wearing suits and heels all day, when I get home, I dress for comfort."

"Clearly," he teased.

I punched him on the arm. "Let's eat," I said, moving towards the table.

"Hey, what was that bizarre dream you said you had?"

"Oh, nothing. Just silly. I was dreaming about a sidewalk with scaffolding around it. It was a little creepy because I could only see the shadow of a man inside the darkness. Then the knocking at the door woke me up. Probably a warning to keep out of dark places."

The expression on his face turned serious. "Then no going up to the roof for thinking time. From now on, when you need to get out of your apartment, make sure you pop across the hall instead."

This was the first time Jeremy had mentioned the roof since that day. But he sounded more concerned about my safety than anything else. I still didn't have the heart to tell him that I'd never go up to the roof alone at night, even if Hugh Jackman were there. Well, okay, maybe if *Hugh* were there, I'd let that rule slide.

When we moved to the couch, fresh popcorn in hand, Jeremy sat closer to the middle than his side. I tried not to make too much of it. After all, we were sharing the popcorn, so it made sense that he would sit close.

I put a pillow in between us and rested the bowl on it. I worried that without the barrier, I'd cuddle up to him without even thinking about it. I just felt so comfortable and relaxed with him.

I spent the rest of the afternoon with my friend, and forgot about the laptop on my desk, quietly whispering my name.

* * *

I hopped into bed that night thinking about the afternoon with Jeremy. I wondered why it was that I was so concerned about not giving him the wrong impression.

Why didn't I want to give him the wrong impression?

Why was it wrong? Why wasn't it the *right* impression?

I'd been single for so long that it seemed like an automatic reflex for me to move away and keep a safe distance.

But most of the time, the men I didn't want to give the wrong impression to were people that I had no interest in. Colleagues, or the occasional sleaze at a bar.

Jeremy was different. I really liked him—he was sweet, thoughtful, caring, funny, charming. Not exactly a bad list of qualities to have. I hadn't really thought about it before, but now that I did, I could admit that he was also good-looking. He was tall, with thick, dark hair and big hazel eyes. He was lean, but not lanky. *Definitely* good-looking.

He had seen me looking like I'd just stepped off the set of a horror movie, and yet, instead of running from the room, he smiled and gave me a goodie basket.

Why was I putting a pillow between us? Why wasn't I jumping all over him instead? Why had I been thinking about a guy who was unavailable, when there was a wonderful, single guy right in front of me?

I slowly drifted off to sleep, still wondering.

In the darkness, I could see the shadow of the man. He was very still, like he was just watching me. Others entered the narrow passageway and I lost sight of his shadow. When the people passed, I saw him again. Completely still.

I heard a creaking noise, but this time the man's head didn't tilt upward. A shadowed object plummeted towards him, striking his head with brutal force before hitting the ground with a deafening crack. The metallic sound reverberated in my ears as I jolted awake, gasping for air.

All of my senses were on high alert. Each shadow in the room suddenly appeared forbidding, the rustle of the wind outside eerily reminiscent of the shadowed object whooshing through the air before its brutal blow.

Was this just a silly dream, or was this dream different? I had dreamed about the incident with Matt, but only after I'd had the vision—at an extremely inopportune time—while I was awake. I'd known it was connected. If this were a premonition of something real, I was both freaked out and somewhat relieved.

Freaked out because it presented a number of concerns, including the escalating nature of what was happening. How long would it continue, and how much worse would it get? I felt an unfair burden of this man's life on my shoulders. *Who was he?*

Relieved because if these premonitions were going to continue, at least they were only occurring during my sleeping hours, and not rendering me mute at work.

My head throbbed. I wasn't sure what it was. There was no *Dictionary of Dreams that Come True* that I could look it up in.

I looked at the clock—4:00 A.M. I quickly did the math. It was 1:00 P.M. in Italy. I started to dial the phone before I could even think about it.

"Pronto." It was Gianni. Thank goodness they must be home for lunch.

"Ah, ciao, Gianni, sono Isabel. Come stai?" I secretly wished Jules had answered. I was too wound up for small talk right now.

"Isabel! Bene, bene, good, good. How was your flight home?" Gianni had an irresistible Italian accent that made everything he said sound like poetry.

"Great, thanks, Gianni. Is Julia home?"

"Sì, I will call her for you. Ciao, Isabel." Gianni must have been able to sense the urgency in my voice because I could faintly hear him whispering to Jules as he handed her the phone, warning her that I sounded anxious.

"Hi, Isy! Are you okay? What time is it there?" She paused as she calculated the time. "It's four in the morning! Why are you up? What's wrong?" Panic quickly entered her voice.

"Nothing, Jules. Sorry to worry you. I just wanted to speak to you. I had a strange dream and—"

She interrupted before I could finish the sentence. "Oh, I see! Well, I was waiting for the next installment. Tell me! What did you dream?" She sounded hyper again and I could visualize her bopping up and down on the other end of the phone.

"Don't get too excited, Jules. I don't know if it was that kind of dream or not yet. That's why I wanted to talk to you. It's kind of like the others, in the sense that I've dreamt it more than once now. But it's different to the others, too, because I haven't seen it, you know, when I've been awake. I can't make out the person at all. All I see is a shadow. I think it's a man, but that's it."

"Geez, why is it always the men that need saving?" she joked. "Okay. Where was the shadow? What happened in the dream?" Jules went straight into analyze mode, exactly what I needed.

"All I know is that there was scaffolding covering a section of sidewalk. The man was under it. Then something fell—I think a part of the scaffolding maybe—and it hit the man hard, knocking him to the ground. The crashing sound—it was so loud." I began to shiver as I thought about it.

There was a moment of silence as Jules contemplated this new information. "Well," she began, "I can see how this is different, but I do think it's real—you know, a vision. Maybe now that you believe in it, there's no need for you to see it during the day? I don't know. But someone is obviously in danger and you're supposed to help them. Problem is, of course, you have no idea who or where or when . . ."

"Ah, as far as problems go, Jules, that's a big one," I pointed out.

"Of course it is. But it's no different to Matt so I don't think this is the end of it. There must be more. For some reason, it's coming through slowly. You said that you've dreamed it more than once right?"

"Yup. Twice now."

"Was it exactly the same both times? Or was the second dream more vivid than the first? Like did you see any more detail, or get a better view?" A light bulb seemed to be going on for Jules.

"Um . . . Yes and no, I suppose. I couldn't see any more of the man, but I could see other people more clearly. In the second dream, people were passing me and walking towards the shadowed man. But he was just staying completely still. It sounds weird, but it was like he was just looking at me and waiting."

"Right, I get two things from that. First, I think you'll dream about it again, and probably keep dreaming about it. Each time, another little piece of the puzzle will become clearer.

"Second—next time you dream it, I want you to pay attention to the people passing you. If you can see them more clearly than the man, perhaps you'll be able to identify one of them and then figure out where or when this might happen."

"Okay. Good idea," I agreed.

"Other than that, try not to worry about it. I don't think

you're expected to perform miracles here. Until you get more information, you couldn't possibly do anything. So time must be on your side. The important thing is to be ready when the information does come to you. And to make sure that you ring me immediately!"

"I will," I promised. "Jules? Why is this happening to me?" I whispered. "Isn't enough, enough? I don't know how much more of this I can take. It's too much."

"I know, honey," she soothed. "I don't know why this has fallen to you, but I do know that you have more strength than you think you have. You're one of the most determined and resilient people I know, Isy. I've always admired that about you. I know it feels overwhelming, because I understand how responsible you feel, but I honestly think it's a gift—it's not meant as a punishment."

I was quiet while I let her words sink in.

"Isy?"

A sigh escaped my lips. "I'm still here. Just thinking about it."

"Whatever happens, at the end of the day, you can only do what you can do. Take it as it comes and try not to worry. Everything will work out, you'll see."

"I don't share your confidence, but you're right, I can't do anything now so I might as well not make myself sick over it."

"Exactly. And remember, Is, you're not alone. I'm here with you. Always just a phone call away," she reassured me, her voice calming. "Now try to get some sleep. You must be exhausted."

"Thanks, Jules. I will. Have a good night. I'll talk to you soon."

"Ah, Isy, before you hang up—just one more question. Have you called anyone else?" she asked slyly.

"What do you mean? You know I haven't told anyone else about this but you." Was she mad? Who would I call—ABC news?

"No, I mean . . . Have you used the telephone number that I emailed you?"

Oh! It all clicked together.

"Good night, Jules," is all I responded before I put down the receiver. I could faintly hear her muttering something on the other end as I hung up.

I managed to get back to sleep, my fears dissipated, at least for now.

8

SURPRISES

MY SECOND WEEK back at work was pretty much the same as the first: hectic. By Friday, I was exhausted.

I'd only had the dream once more during the week. This time I did as Jules had suggested and tried to focus on the other people passing me. Only one had stood out: a woman. She was wearing a dark green suit with a thin, black belt around the waist of her jacket. She had jet-black hair pulled back in a clip, gorgeous green and black stiletto heels to match her suit, and a burgundy leather attaché case.

I tried to get a better look at the street, but couldn't make it out. And so I waited, believing Jules that there must be more to come.

At 1:45 P.M. I headed out to grab a sandwich. Unfortunately, most of the good stuff had already gone by then. Scanning what the seagulls had left behind, I spotted the last remaining Cajun chicken wrap, a tiny beacon on an otherwise dreary day. My spirits lifted. I was at the front of the line and the girl came to serve me.

"Can I help you?" she asked.

"Yes, please. I'll have the—"

"Cajun chicken one right there, thanks." A man in a gray suit with a British accent, probably in his early forties, abruptly pushed in front of me and tried to claim the last wrap! *I don't think so, buddy!*

"Excuse me, I was just ordering that. Perhaps you didn't notice me," I said with a hint of sarcasm.

"Sorry, love, no time. Gotta run." Then he turned to the girl behind the counter, threw her a ten-dollar bill and winked, "Keep the change."

"Ouch!" I screamed. The horrid man stomped on my foot as he pushed back past me.

My mouth dropped open in horror. The rudeness! The complete and utter rudeness! I would've said that aloud, but he'd already disappeared. He was so condescending—*Sorry, love*! Ugh!

He probably thought the British accent was so charming that he could get away with anything. Just he wait until I see him again! He most likely worked in the building, it was full of lawyers. He was probably a partner at another firm and thought he owned the world. I hated people like that. Arrogant ass.

I was still so angry when I returned to my office that I only got through half of my stinky egg sandwich.

When the phone rang, I dumped the other half in the trash. I looked at the caller ID. It was Marie from reception.

"Hi, Marie."

"Hi, Isy. I have a package at reception for you."

"Thanks. I'll come up in a while and collect it. Who's it from?"

"Not sure. You'd probably better come up sooner than later. See you." She sounded cheerful. My packages were usually legal documents. Nothing to get excited over.

Now I was curious, though. My foot still throbbing, I got up and headed to reception on the top floor of our building, which had a stunning view of the San Francisco Bay.

As I got out of the elevator, Marie was smiling at me. She was beautiful, in her mid-thirties, with black, short hair that reminded me of Audrey Hepburn.

"Where's the package?" I asked her, not seeing any parcels on the large counter.

"Over there," she said, pointing to a beautiful arrangement of flowers.

My mouth fell open. "Are you serious? Who sent them?"

"That's what I'm dying to know! They're absolutely gorgeous. Open the card."

My mind raced. Who on earth would send me flowers? Not work—all the long hours were expected, and certainly not worthy of flowers. There was only one person I could think of . . . Jeremy. Oh my Lord. I couldn't think. Was I excited that he sent them? Or worried?

Either way, my hands were trembling as I opened the card.

Since you wouldn't let me take you to dinner, I thought I'd say thank you with flowers. Hope you enjoyed the rest of your trip.

Matt

Oh. My. Lord.

What the?

How?

Why?

Oh. My. Lord.

Marie was talking to me but I couldn't hear her. Not that it mattered, I would need to pick my jaw up off the floor before I'd be able to speak.

My heart was pounding. Since my jaw was still at my feet, and Marie was waiting for a response to her burning questions, I handed her the card. Probably a mistake. That just led to more questions.

"Who's Matt? What is he thanking you for? Why didn't you go to dinner?" After a few moments of silence, she could see she wasn't getting a response any time soon.

"Well, Isy, if I were you, I'd call to say thank you. A girl doesn't get beautiful flowers like that every day. Oh—and from a doctor, no less."

Call? Could I?

Hang on—did she just say doctor? How could she know that? I looked up at her, confused.

She answered my unasked question. "Says right here on his business card—it's stapled to the back of the note. Looks like he wants you to contact him," she said, winking. "Whatever you're doing, honey, keep doing it."

I carried the flowers back down to my desk, my mind in a spin. I couldn't believe he was so thoughtful. That he even remembered me. How did he know where to find me?

My head was telling me not to get too excited but the rest of me wasn't listening. My stomach was doing cartwheels and my heart was flipping. I was practically panting.

"He has a fiancée. He has a fiancée," I kept chanting to myself. But it didn't help, I was beaming on the inside.

I scolded myself. This was exactly why I didn't want to be friends with him. I seemed to turn into a schoolgirl whenever I was around him—whenever I even *thought* about him!

Okay, think. I have to thank him for the flowers, it would be plain rude not to. Should I call? No, that could have disaster written all over it. Email? Yes—much safer.

I opened up the email. I had urgent work on my desk, but I needed to put this out of my mind before I could concentrate on anything else.

I typed: *Dear Matt.* Then I deleted it. Too formal.

Hi Matt

Better. What should I say? After three rewrites—totally pathetic—I finally finished it:

Thank you for the flowers. They were unnecessary but absolutely beautiful. What a lovely surprise.

I hope you also enjoyed the rest of your trip? And of course, stayed off the road ☺

P.S. How did you know where to send the flowers?

Thanks again,

Isy

Tentatively, I clicked SEND.

I stared at the screen. Would he get it right away? Would he respond right away? I had to will myself away from my computer before I went mad. I got up to make a coffee.

On my way back from the kitchen, Harrison caught sight of me and called me into the boardroom. He wasn't alone, but his guest had his back to the door so I couldn't see his face.

"Isabel, please come in."

He was being formal. *It must be a client,* I thought.

I straightened my shoulders and entered the room, sneaking a side glance at his mystery guest.

"Isabel, I'd like to introduce you to Jonathan Hawkins, who as you know is General Counsel at Parkmores. I thought since you are working closely on the Parkmores matter, the two of you should be introduced.

"Jonathan, this is Isabel Cartier, one of the lawyers on my team. She is giving her complete focus to your matter."

I stepped over to Jonathan to shake his hand as he turned to face me.

Then for the second time that afternoon, my jaw dropped to the floor.

Oh. My. Lord. No. It couldn't be. It *couldn't* be.

But it was.

Jonathan was Arrogant Ass from the sandwich bar downstairs—the thief who stole my lunch and stomped on my foot! I was right about one thing: he was a lawyer. But not from a rival firm. No, much worse. He was a client. *My* client.

And now instead of retribution, I was going to have to suck it up and be as sweet as pie to him. Very difficult to do when all you want to do is find his foot and return the favor.

"Nice to meet you, Isabel," he greeted in that smooth British accent.

Oh look, he wasn't brought up in a cave after all. He did have manners.

I forced the stunned expression on my face into a smile, although I sensed that it wasn't that convincing. "Likewise, it's a pleasure, Jonathan. I look forward to working with you more closely." *About as much as I looked forward to growing old and dying.*

A spark of curiosity crossed his features. "You look familiar... Have we met somewhere before?"

Yes—this afternoon! You cut in front of me and stepped on my foot without apologizing, you arrogant ass! "Not formally, no."

Harrison cut in to signal it was time to go. "Please feel free for your team to contact Isabel for anything you need, Jonathan. Like me, she will be available at any time."

Why, does he want to finish off the other foot? "Absolutely. Of course, it would be my pleasure to assist in any way I can. It was lovely to meet you, Jonathan."

"The pleasure was mine," he said, oozing out the charm. *The man with two faces*, I thought. If I hadn't already had the pleasure of meeting him, I may have been fooled into thinking that he was a gentleman. But I knew better.

I excused myself and turned to exit.

"Are you limping?" Harrison asked. I hadn't noticed that I was, but my big toe was still throbbing. Nothing gets past Harrison.

As I turned back to respond, I caught a glimpse of Jonathan. I almost heard his brain click as he figured out why I looked familiar.

"Someone stomped on my foot in the line at lunch today," I explained, enjoying the freedom to point this out, before quickly adding, "by accident, of course. You know how the crowds get at lunch. I'm fine." I needed to play nice. Harrison wouldn't care if Jonathan had stolen my kidney, he was an important client. An important client who now had the color draining from his face.

I went back to my desk wearing a smug smile. The flowers instantly brightened my office and my mood. They really were breathtaking.

I looked at my Inbox—there it was. A reply from Matt. My heart skipped a beat.

Anxiously, I opened it.

Hi Isy

I'm pleased you liked the flowers. I disagree – I think it was very necessary.

You will be happy to know that I managed to stay in one piece for the rest of my trip. Although I did nearly fall into the Trevi Fountain and I wondered where you were to save me.

I was hoping you wouldn't pick up on the fact that I had to look you up to send the flowers. It was a little stalkeresque, huh? I have to admit that I googled you – found your profile on LinkedIn. I hope you don't mind.

But since the damage is already done, I might as well tell you that the dinner invitation is still open across continents. You just have to say when.

When?

Great to hear from you,

Matt

Oh. My. Lord. Again.

He was sweet *and* funny *and* absolutely lovely. *Fiancée, fiancée,* I kept reminding myself.

I was tempted to meet him for dinner until I remembered why I'd declined in the first place. You can't be friends with someone you're attracted to. I already had enough complications in my life.

I hit REPLY to his email.

> I'm horrified to learn of the near drowning incident at the Trevi Fountain. It's an outrage that they don't have life-guards on hand.
>
> Thanks again for the dinner invitation – again, unnecessary. Things have been extremely hectic at work since I got back. I've been eating dinner at my desk every night. Save yourself, though – I'm sure there are still places serving food that isn't in plastic containers.
>
> Please stay away from any large pools of water – you know how dangerous those puddles can be.
>
> Be safe,
>
> Isy

There. That should do it. Leave it light, but make sure it's clear.

I was careful not to ask any questions in my response. Questions would lead to him responding—and it was better to leave it there. Otherwise I'd never leave the office because I'd never get any work done while I was waiting for another email.

I debated whether or not to tell Jules. I was dying to tell her.

Dying. But if I wanted to forget about it—about *him*—telling her would be a big mistake. I decided not to.

As I was thinking about it, I saw a message flash at the bottom of my screen informing me that a new email had hit my Inbox. I gasped. It couldn't be, could it?

I clicked on it, my eyes widening. It was from Jonathan Hawkins.

> Dear Isabel
> It was nice to meet you this afternoon. I have a couple of things I would like to discuss. Can we schedule a time on Monday – say 11am? If you could come to my office, that would be great.
> Regards,
> Jonathan

That was quick. He must have sent it from his iPhone straight after he left the meeting. Honestly, could this day get any weirder? The General Counsel wouldn't generally ever request to meet one-on-one with me, and certainly not without Harrison. I checked my calendar and blocked the appointment. Parkmores' offices were only a few blocks away. Till Monday then.

9

INVITATIONS

WHEN I GOT HOME on Friday night, I found a note on the door from Jeremy.

> It would be a pleasure to serve you lunch tomorrow, my lady. If you're free, just pop this note under my door. I'll drop by at noon.
> Jez

That boy was a total sweetheart. Here was someone who was sweet, funny, charming and fun to be with. And he seemed to enjoy my company, too, despite me answering the door in my pajamas, with bed hair and last night's make-up. I began to feel guilty that I hadn't been easy to get hold of, and never called him during the week to see how *he* was doing.

I pulled the note off the door, smiling. There was more than one reason why I had been looking forward to the weekend. The obvious one was the fact that it gave me some much needed time to breathe. The other reason was that I had come to look forward to the notes on my door, and seeing Jeremy. I had grown to really value our friendship.

Maybe I was getting spoilt. I was so accustomed to Jeremy's visits that I would actually be disappointed—more than that, deflated—if I got home and there wasn't a note.

I put down the flowers I'd carried home and pulled a pen out of my bag. I scribbled *'Absolutely'* and drew a smiley face on the note before slipping it under his door.

As I was lying in bed that night, I couldn't stop my mind from wondering back to Matt. How incredible he was. First impressions really were true. I knew from the moment I met him that he had a certain something about him—an incredible energy that drew you in and made you want to be close to him. Of course, those scintillating blue eyes might have had something to do with it, too.

His email was so sweet, and he'd made me laugh with the whole falling into the Trevi Fountain remark. Oh, if he only knew how much I wished I'd been there with him.

Jules was right about this one. He would be a great friend to have. Any time I was near him or even just had any kind of contact, like today, I was buzzing. He lifted my spirits and made me smile.

I wished that I could've stopped myself there. But my mind made the leap to something more than friendship, and as soon as I wanted that—and I did—I knew the friendship thing could never work. And, more importantly, it would only lead to pain—

mine. If I could get over my infatuation with Matt, I could be friends with him, but I didn't see that happening anytime soon.

I had to be practical. Matt was off-limits. Thinking about him was a waste of time.

I promised myself as I lay there in bed that I would stop fixating on him and let it go. I regretted bringing the flowers home. Now they would be in the apartment all weekend and it would make it very difficult *not* to think about him. But I couldn't bring myself to throw them away. It would be such a waste, and it seemed rude and ungrateful after Matt took the time to send them.

Pushing those thoughts aside, I concentrated on Jeremy and our lunch date tomorrow. Jeremy and I were just friends, but if he wanted to explore that relationship—could I? Would I? Or had I just misread his behavior last weekend and was now jumping to conclusions?

I made sure to set the alarm for the morning. This time when Jeremy showed up, I planned to be properly dressed, instead of looking like I'd just survived a tornado. He wasn't exactly coming early, but I didn't want to take any chances. Plus, I wanted to tidy up a bit before he arrived.

I didn't have any answers to the questions about Jeremy, but I decided that as long as there was even the slightest possibility, I would not close myself off to it. I would just go with the flow and let it all unfold as it should.

The next morning, I took longer than I'd anticipated to choose an outfit. I had to look casual like I normally did—like I hadn't put a lot of effort into it. It turns out that looking like you hadn't put any effort into it actually takes *a lot* of effort. I had settled on my favorite denim skirt and red top when it occurred to me that that was something I'd never just wear at home. So I traded my skirt for an old pair of jeans. That was as casual as I was willing to go. There was no need for him to see me in my sweats again.

Putting away the hoard of discarded wardrobe choices, I suddenly felt ridiculous for all the time I'd spent in front of the mirror. The beauty of my friendship with Jeremy was that we were just ourselves—no pretenses. If I started overthinking it, it could potentially ruin the friendship that I now cherished. I was just about to pull off my jeans and give in to the track pants when I heard a knock at the door.

Jeremy was punctual, it was right on noon. When I opened the door, I was surprised to see that he wasn't carrying any packages.

"Hi, Sleeping Beauty. You're looking incredibly awake this week," he teased, giving me a wide smile.

"Ha ha. Hi, Jez."

"Shame, too, I thought I might've had to awaken you with... What was it the prince had to do to awaken her?" he asked mischievously.

"Give her a kiss," I answered automatically.

"Ah, yes, that's it," he said, a sly smile playing on his lips.

"Do you want me to go back to sleep?" I asked with as innocent an expression as I could muster.

Jeremy cocked his head to the side, surveying me, before his mischievous grin returned. I decided to change the subject before the moment got awkward.

"So," I said, looking in the direction of his empty hands, "if you were hoping for something edible to come from my apartment, I hope you like toast."

"Actually I was thinking since it's such a nice day we could go for pizza at Pizzeria Delfina in Pacific Heights. Do you feel like getting out?"

This was new. We'd been neighbor buddies up until this point and had only hung out inside the apartment building. I wished I'd known we'd be venturing out into the real world while I was agonizing in front of the mirror earlier.

"Sure, that sounds great."

He jingled his keys. "I'll drive. My service is door to door, my lady," he said, bowing again.

"Why, thank you, kind sir. Please do enter my humble abode while I grab my purse and put on my shoes." I gave him a sweeping gesture with my arm to enter.

"Why, I'd be delighted to."

As I was fastening the strap on my wedge-heeled sandals—and wishing I'd gone with the denim skirt after all—Jeremy's eye caught the large arrangement of flowers on the kitchen table. Pretty hard not to miss.

"Secret admirer?"

"Do you mean that you didn't send them?" I asked, sounding hurt. I instantly regretted the joke when he blushed a scarlet red. "Just kidding, Jez!" I added quickly.

"So who . . . ?"

I didn't want to lie to Jeremy. I felt like I was already hiding enough from him. As someone who valued honesty and loyalty in friendship above all else, I still felt terrible about that. But I also couldn't tell him the truth—not the whole truth at least. I settled on telling him the parts that wouldn't reveal my *'quattro ochi'* and potentially result in him canceling lunch.

"They're from a guy I kinda helped avoid getting hit by a car . . ." I started. Jeremy raised his eyebrows in confusion—or was it also jealousy? I wasn't sure. "It was nothing really. He was about to cross the road when I saw a car was speeding up to run the red light, so I pulled him back. That's all. He sent flowers to say thank you. He apparently googled me to find out where I worked."

Jeremy still had an expression on his face that I couldn't quite decipher. "You didn't tell me about this. When did it happen? Where?"

"Actually, it happened while I was in Florence. Just a major coincidence that we're both from San Francisco. But then, not that much of a coincidence I suppose when you can't walk two feet without bumping into another American overseas!" I laughed nervously and—against my will—snorted. I continued quickly to try to hide the snort—like I *could*. "He was traveling with his fiancée." There, that should clear up any confusion.

"Huh."

There was an awkward pause. *What was he thinking?* I wondered.

"They're really nice flowers. He must be *very* thankful," he finally said, the hint of sarcasm just barely masked.

I shrugged, eager to close the subject.

Jeremy didn't take the hint. "Did you say that he *googled* you to find out where you worked?"

I nodded as I got up to get my purse.

"A little stalkerish," he muttered under his breath. "*And* he has a fiancée?"

I sighed. He was clearly going to harp on this. "What's your point?" I asked, crossing my arms defensively.

"My point, dear, innocent Isy, is that a guy would never go to the trouble of finding out where you work to send you flowers if he wasn't hoping to get a little something for his efforts."

I rolled my eyes at him. "Don't be so suspicious, it's not like that," I replied indignantly.

Yet, as much as I tried to dismiss the accusation, there was some small part of me that delighted in the possibility that it *could* mean something. That Matt really was attracted to me and felt the same pull. Was that awful? But my fantasy necessitated his fiancée suddenly deciding to leave him and I couldn't imagine that ever happening. And I certainly didn't plan on being the other woman.

"Just be careful, that's all I'm saying. I'd be wary of his intentions."

"If he were a womanizer, he'd take a more direct approach. He asked me to dinner *with* his fiancée. Don't worry, I'm not an idiot. Let's go," I said, picking up my keys and ending that particular conversation.

He muttered something unintelligible under his breath as he got up from the couch, before taking a deep breath and giving me a warm smile. "After you, ma'am."

Jeremy was a little old school. When we got to his car, he opened the door for me. I felt slightly uncomfortable, given how unaccustomed I was to anyone opening a car door for me, unless I'd just pulled up in front of a hotel or valet parking. But it was sweet.

We chatted in the car as he drove, discussing the events of the week.

"You will never guess what happened to me yesterday!" I exclaimed, knowing Jeremy would get a kick out of the Jonathan fiasco.

"What? Did you save someone else's life that you haven't told me about yet?"

"Haven't I told you about me breaking up that bar fight? Lucky for my black belt."

Jeremy's head whipped towards me and he had to swerve sharply to correct his steering.

"Jez, I'm kidding! Goodness, it's nothing that exciting. The story is going to seem very boring after that, trust me. It's a work story." I rubbed my eyes. A black line marred my vision, like I had an eyelash in my eye.

"Sorry, go on. I promise to at least *look* interested. Although it will be difficult after the superhero bar maiden image I just had going. I was envisioning the costume." He smirked, his tone turning mischievous again.

I didn't take the bait this time. Instead, I ignored him and went on. "So, I was standing in line at lunch—"

He cut me off. "Riveting so far," he teased.

"Give me a chance! And this really rude guy pushes in front of me—" I paused as I noticed his raised eyebrows continuing to question the interest level of the story. "Fine," I said petulantly. "To cut a long story short, he stole my lunch, stomped on my foot—without apologizing—and then turned up in the boardroom at my firm!"

This time I paused for effect.

"Turns out," I continued, "that he's—"

Not an eyelash. Nope. It was happening again. I was seeing

something. I rubbed my eyes. *Not while I'm with Jeremy! Please!* I shifted uncomfortably in my seat.

All I could see was a face in shadow. Not an entire image, like my usual dream. Just a face.

I conceded defeat. There was no point fighting it. The sooner the vision came, the sooner I could launch into damage control. I squinted. *How silly,* I thought, *like that would help.*

I was vaguely aware of Jeremy speaking to me, but it was like someone had turned down the volume and it was only background noise.

I tried to get a better look at the face, but it was too dark.

Then, suddenly, as if someone switched on a light, the face was illuminated, as clear as day. It was a face I knew, a face I recognized. Then the image was gone.

"Jonathan!" I screamed.

"Who? Who is Jonathan?" Jeremy asked, confused and no doubt concerned by my lengthy silence and weird behavior.

My focus turned back to Jeremy. I felt my heart rate accelerating and tried to compose myself. Jeremy was going to think I was a nut case, the work story wasn't worth getting that worked up over.

"Jonathan is my client on a big matter I'm working on. I'd never met him before, he's pretty high up the chain over at Parkmores. He heads up their in-house legal team—General Counsel to be precise."

"Oh. So the big highflying lawyer is a lunch stealer? Don't they pay him enough?" Jeremy was amused, but there was still a lingering note of concern in his voice. At least he was pretending not to notice my few-cards-short-of-a-deck behavior, so I decided to count my blessings.

I didn't bother correcting him about the fact that Jonathan had paid for his lunch. I was too entranced by what I'd just seen and desperate to make sense of it. I was totally bemused. And in that moment, I felt completely alone.

I cracked open a window, desperate for air. It felt like a truck had just rammed into me. Except no help was coming. The truck's tires were still spinning, pressing into me.

Was it because I was just talking about Jonathan, thinking about him, that I saw him? I quickly dismissed that hypothesis, doubting it was my imagination. But I hadn't seen the sidewalk from my dreams, just his face, so were the two definitely connected? Was Jonathan the man I'd seen under the scaffolding, or did it mean something else? Was he the answer to a different question, one I hadn't even asked?

I needed more conclusive evidence to be certain.

I wished that Jules were on speed dial right now.

If it was a piece of the same puzzle, I was still confused. Surely I wouldn't have to save Jonathan? That would be ironic. Jonathan didn't fit my idea of the vulnerable. So far, the people I'd seen in my visions had been amazing people. Jeremy and Matt. Both were good, decent, wonderful people. Both had so much to offer. Protecting them made sense.

But Jonathan?

It seemed odd to me that Shadow Man and Arrogant Ass could be one and the same. There could be some other explanation that was yet to reveal itself.

I wasn't sure how I felt about it if they *were* one and the same, what that even meant. On the plus side, saving Jonathan had to earn me credit with Harrison, I thought smugly, until the stress and uncertainty pooling around me drowned out my diverting thoughts. *How could I know for sure?* I decided if it really was Jonathan under the scaffolding, I would see it more clearly in another vision.

We stopped at a traffic light and I gazed enviously at a group of young girls crossing in front of us, laughing without a care in the world.

"Isy? Are you listening to me?" Jeremy was eyeing me with concern.

"Sorry, Jez, I missed that. What did you say? Oh, I love this song!" I turned up the radio for a chance to take a moment to regain my focus.

* * *

Monday morning came around quickly. I hadn't slept much over the rest of the weekend, my mind in a spin. I wasn't able to reach Jules, and my inner turmoil festered like mold baking in the hot sun.

I stood in front of the mirror, staring at the dark circles under my eyes. If my anxiety over his possible connection to the scaffolding incident wasn't enough, I was also puzzled by the highly unusual nature of the meeting. Taking a deep breath, I reached for the concealer. I was determined to mask my nerves, look my best and walk in confidently. I put on my favorite suit, a gray-blue fitted jacket and skirt falling just above the knee, accompanied by a light blue silk blouse. I paired it with my favorite pair of black stiletto heels with the strap around the ankle. The kind of shoes that were made for sitting, not walking.

I hopped on a cable car to his office. It was only three blocks away, but that was three too many for my stiletto heels. I had no idea what he wanted to discuss, so I carried my Burberry tote bag with my iPad and a progress update on where everything was in regards to his matter. If he asked me probing questions about anything too specific, I was going to have to wing it. There were too many documents to carry with me without knowing the precise purpose of the meeting.

From what I had heard from Harrison, Jonathan was pretty hard-core. He often sent Harrison emails in the early hours of the morning and over weekends, expecting prompt follow up. He was meticulous, hard-working, demanding, and well regarded at Parkmores. He set the bar very high and I knew Harrison thought highly of him.

He had a large team working for him and shouldered a great deal of responsibility. He liked to know who was on his team at Barkleys, but other than the occasional email or phone call, he usually only gave his limited time to the most senior members of the team—partner level, or occasionally senior associate. More often than not, he dealt directly with Harrison.

Harrison was extremely surprised when I told him that Jonathan had requested a meeting with me. More than surprised, he nearly choked on the sip of coffee he'd just taken. He rewarded me with a look of approval. At least this would help win back his confidence in me, so long as I didn't allow my latest vision paranoia to throw me off my game. Or worse still, if I reverted to visionary status in the middle of the meeting. Any episodes of the 'quattro occhi' variety would be a complete disaster. I had to remain in professional mode. I sent a silent prayer up to the heavens. *Please do not let any catatonic events occur in front of Jonathan.*

I waited in the reception area at Parkmores, expecting to be there for a while given I was ten minutes early and Jonathan would most likely be running late. With so many demands on his time, I doubted he would worry about keeping me waiting.

The reception area was plush, boasting the company's impressive bottom line. I perched myself on the edge of the huge red leather couch, trying to look ladylike in my skirt, and flipped through a copy of *Harvard Business Review*.

I'd only been there for a couple of minutes when I heard a voice.

"Isabel, I'm so glad you could make it."

I looked up, surprised. Jonathan was standing there with his hand extended to me. I stood quickly—too quickly—knocking the magazine off my lap and onto the floor. So much for looking demure.

I took his hand and smiled. "Good morning, Jonathan. Thank you for the invitation."

"Shall we go downstairs to the café?" he asked.

Café? I assumed we would have the meeting in his office or a boardroom. Maybe this would be less formal than I'd expected.

"Sure. Lead the way." I quickly retrieved the magazine and tossed it back on the table.

Jonathan gestured for me to enter the elevator before him. When the doors opened on the first floor, he held them open—blocking the sensor with his arm—and again waited for me to exit first. Once we reached the café, he asked me if I was happy with the table he selected before sitting. All of these gentlemanly gestures did not go unnoticed.

He waited until we ordered our coffee before he started talking.

"So, Isabel, I'm sure you're wondering why I asked you here today," he started.

I was wearing my professional mask, preventing my thoughts from shining through. His mask was just as impenetrable.

"When I met you in the boardroom on Friday, I realized why you looked familiar . . . And when I saw you limping . . ." His voice trailed off as he shifted in his seat. A crack slowly appeared in the armor, his discomfort slipping through.

Was *this* the reason for the meeting? I was surprised he would bother to take the time to meet with me to discuss it. As much as I initially had wanted retribution, I couldn't help but feel a little sorry for him now. His embarrassment and remorse were clear—even if it was only because he'd gotten caught.

I cut in. "It was nothing, nothing at all," I reassured him.

The waitress interrupted, bringing us our coffee. He thanked her and waited for her to leave before continuing.

"No, it was inexcusable," he said with his eyes staring at the latte in front of him. "I owe you an apology." He looked up at me and continued. "I'm sorry for the confusion—for my actions that day. I don't want you to think that that is my normal behavior. To have been so rude, it was . . . well, inexcusable."

"Apology accepted," I said quickly. "Although there was no need. I understand. We all have our days."

His rigid posture relaxed a little. "That was a particularly bad one for me. Not that it's any excuse, but my head was somewhere else. There's just so much going on at the moment. I also wanted to thank you for being so gracious and not mentioning it to Harrison."

"Of course. There was no reason to mention such a minor incident. I have to say that I think it's very gracious of you to take the time to apologize."

"It was the least I could do. I didn't want that to be your impression of me."

He looked so sincere, I wanted to reassure him. For someone in as high a position as Jonathan, a gesture like this was particularly rare. "Harrison has only ever spoken very highly of you. I know he holds you in the highest esteem—as do I."

The intensity in his eyes faded and he smiled. "Thank you, Isabel. I do appreciate that." He leaned back in his chair. "So tell me—how long have you been at Barkleys?"

"Three years now. It's a great firm and I really enjoy working with Harrison. I'm learning so much," I responded.

"Harrison is a genius. I have no doubt you'd learn a great deal from him. I'm very happy that he's brought you onto the Parkmores team."

"Thank you."

"So, tell me a little about yourself. Do you have a family?" he inquired, stirring sugar into his coffee.

"Just my parents. I don't have any children. Yourself?"

"I envy you. I'm married and have two children, Dalia and Samuel—we call him Sammy." He pulled out his wallet and showed me a picture of the two children sitting on Santa's knee. They were adorable.

"Dalia is seven and Sammy is five," he explained, pride shining in his eyes.

"It's me who should envy you—your children are beautiful."

He nodded. "I meant it in the sense that you don't have to feel guilty about anything. You don't have anyone pressuring you about the time you spend working, anyone to get angry with you because you get home late or have to work on the weekends. Spouses don't seem to understand that's what's expected in our line of work. As if I enjoy missing out on the children's school recitals."

"Oh, I see. On the other hand, I go home to an empty apartment. At least you have someone who misses you."

"I suppose you're right. But enjoy the time you have now to focus on your career, to make it your priority without having to feel guilty about it. I'm sure you're one of the up-and-coming lawyers and with Harrison as your mentor, you can reach as high as you want to go."

"Thank you, Jonathan. That's very kind of you."

He leaned forward, jiggling his brows. "I bet he's making you work for it, though. A lot of long hours and weekends?"

"That he is. I don't have a life outside the office."

"Well, take my advice: if you start dating, make sure it's someone who understands your work. That will make things easier for you both."

"Ah, but if your wife had the same work pressures you do, your children would be running the house—they'd probably think it was Christmas every day and party."

He chuckled. "True, they would. I suppose if she had been a lawyer, too, she wouldn't want to take time off to raise the children. You work too hard to just give it up."

I resented the boxes that women were usually put in, especially when it came to careers and motherhood. "I know female lawyers who manage to juggle both, some are even able to work part-time. Everything is about balance."

"I never understood that word—balance. It just means that something's gotta give." There was a touch of sadness in his eyes.

I thought about that for a second. I certainly didn't have a lot of balance in my life at the moment—and it seemed impossible to fulfill my responsibilities at work and manage to have any balance at all.

"I guess that's true. I think it just depends on what you want more—and what you're willing to give up to get it," I conceded.

"And sometimes it's just about what you *need* to do," he said in that same matter-of-fact tone.

I thought about my vision of him. Regardless of whether or not it was him under the scaffolding, anything like that could happen to anyone of us, anytime. I seized the opportunity to point this out, knowing I might not get another chance.

"I understand what you mean. In order for me to fulfill my responsibilities at work, I need to work the hours I do. There's no way around it. But I was recently in Florence and I witnessed a man almost get hit by a car. He could've died or been seriously injured. In that one fleeting moment, his whole world could've been changed, or his life could've been ended.

"I've been thinking about a lot of things since then. About how fleeting life is, how it only takes a second to change everything. How we really have to value what we have, while we have it."

I was getting a little philosophical for a coffee meeting with the General Counsel at Parkmores, but for some reason I felt comfortable with Jonathan, and he seemed to have let his guard down with me, at least for the moment.

"You were recently in Florence?" he asked, his interest piqued.

I suppressed a sigh. He had missed the point entirely. "Yes, a couple of weeks ago. I went to visit a friend—for her wedding," I added. For some reason, I still felt the urge to cover my tracks.

"That sounds exciting. A vacation sounds great. I don't even remember the last time I had a day off. There's just too much going on—always is, it seems. Speaking of which, I should probably get back." He cleared his throat, shifting his tone. "Thank you for coming down to speak with me, Isabel, I appreciate it. And I'm pleased we had an opportunity to clear the air. I look forward to working with you." He flashed me a smile as he rose from the table.

"It was my pleasure. Thank you again for the invitation. I hope to see you soon," I said, shaking his hand. *Hopefully not under a pile of metal*, I thought.

As I sat in the cable car on my way back to the office, I thought about our conversation. It's amazing how easy it is to misjudge a person. You can meet someone on his or her best day or worst day, and you never know which it is. We never know the reason behind why people behave the way they do. Someone who has just yelled at an innocent shopkeeper may have just had their heart broken. Someone who makes a fool of themselves may have just lost their job. Everyone has a story. Yet we judge using the same yardstick, we factor none of that in when we characterize the people we meet. We let one moment form our judgment, one speck of time stretch out to fill in the rest of the whole, a thousand missing pieces.

* * *

I managed to reach Jules that night and was eager to discuss all of this new information. If it was Jonathan, I knew the *who.* But I still didn't know the *where*, or even more worrying, the *when.*

"I can't believe you met him and he's your client! Wow, this is getting more interesting by the second," Jules said excitedly.

"But I've got no idea where or when. And now because I've met him and gotten to know him a little, I feel more responsible for him. How do I figure out when? I can't exactly follow him around."

"The *when* I'm not sure about yet. But as for the *where*—now that you know who it is, you could probe him. Subtly, of course."

"You realize the fact he's an important client makes it trickier, Jules. I mean, I can't risk sounding like a loon in front of him."

"You won't. Let's look at what we know for certain. We know it's Jonathan—"

I corrected her. "We *think* it's Jonathan. I hate not having all of the facts. What if there's something I'm missing?" I had no idea what the rules were with these visions, or even *if* there were any rules. How could I be expected to do my due diligence?

"Isy, there's no opposing party trying to conceal evidence from you. If you saw Jonathan in a vision, it's him under the scaffolding," she insisted. "You have to trust your intuition. Forget your head, what does your gut tell you?"

Allowing myself to respond automatically, without pausing to analyze it this time, I answered her. "It's him."

"Good. So, we also know where he works," she continued. "You said the other people who were walking towards him were all in suits, right? So it's probably somewhere close to his office. On your lunch break—yes, this means you will actually have to *take* a lunch break—go and investigate. Walk around the streets nearby and see if you can find the place."

I thought about it. "That's a good idea, it's worth a try. At least I'll feel like I'm doing *something*. Thanks, Jules. Should I put you on a retainer or something?" I quipped.

"Girl, you couldn't afford my hourly rate."

"Put it on my tab. I'll let you know if I find out anything more. By the way, I feel awful—I'm always calling to talk about the madness in my world, and I haven't asked you how things are going with you?" I admitted guiltily.

"Lucky for you, I'm not sensitive," she said with a chuckle. "Things are well. Nothing as exciting as saving the world, one person at a time. I'm proud of you, Isy, for keeping such an open mind about everything. I know it was a stretch for you—a splash of mayhem in your usually ordered life."

"I have you to thank, Jules. I would've gone mad without you."

"You know I'm happy to be involved in any way I can—even if it's just as the good-looking sidekick." She laughed and I could envision her playfully flicking her hair.

As always after speaking with Jules, I felt better when I hung up the phone. I had a mission. There was something proactive that I could do to try to get another important piece of the puzzle. I would walk through every street in the city if I had to. I only hoped that time was still on my side.

10

SMALL MIRACLES

THE NEXT DAY AT LUNCH, I skipped a Continuing Legal Education session to roam the city streets looking for the path in my vision.

An attendance sheet would be circulated at the session, meaning my absence wouldn't go unnoticed. I debated whether ditching it was such a good idea, but I felt a sudden sense of urgency in finding where the vision would take place. I was learning that I'd need to make choices; these visions came with both the gift of being able to make a difference in someone else's life, and the responsibility that went along with it. That responsibility would sometimes come at a price.

I started to feel empathy for Clark Kent and the challenges he faced every time he ran out of the office to help someone. But I was no Superwoman—I was just an ordinary person, living an ordinary life.

I ruminated on how long the visions would continue—*if* they would continue. The burden they carried felt like the repressive weight of a mammoth hitching an unsolicited ride on my back. I hadn't asked for it, nor given my consent. I'd been carelessly thrown into the volcano and left to find my own way out. I wouldn't undo any of the events of the past couple of months. I was thankful that I had been able to help Jeremy, Matt and—hopefully—Jonathan. But if I had a choice, if someone asked me if I wanted to make it all stop after this, would I say yes? I knew the answer: I would.

I was cognizant that there was a good chance the day would come when the price was a costly one. Today I was only skipping a lunch session. One day it would be more significant than that. If the visions continued, my resolve would be tested.

I only hoped that when that day came, I made the right choice. Whatever that would be.

But a part of me was resentful for the toll that would be demanded, the sacrifice that would be claimed. I would be unwittingly paying a steep toll to cross a bridge I never planned to cross. I prayed whatever was on the other side would be worth the heartache.

As I walked through the city, I felt a pull drawing me in a certain direction and my feet dutifully obeyed. The sun briefly broke through the clouds, warming my skin. I remembered what Julia had said about lessons. The people in my visions each helped me on my own journey. There was something I needed to learn from them. Although I didn't understand how or why this was happening, I believed Julia about that. It had so far proven true.

I pondered what it was that I was supposed to learn from Jonathan. I considered him to be a glimpse into my own future: the sacrifices he made in regards to his family, the pressures he faced. Perhaps it was a sign that I shouldn't have children, I didn't know what kind of mother I would be. Although I was very far from having to make that kind of choice, so there had to be something else I hadn't considered.

Chewing my lip, I turned the corner and instantly glanced upwards.

There it was.

The enclosed section of path.

More than just looking the same as my vision, it felt like the place—I could *feel* it. It was like someone whispered it into my nervous system and my whole body responded. I was acutely aware of the pure energy that was the essence of my being. I felt an assurance—and calmness—within me that I never had before.

I *knew.*

The energy force was strong, pulsating through me and sticking my feet to the ground. I couldn't move. My rational mind told me how silly that was, I couldn't stay here forever. The vision with Jonathan could happen tomorrow, next week, next month.

But it was going to happen today.

This knowledge had nothing to do with logic. It had everything to do with the truth that vibrated through my core.

I checked the time—1:32 P.M. I had half an hour before I needed to be back at the office. It would make sense that Jonathan was out at lunch, too, so I felt sure it would be soon.

Each minute that passed felt like a lifetime. My eyes were fixed on the path refusing to look away for a second, terrified that I would miss Jonathan and not make it in time.

People bumped and pushed past me, but I barely noticed the

jostling. My eyes darted from person to person walking through the enclosed section of path, scanning for both Jonathan and the woman with the dark green suit and burgundy attaché case.

When the number of people on the street started to dwindle, and it felt like an eternity had passed, I dared to risk a quick glance at my watch. It was now 2:07 P.M.

I had a 2:30 P.M. meeting at Parkmores with their marketing team and two members of their in-house legal counsel. We were reviewing some of the advertising and other marketing material that was under investigation by the FTC to determine whether or not it was deceptive.

I had left all of the paperwork I'd prepared for the meeting back at the office, meaning I'd have to return there first before heading over to Parkmores. I would need at least twenty minutes to make a mad dash there in time.

That left just enough time if I abandoned ship and hightailed it now. My mind told me to hurry, but my body didn't respond. My muscles didn't move an inch.

I was being tested sooner than I'd thought. I would've been seized by anxiety—knowing the war zone I was going to face when I returned to the office and faced Harrison—if it wasn't for the fact that I still had that energy force running through me. The sense of assuredness and calmness was still there. My head was screaming to panic, but before the fear could rise in me, it was smothered by that reassuring energy that wrapped around me like a protective embrace.

I could not leave.

Another five minutes were swallowed by the clock, rendering it impossible to make it to the meeting on time. Without shifting my gaze from the path, I reached into my bag and pulled out my phone, using voice command to dial.

My secretary answered immediately. I had no idea what I was going to tell her.

"Good afternoon. Barkleys. This is Elizabeth," she chirped.

"Liz, it's Isy. I need you to please call Amanda at Parkmores immediately about our two-thirty appointment—"

"Hey, Isy, I've been trying to find you!" she interrupted. "She called half an hour ago to say they had to reschedule. Something urgent came up with their Board."

It was the sweetest news I had ever heard, like hearing your winning numbers being called in the lottery.

I backtracked as quickly as I could, trying to hide the relief in my voice. "Yes, I spoke to her secretary. I was going to ask you to find out when it was being rescheduled for, because the phone cut out. I'm sure their urgent matter will take the rest of the afternoon anyway, so there's no need to worry about it. Thanks, Liz, I'll see you when I get back. Hopefully won't be too long. Bye."

I disconnected before she could ask any questions regarding my whereabouts. I had no idea what I would say when I got back. I shifted all of my focus back to the task at hand.

Then I saw her. She was immaculately dressed—exactly as I'd seen her before—with her dark green suit, sleek stiletto heels, burgundy attaché case and jet-black hair pulled up in a clip.

She was across the street talking to someone. I searched frantically for Jonathan but I still couldn't see him. I crinkled my forehead. Where was he?

The woman kissed her companion goodbye and crossed the

street, walking towards me.

I vacillated between which direction Jonathan would be approaching. In my vision, I had only seen him in shadow, and he had been still.

The woman was about to enter the enclosed part of the sidewalk. Whipping my head around, I took one last look behind me—to make sure Jonathan wasn't approaching from behind—and then bolted into the scaffolded tunnel. I slammed into something—*someone*—hard. I lost my balance and started to swing back before he grabbed my shoulders to steady me.

"Are you all right?" he asked.

I recognized the voice immediately. Jonathan.

How did he materialize out of thin air? I'd been watching so closely . . .

I heard a faint creaking sound. I lifted my hands to his chest and pushed into him as hard as I could. We both stumbled and he took a step backwards to regain his balance.

"What are you—" was all he managed to say before the metal hit the ground with a crashing thud that vibrated through the enclosed space and flooded our ears.

He jumped, immediately pulling me closer towards him and dragging me back two more steps, out from under the scaffolding.

The sunlight was momentarily blinding. He blinked, surprise sweeping over his features.

"Isabel? How did you—?" His eyes darted back to the scaffolding, focusing on the more pressing question. "What was that?"

"I don't know. It sounded like metal from the scaffolding, unless it was part of the building fascia," I answered.

His attention turned back to me. "Why did you push me? How could you have known it was going to fall?"

"I heard a creaking sound and it just kind of all happened so fast. I get a little claustrophobic and I wanted to get out of there—you just happened to be in the way," I told him. I was impressed with myself, that sounded like a reasonable explanation for the bizarre events that had just unfolded.

"But you seemed to be running from a distance . . . I suppose it did happen so quickly. I didn't hear anything."

"I didn't see you approaching. Where did you come from?" I asked him curiously, trying to shift the focus back to him.

"I came through the alley," he explained, pointing behind him. "I can't believe that just happened. I'm going to call the authorities—that is a hazard! Do you realize that we could've been seriously injured?" The outrage was apparent in his voice.

"Yes, we could have. Thank God we weren't." *Hint, hint.*

"Thanks to your claustrophobia, supersonic hearing and little regard for pushing people around," he said in a playful tone as he started to make the call.

I laughed under my breath—if only he knew. Relief washed over me. It was over.

I took a mental tally. Jonathan rescued: check. My story believed: check. My client meeting crisis averted: check.

All in all, life was good. I smiled smugly—if only this could be included in my performance review at work. After all, I'd just saved one of our biggest clients.

I groaned. *If only.* So much for earning credit with Harrison. Instead, I was more likely to be interrogated by him regarding my whereabouts. He was probably polishing his pistol right now.

Jonathan was busy guarding the sidewalk, instructing other pedestrians to walk around and making sure that no one entered the danger zone.

"I'll stand on the other side," I offered, "until they come to rope it off."

He looked at his watch. "I hope they come quickly," he said as he dialed the phone again.

Me too, I thought.

By the time I got back to the office, it was after 3:00 P.M.

I snuck in, hoping to get to my desk without Harrison noticing. I immediately pulled up a file and started typing, like I'd been working for a while.

Harrison was at my door in a flash. "Liz asked me if I knew where you were earlier, so she could tell you about the rescheduled meeting. There wasn't anything in your diary," he accused with raised eyebrows, looking at me suspiciously.

I swallowed. I decided to lie about the meeting and pray I didn't get caught. It was the only way. The rest of the story would hopefully overshadow that detail.

"Yes, I spoke with her. I knew about the cancellation. Sorry I was delayed, Harrison. I ran into Jonathan Hawkins—quite literally. There was a collapse under some scaffolding and we narrowly avoided serious injury. I stayed with him and made sure we warned people until the police came and roped off the area."

His eyebrows shot up. It took a lot to get a reaction out of Harrison, he was usually so composed. "What? Are you okay?"

"Yes, we're both fine, thank you. It just narrowly missed us. Luckily no one was hurt."

"Yes, that is lucky. The scaffolding company will have a serious legal issue on their hands. Do you know which company it is? You should talk to the litigation team—might be a prospective client."

Trust Harrison to see the silver lining.

"I'll let you get back to it. I'm glad you're okay. That's quite a coincidence that you ran into Jonathan . . ." he mused.

His look of suspicion told me he was wondering if we had really just run into each other, or if we had actually *planned* a secret rendezvous. I could see the thoughts coming together in his mind—first the impromptu meeting, and now this. He gave an almost imperceptible nod, seemingly in answer to his unspoken thoughts.

That was the last thing I'd anticipated, for Harrison to think I was having an affair with a client! It was hardly professional. Not to mention the fact that Jonathan was married! But if this was the only consequence—given how much worse I thought this conversation was going to go—I would take it (reluctantly).

"Yes, it's a small world," I said, trying to keep the indignation out of my voice. *And I'm offended at the intimation!* I mentally added.

Harrison turned and left my office, still wearing the look of contemplation on his face.

I had somehow pulled a rabbit out of a hat. Or perhaps someone else had for me. The rescheduled meeting was such a blessing. Perhaps someone was helping *me*.

I felt a tad guilty about my earlier feelings of resentment over having to bear the consequences that came with the responsibility of my visions.

Maybe it would be okay. Maybe I wouldn't be expected to

make too many sacrifices after all.

Or maybe this was just the beginning.

* * *

I managed to get through the rest of the week without any mishaps—or visions. But I was starting to become much more attuned to my environment.

As I was scanning the business papers one morning in the kitchen, I suddenly had the urge to lift the paper from the table. A few seconds later, James, a first year law graduate, accidentally knocked over his coffee, spilling it across the table. Had I not moved the paper, it would have been soaked.

I smiled to myself, knowing my intuition was getting stronger.

When I got back to my desk, I eagerly opened my email. I had a good feeling and presumed Jules had written.

I was partly right, there *was* a non-work related email, but it wasn't from Jules.

> Hi Isy,
>
> Just a short note to see how you're doing? I hope things have eased up at work for you and you're getting some time for yourself.
>
> Anything new going on?
>
> We just picked up our photos and Eliza (my fiancée) is going crazy putting an album together. Did you get any good shots of your trip?
>
> Hope you're well,
>
> Matt

I was surprised, I hadn't expected to hear from Matt. Maybe the man was in desperate need of friends. I was in a good mood so quickly replied without worrying too much about it.

> Hi Matt,
> All good here, thanks. The usual – work, work, potential near-death accident, more work.
> How are you?
> I unfortunately didn't take too many photos while I was away – I'll have to Photoshop my head into the background of some of your photos in Florence to make my own album ;-)
> So – where was your favorite place that you visited?
> Isy

A reply came through not even five minutes later.

> I'd have to say Florence. It's a beautiful city – and it comes with a good story. How often can anyone say that a lawyer actually *helped* them?
> Only joking. I come in peace.
> I'll send you some of our photos of Florence. I'd like to see an advance copy of the *Where's Isy?* book, though.
> Now what was that you said about a near-death experience?!
> Matt

I laughed and hit REPLY.

Keep laughing now because you won't find it as funny when you get my bill...
Florence is one of my favorite places as well. I'd also add Paris and Prague to the list. If you haven't been to the P cities, perhaps you can take Eliza on your honeymoon.
As for the potential accident (I admit 'near-death experience' was for storytelling effect) there was a collapse under some scaffolding which narrowly missed my client and me. But I'm here to serve and protect – no one gets injured on my watch.
Go forth and prosper, Peacekeeper
Isy

I added the joke about protection knowing he wouldn't understand how close to the truth it was in my currently crazy world.

I marveled at my ability to talk about his fiancée and their honeymoon so nonchalantly. Perhaps I was maturing and getting over my ridiculous infatuation. Perhaps we *could* be friends after all.

It took him less than ten minutes to reply, not that I was counting . . .

We're planning our honeymoon at a resort in Koh Samui – well, I should say that Eliza is planning it. All I have to do is agree and nod my head.
You are truly one of a kind – lawyer by day and fearless rescuer by night. I never knew such a person existed. But I'm glad that you do.
One of these days you may need rescuing yourself, you know. I'm always at your service.

> Since you're busy during the week, how about a week-end? Eliza and I are having a few friends over on Sunday afternoon for a casual BBQ. We'd love it if you could come. Bring a friend.
> Hope you can make it.
> Cheers,
> Matt

I wasn't *that* matured yet.

> Thanks for the invite, Matt, that's very kind. Unfortunately I already have plans this weekend. Sounds like fun, though – have a good time!
> Isy

I think it would be better if Matt was more of an *e-friend.* The type of friend you have that you only ever keep in touch with electronically—email, text message, Facebook, that kind of thing. Without modern technology, I think I would cut the number of friends I had in half.

11

POINT, SET, MATCH

IT WAS TRUE that I had plans on the weekend—only it was on Saturday instead of Sunday. Technically, though, I took some pleasure knowing that I hadn't really lied. I may have led him to believe something that wasn't true, but I hadn't actually *said* something that wasn't true.

I conceded that this was perhaps only a lawyer's distinction between fact and fiction, but it still made me feel better.

On Saturday night, I headed to a dinner party hosted by my friend, Rachel, at her home in Bernal Heights. Rachel and I had met during our second year of college. She was one of those people who you instantly got along with—bubbly, outgoing, upbeat. We had completely different views on just about everything—religion, politics, justice, who should win *The Voice*—but none of that ever mattered. We always agreed to disagree and continued our conversations with good humor.

We didn't see each other as often as we used to, but when we did, it was like no time had passed at all.

Rachel had been busy in recent weeks with her new boyfriend, Neil. She organized the dinner for a few friends to meet him, and I was looking forward to getting to know the new man in her life.

I arrived with a bottle of wine and an eager smile. I gave her a huge hug when she opened the door.

"Hey stranger, so good to see you. Come in." She gestured towards the dining room where the group was gathered. The dining table was beautifully laid out with pale green place settings and a sprinkling of yellow rose petals. Three caramel-scented candles ran down the center, their fragrance dancing through the air. Scattered on the surrounding furniture, more candles illuminated the room with an orange glow.

Two other couples had already arrived. Ian and Sally, who both worked with Rachel at the recruitment agency, stood in the corner chatting to Michelle, Rachel's oldest friend, and her husband, Jordan.

My eyes automatically landed on the stranger in the room, the new boyfriend. Neil was tall and stocky, with sandy hair and glasses. I knew absolutely nothing about him, except his name and the fact that he was dating Rachel. He didn't seem to be her ordinary type on the surface. I was eager to speak to him and find out more about him.

Rachel walked me over and introduced us. "Isy, this is Neil." She turned to Neil and touched his arm. "Neil, this is Isy, my friend from college that I told you about."

Neil extended his hand to me. "Nice to meet you."

"Likewise," I responded and took his hand. The moment my hand touched his, a sense of foreboding blasted through me, making me shiver. Instinctively, I wanted to jerk away, eager to shatter the path of negative energy that seemed to flow into me from Neil. But I couldn't appear to be rude for Rachel's sake. I tried to smile and act completely normal. "I don't know what you've heard, but don't judge me from my college days—Rach was a bad influence." I tried to keep my tone lighthearted, but even I heard the nervousness in my high-pitched voice. Neil threw me a dismissive look, like he'd summed me up already and wasn't interested in any further pleasantries.

Rachel, God bless her, picked up the conversation. "Yeah, like anyone could make *you* do anything that you didn't want to do," she said as she rolled her eyes at me. "Isy is a strong-minded person, everything is black and white. I've always admired her conviction, although I don't think we've ever agreed on anything in our lives—well, except maybe for our mutual love of Kings of Leon and cosmopolitans."

I laughed, feeling a little less uncomfortable. "Hey, that's why you're so brilliant—and dangerous. Most of the crazy things we did you somehow made me think were *my* idea. Pure genius. I still don't know how you managed it. You are one of a kind, Rachel Wesley. When you walk into a room, the whole atmosphere changes." I turned to Neil. "She's the life of the party. But I'm sure I don't need to tell you that."

I had to force myself to make eye contact with him, the guy gave me the creeps. But despite my best efforts to be cordial, he shot me a disapproving look. There was an awkward moment of silence before he turned to Rachel and said, "Your other guests have been here a while. Don't you think you should serve the first course?"

I tried to convince myself that I was mistaken when I detected a tone of forcefulness in his voice. Rachel had always scolded me in the past for judging people too quickly. I tried to stay open-minded, I'd only met the man two minutes ago. Remembering the bad start that Jonathan and I had gotten off to, I convinced myself that the bad vibe I'd sensed when I shook his hand didn't mean he was a terrible person. He may have just been having a bad day and wasn't in the greatest mood.

Without saying a word, Rachel turned and headed to the kitchen. Neil announced that the first course was about to be served and instructed us to sit.

My eyes followed after Rachel, whose robotic compliance struck me as more submissive than her usual self.

The first course of mushroom soup was consumed during a discussion of baseball and golf. Neil seemed to do most of the talking. When he finished his soup, he gestured towards Rachel to take the plates away.

Open mind, I reminded myself.

Much of the same conversation continued during the main course. I stayed quiet for the most part, observing the scene. Most of the time, Rachel either remained silent, or nodded her head, adding, *"Yes, for sure"* or *"Absolutely"* after Neil made a comment. If she did start to say anything more, she was usually interrupted.

I was struggling to keep my mind open, knowing it was about to slam shut with a thud. The jury was on its way back from deliberations and the verdict was about to be read.

I wondered what the attraction was, what kind of hold he had on her. For Rachel's sake, I needed to get along with Neil. I tried to look at him through her eyes to find what she saw.

The conversation turned back to baseball and the topic of A-Rod's doping scandal, the discussion centering on whether he deserved the title as one of the greatest baseball players in history.

Unsurprisingly, Neil wasn't as opposed to performance-enhancing drugs as the rest of the table. "At the end of the day, it doesn't matter. Just like Lance Armstrong. Everyone throws their arms up in the air at the mere mention of doping, but both of these guys made a ton of cash getting to the top, and even if their titles go, their money never does. A-Rod's earned hundreds of millions of dollars. Whatever he did or didn't do, it worked for him, didn't it?" he challenged.

The other mouths at the table gaped open, leaving a window for Rachel to get a word in. "Well, I don't think PEDs are fair, but regardless, I'm not a huge fan of his," is all she said before Neil cut her off.

"Well, I don't think A-Rod would care too much, love. You know even less about sport than you do about cooking." He dismissed her with a snicker and continued talking to the boys.

Rachel looked down at her plate, her cheeks flaming. Wordlessly, she began to clear the table for dessert.

I could not believe my eyes. This was not the Rachel I knew. The Rachel I knew would've had a response to that. The Rachel I knew would never date someone who berated her. If that wasn't bad enough, the Rachel I knew was an excellent cook and how anyone could insult her cooking was beyond me. She had clearly spent all day preparing this meal—a meal she had prepared in *his* honor.

The blood rushed to my face. Anger started in the pit of my stomach, growing from an ember into a raging fire that boiled my blood. My mind slammed shut with enough force to cause a tsunami. The foreman had just read the verdict, and it was *'Asshole.'*

I was itching to turn to him and respond, "I'd heard about that ape they taught to talk, but I wouldn't have believed it until I saw you sitting here with my own eyes." The words were bubbling in my mouth. I restrained myself, knowing it would only make Rachel uncomfortable and risk ruining her dinner party. Plus I didn't want to insult the poor ape.

I glared at Neil with contempt. How dare he turn my beautiful, vibrant friend into such a deflated, solemn woman!

The anger turned to outrage, which traveled through my bloodstream and took hold of every cell in my body. I fought to control myself, to sit politely and smile. But the fire that now threatened to consume me would not permit it. I continued to glare at Neil but he was too self-absorbed to notice. I managed to rise from my chair to see if I could help Rachel with dessert.

"How are you going, Rach?" I asked her, peeking my head in the kitchen.

"Good." She smiled back at me like nothing was wrong. "I hope you're enjoying dinner. I've made cheesecake for dessert so I hope you're not full."

I wanted to ask her what on earth she saw in him, but I knew it wasn't the time or place.

"I can definitely find room for cheesecake. Everything has been so lovely. You've completely outdone yourself, Rach, really. You're a magnificent cook—just one of your many talents." If I wouldn't let myself say anything about the pathetic excuse for a man in the other room, I would at least try to counter his insults with some well-deserved praise.

"Thanks. I hope the food was okay." Doubt clouded her eyes and I knew who put it there. I didn't think there was room in my body for any other emotion after the outrage had flooded my system, but sadness managed to pierce my heart.

After dessert, we moved into the living room to play a game of Pictionary. Since there were odd numbers—I was the extra wheel—Rachel captained a team with Ian, Sally and me, while Neil captained the other team with Michelle and Jordan. I was thankful that I wasn't on Neil's team. I wanted to kick his butt, and since I couldn't do that physically, I was hoping to do it Pictionary-style.

The scores were even halfway through the game. Finally it was Rachel's turn to get up and draw. She looked at her card: a movie title. As soon as she picked it up, I knew what it was. It was the same intuition that had told me to lift my paper in the kitchen at work before James spilt his coffee. I couldn't describe how I knew, I just did. It was a sense of *knowing*. Like someone had just told me without me ever hearing the words. My ears didn't hear it, my eyes didn't see it, but the *knowing* resonated deep within me. The answer was *Pretty Woman*. Before Rachel even picked up the pen, I was certain.

She drew a sketchy image of a woman. I waited for her to draw most of it so it wouldn't look suspicious if I screamed out the answer too quickly.

While she was drawing, Neil felt the need to add commentary, skewering her with a supercilious look. "Geez, you draw even worse than you cook."

My entire body trembled with rage. The blood ran to my face

and my hands curled into fists. Primal instinct won out as my body prepared for battle.

Control yourself, I silently chanted to myself.

"A girl," Sally cried out.

"A woman," screamed Ian.

"*Pretty Woman*!" I yelled with satisfaction.

"Yes!" exclaimed Rachel.

"Good work!" I cried, giving her a high-five.

Neil, being the misery-lover he seemed to be, could not let the positive mood go unspoiled. "Good? That looks more like a bad self-portrait than a pretty woman," he huffed.

That did it! *Drop dead, asshole!* All of the effort I had expended trying to control myself and keep my mouth shut now refocused. The rampant fury exploded, pleased to have a target to fire upon.

"Well, when it's time to draw *Planet of the Apes*, you can have the first crack. I'm sure *that* self-portrait would be a work of art. Because everything *you* do is superior to everyone else."

The words spilled from me like lava erupting from a volcano before I had a chance to stop them. They heated the room and engulfed everything in their path, leaving a wake of destruction. Everyone suddenly fell silent, all eyes in the room darting around not knowing where to look.

Observing the damage, I felt horrible that I had caused a scene at Rachel's dinner party, no matter how much I felt it was deserved.

I tried to break the silence and shift the mood, laughing awkwardly. "You know how competitive I can be when it comes to Pictionary! Of course it's just a game. Your turn!" I screeched, trying to sound overly enthusiastic.

I fooled no one.

Neil was fuming that I had ridiculed him. He liked to dish it out, but he didn't like to take it.

"Perhaps we should all do self-portraits. What exactly do you do, Isy?" Neil's tone, particularly as he said my name, was acidic.

Without skipping a beat, I turned to him and responded. It suddenly occurred to me that I had no idea what *he* did.

"I'm a lawyer. And you, Neil?" I asked with exaggerated innocence.

"Figures," he mumbled snidely. "I'm a tax accountant." It seemed to me that he puffed out his chest as he responded, announcing his profession like it was the most admirable in the world.

I knew I should stop myself, I'd already caused a big enough scene. But it was just too tempting not to hit the ball back over the net. "Well then, I guess you can count. Now let's see if you can draw."

I had to stop myself from laughing, he looked like a cartoon character with steam blowing out of his ears. He was so infuriated that I'd had the nerve not to bow down to him, it looked like he might actually wet himself.

"Can *you*?" he hissed at me.

"No, I never said I could. I only draw stick figures," I responded without pause. My tone was light, playful, like a cat toying with her mouse. "I also can't cook." I laughed, throwing the last comment in for fun.

This seemed to only infuriate him more. It would be difficult to insult me if I wasn't claiming to be anything more than I was. And he knew it. There was a long pause while he tried to think of a response.

"So, you're single then, are you?" He said it more as an announcement, rather than a question. The single card—*that* was what he was playing? He had to do better than that if he wanted to play with the grown-ups.

"Yes. A lot of men seem to feel threatened by me," I said, stirring the pot. "You know the type—the Tarzan wannabes who have to beat their chests and put other people down to make themselves feel better." I knew I needed to control myself, but I was starting to enjoy this way too much. It was just too easy to bait him. "But, like the cavemen they are, they only have one-syllable snide remarks so they're usually easy to put back in their box."

There was another long pause. Mr. Smarty Pants wasn't very adept with the comebacks.

"As long as you don't mind becoming an old spinster," he spat, finally finding his voice.

Better than being an asshole is what I wanted to say, but I thought better of it. I needed to regain my self-control and try to salvage what was left of the evening. Everyone had witnessed this interaction in silence. The air was so dense, it felt like a wet blanket had shrouded the room. I wanted to move on and shift the mood. At least open a window.

"What I want is to not grow old while finishing this game," I said, laughing. Let him have his last remark, maybe that would shut him up for now. "Who's up next to draw on your team?"

The rest of the evening passed without further incident, but Neil was in a foul mood. The grumpier he behaved, the bubblier I became, trying to even the energy in the room.

I attempted to make peace when I said goodbye at the end of the evening.

"Good night, Neil. I guess you proved you can definitely draw better than I can." I smiled as I extended my hand.

Neil didn't accept my olive branch. He barely touched my hand, eager to dismiss me. But the moment my hand brushed his, I was gripped by a sudden rush of dizziness. The room spun. Caught off guard, I sucked in a breath and closed my eyes to steady myself. Then so quickly, I almost wasn't sure if it had happened, an image of Neil sitting in front of a bench conducting something that looked like a science experiment swam into my vision. I didn't know exactly what it was, but I got the distinct impression that it wasn't good. I heard the muffled sound of sirens before the scene cleared with a flash of light. And just like that, the dizziness passed, and I opened my eyes to see Neil again. This time he was snickering, probably hoping I was sick, the spiteful bastard.

I tried to act normal and resist the urge to grab Rachel's hand and run. Who knew what this guy was mixed up in? "I'm sorry, I just had a dizzy spell, don't mind me."

I turned to Rachel who looked concerned. "I'm fine, just light-headed for a moment. All good. Good night, Rach. Thanks so much for the incredible dinner." I hugged her and whispered, "I'm really sorry. I hope I didn't ruin the evening. Dinner soon?"

She pulled away. "I'll walk you out." Her formal demeanor indicated she wasn't exactly thrilled with me. My stomach twisted.

As soon as we stepped outside and she closed the door, I tried to apologize again. "Rach—"

She lifted her hand and cut me off. "I don't want to hear it. I can't believe you! How could you? You knew how important this dinner party was to me. You made everyone uncomfortable!" She was shaking her head and I was surprised to see her hands trembling. I was laden with guilt. Rachel and I hardly ever argued. Not seriously, anyway.

"I . . . I wasn't thinking. He just made me so angry. I didn't like—"

"Exactly! *You* weren't thinking! He made *you* angry! *You* didn't like him! Are you listening to yourself? It's all about *you*! Maybe if you'd stop to think before you felt the need to share your condemnation with everyone, you could have acted more civilized! God forbid someone doesn't live up to your standards. You could have pretended that, for once, it was about *me*!"

Her words were like a slap across the face. I knew I was in the wrong, but Rachel had never been this angry with me before, or this hurtful.

My voice quivered, barely a whisper. "I'm sorry, Rachel. I was going to say that I didn't like how he spoke to you. I was trying to protect you." An unbidden tear escaped and I hastily brushed it away.

Rachel's breathing slowed, her voice softening. "It's not your job to protect me. And it's not your place to say whether or not you like it. I'm an adult—it's my decision and you need to respect that. Thinking you know better than me is insulting and demeaning. And frankly, you haven't helped me at all. You've put me in a very awkward position. Neil is fuming. He's not exactly going to want to invite you over again any time soon."

What could I say to that? She was right, Neil would love to see the back of me for good. Had I just threatened my friendship with Rachel? Surely our friendship was stronger than one disagreement over a guy. Especially *this* guy. At least, I hoped it was.

I fought the urge to comment on the fact that she was blasting me, but she let Neil walk all over her. And as much as I'd egged him on, it had taken two to tango—where was his culpability in all of this?

Pointing out any of these arguments would only cause more friction between us, and I seriously doubted that Rachel would see reason about Neil right now. If I wanted to raise my concerns with her, it would have to be another day. But I guessed I'd forfeited the right to discuss him with her at all, she'd never listen now. I'd been upset that she was letting him rule over her, but trying to make her decisions for her wasn't much better, even if I had good intentions.

I should have taken a different tactic. Criticizing her choice of boyfriend wasn't helpful when she was being criticized enough by said boyfriend. I should have reinforced that I was in her corner, first and foremost, before helping her to see that she deserved better. She wouldn't listen to me about Neil disrespecting her if she felt like I was doing the exact same thing.

Bile rose in my throat, the thought of being compared to Neil making me nauseous.

"I'm really sorry I ruined your dinner party, Rach. Truly I am. I don't want this to come between us, you mean too much to me. I will respect your choices. I only want what's best for you."

She sighed, her anger dissipating. "I know you do. And I'm sorry I was so harsh before. I'm just really stressed out and this was kinda the last straw."

Guilt crashed down on me, knowing I'd made things worse

for her. I was leaving Rachel with a very unhappy Neil and she would be the one to endure his bad mood.

"God, Rachel, that was the last thing I wanted. I'm so sorry. I know you probably don't want to talk, but if you do, I'm here. Whenever you want."

She nodded, and I wasn't sure if she was agreeing that she didn't want to talk, or that she did. "Look, I'd better get back inside. Neil will be waiting."

She hugged me but there was no warmth in it. As she opened the door, I heard her take a deep breath, bracing for whatever await her inside.

I worried about how long this relationship would last, fearing that Rachel would lose her sense of identity with Neil. I wanted her to be happy and unless Neil underwent a personality transplant, I didn't see that happening any time soon. He was so negative towards her and she seemed to take his criticisms of her as gospel.

But as she'd just demonstrated, there was some fight left in her. Hopefully she would see what he was doing to her and stand up for herself.

As I walked back to my car, I prayed she'd be okay. Not only didn't I like the way he treated her, I didn't trust him. *What was that flash I saw of him?* I pondered. I couldn't quite put my finger on it. It wasn't so much what I'd seen that sent a shiver down my spine, it was the ominous energy it expelled. It didn't feel so much like a premonition that required intervention, as it did a warning of some kind. A big, flashing neon sign reading: CAUTION: HANDLE WITH CARE.

I didn't exactly know what he'd been doing, but something

instinctively told me that he was up to no good. The sirens I'd heard literally screamed *trouble.* This had to be different to the other premonitions I'd had, I couldn't be expected to try to help someone as abhorrent as Neil, especially if the police were involved. I mean, what would I be expected to do—drive the getaway car? I laughed at the thought. I'd lock the doors and keep edging the car forward every time he tried to reach the door handle. If Neil was mixed up in something he shouldn't be, that was certainly *his* problem. It wasn't going on my to-do list. My concern was for Rachel. She wasn't in the flash I'd seen, but I didn't want him dragging her down.

An idea occurred to me: what if I called the police? I imagined waving to him as the police hurled his butt into the car, and a smile slowly spread across my lips. I instantly dismissed the thought—the sirens were there without my intervention. That would happen without me. *So then, what was my role, if anything?* I mused. Given that Neil getting caught was the best thing that could happen to Rachel, I had zero intention of trying to prevent it. The best thing I could do would be to try and get her away from him, or, failing that, to be there for her when the police did that for me.

I didn't know whether I should say something to her about Neil's possible illegal activity. I could imagine the look on her face as soon as she heard the word *premonition.* And that was on a good day. Now that she was furious with me, even if she believed what had been happening to me, she'd think the image I'd seen of Neil was deliberately conjured to reaffirm my dislike of him, that I was merely seeing what I wanted to see. That was the best-case scenario. Worst-case scenario she'd think I was making the whole thing up as a ruse. Without proof of some kind, the accusation could destroy our friendship.

I decided that if she wasn't ready to hear the truth about Neil, then no good could come of it. It would only drive a bigger wedge between us, and in the process, drive her closer to *him*. But the premonition worried me—whatever Neil was up to was serious and I didn't want Rachel to get caught in the crosshairs. Maybe the whole point of the premonition was to warn her about him. *Why else would I have seen it?* I needed advice.

* * *

I called Jules as soon as I got home but I couldn't reach her. I went to bed but tossed and turned most of the night, thinking about the evening.

The next morning, when I was still unable to get the past evening's events out of my mind, I decided to call my mom. I hadn't spoken to her for more than a quick hello since I'd gotten back from Florence, so I felt bad that I was calling mainly because I needed help with a problem.

I was an only child. My parents had tried for more children after having me, but had been unsuccessful. We didn't have a lot of close relatives. My father's parents immigrated to America from France when he was very young and unfortunately both died in a car accident when he was still a child. My mother had one sister who lived on the east coast with her two sons. I had seen them once in the past five years.

Mom answered the phone on the third ring.

"Hi, Mom. How's it going?"

"Belle! Well, isn't this a nice surprise. I was beginning to wonder if you'd moved countries without telling me. How are you, sweetheart?"

"Sorry I haven't called much lately, Mom. Just had a lot on my mind. How's Dad?"

"He's good. He's out tinkering with the car. You should come up for a visit, maybe stay the weekend. We'd both love that, Belle."

My parents lived in Napa Valley, having moved there against my will when I was fifteen years old. I moved back to attend Berkeley after high school. Napa Valley was only an hour or so north of San Francisco, but I didn't make it up there to visit as often as I should.

"I promise I will soon, Mom, and I'll stay the whole weekend. We can have a movie night with Cary Grant and popcorn, just like we used to."

"That would be lovely, Belle. I'll get the movies ready," Mom promised enthusiastically. "So tell me what's been on your mind that's been keeping you so preoccupied."

My mother was a very straightforward, matter-of-fact kind of person. She would often say, *'I call a spade a spade, you know'* after she'd given an unapologetic, frank opinion. It was one of her best—and sometimes one of her worst—qualities. You always knew where you stood with Mom.

She had always praised me for my judgment and rational approach to life. It was for this reason that I'd been reluctant to share my tales of premonitions and near-death experiences with her. If *I* thought that I was edging on borderline *Twilight Zone*, then I could only imagine what my mother would think. It was a conversation I certainly wasn't ready to have, at least not until I knew what I would say.

What had been keeping me preoccupied since last night was a different story, however. I knew Mom wouldn't scold me for the incident and she would have sensible advice about what was best to do now. I would just ignore the oh-yeah-I-had-a-premonition-that-he-may-be-doing-something-illegal part of the problem.

"Actually, Mom, something happened at a dinner party at Rachel's that I feel really bad about and I'm not sure what to do about it. I want to warn her but I've already made a mess of things and I'm worried I'll only make it worse. I'd love some advice."

"Of course, Belle. What happened?"

I proceeded to give her a play-by-play of the events of the previous evening. I may have exaggerated slightly for storytelling effect, but I gave her a fairly accurate description.

"That's a tricky one," she responded. "You know I like to call a spade a spade"—my lips twitched hearing the familiar words—"so I can see why you called him on it. His behavior was inexcusable. But in this case, sweetheart, I think it would have been better not to have caused an argument in the middle of the party. I doubt she'll want to listen to anything else you have to say."

Great, even my straight-talking-make-no-apologies mother had better sense than I did.

"But Mom—"

"Belle, you were at a dinner party meeting your friend's boyfriend. He was not being rude to you. If Rachel had a problem with the way he spoke to her, then *she* should've been the one to say something. Maybe she wanted to deal with it privately."

"But—"

"I know your heart was in the right place—you were only trying to protect her. But she's an adult, sweetheart. It's up to her to decide how she wants to be treated and whom she wants to date. You can't decide for her. I would've advised for you to meet her after the dinner party to speak privately about it.

"But since what's done is done, I don't see any point in you making yourself sick over it. From what you said, you didn't say anything overtly offensive—well, except for the *Planet of the Apes* comment . . . That was bad. I agree he deserved it, but you stooped to his level. I think it would be best now to give Rachel some space. It's quite clear that you don't like him, so I doubt she'll want to invite you over again in a hurry to all sit down together."

This was exactly the sentiment that Rachel had shared. I was burning to tell my mother about the premonition and why I was still harping on this when I'd already put my foot in it. Without sharing my concerns about that, I seemed like a dog with a bone. I tried to explain, without explaining, so she'd understand the seriousness of the situation.

"But Mom—this guy looks really shifty. I wouldn't be surprised if he was up to no good. Illegal stuff, I mean."

"Do you have any proof of that?"

Exactly the question Rachel would ask. The one I couldn't answer. "Well, not exactly . . ."

"Then I certainly wouldn't be making things worse with unfounded accusations. I would give her a quick call to apologize. Give her some positive reinforcement—tell her that you only want her to be happy and that she deserves to be treated like the incredibly wonderful person she is. Tell her that you respect her decisions and you're there for her no matter what. Then leave it at that. When she's ready to talk, she'll let you know."

"I kinda said that already. Well, to that effect anyway."

"Then let it go, Belle. You can't do any more than that, but give her space. What's done is done."

I wished now that I had been able to put the evening on pause and call Mom *before* the incident. I'd been convinced that she would've torn him to pieces without mercy. I realized that maybe things weren't always so black and white, that perhaps my mother sometimes had a different perspective to what I would assume.

It dawned on me that I, of all people, should learn to expect the unexpected. Sometimes things came with a clear label—indisputable fact—and sometimes nothing was what it seemed. There were always so many ways of looking at the same thing, it just depended on what angle you looked at it from.

I thanked Mom and hung up the phone. This was one vision that I couldn't control. Rachel would never listen. And Neil didn't deserve any intervention on my behalf, he was making his own bed.

12

WARM EMBRACE

ANOTHER WEEK PASSED without any more visions, affording me some much needed breathing space.

The vision blackout also accorded me more time to worry about Rachel. I took my mother's advice and tried to let it go for now. I could only be there for her if and when she needed me.

Although I hadn't had any new visions, the *knowing* I had experienced at the dinner party had been occurring in increasing intensity and frequency. This feeling I had of being attuned to my environment was growing by the day.

When I was leaving my apartment for work on Monday, I suddenly put down my purse, went back into my bedroom and changed my blouse, selecting a navy blue one to replace the white I'd been wearing. The instinct had been so strong that my feet turned around at the door before my head could even catch up.

I didn't think of it again until later that day when someone bumped me in the kitchen and I spilled my coffee straight down my top.

I should cut back on the coffee, I thought. But once I'd dried it off and put my jacket back on, it was difficult to see the mark.

Oh, that explains this morning. Strange . . . If I had the instinct to change my blouse, why couldn't I have known to avoid being bumped and prevent the spill completely?

Little things like that were happening to me more and more. I seemed to be tapping into a different frequency, the transmission providing answers to questions I hadn't even asked.

But I was yet to learn to control it and I had no idea what was coming later that week.

On Thursday evening, I was at work when I heard my phone chime. I picked it up and looked at the message.

> HEY ISY. CAN U PLS LET ME KNOW WEN U GET HOME – NEED 2 SPEAK WITH U. DONT WORRY IF IT'S LATE. JEZ

I stood motionless for a second, too worried to move. This was not like Jeremy. Something was wrong.

Ignoring the pile of paperwork on my desk, I immediately text him back.

> LEAVING THE OFFICE NOW – B HOME BY 7

I quickly shut down my computer and grabbed my purse. I flew out the door before anyone—particularly Harrison—had an opportunity to stop me or ask for any status reports.

When I got home, I went straight to Jeremy's apartment. He opened the door as soon as I knocked, like he'd been waiting.

"Jez, how are you? Is everything okay?" I asked him, the panic rising in my voice.

"Calm down, Isy, you look like you practically ran all the way home. I didn't mean to frighten you. I just wanted to see you. Let's go to your apartment, so you can relax and change your clothes."

He tried to give me a reassuring smile, but it was half-hearted and I knew it was solely for my benefit. Something serious was definitely troubling him, the pain was evident in his eyes. My heart sank.

"Okay," I agreed hesitantly.

I put down my things and kicked off my heels but didn't hurry to change my clothes. He needed to tell me something and I braced myself.

"So, I didn't see you last weekend. What's been going on with you?" he asked, leaning on the edge of the couch. He folded his arms across his chest, almost hugging himself. His voice was quiet, like he couldn't muster the energy to speak any louder.

"Same, same," I told him, in a hurry for him to forget the small talk and get to what was important.

"Work?"

He was stalling—why? Was it so bad that he couldn't say the words aloud? "It's okay, well except for the part of me landing in hot water last week. But it's nothing to worry about, it's just work." There was something much more important to worry about. I fought the urge to shake him to get it out of him. I had to let him tell me in his own time.

"What do you mean?" he asked, his eyebrows pulling together.

I mentally chastised myself for bringing this up at the worst possible time. I elaborated as quickly as I could. "I nearly missed a client meeting because . . . I was out . . . at lunch. Thankfully the client rescheduled, or I would've been toast."

"You know, Isy, no matter what happens—and I know how important your career is to you—I will always be here for you. Just as you were here for me when things weren't going so well." His eyes were so soft, so sincere, that he nearly brought me to tears.

I moved closer to him and squeezed his arm. "You're too good to me, Jez."

"I mean it, Isy. We all have our good times and our bad. The wheel is always turning—sometimes we're up and sometimes we're down. The only thing that really matters in the end is who is still there beside you."

His eyes glistened. I closed the remaining gap between us and gave him a hug, eager to comfort him. "Ditto," I murmured. I leaned back so I could look up at him, but kept my hand on his arm. "What's wrong, Jez? You know you can talk to me about anything."

He nodded, giving me a sad smile. "I just wanted to see you to let you know that I'm going to Phoenix for a little while. I'm not sure for how long. I'm on a flight first thing in the morning. My sister needs me."

His gaze shifted and some long-ago memory seemed to shroud his eyes.

"Did I ever tell you that I was adopted?" he asked, meeting my eyes again. I shook my head. "You know, everyone's experience is different. Some people feel this terrible rejection, thinking they were unwanted. But for me, the opposite was true. No one was more wanted than I was. My parents jumped through so many hoops to get me. Every single day I knew I was loved. Sometimes I felt like something was missing, but . . . I don't know. It was a weird feeling, like a piece of me was missing—like I wasn't whole—but it had nothing to do with my parents. I know that sounds strange, I can't really explain it. My mom thought it meant that I wanted to look for my biological parents, but I never really felt the urge. I know who my mom and dad are. And I couldn't have asked for anyone better." He took a steadying breath, his voice soft. "My older sister, Belinda, was so protective of me. Fiercely so. She's always been there for me. I need to be there for her now."

His eyes were shrouded in memories again, the sadness pooling around him.

I squeezed his arm. "What—what happened?" Seeing his struggle, I quickly added, "You don't have to talk about it if you don't want to."

He paused, taking a deep breath before continuing. "My niece—she's only five—she had a serious accident today. She's in intensive care. Belinda called earlier. I need to go to Phoenix to be with them."

I could see him fighting the emotion as he said the words, but his eyes welled up as soon as he mentioned his niece. Now I understood his introspection about being there for the important people in your life. Why couldn't I have had a premonition to prevent *this* accident from happening? I couldn't bear to see Jeremy in pain.

I wrapped my arms tightly around him. "Oh, Jeremy, I'm so very sorry to hear that. That is awful news, but I'm sure she'll be okay. My thoughts and prayers will be with you." I squeezed him more tightly.

"Thanks, Isy. It's just such a . . . such a . . . shock." His voice was beginning to quiver.

I pulled back a little to look at him again. "I know. How did it happen?" I wasn't sure if this was the right question to ask, discussing the details could make it worse.

He looked past me to an unmarked spot on the wall, speaking slowly. "Belinda was changing Audrey's clothes after school when they discovered a bird's nest outside her window. Belinda left the room for just a minute when she heard Audrey scream. She said she ran downstairs and found Audrey lying next to the house . . ." His voice trailed off, but he cleared his throat and continued. "She'd fallen out the window. We can only guess that she'd been trying to reach for the bird's nest. She was just lying there, unconscious—" His voice broke.

His cheeks glistened with the wayward tears that had managed to escape and my heart broke for him.

I kissed his right cheek and gently caressed his left, wiping the tears with the back of my hand.

Our eyes locked. The intensity of emotion was so strong, it almost felt like another entity in the room. His eyes, brimming with pain, searched mine.

"I know you want to be strong for your sister, but you don't have to be strong now," I whispered, trying to give him permission to let go and release the whirlpool of emotion inside him.

More tears began to stream down his face, but I could see him still resisting. "It's okay to let go," I whispered again.

He buried his face in the top of my hair and held me closely to him.

We stayed like that for a few moments. I could hear his uneven breathing as he tried to suck the air into his tightening chest.

I pulled back to examine his face. His eyes were still searching.

I kissed his right cheek again. As I moved to kiss his left side, my lips brushed his.

And then it happened—too quickly to know what was happening, or to stop it.

His lips were on mine. Gentle, but passionate.

I realized what he had been searching for: comfort.

The intensity of emotion in that moment—pain, fear, worry, anguish, desire—bubbled to the surface and spilled over with unrelenting force.

His soft kiss was replaced by one with more urgency and need. He crushed me to his chest, locking his arms around me and pulling me up to his mouth.

I responded. I didn't know whether it was because he was deeply hurting and needed me, or because this was the natural path of our relationship. I only knew that in that moment, I couldn't pull away.

Eventually, he came up for air. He leaned his head back so he could look into my eyes. I'm not sure what he saw there.

He gently placed his hands on either side of my face, continuing to stare deeply into my eyes—my soul—and kissed me again. His hands were warm and my skin quickly heated under his touch.

He made his way to the inside of my jacket and a heartbeat later it fell to the floor. He locked his arms around my waist again.

I brought my arms up and closed them around his neck.

"Are you sure?" he whispered.

"Yes," I murmured.

It took him only a second to reach for the buttons on my blouse. Soon that was on the floor, too.

So swiftly that I didn't realize what he was doing, he leaned down and swooped me up into his arms and carried me into the bedroom.

* * *

The next morning, streaks of sunlight announced the new day, beckoning me to awake. I reached over to the other side of the bed. Jeremy was gone. There was a note on the pillow.

> Morning, Isy.
> I'm so sorry that I had to leave, but I had to catch my flight. You looked so peaceful I didn't want to wake you.
> Thank you - for everything.
> I will call you.
> Jez x

My head was spinning. In the light of day, I wasn't sure how to interpret the events of the previous evening, or even how I felt about it.

Thank you—for everything.

What did that mean? What was I hoping it meant?

Something about last night, as wonderful as it was—as gentle and genuine and caring as it was—filled me with a sense of foreboding. I couldn't quite figure out why.

I cared for Jeremy, more than I had cared for any other man before. I felt close to him, I could trust him wholeheartedly, and I knew he would be there any time that I needed him. I didn't need to try to be perfect to impress him. He knew how to cheer me up when I was feeling down, he made me laugh, and he wiped away my tears. And he'd allowed me to do the same for him. Being with him was just so natural, so effortless.

Then I realized what it was that had been bothering me, why it just didn't feel right.

Jeremy was my friend, my true friend. I loved him. I adored him. There was no way I would ever want to risk that by complicating our relationship with romance. I couldn't bear to lose what we had, couldn't even bear to think about it. We had both been a little hesitant and cautious last night, like we knew that we were doing something we probably shouldn't.

I sighed at this sudden epiphany. I was worried about how this would affect our friendship. The last thing I wanted was to hurt Jeremy. I shuddered at the thought.

This was probably why as much as I trusted Jeremy, as much as I was comfortable being a blubbering mess around him, I still hadn't confided my biggest secret to him. I couldn't risk any possibility of him looking at me differently. That would *kill* me. Irrespective of that fear, he was always worrying about me and I hesitated to further burden him with yet more of my drama.

There was no way I could talk to him about any of it now. Not now that he had so many more important things to worry about. I couldn't do that to him.

What will I say if he calls me? I mused. I would have to play along so as not to hurt his feelings, but I didn't want to play along so well that the truth would be a complete and utter shock to him when we eventually did talk.

I rolled over and buried my head in my pillow. "Why?" I wailed over and over again.

Then another thought hit me and interrupted my hysteria.

Thank you—for everything.

That didn't sound like the note of someone who was about to profess his love. If anything, it sounded more like the parting words of someone who was about to move out of the building and change his name. Part of me felt surprisingly indignant about that, but I quickly swept that aside and let the relief calm me.

Perhaps Jeremy felt just as confused and awkward as I did.

Perhaps this was something that we could laugh about when he got home.

I wasn't sure. Right now, it didn't matter. Right now his only thought would be of his niece and whatever happened last night would pale in comparison. *Dear God, please let his niece be okay.*

The last thing I wanted was to make anything more difficult for Jeremy, or for him to feel awkward. I thought about my intuitive abilities that were beginning to manifest and wondered: why couldn't I have predicted *this* mistake?

I sighed and pulled the covers over my head. Although it was a mistake, I would probably do it all over again. Jeremy had needed me last night. And our relationship had been building to something. It was only a matter of time before sexual tension threatened our friendship.

Now that we knew we'd ventured into dangerous waters, those

thoughts would be exiled. The curiosity had been satisfied. Any potential desire to take the relationship further—and potentially ruin everything we had—was gone.

My alarm went off, interrupting my ruminations. I would have groaned at the idea of going to work, except today I had things in better perspective.

I said a prayer for Jeremy and his family and got up to face my day.

13

LEAP

I DIDN'T HEAR from Jeremy on Friday. I wondered whether I should call him to let him know that I was thinking about him and hoping everything was okay. I didn't want to intrude on his family time, though, and so I resisted the temptation. *He would call me if he wanted to talk*, I told myself.

Saturday came and went without any news.

By Sunday, I was half out of my mind, thinking the worst. I had dialed his number a half dozen times and hung up just before the call connected.

My mind was racing: What if the news was bad and his niece had—

No, it was too awful to even consider. Maybe he just didn't want to speak with me after the other night.

I focused my nervous energy on cleaning. My bathroom sparkled so brightly, it was practically luminescent.

I jumped so high that I nearly hit the roof when the phone

rang later that afternoon as I was coming out of the shower. I looked at the caller ID.

"Jeremy? How are you?" I asked hysterically.

"I'm . . . okay, Isy. How are you?" He spoke softly and I could hear the fatigue in his voice.

"Fine, fine," I blurted. "How is she?" I was afraid to ask, but there was no way of getting around it.

"She's doing a little better, thank God. There's still a lot of swelling so they can't be sure about . . . the future. But she's going to make it."

I breathed a sigh of relief. "I'm so glad to hear it. How are you holding up?" I asked.

"Okay, just a little tired. I'm sorry I haven't called earlier."

"Don't be, that's the least of your worries. I'm just happy that she's doing better. You probably haven't slept at all. Or eaten."

"I'm fine," he reassured me. "I just wanted to give you a quick call to let you know. I'd better get back now. I'll try to call again soon," he promised.

"If there's anything you need me to do, just let me know. I'm thinking of you all."

I hung up the phone feeling grateful that things were looking more promising. He had mentioned possible complications in the future but I was staying positive.

I was also grateful that it had not felt awkward between us, although that was undoubtedly because he had more important things to worry about. Regardless, I still had the feeling that Jeremy wanted to pretend it had never happened as much as I did. I decided to stay positive about that as well because there was no way I would let this hiccup destroy our friendship.

Although I knew it wasn't only up to me.

I closed my eyes and said another prayer for him and his family. Everything would be okay, I was sure of it.

When the alarm clock went off the following morning, I didn't grumble that it was Monday. I was still feeling the same sense of gratitude. I had so much for which to be thankful.

Harrison passed my office later that morning and stuck his head in. "Morning, Isy. Jonathan is coming by soon. Make sure that you have the depositions ready in case he wants to see them."

"Morning, Harrison. Sure, no problem." I smiled as I pointed to the paperwork on my desk.

He nodded and disappeared.

Jonathan. It had been a while since I had seen him. I was wondering how he was. Every day that he had since that near miss was a blessing. Of course, I couldn't tell *him* that. I wished that I could, though; it may have given him a different perspective when it came to quality time with his family. The image of Jeremy's niece was making me see that all the more clearly.

I turned back to my computer. There was an email from Jules, asking me what was happening with Jeremy and his family. I had emailed her last Friday to tell her what had happened, but neglected to call to update her last night.

I quickly typed her a response, reassuring her that things were looking more positive.

A reminder popped up on screen and I started filling in my timesheet from the previous week. It was the bugbear of all lawyers who had to record every six minutes of their time. I usually made sure my timesheets were submitted every Friday, but with the stress of what was going on with Jeremy, I neglected this duty last week.

As I was assigning the time I had spent at two client meetings, I saw a flash.

My fingers paused on top of the keyboard. My whole body was still.

It was a merry-go-round of information, all coming too quickly, twisting and turning. I heard bells, laughter, footsteps, a loud thud, screaming. It was like watching something in fast-forward and only catching every second frame.

I held completely still and closed my eyes. I attuned to my sensory constitution and, like a tide washing ashore, let the familiar feeling of calm sweep over me. Finding my center, I consciously slowed my breathing and waited.

There it was. California Street. I couldn't see anything in the background that told me this, but I knew it. I felt it. I could see the tracks and the cable car that was stopped as it picked up passengers. I could hear the two girls laughing as they boarded the car.

The footsteps belonged to a man in a suit, walking briskly, crossing the road. I focused to see his face. It was as if he turned his head and looked straight at me in response, like he knew I was there.

Jonathan.

He stepped out to cross the tracks behind the stationary cable car, not realizing that another one was approaching from the opposite direction.

"No, Jonathan. *No!*" I screamed.

I knew the rest. I did not want to see. I opened my eyes as quickly as I could.

Ashley, a senior associate with the neighboring office, poked her head in.

"Are you all right, Isy? I heard screaming." She looked at me curiously, tapping her foot.

"Sorry, Ashley, I was just getting worked up over an email. I'll keep it down in here," I told her, blushing.

"Okay, then." She gave me one last dubious look and disappeared around the wall.

I was trying to make sense of what I saw. Jonathan—*again*? How? Why? I could see how taking care of Jonathan could potentially become a full-time job.

Why was this happening again? Freak accident? Or something more?

I didn't have time to think about it. The scene of the vision was two blocks away and I still had to get down thirty-seven floors before I could start my dash over there. Something told me that I had to hurry, the time was close.

I flicked off my heels and pulled on my flat walking shoes under my desk. I wouldn't be able to run fast enough in four-inch heels.

I flew out of my office, praying no one saw me. I had no cover story. My mind was focused on only one thing and I wasn't pausing to think of any believable lies that could explain why I was running out of the office like a bat out of hell.

A bat that had the foresight to change her shoes.

The elevator ride took an eternity. Why was it that when you were in the biggest hurry you stopped on every floor? And why were some people so lazy that they couldn't take even a single flight of stairs? Ugh!

When the doors opened on the first floor, I sprang into action. I raced across the large foyer of the building and flew out the door onto the street, running so quickly that I nearly bowled over the man who was entering the revolving doors.

"Sorry," I screamed as I ran on, not turning back. I could only hope that my speed did not allow Andrew Maloney, a partner at Barkleys, to recognize me. But I had no time to worry about it even if he had.

I made it there just as I could faintly hear the girls laughing in the distance. I was on the other side of the street and considered screaming out to Jonathan, but I was afraid that he might not see me in time. He was still hidden from view behind the stationary cable car. As soon as he stepped out, it would be too late.

The other cable car was approaching from the opposite direction, about to move past the stationary one on the other line.

There was only one thing left to do.

My feet reacted before my head did. If I'd had time to think, to process what was happening, I might have looked out for the motorcycle.

Instead, I leaped onto the road. The motorcyclist nearly lost control of his bike as he reflexively swerved around me, trying to avoid slamming straight into me.

I would've gestured an apology—or more likely, *wet myself*—if I'd had time. But I was halfway across the road with the destination my only focus. If I wasn't fast enough, both Jonathan *and I* would be road kill.

The approaching cable car started dinging its bell furiously. The gripman saw me running directly into his path but he wouldn't have time to stop. The historic cars were built like tanks and required a lot of stopping distance to pull up completely.

And like tanks, getting hit by one was not a good idea. It was capable of literally ripping a person in half.

As I leaped in front of it, eyes squeezed shut in fear, it occurred to me that the frantic ringing of the bell should have been enough to stop Jonathan from stepping into its path. Why didn't this occur to me *before* I leaped in front of it like a suicidal maniac? I obviously didn't think this through. *Please don't let my stupidity kill me.*

It was true that your life flashed before your eyes during a near-death experience. My whole life was on film, slides of all the key milestones flickering before my eyes. My childhood, graduating law school, moving into my first apartment, that first day at Barkleys, meeting Jeremy.

Time slowed down and the seconds stretched like a rubber band—until it snapped back again and the clock resumed its regular pace. I took one last leap forward and—miraculously—cleared the car just as it flew past me, the gripman still ringing the bell in fury.

I did hit into something, though—or rather, someone. I looked up as he grabbed my arms to steady me and saw that I'd slammed straight into Jonathan. Déjà vu, anyone?

"Isabel?" he asked, confused. He looked in the direction of the car that had just passed. "What are you doing? Do you realize that you nearly got yourself killed?"

Yes, actually, I do! Do you realize that I just dirtied my underwear trying to save you? "Hi, Jonathan. How are you?" I smiled meekly, wiping the sweat from my forehead.

"What are you doing here?"

Ugh. No cover story. Ugh, ugh, ugh. This was so unfair. I should be getting a medal or something, not having to cover my tracks.

I willed a decent lie to enter my mind and spill from my lips.

Nothing. My mind was still reeling from very nearly becoming a pancake and had shut down for business.

So I went with the truth—partially. I was going to sound insane regardless and I was too exhausted to worry about it. "I thought you were going to step out in front of that cable car, so I crossed over to stop you."

I never thought I looked good in white. My skin was too pale. *Were all straitjackets white?* I wondered.

"You *what*?" he asked in disbelief. I followed his gaze to the other side of the road, realizing there would be no way I could've seen him from there.

"Yup—so that's twice now, huh? Lucky for you that you have a guardian angel. You need to keep better watch next time," I said jokingly, hoping that my smugness would convince him that I *had* seen him—in the conventional way one normally sees, that is.

"How could you have seen me? And why would you be so reckless? And—"

"Are you heading over to Barkleys? We can walk together," I interrupted. I was trying to distract him, but I cringed realizing he would probably retell this story to Harrison.

I turned and started walking towards the office with dread. Jonathan followed.

"Yes. What are you doing here?" he persisted.

My mind was rebooting, weaving a new web. One that would

either make things better or worse—much, much worse. "Jonathan, I feel that I can trust you. I know you're a client, and I really shouldn't tell you this, but—" I paused as I looked up at him to search his eyes and gage his reaction.

He looked open to listening to me. I decided to continue.

"If I tell you something, can you please keep it between you and me, and not tell Harrison?" I asked him earnestly. He would either say yes—in which case, Harrison would not hear this story—or he would say no and I would use that as an excuse to not answer his questions. It was flimsy, but it was all I had.

He looked down at me. "I believe I can do that, so long as it is something personal and not something that would affect Parkmores."

"No, it's definitely personal," I reassured him.

"Then I believe I can return the same courtesy that you once showed me," he said, giving me a knowing smile.

I smiled back. "Thank you, Jonathan. You see, I was out because . . . well . . . let's just say that I was . . . considering my future at Barkleys—"

He cut me off, filling in the blanks and ending my discomfort. "I see—you're coming from a job interview. I understand. But—" He eyed my empty hands and choice of footwear with confusion.

"I didn't want to look conspicuous, so a friend had the things I needed waiting for me," I lied.

"Oh. You are resourceful, aren't you?" he commented, seeming to be impressed. "You know, Isabel, I wouldn't want to poach you, but if you were ever entertaining the idea of leaving Barkleys, I would be more than happy to consider having you join my team."

I was speechless.

"Just something to think about," he continued. "I would rather have you working *for* me than against me." He winked. "Don't worry, I won't mention to Harrison that I saw you."

"Thank you, Jonathan. You don't know what a relief that is."

"You're welcome," he said, smiling conspiratorially like we shared a secret. Then he cocked his head to one side, seeming to remember something. "Were you really worried that I was going to be hit by that cable car?"

"Ah, yes."

"And that's why you were running?" he clarified.

"Yes."

"That's silly, you needn't have worried. There was no chance I would've stepped in front of that car. The way the gripman was ringing his bell like a madman possessed, no one would charge in front of it—except you, of course. I suppose I should thank you for the gesture, though. It was very brave—and very foolish."

I was right about the darn bell. *I must remember that for the next time I nearly kill myself.* Sometimes less dramatic gestures are enough to change the outcome of a vision. If I wasn't careful, the next vision I had would be of me.

"You're welcome," I replied.

"So I guess it is you who should heed your own warning and be more careful," he said smugly.

Clark Kent used to look like a bumbling idiot and not be able to tell the truth, either, I thought.

Ugh. I really needed to stop comparing myself to fictional superheroes. I wasn't fictional and I wasn't a superhero. And I certainly wasn't made of steel.

When we got back to the office, I asked if Jonathan would mind entering first. My plan was to ensure Harrison was distracted, and sneak in via the entry that took me by the restroom. If anyone asked, I planned to tell them I wasn't feeling well in the lower region. No one ever asked for details after you told them that. Once upon a time, I would have been mortified by the idea of saying such a thing, but now I was clinging to it like a life raft in a stormy sea.

I quickly sat down at my desk and tried to look busy, like I'd been there the whole time. I opened my email to check if I'd missed anything urgent. There it was: another email from my newest e-friend.

> Hi Isy
> How are things?
> I have a break tomorrow around lunch. Hoping we can catch up for a bite – or coffee if you're pressed for time. I'll come to you. Anytime between 12 and 2 – whatever works best for you?
> Before you say no – remember that a person can only take so much rejection... So be kind.
> Hope to see you,
> Matt

I was frozen in my seat. What the? Tomorrow? Come *here*?

I wanted to scream, *No*. But how could I when he was the one going out of his way to come to me and the way he asked was so . . . endearing.

This definitely did not fit into my definition of an e-friend. He had missed the whole point of the 'e.' Of course, I hadn't exactly explained my e-friend theory to him, so I couldn't be upset that he had bypassed the 'e' altogether.

My hands began to tremble. I contemplated the emotion that was causing this physical reaction—was it fear? No, it was *excitement.* I was nervous.

He was just stopping by during the course of his day, I told myself. He would be alone. Alone was good. Or maybe alone was bad.

I decided that I couldn't say no. It was just coffee. I hit REPLY.

> Matt,
> How about coffee at 1:30pm? I'll meet you at the coffee shop at the bottom of my building.
> The kind one
> ☺

That should be safe. Definitely no more than half an hour.

His reply was almost immediate.

> Thank you, oh kind one. Look forward to seeing you then.
> Matt

My thoughts were like a tornado, spinning out of control. I scolded myself for the lightning flashes of imaginary grandchildren reappearing in my mind. I wouldn't give this another thought if it were any other friend coming to meet me. I couldn't let myself make more of it than it was. It meant nothing, and more importantly, it *couldn't* mean anything. I replaced the forbidden images with thoughts of the twenty-eight cats I would likely have someday if I didn't stop being distracted and romanticizing things that could never happen. I had to stay focused on what was real. Matt may as well be Hugh Jackman, it was never going to happen.

I got up to refill my coffee and clear my head before getting back to work.

As I passed the boardroom on my way to the kitchen, I caught a glimpse of Jonathan with Harrison.

The rhythmic echo of my heels clicking on the kitchen floor tile sounded like a ticking clock. My mind started to wonder, thinking about the strange events of the day and the fact that Jonathan had now been the star of not one but *two* of my visions.

Was he just accident-prone?

Or was there a reason why I was meant to help him again? Could the real purpose of our interactions not be about scaffolding and cable cars, but something else?

I had no idea. Unfortunately, I wasn't the Dalai Lama. I wished I had him on retainer, too.

14

CAFFEINATED CONFESSIONS

LATER THAT EVENING, I picked up the phone and dialed my guru of visions, Julia. Before I let her respond about Jonathan, I let it slip about my coffee with Matt the next day.

"Really?" she breathed down the phone with mild amusement. "I wish I were a fly on the wall to watch this."

"That's not very nice, Jules. Are you intimating that I'm going to embarrass myself?" I asked, not hiding the annoyance in my tone.

"Not at all. As long as you don't overthink it. I know you—you'll be worried about how every syllable will be construed. I would think that if this whole experience—this whole gift—would teach you anything, it's that life is so much bigger than the trivial everyday things most of us worry about. There is meaning everywhere, but not the kind of meaning that they cover on the entertainment news—or in the office," she added.

"Yeah, yeah," I responded, humoring her. "You think that maybe in the whole scheme of things we're supposed to be friends, and it has nothing to do with romance, so I should get over it."

"Not that you should get over it—that you should be *open* to it," she corrected. "I'll stop nagging you about Matt, though. I know you have to do what's right for you. I'm not there, so I can't tell you what's right. Now let's talk about Jonathan—that is so interesting!"

I was grateful for the change of topic. "But what do you think it means?" I breathed, looking for enlightenment.

"I don't know, I'm not Oprah. But there must be a reason. Maybe the purpose is for you and Jonathan to become closer friends, for you to trust each other. Maybe the real purpose will come later. He already helped you with Harrison today. Maybe you should take him up on his offer to go work for him."

"He only had to help me since I was in that situation because of *him*," I pointed out. "How would working for him help? I doubt I'd be getting any free rides. I'd have to start from the ground up again, building my profile in the company."

"Well, I don't know. This is all new to me, too. Maybe he could give you a reference for another job or something. Or maybe it will be you who has to help him with something—unrelated to life and death situations, I mean. I think you should be patient, the reason will reveal itself eventually."

"So long as this doesn't keep happening over and over because I'm not getting it. I don't know how many more times I can pretend that I was 'just in the neighborhood.' He'll start to think I'm stalking him soon. Or how many more times I can get away with it at work. Or how many more times the guy can get in harm's way. Or how many—"

She cut me off. "Okay, I get it. So are you more worried about his welfare, or about everyone's perception of you?" she asked in a tone that I considered to sound a little too smart-alecky for my liking.

But what annoyed me most was not her tone, it was the fact that she was right. *Didn't I have a right to worry about how everything affected me, too?* The danger I'd put myself in had been a result of my own poor judgment, but running out of work had been unavoidable and that came with its own risks.

I fidgeted with my hair, curling it around my finger. "So . . . you think that maybe this whole thing with Jonathan is to test me and to stop me being so self-absorbed?" I asked so quietly that I wondered if Julia had even managed to hear me. Then I lifted my shoulders, the memory of leaping in front of that cable car flooding back. "Because I've got to say, after today, I kinda object to that label."

Her tone became softer and there was no judgment in her voice. "I don't know, Isy. Like I said, this is all new to me, too. I can only imagine how hard this must be for you. I can't judge you when I'm on the other side of the world and the biggest dilemma I have in my day is whether to get a prosciutto focaccia for lunch or a brioche. And you're right—when the key moment comes, you've proven that you're anything but selfish. I'm not judging, I didn't mean to sound like I was."

"That's okay, Jules, you weren't completely off base. And with all of the questions I've been throwing at you, what you have for lunch does not make the list of things you have to worry about."

"Thanks, Is, but you're doing all of the hard work. I'm just commentating by the sidelines. I think you're to be congratulated, by the way. It's a shame that no one knows what you've faced, or what you've managed to do, or you would be awarded the Medal of Honor for Bravery and get the recognition you deserve."

"I would have gone mad if I hadn't been able to talk to you about it. And your insight has helped more than you'll ever know. Plus, if we had switched places, I know you wouldn't have struggled for a second, you wouldn't have given a second thought to how it would affect you. You're the true hero—the one who doesn't think of your own needs first."

I considered myself the unlikely choice between the two of us. I was so caught up in my own world, always looking inward. Jules would be so much better equipped to handle it.

"How's Jeremy's niece going?" she asked, switching topics.

"She's still in ICU. I've messaged him a few times, but I've been trying to give him space. He turns the phone off at the hospital. I'm just praying she'll be okay. I can't even think about . . . the alternative." My throat closed.

"I'm praying for her, too. She'll be okay," she reassured me.

"She has to be."

"Well, let's not end the call on such a sad note. Tell me something funny or trivial after all of these serious topics. What are the Kardashians up to?"

My lips twitched. "I can't tell you what they're doing, but I do have some gossip to tell you. I went to dinner at Rachel's and met her boyfriend not long ago." I was dying to get Jules's take on this, but hadn't wanted to do it over email. There was no way I'd ever put the details of my bizarre life in writing.

"Oh, what's he like?" she asked excitedly, assuming that this was just some let's-dish-about-the-new-boyfriend gossip.

"He's an absolute and total asshole," I replied bluntly.

"He can't be that bad, Isy."

"Worse, Jules. I mean it. He completely berated her all evening. He's rude, arrogant, demeaning—you give me a bad adjective and if we google it, we'll find his picture." I conveniently left out my faux pas relating to the evening—Jules wouldn't tell me anything I hadn't already heard about the error of my ways—and skipped straight to the part where I needed her input. "But it's not only that. I had the weirdest experience. When I touched his hand, I saw a flash of him in a garage or workshop doing something highly suspicious."

"You mean like a vision?" Jules was instantly intrigued.

"No, different. It felt more like a warning, like I was connecting to his energy or something. Trust me, it would be a gigantic cosmic joke if I were expected to help this guy, in any shape or form. Not that he'd listen to me regardless."

"Isy, I know you don't like him, but if he needs help—"

"What? No way, Jules. You're only saying that because you don't know him. Besides, I think the only danger he faces is being arrested. And that is absolutely his own fault and his problem. I'm all for it, in fact." There was no way I was going to let Jules guilt me into worrying about Neil. He was an adult and he was responsible for himself. No one was making him behave the way he was.

"What do you mean *arrested*? What exactly did you see?"

"I'm not sure exactly. He was sitting at a bench cooking something up and then the next thing you know I heard the sirens. I assume the police were about to bust him. Just a feeling, call it intuition."

"What do you mean 'cooking something up'? As in food, or chemicals?"

"Well, I don't mean that he's in trouble for burning a meal. Chemicals, of course." My voice was heavy with sarcasm, but Jules ignored it.

"Then it's probably a meth lab, or something similar."

"You think it could be that serious?"

"The police wouldn't be there to bust him over a chemistry set, now would they?" she retorted, matching my earlier sarcasm.

"Well then, he's definitely on his own. No way would I ever help him get out of that, the low life."

"Maybe it's like you said, more of a warning. It would certainly explain his bad behavior if he was using. You should worry about Rachel."

I don't know why I was so naïve but him *taking* drugs hadn't really crossed my mind up until now. Maybe because he didn't fit my idea of what a drug addict looked like, but then, I was learning not to judge anything based on appearance alone. Some addicts were high-functioning members of society, and Neil could be dealing to fund his habit. It certainly would explain his moodiness. "Do you think Rachel's in danger? That he could be violent?" I asked, chewing the inside of my lip.

"I don't know. You need to take the subtle approach when you speak with her, otherwise she might become defensive. You can't make her leave him. Being too forceful about it may make her withdraw from you completely, so tread lightly."

Once again, my past deeds were biting me in the ass. And once again, everyone else seemed better equipped to deal with these types of situations. "Um, yeah, so it's probably too late for that. Consider her defensive."

"What? Why?"

"Ah . . . don't give me a lecture because I've heard it all before, but I already . . . let's say, 'demonstrated' my dislike for him. And she was angry about it. Told me to butt out. So she won't listen to me about him now."

"This is huge, I can't believe you waited so long to tell me."

"I tried calling you the night it happened but you were out. And to be honest, I've gotten so caught up in everything else that's been going on, I kinda pushed it to the back of my mind . . ." I admitted, feeling completely guilty that I had prattled on about coffee with Matt when Rachel could potentially be dating a drug-dealing addict.

"Isy, I get it. You're worried about so many things at the moment, you probably feel like your head is about to explode," she empathized. "Forget about it now and try to get a good night's sleep. Tomorrow's a new day."

I promised to keep Jules posted if there were any new developments and to send her a quick email after coffee tomorrow. I hung up the phone, thankful for my friend who was sharing this experience with me.

I decided I'd invite Rachel to dinner and try to talk to her about Neil. At the very least, I could see for myself that she was okay. I called her number, but there was no answer. I left her a voicemail to call me back. Until she did, the incessant worrying wouldn't help anyone.

* * *

The next day I decided against going to get a sandwich for lunch. I felt too nauseated. I settled on some crackers from the kitchen instead.

I went down to meet Matt with butterflies in my stomach. I searched the tables for him, scanning the coffee shop.

I felt a hand on my shoulder and turned to see it was Matt.

"Hi, Isy. Great to see you." He beamed his killer smile at me.

"You, too, Matt."

I hesitated. I didn't know what I was supposed to do. Kiss him on the cheek? Shake his hand? Nothing? It was beginning to feel awkward as we both stared at each other, neither of us moving.

Matt finally broke the silence. "Shall we sit?" he asked.

"Sure."

I waited for him to lead the way, but he must have been waiting for me because we both just stood there, frozen.

I knew this was a mistake, I shouldn't have agreed to it, I thought.

Matt smiled at me and led the way to the table.

Looking around at the other tables after we'd taken our seats, Matt asked, "Is there table service here, or do you have to order at the counter?"

Ugh. It was the latter. I knew that. It had completely slipped my mind. Now I looked like an imbecile.

"Oh, that's right, you have to order at the counter. I'll go—" I said as I started to rise from my chair, bright red.

Matt cut me off. "Nonsense, I'll go. What would you like?" he asked, already standing.

"Ah, a soy latte, please."

He nodded and went to place the order. I felt bad that he was paying for me, even though it was only coffee.

He returned and sat down, smiling. "I'm happy you could make it today, Isy."

"Thanks. Me too."

Silence.

"Thanks for coming to meet me here," I finally added.

"Not a problem. So, what's new with you?" he asked, gesturing with his right hand.

A couple of things happened in the moments that followed.

Matt's hand accidentally knocked the sugar container and it tipped off the table. Before it could fall to the ground, I reached out and caught it.

That would all be normal, except for one thing: I reached out and put my hand in place *before* the container fell. A split second before Matt's hand knocked it, my hand was already in place to catch it. I'd sensed it was about to fall and instinctively flung my hand out.

I hoped that Matt didn't notice . . .

Unfortunately, he did.

As I was putting it back on the table, trying to act completely casual, he stuttered, "How . . . how in the world did you catch that?"

"Fast reflexes." I shrugged. "So what's new with you?" I blurted, trying to steer the conversation away from what had just happened.

He wasn't distracted. He was still staring at the container.

"But . . . I know this sounds strange, but—"

"Yes," I told him, eager to move this conversation along.

"What?" he asked, confused.

"Yes, I did see it fall before I reached out—to answer your

question."

"No," he responded slowly, "That's what I was *about* to ask you. You answered before I had a chance to ask. Just like the way you reached out before I'd even knocked it."

Oh crap. Had I really answered a question I thought he was going to ask, *before* he asked it? I had heard it so clearly in my mind that I thought he really had asked it—*aloud.*

He locked his eyes on mine. "Isy, there's something you're not telling me. I can't understand any of it, but I'm sure there's an answer that will clear it up. Please tell me what it is so I don't think I'm seeing—and hearing—things."

So he *doesn't think that he's seeing and hearing things.* How ironic.

What could I tell him? A lie would be more believable than the truth.

I looked back at him, carefully transforming my features into a mask of innocence. "You're making a big deal out of nothing, Matt. I have quick reflexes. I answered a question you were obviously going to ask—I didn't have to be a genius to figure that out."

There was a long pause while he continued to look at me, seeming to evaluate my response.

I tried to change the topic of conversation again. "So you never told me when you're getting married. Have you set the date?" I inquired, trying to feign enthusiasm.

"June," he responded flatly, without breaking his lock on my eyes.

"Sounds perfect. You must be busy with the planning. Where are you having it?"

"I don't know, some fancy reception. Eliza is very particular about what she wants and she prefers for me to let her take care of it. I would just get in the way."

He was still staring at me intently. He answered mechanically, his concentration unwavering from his previous thoughts. The waiter brought us our coffee and he thanked him without unlocking his eyes from mine.

When he started to speak again, the serious look in his eyes faded into one of kindness and understanding.

"It has not escaped my attention that there is something different about you, Isy. I mean that in a good way. I noticed it when I first met you in Florence. You are absolutely intriguing. Maybe that's why I want to get to know you better. You're unlike anyone I've ever met before.

"I can't quite place my finger on what it is about you that makes you so unique, but I know it's there. Something I can't quite figure out. Like I said, I knew it from the time we met. There was something about you that day. Something about the way you pulled me back from the street. Something about the look in your eyes when you did—like you were relieved.

"I always thought that was strange—it happened too quickly for you to be relieved. It made no sense. And you appeared out of nowhere. How could you possibly have seen the car from behind me?" He paused, searching my eyes for answers and holding me prisoner in his gaze.

If he saw anything in my eyes now, it would be concern. He was observant. I was not as clever as I'd thought, he would see through any lies I told him.

I felt like he was looking straight into the depths of my soul. I shifted awkwardly in my seat. I felt naked, exposed.

"You can trust me, Isy," he promised, sincerity warming his expression. "I want to be a friend to you. I won't betray your trust."

The conversation I'd had with Julia replayed in my mind. She had wondered whether the reason I kept seeing Jonathan was in order to build trust. This was something that I clearly had a problem with—trusting people.

Maybe Julia's same hypothesis could be applied to Matt. Maybe I *should* trust him. I certainly wanted to.

I sighed. It was too hard to try to lie to him and I was sick of all the subterfuge. But it was equally as difficult to completely let my guard down, to bare my soul. I would've felt less uncomfortable—less naked—if I had been sitting across from him without any clothes on, than I did thinking about revealing the most personal thing about myself and trusting him so completely.

He waited for me to speak. He seemed to appreciate how difficult it was for me and gave me some space to reflect.

"Okay," I finally responded.

He gave me a reassuring smile and leaned in with anticipation.

"You were right about Florence," I admitted. Might as well start from the beginning. "I couldn't see the car from where I was standing. It wasn't that I could see the car then—in that moment—but I had seen it. I'd seen it earlier in . . . a . . . I just knew that it was going to happen." I wasn't ready to use the word *vision*. I didn't want him to think I had a crystal ball and a wand in my closet.

"Like a premonition?" he asked, not at all fazed by what I was telling him.

"Yes, something like that."

"Which is what just happened now—with the container," he clarified.

"Not in exactly the same way, but yes."

He leaned back for a moment, looking satisfied with this revelation. "So you knew that I would be hit by that car and you ran to save me?"

"Yes."

"Wow." He reached over and touched my hand gently, looking at me with gratitude and affection. "Thank you. I mean, you went out of your way for me, it wasn't just by chance. You really saved me."

I blushed. I'd expected surprise, ambivalence, possibly ridicule, but not gratitude. It felt nice.

Probably too nice. I moved my hand away.

"So, does that kind of thing happen often?" he asked, those blue eyes sparkling with curiosity.

I was so relieved that he had reacted so well and I could feel comfortable talking to him about it, everything spilled out at once. The wall was down, I might as well invite him in and show him around.

"Four times so far. Jeremy was the first, you were the second, and both the third and fourth times were Jonathan. I'm yet to figure out why that is—that Jonathan has been twice, I mean. It's all just so confusing to me. I don't really understand any of it yet. The only other person who knows is Julia—my best friend, the one I told you about in Florence. I haven't dared tell anyone else. You have to promise me that you won't say a word to anyone—not even your fiancée."

"It'll stay between us. You have my word," he promised. His eyebrows pulled together in contemplation. "So did you come all the way to Florence to save me? Or did you only see it was going to happen when you were already there?"

"I saw it before but I didn't know it was in Florence. I went there to see Julia—she's the only one I could talk to about what was happening to me."

"So what happened to this Jonathan?"

"The first time, he was nearly hit in the head in a construction zone. The second time, it was a cable car," I explained.

"And Jeremy?"

I didn't want to betray Jeremy's trust by telling Matt something that personal about him. Jeremy deserved his privacy.

"Accident of sorts. So you don't think that I belong in a circus? Or that I'm delusional?" I asked him incredulously.

"No, why would I? I have directly benefited from your premonitions. Who am I to judge you for them? I'm happy that you trust me enough to talk to me about it. I really am. That's a major thing to keep to yourself. It must be hard to deal with, you must feel alone sometimes. And your friend is so far away. I want you to know that you can talk to me about it anytime you want."

"Thanks, Matt. You don't know what a relief it is to be able to."

He smiled warmly at me and leaned over to touch my hand again. The wall was gone. He seemed pleased with himself that he'd finally been able to climb over it and discover what lay beyond.

"You know," he said, "when I realized in Florence that I could've been hit by that car, it made me think about my life and what was important to me. I have a brother who I hadn't spoken to in a long time. We'd had a falling out. After that, I realized I might not always get the chance to make amends with him, to make things right between us. Before that, I always thought there was time—it was something to do *one day*. It really changed things between us.

"It taught me that you can't leave unfinished business thinking that you'll take care of it tomorrow, or the next day or the next. You need to tell the people you love that you love them, while you have the chance.

"I don't know what happened with Jeremy, but I'm guessing that something major changed in his life as well.

"So—and I'm only thinking aloud here—what if the reason this Jonathan guy has popped up twice is because whatever he was supposed to change, or do, or realize—he never did?" He noticed my raised eyebrows. "It's just a theory. I don't really know what I'm talking about, I just like to sound like I do." He laughed, winking at me.

But it made sense, perfect sense. From what I could tell, Jonathan's life was exactly the same as before. He never seemed that fazed, never seemed to appreciate how close he could've come to a serious accident. If anything, both times the events happened, the only thing he seemed concerned about was my strange behavior. It had shone a spotlight on *me*, rather than him.

Maybe it was the way I was going about it. *But what other way* could *I go about it?* I wondered. What is the *right* way to try and save someone? It never occurred to me that there could be a wrong way before. I thought the 'saving' was the only purpose, the only evidence you needed of success.

"I think you're absolutely right," I told Matt. "I can't believe I've been thinking about this for so long and you came up with that in a few minutes." I smiled at him in awe. "Since you're so insightful, perhaps you can figure out another problem."

He sat back, clearly impressed with himself and enjoying the compliment. "Hit me."

I lowered my voice. "I think my friend might be dating a drug dealer. I just got this intuitive sense when I met him and I saw a flash of him making the stuff, but then I heard sirens so I think he's about to be busted."

Matt furrowed his brow and leaned in to me. "Be careful, Isy. He might be a desperate man, and desperate men can do horrible things. I wouldn't say anything to make him suspicious of you. If he's about to be busted, steer clear and don't intervene."

"What about my girlfriend, though? I don't know what to tell her, she'd never believe me if I told her what I saw."

"Then be there for her if she needs you, but don't get involved. If she doesn't believe you, she might tell her boyfriend and you don't know what he'd do."

I hadn't considered that. Perhaps I'd be putting her in *more* danger. *Maybe I really should just let it all unfold as it was supposed to.*

"Thanks, Matt. That's good advice." He really was a fountain of insight. Jules had been completely right about him, about being friends. I felt foolish now for overthinking it so much. "Conversations about premonitions and drug dealers—nothing too heavy for an afternoon coffee, huh?" I joked. I scanned the room again, concerned about eavesdroppers, and noticed that the tables around us were empty. "Oh crap, what time is it?" I looked at my watch. “It’s after two, I’m late. I have to get back to the office. I’m so sorry to run out on you. I’m probably making you late, too!” I blurted as I leaped up from my chair.

“No, I’m okay. I’d like to continue this conversation another time, though. I hope you will do me the honor again soon?”

“That sounds nice. As long as we’re alone,” I clarified, reminding him of his promise to keep this between us.

“Of course. Perhaps another coffee or lunch sometime, or drink after work?” he offered, rising from his chair.

“Deal. Thanks for coming, and for listening. Gotta run!” Without even thinking about it this time, I leaned over to kiss him on the cheek. It seemed like the natural thing to do and I hadn’t paused to think about it until it was done.

But he didn’t look awkward at all. He just gave me a big smile and squeezed my arm.

15

NO GOOD DEED GOES UNPUNISHED

I WAS STILL on a high the following week from my coffee with Matt. I had trusted him with the most terrifying secret about myself, the thing I thought would make him judge me and question my sanity. He'd rewarded me with acceptance, understanding, clarity, and even gratitude.

Matt wasn't a hocus-pocus kind of guy. He belonged in my world, the world of the rational. Yet he believed. He didn't just believe me—he believed *in* me.

More than that, he had actually been able to help me by providing an insight into the Jonathan repetition saga. It was his logical thinking that allowed him to see the pattern, to solve the puzzle.

Matt had been a true friend to me. I couldn't try to shut him out anymore, nor did I want to. Trust was a two-way street.

I tried to schedule a catch-up with Jonathan. I had an inkling that his lesson somehow related to the time he spent—or didn't spend—with his family. Although I couldn't be sure. I needed more information.

I had no idea how I could convince him to focus more of his attention on his family. I knew I had to try, but I doubted it would be easy. The man nearly died twice and didn't bat an eyelid. It was all in the course of his day, between meetings.

Although, in his defense, Jonathan didn't realize how close he had come. The incident with the cable car didn't help, I'd created too much of a distraction. I had no idea at the time that I was an actor in a play and I got my stage queue wrong. *If this was such a precise art form, perhaps someone should supply me with a script, rather than just a preview,* I thought.

I had a feeling that this act might be on a loop and we could be forced to re-enact it over and over again until we got it right. We had two scenes already and neither hit their mark. Would there now be a third? Another scene to try and teach Jonathan to value his life and his family? To remind him what was important?

The question that had me the most worried was: How would I know what I had to do if faced with a similar situation? I didn't exactly have time to devise a plan the last time. If I had dawdled, Jonathan would have stepped in front of that cable car. Play over. Curtain closed. I didn't want to even think about how close I'd been to having the curtain closed on *me*. I couldn't bear another Jonathan replay. I had no intention of taking my final bow, and I was afraid that without intervention, Jonathan would be taking his. I learned after my harrowing daredevil jump in front of that cable car that sometimes a more subtle approach was all that was needed. From now on, I intended to avoid the dramatics and welcome back some normalcy in my life. I wanted off this stage, for good.

There was only one thing to do: I had to talk to him, in a safe environment where there were no cable cars or scaffolding. No trains, buses, airplanes, fires, explosions, rock climbing, skydiving or, God forbid, whatever else could go wrong. Somewhere I wasn't panic-stricken and I could actually breathe.

Jonathan wasn't making it easy. He rejected my invitations to coffee, citing his heavy workload and undoubtedly believing me to be too friendly since it was against protocol. So I decided to take him up on his offer of discussing a potential role for me at Parkmores. If Jonathan only had time to talk about work, I had to give him a justifiable reason to see me.

He accepted my latest invitation and scheduled a meeting on Friday afternoon—in four more days. I only hoped that the opportunity to speak with him, even under this pretense, would be enough.

In the meantime, I had one more conversation to get through, the ramifications of which could potentially destroy my friendship with Rachel. I resigned myself to tread very carefully, just as Matt had suggested, but I ignored the rest of his advice to let things lie because I couldn't shake the nagging feeling that I needed to talk to her. Like a pesky fly that couldn't be squatted away, there was a persistent buzzing in the back of my mind urging me to make sure she was all right.

Anxiety seeped into my chest, making my heart hammer. This could be a complete disaster. Rachel and I hadn't really spoken since her dinner party. I only hoped she'd had enough time to let go of her anger and perhaps see things differently.

I made my way down to the bar to meet her after work on

Monday. She had already forewarned me that she couldn't stay long because she was having dinner with Neil.

She was there when I arrived, sitting at a table in the corner.

"Hey, Rach. How are you?" I gave her a hug.

She looked weary, but she gave me a hesitant smile. "Good, and you?"

"Great, just busy as always."

We had a few minutes of small talk before I couldn't take it any longer; there was an elephant in the room and we were both trying not to look at it.

"Listen, Rach," I started. "I just wanted to apologize again for arguing with Neil at your dinner party. I feel awful. I know how much trouble you went to and the last thing I wanted was to make you or the other guys feel uncomfortable." I tried to convey my sincerity to her, the remorse evident in my voice.

"I appreciate that, Isy. But I know you too well—there was no mention of Neil in your apology."

Oh crap. No freaking way would I ever apologize to him, the dirtbag deserved everything he got. I could avoid insulting Neil if we avoided talking about him, but it was going to be hard to camouflage the disgust in my voice if I had to acknowledge him. Suddenly the oppressive elephant in the room jumped onto my lap, taunting me. The weight of it was palpable, sucking the air out of my lungs. How could I delicately tell her that her boyfriend was not who she thought he was, and I actually knew that better than she did? I couldn't, she'd never believe me. The whole reason I'd avoided this conversation until now. But I had to say something. I'd never forgive myself if Neil hurt her.

She raised her eyebrows at me. She'd laid her cards on the table and was now waiting for me to reveal my hand.

I started fidgeting with the napkins while I gathered my thoughts. "I can't tell you who to date, Rach. I know that. I just want you to be happy. I worry about you. I mean, how well do you really know Neil?" Just saying his name left a bad taste on my tongue.

A flash of anger distorted her features. "How well do *you* know him? You met him once and you think you know him better than I do?"

I sat back to put some space between us. We were off to a very bad start and one thing was clear: me arguing with Rachel was not going to help either one of us. "I'm sorry, Rach. You're right, I've only met him once. I was just concerned about the way he treated you. I just had an intuitive sense about him that maybe there's more to him than meets the eye—"

"*Intuitive* sense! Are you shitting me? Since when do you frigging talk about intuitive senses? What kind of lame-ass bullshit is that? Just admit you don't like him! You always have to judge people, and if they don't live up to your expectations—the *Rulebook According to Isy*—then forget it, there's got to be something wrong with them. Did you ever think that maybe there's something wrong with *you*? That maybe there's a reason that *nobody's* ever good enough for *you* to date? That it's extremely damned difficult to fit into your idea of worthiness?"

Ouch. The anger radiated off her in waves, destroying everything in its path. We were right back where we started and Rachel had gone for the jugular. That's one thing about friends: they knew where to hit you where it hurt. My eyes started to well up. *Rulebook?* If there were one, it certainly wasn't me who'd written it. I wanted to hang up my do-gooder cape and tell her to run back to the dirtbag because I was sick of being the bad guy! I was sick of having my life turned upside down, and sick of having responsibilities for people that I hadn't asked for, especially when those people were dumping all over me.

Repressed anger clawed its way out of me. "You know what, Rach? I've spent plenty of time recently wondering what's wrong with *me*. And you know what I realized? The only thing wrong with me is that I've been spending so much of my damn time worrying about everyone else—like you! And you know what else? If you don't want my help, I have better things to do! Like helping the people who *do* want my help! Or worrying about myself for a change!"

My face burned with fury. The unleashed beast was ready to swing its claws. I was just about to tell her that if she thought Neil was so hot, and I was so damaged, then I couldn't help her anyway.

But this time, I swallowed the words burning my tongue. I recognized this kind of capricious behavior. Rachel had become accustomed to being attacked and now she was learning to become the attacker. She wasn't going to listen. And I couldn't make her. Pulling out my sword and battling her would help no one—except maybe Neil who would probably prefer that she never speak with me again.

Rachel's voice raised an octave. "Maybe you *should* worry about yourself! I never asked for your help!"

I needed to diffuse the escalating time bomb—fast. Our friendship meant too much to me to let this go any further.

"Rachel, I'm sorry you feel that way. I only had your best

interests at heart. But if that's the way you feel about me, then I'll keep my distance for a while and give you some space."

"Well, maybe that's best. Neil isn't exactly your biggest fan."

That did it. So much for the high road. "So you let Neil decide who your friends are now? Geez, I thought years of friendship meant more than that." Unfortunately, I'd picked up the bomb and given it a shake.

That really pushed her buttons and sarcasm oozed from her pores. "Oh, so you're upset that you think I'm letting *Neil* dictate who I can hang out with—instead of letting *you* be the one to do that?"

My jaw dropped. *She was comparing* me *to Neil?* I thought indignantly. No way! I wasn't trying to control her, I was only trying to protect her. I guess it all appeared the same in her eyes. I slumped in my chair. She was right about one thing: If I could have my way, she'd drop him like a hotcake. Maybe I *was* trying to control her. Her mistakes were hers to make. If this was what she wanted, then so be it. Mom, Jules and Matt had all said the same thing: tread lightly, just support her. My job as her friend wasn't to stop her from making mistakes, it was to help her pick up the pieces afterwards.

"I have no right to tell you who to date and decide whether or not Neil is good enough for you. It's only because I love you so much that I want the very best for you. If you think that's Neil, then that's your decision. It's your life. I value our friendship, Rach. I don't want to lose that."

Her eyes softened. Rachel was sick of being criticized; her reaction was a by-product of spending so much time with Neil. I didn't have to like it, I just had to understand it. "I'm sorry, too,

Isy. I know you mean well and I'm sorry I was so hard on you, but I'm sick of people telling me what to do. I couldn't bear it from you, too."

"Consider this entire conversation stricken from the record. An amendment to the—what was it? *Rulebook According to Isy*?"

"Um, yeah, I'm sorry about that. I didn't mean it."

"Sorry about what?" I asked, giving her a quizzical look and feigning confusion.

"About the—Oh. Right." She smiled.

I couldn't help Rachel if she didn't want my help, I had to accept that she was responsible for her own choices. This wasn't a burden for me to carry. I had enough drama in my life, I certainly didn't need—or want—to add to the insurmountable stockpile. I needed to focus my energy on those things I *could* control, everything else was futile. And as for Neil, help would eventually be on the way. And it would be wearing a police uniform. I knew I shouldn't take pleasure in that, but justice really was sweet.

16

NINE LIVES

"ARE YOU COMING, ISY?" asked Ashley, the senior associate with the office adjacent to mine.

It was our weekly practice team meeting, scheduled for one o'clock on Tuesday. Working at a law firm, it was common practice to schedule meetings over lunch—in order to protect the time for billable hours. The only good thing was the gourmet sandwiches and wraps they provided.

"On my way," I replied as I rose from my chair to head to the meeting on the thirty-eighth floor.

These meetings included all lawyers in our practice team—from the most senior to the most junior. The purpose was to discuss clients and workflow, make announcements and share matter updates or new regulations that we needed to be across in the practice. Senior Partner, Diana Morrison, chaired the meeting. She went through the first item on the agenda: criminal sanctions for cartels.

She had just started to discuss the issue of evidence and the difficulty in proving allegations of cartel behavior when I heard a loud screeching sound followed by two loud crashes.

Being on the thirty-eighth floor, we should have been insulated from the street noise far below, but it was so loud that my head jolted towards the window. Tammy, a first year graduate sitting next to me, noticed my response. She gave me a look with raised eyebrows.

"Did you hear that?" I quietly whispered.

"What?" she mouthed, her eyes back on Diana. As a graduate, she was keen to make a good impression and I sensed that my interruption was unwelcome.

I turned back to face Diana, but I could no longer see the room. In front of me loomed the street corner about a block over from my building.

Oh no, here we go, I thought as panic started to break over me like a tidal wave. This was the most incongruous place for this to happen. Conceding it was inevitable despite my protest, I tilted my head down towards my notepad and tried to shield my face. I had no idea what I looked like when I saw a vision, but from the reaction of the people who had seen me, it was far from normal. Of course, staring vacantly at a blank page wouldn't exactly look normal, either, nor would it help me feign interest in the meeting. But it was the best I could do under the infelicitous circumstances.

I could see the intersection. A blue Toyota Camry traveling east down California Street seemed to speed up as the light turned red. The driver either panicked, or was just reckless. As the car tried to make a left turn in front of a cable car—what was it with cable cars lately?—it lost control. The driver slammed on the brakes, the tires screaming in protest against the road. Thick smoke from the burning rubber pervaded the air. The car mounted the sidewalk and slammed—hard—at a forty-five-degree angle into a brick wall. Ricocheting off the wall, and still screeching, it barreled down the sidewalk with pedestrians scrambling to jump out of the way. A man sprinted in the wrong direction and was trampled by the out-of-control car, before it finally came to a crashing stop after plowing into a pole.

My heart beating frantically, I forced myself to examine the pedestrian lying broken, thrown like a rag doll. But I knew. *I knew.*

It was Jonathan.

I gasped in horror at the sight of his mangled body. My stomach revolted as the blood drained from my face.

Scene three. It had not waited until after our meeting on Friday. It was going to happen today.

"Isy!" The frustration in Diana's voice snapped me back to the present. How long had she been waiting for a response? A while, judging by her stormy glare.

I shrank back from her, turning bright red as I became conscious of all eyes in the room on me. Tammy shifted herself in her chair, leaning as far away from me as possible. I could just imagine my next performance review: *Apathetic. Lacking commitment. Disappointing.*

"Since you appear to be so interested in this topic," Diana continued sternly, "perhaps you would care to prepare a presentation at our next CLE?"

Our next Continuing Legal Education session was on Friday.

"Of course. Sorry, Diana," I said quietly as I slipped down in my chair.

Panic replaced the embarrassment I felt. What could I do? This accident would happen today. Soon. But I had no idea *how* soon.

I couldn't just walk out of this meeting—especially now after having been berated for not paying attention—and disappear for hours. I might as well pack up my office on the way out.

Perhaps I could just wait until the end of the meeting and then disappear as everyone headed back downstairs. That could work, I thought.

I tried to discretely look at Tammy's watch instead of my own. If I got caught checking the time, it wouldn't help my predicament. Forty-five minutes to go. I just needed to wait another forty-five minutes.

Forty-five minutes and I could save my job.

Two minutes slowly ticked by, each second taunting me. I was gripped by a sudden rush of guilt. *What if I saved my job at the cost of saving Jonathan?*

This was it. The sacrifice I knew had been coming. It was here. I had to choose.

The image of his mangled body flashed in my head, beckoning me to act. A wave of nausea hit me so strongly that I wondered if I would be sick right there in the room. I instinctively put my hand over my mouth.

Although I felt physically weak, it was another kind of weakness that plagued me. Remaining in that chair made me weak in spirit, weak in courage, and weak in character. *Why was this happening to me?* Why was I put in this situation? Hadn't I done enough already? Shame warred with indignation.

Shame won. The guilt of not trying to save him would ruin me. My hands began to shake. I gripped the edge of the table to try and pull myself up from the chair. I had to leave—now. I had to pull it together—now.

I was about to walk out of a room while Diana was speaking, in front of every partner in the practice. I was about to walk out after having already been reprimanded.

I gasped for air, an unbearable weight pressing down on me. I had no time to crumble. I had to get downstairs. I couldn't bear it if my weakness cost *more* than my job. So much more.

Perhaps Jonathan's lesson to learn was also my own.

"Isy, you don't look well. Are you okay?" Harrison asked from across the table.

I looked up at him. "I don't feel well, I feel faint. I'm sorry, would you please excuse me?" I said softly.

He looked at me for a long moment. "Tammy, please go with Isy to make sure she doesn't faint. Take her to the Wellness Room on the thirty-fifth floor," he instructed.

Tammy glared at me. The 'Wellness Room' was a small room with a cot to lie down. I hadn't even heard of it since my orientation with the firm three years ago.

This was good. Harrison had given me the green light to leave the room, even though there would be questions later. This was also bad—Tammy was my chaperone. She would be dying to run back and tell everyone that I ran out of the building.

We walked to the elevators in silence. When the doors opened, I stepped in. Tammy tried to follow but I held up my hand.

"Look, I don't need a chaperone. I can make it there by myself. You don't want to be here as much as I don't want you here. Just wait a minute and then go back to the meeting," I instructed.

"But Harrison—"

She started to protest but I cut her off. "I will tell Harrison you came with me," I said as the doors closed, leaving her standing there with a worried look on her face.

I quickly hit the button for the first floor. When I stepped out onto the street, it occurred to me that I didn't have a plan.

A thought pulsed through me. This scene was a variation of the same accident as before—in a nearby location where once again Jonathan would be hit by a moving vehicle. Was there some hidden meaning in that? A scene destined to continue to repeat itself, escalating each time? Or merely coincidence? I didn't have time to ponder it. As I scurried up the street, my eyes locked on the intersection that could change everything.

I crossed over California Street, towards the corner of the accident, and monitored the traffic near the intersection. No sign of a blue Camry approaching.

I couldn't wait at the corner. The car would hit straight into me. I had to approach from where the car ended up, not where it started. *If only I could be certain from which direction Jonathan was walking*, I thought.

I wondered how long it would be. How long I would be waiting. As I approached the spot that would be the last resting stop for the Camry, I tried to think of a plan. *At least I've got more time than the last time.*

Wrong.

No sooner than the thought entered my mind, I heard the screeching tires behind me.

I frantically searched for Jonathan. He wasn't ahead of me. I turned to look behind.

I caught sight of him just as the car mounted the sidewalk. In that moment, I saw the surprise—and the fear—in his eyes. He turned his body to run towards the road and get off the sidewalk. He didn't realize he would be running straight into the path of the car.

I was standing by the pole. I leaped towards him, crashing into him as he started to sprint in my direction.

"Back!" I screamed as I swung around him and tried to pull him towards me against the wall.

He was stronger than me, and for a split second he resisted, still wanting to go forward. But the gentleman inside him lurched in front of me against the wall, shielding my body with his.

It all happened in an instant. The car ricocheted off the brick wall, flew past us and crashed straight into the pole, finally coming to a stop. We heard the roar of the collision and the eerie silence that ensued. I slumped in his arms. It was over. I could breathe again.

Slowly, he pulled his body from mine. His head jerked towards the car and then back to me.

"Isy!" he cried with surprise. "Are you okay?"

"Yes, yes, I'm fine. Are you?"

"Yes. Just in shock. That came out of nowhere. You . . . you came out of nowhere, too . . ." He spoke slowly, the confusion and shock elevating the pitch of his voice. He turned his head and eyed the car and its final resting place. "If you hadn't pulled me back—"

A woman in her forties jumped out of the driver's side, twitching her head back and forth as she surveyed the scene, then slumped to the curb. At the same time, a teenage boy opened the door from the passenger side and stepped out.

Thankfully, both of them appeared unharmed, although the woman was clearly in shock, gasping for air and fanning herself frantically with her hands. The boy went to her side and sat quietly beside her.

Three people on the street immediately ran to their aid and called 911.

I was surprised the driver was a middle-aged woman. I'd mistakenly presumed by the driver's risk-taking behavior that it was a young man behind the wheel. But nothing was ever what it seemed. I should know that by now.

My heart thumped with gratitude, relieved there hadn't been any fatalities.

Jonathan turned to approach them. I pulled his arm back.

"She's in shock," I said. "Too many people surrounding her might make it worse. It looks like they've already called for help. We should wait here."

He turned back to me and nodded.

"I think you should let the paramedics look at you, too. You might be in shock as well—understandably so," I told him.

"Me? What about you? You were just as nearly crushed as I was. Why do you seem so calm?" he asked.

I held up a shaking hand, the tremors visible. "Not so calm. But I saw the whole thing unfolding—I was looking in that direction. Whereas it all happened behind you—that would've been much worse, not knowing what was happening," I tried to explain.

"Still . . ." he muttered as he considered that explanation and appraised my status.

"What are you doing here?"

"I'm supposed to be meeting someone." He pointed to the restaurant a few doors down from where we were standing.

I turned my head in that direction. There were swarms of people standing in front of the restaurant, the patrons inside rushing out to see what was happening.

"Jonathan, mate!" A man approaching us screamed out in an unmistakable British accent as he caught sight of him.

"Dave! Sorry I'm late. As you can see, a bit of drama here."

"Are you all right, mate?" his friend asked him, while giving me the once-over with a raised brow. His eyes darted between us, clouded in suspicion.

Jonathan rolled his eyes, obviously catching his friend's expression. "Yeah, the car whirled straight past us. Isabel works at Barkleys nearby," he explained.

"Oh." This appeared to satisfy him and quash his mistaken presumption of some tawdry affair between Jonathan and me.

Sheesh. Why does everyone think we're having an affair? I wondered as I pulled on my skirt, making sure it wasn't hitched higher than it should be.

"Dave, can we take a rain check?" Jonathan asked. "I think I'll wait for the police and paramedics."

Dave shot me another quick glance. "Sure, mate, no worries. I'm just glad you're okay. You could've been a goner!"

"Yeah, that was a close one," Jonathan said, nodding his head.

"Give me a call to reschedule. Take it easy, mate." Dave gently slapped him on the back and turned to leave.

The distant sound of sirens sang their reassuring tune. The

police were the first to arrive at the scene—all three cars.

"That was quick," I noted.

"Hopefully the ambulance isn't far behind," Jonathan added, glancing at the curb. The woman was visibly shaken. The teenage boy was still sitting quietly beside her.

I wrestled with the desire to tell Jonathan how close he had come to ending up under that car. "I'm so glad no one was hurt. It really puts things into perspective, though, doesn't it? I mean, one minute you're here and the next you could be gone. Makes you think about what's really important in life."

He nodded. "I know. It might sound strange, but in that moment, my whole life flashed before my eyes. All I could think about were Dalia and Sammy."

Hallelujah! Music to my ears. "It doesn't sound strange at all. You know what's important to you, and nothing could be more important than your children. It makes sense that you were thinking about them." I beamed. Jonathan was finally seeing the bigger picture. I was witnessing it, right here before my eyes. Thank goodness, I really didn't want to play chicken with any more cable cars or out-of-control vehicles. I feared rock climbing would be next. If either Jonathan or I had nine lives, we were quickly using them up.

"I had a fight with Miranda—my wife—this morning. If the last words I'd said to her had been—" He paused suddenly, not wanting to tell me what he'd said. "It would've been awful," he confessed, lowering his eyes and shaking his head.

"You can't worry about that. The important thing is you go home tonight and tell her how much you love her. I'm sure she knows but it's always nice to hear." I smiled, feeling a weight lift.

I could practically hear the harps, the heavens were smiling, too.

"You're right. I think I'll pick her up some flowers. Gosh, I haven't done that in years. Maybe I shouldn't—she might think I'm having an affair."

I laughed, releasing all of the built-up tension. More sirens reverberated through the street as the ambulance approached, drowning out the chatter of the surrounding crowds. "Good, here they come. I have to get back to the office, but please let the paramedics look you over, okay? The police will probably want statements, but there seem to be more than enough witnesses."

"Hey there, miss," he said as he grabbed hold of my arm. "You're not going anywhere. If you think I need attention—which I don't—then *you* must need attention. I doubt Harrison would say anything about your whereabouts when he finds out what happened."

Holy . . . I had to come clean. I didn't want Jonathan to tell Harrison and shatter my sickbay alibi. "Jonathan, can you please not mention this to Harrison?" I pleaded, that familiar sense of déjà vu washing over me.

He cocked his head to the side. "Why?"

"Um, you see, I was . . . um . . . in a team meeting and I left because I wasn't . . . ah . . . feeling well. If Harrison finds out I was here—it might be difficult to explain."

"I see. You skipped out on a team meeting. I certainly hope you won't be doing that when you come to join my team. I'll have to keep a close eye on you." He winked. "You know, I think you just saved my life. If you hadn't pulled me back, I'd be under that car right now, instead of arguing with you. Not only is the job yours if you want it, but I think I'll have to fight for a pay rise for you."

I grinned. "We'll talk about it on Friday. We're still on for our catch-up, aren't we?"

"Of course."

"Great. I'll talk to you then. I really have to go."

"Isabel, wait!" he screamed after me. But I was already running past all of the onlookers and heading back to face the music.

I looked at my watch as the elevator doors opened on the thirty-seventh floor. It was just before two o'clock. If I was lucky, I would be back at my desk before the meeting ended.

But luck wasn't on my side. Today had to be the day the meeting finished early.

Harrison was in my office before I had time to sit down.

"You look better. Where were you?" he asked, his tone accusatory.

"In the Wellness Room, like you instructed," I answered.

"No, you weren't. I came down to check on you."

Holy mother of... "Oh, I decided to go down to the pharmacy to get some pills. They made me feel a lot better." Good, very plausible. *And the Oscar goes to . . .*

"I went downstairs to the ATM. And on my way up in the elevator, Thomas from M&A told me that he saw you among all the onlookers staring at some accident nearby."

Mental note, Thomas was off my Christmas card list. Not that there would be a Christmas card list—I was a dead woman walking. I was slightly annoyed that Thomas had left out the part about me nearly being killed. Clearly he hadn't seen *that* part to report.

"They didn't have what I needed at the pharmacy downstairs

so I went to another one down the street. And I wasn't an onlooker, I was a *witness*," I corrected him. "A car ran straight into the sidewalk and nearly hit into me. I was waiting for the police and ambulance to arrive." If I was going down, I was going down swinging.

"Why didn't you say that in the first place?" He was still eyeing me suspiciously.

Hello! Nearly killed here! How about asking if I'm okay? "I don't know, I guess I should have. I'm still feeling out of it, must be the migraine—not to mention the adrenaline from the accident."

He seemed to appraise my response. Finally, he said, "I'm glad you're okay then," and left the room.

Something told me that he wasn't convinced. Perhaps I responded too calmly for someone who was nearly run over. And it was a significant detail that, under normal circumstances, I would've included in the explanation of my whereabouts. No wonder he was suspicious.

I sighed. If I'd known Thomas Blabbermouth had seen me, I would've gone with the second pharmacy story from the outset and permitted Jonathan to tell colorful tales of my heroics. Hearing about another Jonathan rendezvous would have almost certainly confirmed Harrison's secret romance supposition, but—ironically—that may have afforded me some protection in my next review.

As it was, partners had to submit their nominees for promotion in the coming weeks. I very much doubted that my name would be on it.

17

AWAKENING

I CALLED JULES that night to fill her in on the incredible events of the day, how I'd only just made it there in time and how my momentary indecision had nearly resulted in a different outcome.

"But you made it, Is. Don't feel bad about it. When it came down to it, you had your priorities in order. You're allowed to be worried about your job. It's not selfish to be concerned about your own life, it's perfectly natural," she reassured me. "Plus, do you realize that you risked your life today—again? If that's not true heroism, then I don't know what is."

"I suppose I didn't really think about it. It happened so fast, the adrenalin took over. I never really felt like something bad would happen to me. I had the benefit of knowing how to steer clear of the car."

"You're not invincible, Isy. I'm starting to worry about the risks you're taking. Your visions seem to be becoming progressively more dangerous, and as the level of intensity goes up, your aversion to risk goes down. You may have *felt* like you weren't in danger, but I'm worried that's because you're starting to think these crazy antics are part of the job. I know I'm the one who encouraged you to take action, but I didn't mean to start risking your own life."

I chewed my lip. When did things go so far that Jules was now the one having to reign me in, instead of push me? Was I really developing a superhero complex? I pushed the thought away, something to ruminate on later. Right now I was concerned with the more mundane things in my life—like keeping my job. And not the one that Jules was referring to, even though I found her choice of words interesting. I always strived to achieve, pushing myself to succeed—had I in fact turned this into some sort of 'job' in my mind and started applying the same principles? To what end? What would it cost me? What was I willing to give up to prove myself? I couldn't let the rest of my life fall apart. I'd worked too hard.

"Try not to worry, Jules. For some reason, in that moment I felt safe. I can't explain it. But I understand what you're saying and I promise I'll think about it. It's my real job that's worrying me right now. It feels like everything is starting to unravel. It's getting so much harder, Jules. Harrison has been really suspicious lately. He's noticed the difference. I really doubt he'll recommend me for a promotion now. I might have to take the job at Parkmores because I don't know how much longer I'll have one at Barkleys if this continues."

"I don't think you should take that job. You said it yourself, it would be just as much work and you would have to prove yourself all over again. You'll only end up in the same situation. At least where you are, they know the quality of your work. They know how dedicated you've been for the past three years."

"That may not be enough if I keep running out and making up excuses," I admitted.

"Don't worry about it now, you've got enough to deal with. But if you're talking about what's best in the long-term, I think you should consider more options than just Parkmores. As you said, this whole thing with Jonathan seemed to be to teach him about what's important—not to get caught up in the everyday stresses of his work, to focus on the bigger picture.

"At the moment, it's like you're juggling two very demanding jobs. Something will eventually have to give. I know being a lawyer is what you always thought you'd be good at—and you are—but you never stopped to ask yourself if it would be what truly made you *happy*. Being good at something doesn't automatically mean that it's the right thing for you."

I repressed a groan, preparing to hear the same old lecture. I resisted the urge to put down the phone for a few minutes and get myself a snack.

Jules prattled on with her speech. "You're stuck on their merry-go-round. You're juggling competing priorities—it's not surprising you're so panic-stricken all the time.

"Just think about it. I know how hard you've worked, and it's all you know. I get that you're not just going to suddenly throw it all in, but would you consider working for a smaller firm?"

My mouth dropped open. Although Jules couldn't see me, she sensed my reaction and quickly delivered the rest of her monologue.

"Hear me out for a second. A smaller firm, one that didn't keep the stakes so high, one that didn't expect everything else in your life to come a distant second. There would obviously be trade-offs: less money, fewer perks and smaller clients. But think of the *rewards*—less stress and more time for yourself. You would be able to step out of the office when you needed to without having to worry that the firing squad was guarding the door. You'd have more time and energy to invest in your *own* life. You may not be a parent yet like Jonathan, but you're on the same path that he is. When was the last time you even went to visit your parents?"

Again, I remained silent. I hadn't seen my parents in a while, but I wasn't about to confess that now. This was my life. My concern stemmed from not having enough time to invest in *my career*, but Jules had turned everything around.

"It's just something to think about, in the back of your mind. Sit on it for a while. See how things go at work and how you feel about everything. That's all I'm saying. You deserve so much, Isy. I don't want you to have to be constantly stressed out because all the pieces don't fit together the way that they should."

I twirled a lock of hair around my finger. Usually when Jules was negative about the amount of time I invested in my career, I rolled my eyes and cut her off. I was determined to achieve the goals I'd set for myself. But this time I didn't argue so vehemently. The doubts about my ability to continue on this path, doubts that I'd pushed away, were starting to bubble to the surface. I felt like I was living in a house of cards, one wrong move and it would all come crashing down.

Still, I wasn't ready to let go—to let go of the dream. The

dream may have been flawed, but it was mine. I was a lawyer at the most prestigious, respected firm in San Francisco. A position that had become part of my very identity. I wasn't sure who I was without my desire to join the most elite on the partner fast track.

Moving to a small firm after being at Barkleys was like going from the best, premium brand of chocolate to an unknown home brand. It was still chocolate but it didn't taste as sweet. There was no lure, no shiny packaging. No frills. Not really enticing to me.

I remained silent on the other end of the phone while these thoughts swirled around me, only offering more confusion and uncertainty. Finally, Jules broke the silence.

"Isy, don't you think it's weird that you weren't worried about endangering yourself at that accident scene today, but you're worried about what Harrison said because of it? Doesn't that seem kinda skewed in the wrong direction?"

I untangled the hair from my finger. "No, actually, it doesn't. I'm not concerned about the accident because it all happened so fast and I didn't feel in danger in that moment. It was a visceral reaction. Maybe I'm delusional, but I have to trust my instincts. You taught me that. What I *am* actually in danger of—the danger I *know* is omnipresent—is ruining my career and killing any chance of promotion. All of that hard work just flushed down the toilet. I don't know how long I can continue like this. My only hope is that Jonathan has finally got it, whatever it was he needed to get, and that will be the end of it. At least for a very long while."

"Okay, Is, I'm sorry. I get how hard you've worked," she placated.

My breathing slowed and I relaxed back into my seat.

"So then, let's do a recap, shall we?" Jules suggested, shifting gears. "First it was Jeremy—where we first learned that you have a gift, and you can really make a difference in people's lives. Then it was Matt—the message he seemed to have for you was about following your passion and not closing yourself off to people. Then it was Jonathan episodes one, two and three. His lesson seemed to be about priorities. How did I do?" she asked me, clearly feeling proud of her summation.

My lips curled. "I think that sums it up quite well."

"Well, I wonder who's next," she voiced excitedly.

"Hopefully no one! That was my point. I think I've earned a break. I need to de-stress before I end up with a stomach ulcer."

"Well, if you think that Jonathan has 'seen the light,' that should be the end of his dramas."

I nodded, leaning forward. "I think he has. You should have seen him, he was pretty shaken. I'll see him on Friday and find out if it's stuck. I certainly hope it has, I don't think I'm cut out for any more of Jonathan's surprises."

"Good luck, then. Send me an email after you meet with him. I have to say again, Is, how proud I am. I don't think I could've done what you did. You saved his life—again. You're a true hero," she praised me, admiration peppering her voice.

"Thanks, Jules. That means a lot coming from you. Talk to you on Friday."

I hung up the phone and started twirling my hair again. I had no idea how to resolve these new challenges in my career without losing everything. But as a lawyer I was trained to find loopholes, and I was determined to find a solution that would allow me to hold on to everything that was important to me.

That night, I tossed and turned while thoughts of these ubiquitous challenges spun around me in an endless loop. My mind was in overdrive; as soon as one concern manifested, another quickly took its place, the relentless spinning making my head ache. I pulled the covers over my head and tried to block out the world.

When I eventually managed to get to sleep, it was not restful. Images of Neil in a garage workshop haunted me, the sound of sirens still ringing in my ears when my eyes snapped open. A chill crawled across my skin. There was something important about that sound, but I couldn't quite put my finger on it.

I groaned, turning over and pulling the covers back over my head. I was *not* going to stay up worrying about this, especially after a day like today. I'd tried to warn Rachel and she'd thrown it back in my face. I was not going down that road again. And as for Neil, nothing had changed. The best thing for Rachel was for him to be arrested. I was adamant that I wouldn't try to intervene in that outcome.

I had a feeling the time was drawing near. *Good,* I thought, *the sooner the better.*

I got up for a glass of water, trying to wash away the images of Neil, his memory like a bad taste in my mouth.

* * *

As I was leaving the office to meet Jonathan on Friday, my phone chimed. I picked it up to see who it was, hoping it wasn't Jonathan telling me he couldn't make it.

It was a message from Jeremy.

HI ISY. THANKS 4 UR MESSAGES. AUDREY IS IN THE CLEAR. SHE'S DOING WELL. COMING HOME TMW. JEZ

My skin warmed. A smile broke over my face, lifting my spirits like the sun breaking through the clouds. The storm was passing, everything clicking into place. Jonathan. Jeremy's niece. The world seemed far less foreboding, my worries washing away like dirt circling the drain. My feet twitched; if I weren't in the office, I would've jumped up and down. I texted him straight back.

THAT'S FANTASTIC! SO HAPPY 2 HEAR IT. LET ME KNOW WHICH FLITE. WILL PICK U UP FROM THE AIRPORT :)

I picked up my Burberry tote bag and practically skipped past my secretary, explaining that I was heading out to meet with Parkmores, purposely being vague about precisely who it was that I was going to see.

As I was walking over to meet Jonathan, excitement fluttered in my stomach with the thought of seeing Jeremy. Then I remembered the last thing that had happened between us before he left and my palms grew sweaty.

It seemed like a lifetime ago, I'd forgotten all about it. But I would have to face it when I saw him. I prayed it wouldn't be awkward.

As my stomach started to twist, I refocused my thoughts back to Jonathan. *One problem at a time*, I thought.

I walked up the stairs to Coffee Haven, the meeting place Jonathan suggested. Instead of me going to his office, as would normally be the case, he volunteered to come to me. We were meeting near the scene of the accident—I wondered whether that was just a coincidence or if he'd deliberately chosen the location.

Jonathan was already seated when I arrived. He gestured me over to his table.

"Hello, Isabel. Lovely to see you." His smile was luminescent.

"Thanks, likewise. I'm surprised you're here, I thought I was early. I hope you haven't been waiting long."

"Just long enough to order our coffees," he said, waving his hand at the cups on the table. "Soy latte as I recall?"

"Thank you, yes. I can't believe you remembered."

He gave a nod, clearly impressed with himself. "So, how are you feeling after the other day?"

"I'm good. What about you? You certainly seem very happy today," I noted.

"I am. It's a good day to be alive." The warmth in his smile hitched up another notch. "And it's amazing how something as simple as flowers can make my wife so happy," he added, giving me a wink.

"I'm pleased to hear it." I was *very* pleased to hear it. "You look . . . I don't know, like a whole new man."

His eyes were shining, making his face glow. He sat relaxed in the chair. "Life is funny, isn't it? What we want most can change from one day to the next." He took a sip of his coffee, reflective. "I realized that on Tuesday, among other things." He paused, leaning back in his seat and taking another sip.

I edged forward, willing him to continue. My heart was in my throat. *What else did you realize? Put me out of my misery, the suspense is killing me! And please, let it be good . . .*

He gazed at me intently. "I know I'm being quite candid with you, Isabel. And it's certainly not my usual style, especially with colleagues. But for some reason, I feel like I can share these things with you. Maybe because you were there with me when the car could have killed us. Maybe because I see a lot of myself in you when I was your age and working towards building my career."

"Yes," I encouraged, "I feel the same way." *Tell me before I hit you.*

He nodded. And yet, frustratingly, he was in no hurry to continue.

"So, what other things did you realize?" I probed, so close to the edge of my seat that I risked falling to the floor.

"Oh, yes. What I realized is that although I love my family, I've let them take a back seat to my work. I suppose that's because I thought they'd be more forgiving than my company. But when I arrived home with flowers and I saw the look on my wife's face, I remembered that once upon a time, before we were married, she was all I could think about. The things I used to do, like a love-struck teenager," he grinned to himself as he shook his head, recalling the memories.

"For the first time in a long time, she looked at me the same way she used to look at me then. And I realized how close I'd come to losing that. I don't want to miss out on my children growing up. I want to be there for them. I want them to know how much I love them. I want them to know that they mean more to me than anything else in the world."

Oh, thank God. I expelled the breath I'd been unconsciously holding.

"So I've decided to take a week off next month and take a

family vacation. You should've seen the CEO's face when I told him. I can't remember the last time I did it. Clearly, either could he." He chuckled, looking much younger than I'd ever seen him. "I wanted to tell you because depending on how you decide to proceed with the job offer, we'll need to either lock it in before I go, or wait until I'm back."

I was smiling so widely my cheeks were starting to hurt. His revelations were more than I'd hoped. There wouldn't be any skydiving, we were both saved.

"Actually, that's perfect," I told him. "It gives me time to think about it. Can we talk again when you get back? That would also give me an excuse to see you and hear all about your trip," I added enthusiastically. "I'm so pleased you're going."

He nodded. "Take all the time you need. And thank you. I wouldn't be going if it weren't for you. I don't know what it is about you—you seem to always be running straight into me when there's danger. Maybe you were right about being my guardian angel," he mused.

I laughed nervously—and snorted. *Ugh,* I wanted to hide my face. Since I doubted very much that a real guardian angel would ever do something as undignified as snorting, I was sure that answered his question. But the guardian part was at least somewhat true. Although it finally looked like I was retiring. For good. And not a moment too soon.

He continued, politely ignoring the embarrassing snort. "I can't seem to stop myself with you, being so candid and sharing too much information. I'll have to stop that if I become your boss," he said.

"I hope that regardless of whether I join your team or not,

or even whether I stay on the Parkmores team at Barkleys, we'll always be friends."

He smiled warmly in response, but we both knew he would maintain a professional distance if I joined his team. "So, has your perspective on life changed at all since Tuesday? Or are you still the unerringly calm Isabel, taking everything in your stride?"

My lips twitched hearing him describe me as calm. Lately, I'd been anything but calm. The term *nervous wreck* seemed to fit better.

"Actually, I'm taking a leaf out of your book. I need to figure out where I'm headed, though, before I can re-evaluate how I spend my time. So in that sense, I'm a step or two behind you, but I'll get there eventually," I assured him.

"I have no doubt you will. You'll have a family of your own soon enough, if that's what you want. Frankly, I'm very surprised you're still single."

I flushed crimson and quickly changed the subject. "So where are you planning to go on your vacation?"

"I'm letting the family decide. So far, we have votes for LA—Dalia wants to go to Disneyland, but Miranda says she doesn't want to leave the beach—and camping, which is clearly Sammy's choice. I'm letting them fight it out. Somehow, though, I think poor Sammy will lose out. I doubt the girls will agree to see the inside of a tent," he said, laughing at the idea.

"I'm sure it'll be perfect, wherever you go. Maybe you can pitch a tent in the backyard another weekend, just for the boys," I suggested.

"Actually, that's the great idea. Sammy would love it. I'm just happy to spend time with my kids where I can focus on them, instead of only half listening while I'm looking at my email, or worrying about something. I intend to get down with them in the sand, or the mud, wherever we are. I'm going to have a mountain of work waiting for me when I get back, so I'd better make the most of my time with them." He lifted his cup and swirled his coffee, temporarily lost in his thoughts. "The big trip will be over the holidays—we're going to England to visit family. We're all looking forward to it. My parents can't wait to see the kids." His enthusiasm was contagious and I couldn't wipe the smile from my face. He cleared his throat, his tone turning professional again. "But enough talking about me, you wanted to talk about the job. Do you have any questions about working at Parkmores?"

"I could definitely learn a lot from you. To be completely honest, my only reservation is about the hours. When I leave Barkleys, I want to be able to take more time to explore other interests," I admitted.

"I won't lie to you, it would be a lot of work, but I daresay not quite as onerous as Barkleys. And you won't be expected to do the same hours I do. The team works closely together and the extra resource will share the burden, so the demand on you won't be unreasonable. That said, there will be times when the workload will necessitate longer hours. It's the nature of the game, but I don't have to tell you that.

"Think about where you want to go in your career. Your experience would be invaluable on our team, but it has to be what you want. I could always ask Harrison to send you out on secondment, so you can get a better feel for our company. Of course, I won't tell him that. He knows I need more resources, so it would be a logical request. What do you think?"

A secondment was a temporary assignment of a law firm's lawyer to an in-house legal position with a client. It was commonplace in Britain and Jonathan was an advocate of the benefits: It allowed the client to secure an additional resource who had experience with the business and could hit the ground running, and afforded the law firm the opportunity to strengthen ties with its client. Most importantly, it offered me a chance to get away from Barkleys for a while. This could be my saving grace, it would give me some breathing space from Inspector Harrison and buy me more time to figure out what to do. Although no need to articulate my motives to Jonathan.

"Actually, I think that's an excellent idea. If Harrison agrees, it would be a good opportunity to see how I'd fit into the team there."

"Great, it's settled then. I should probably head back now. It's been a pleasure catching up with you, as always," he said as he lifted his glass to take one last gulp of his coffee.

"Thank you, Jonathan. I really appreciate all of your help—and your support."

"Any time, Isabel. I mean it. I'd better get back now but I'll talk to you soon."

He gently placed his hand on my shoulder as he said goodbye. He was still smiling as he turned to leave. He looked renewed.

18

ANTICIPATION

MY STOMACH WAS flipping with nerves as I was driving to pick up Jeremy from the airport on Saturday. I hadn't let myself think too much about it before he got back to San Francisco, but now that I was about to see him, a cloud of apprehension settled over me. A thousand questions burst into my mind.

What if Jeremy thinks what happened the night before he left was the beginning of a romantic relationship between us?

What if he wants to pick up where we left off?

What if he wants to kiss me when I greet him at the airport?

Oh dear Lord—what if he's in love *with me? How can I possibly tell him that I just want to be friends without crushing him, without ripping his heart out and breaking it into a million pieces?*

What if things will never be the same between us?

The mere idea of hurting Jeremy was abhorrent to me. My stomach somersaulted. My hands were shaking as I gripped the steering wheel, my knuckles turning white. I couldn't bear to look into his eyes and see the hurt and know that I put it there.

I drifted to the gate, fidgeting with my hair. I'd chosen a black turtleneck and an old pair of jeans. I didn't want to wear anything too feminine or alluring. I pulled my hair back and wasn't wearing any earrings or make-up.

Poor Jeremy.

I caught sight of him as he exited the gate and waved him over to me. He looked really good. Stubble shadowed his jaw and he was wearing a red T-shirt that hugged the lines of his muscular chest—very sexy.

I started wondering why I'd been so adamant about the friends thing. *Maybe I shouldn't have been so hasty . . . Maybe if he wants to kiss me, I will let him . . . Darn, should've put on some lip gloss.*

No, no, be strong, there was a reason why I didn't want to go there, why I didn't want to play Russian roulette with Jeremy. I just couldn't remember it right now.

My stomach was still flipping as he shambled over to me. I couldn't help but notice that his pace slowed as he drew near, stopping more than an arm's length away. *Any further and I'd need a walkie-talkie*, I thought.

"Hi, Isy. Thanks for picking me up from the airport. You really didn't have to, I could've gotten a cab." He looked at me like he wished he had.

It occurred to me that I could have overestimated Jeremy's desire for me just a tad. *Or maybe it was the turtleneck and general librarian look I'd gone for.*

"Don't be silly, of course I was going to pick you up. So tell me about your niece. I'm so happy to hear that she's doing so well, that's such a relief." I wanted to give him a hug, but the space between us felt insurmountable, an impenetrable invisible brick wall. I repressed a groan, keeping the smile plastered to my face like a marble statue. I tugged on my turtleneck and brushed my fingers behind my ear, making sure there were no stray hairs out of place. *Ugh, this is even worse than I'd imagined.*

"So, fill me in," I begged, spinning on my heel and motioning towards the exit. At least if we were walking, it wouldn't feel so awkward. "How's your sister?"

He updated me on everything, filling in the time back to the car and most of the ride home. I stole inconspicuous side glances at him when I could. He looked drained but relieved, like a soldier returning home having just won the war. I imagined that's what he probably felt like, given the trauma he'd just experienced and the miraculous outcome in the face of so much fear.

The obvious undercurrent of awkwardness was heightened in the car, the small space heating and expanding it until it felt like a third entity crammed between us. He was acting too polite, signaling he was afraid to offend me in some way.

When he asked to change the radio station, his hand accidentally brushed against mine as we both reached for the button. He immediately pulled his hand back, his face turning crimson.

The cause of his discomfort—merely brushing against my hand—was so insignificant that his reaction was magnified, like a flashing neon sign in the car.

Something had definitely changed between us and Jeremy didn't know how to act around me anymore.

As much as I worried that this awkwardness would translate into the end of our friendship, I realized it also meant we possibly shared the same concerns. He didn't want the lines of our friendship being blurred with romance any more than I did.

Maybe he was worried that he would hurt *me*. That I was the one who was desperately in love with *him*. That it would be *my* heart shattered into a million pieces. The irony didn't escape me.

When we got back to our apartment building and I invited him over for lunch, he tried to make a run for it, citing his fatigue from the trip. I wasn't allowing it, though. If I let him start avoiding me, it would be even more awkward and difficult to talk about it later.

I insisted, using the excuse of the food I'd organized for him.

"Just collect the groceries I got for you and stay for a quick bite," I urged, unlocking my front door. "I've got a whole heap of cold cuts and Turkish bread from the deli. At least make yourself a sandwich." I flashed him an encouraging smile.

"You didn't have to do that, Isy, really." I could see the resistance on his face warring with what appeared to be a sense of guilt. I knew if I persisted, he would succumb.

"Nonsense, of course I did. Isn't it the same thing you did for me when I got back from Florence?"

"I suppose, but—"

I cut him off. "But nothing. We're friends and that's what friends do. Come in."

I was quick to use the *friends* word to try and alleviate some of his possible concerns that I was going to throw myself at him as soon as I got him inside. If the awkwardness weren't hanging so thickly in the air, I might have made fun and asked him what kind of wedding cake he'd like. But this wasn't the right time for teasing. That kind of joke could send him straight to the emergency room with a coronary.

He sat down at the table so reluctantly it looked like he was afraid it would be his last meal.

Hey, you could do a lot worse! I thought, suddenly insulted.

I chuckled under my breath. After all of my fears this morning, I should be thankful. Instead, I was letting my ego get bruised by the fact that the idea of a relationship with me was repellent to him when I felt the exact same way he did.

I let him make his sandwich before I started talking.

"As you know by now, Jez, I'm the type of person who likes to call a spade a spade—" I paused, realizing that my mother's words had just flown out of my mouth. I watched him freeze in place with his mouth half open to take a bite of his sandwich.

I continued, wanting to get this over with quickly. The tension in the air was as thick and suffocating as a wet blanket and Jeremy still didn't look like he'd taken a breath. "I don't want things to be awkward between us, there's really no need. Can we please just forget about what happened before you left for Phoenix?"

His jaw relaxed a little and he slowly closed his mouth as he processed my request with obvious relief.

"I mean, not that it wasn't great, because it was—"

"Oh, yeah, absolutely, it was—great," he agreed, still looking uncomfortable but less likely to drop dead from a heart attack at any given moment.

"Yes—great. Definitely."

"Definitely," he chimed in again.

"It's just that we don't want to ruin our friendship. I value you too much as a friend to ever do that."

"Yes, yes—me too. You're such a good friend, I definitely

wouldn't want to . . . risk that," he concurred, echoing my sentiment. His expression suddenly grew somber. "After the horrible mess with Becca, I just couldn't bear to go through something like that with you. We could never have a casual relationship, you and me. There would be too much pressure. I couldn't bear to have you hate me if I messed things up . . ." he whispered.

He busied himself inspecting his sandwich, avoiding eye contact. I could tell it was hard for him to admit his innermost fears. He hadn't mentioned Becca for such a long time, I'd forgotten just how much it had affected him. I was an idiot for not realizing sooner that the breakup had happened during a time in his life he'd rather not revisit, when everything had seemed to collapse around him. My Jeremy always seemed so easy-going, so composed, I had to remind myself that his past experiences were still bound to haunt him and he would be even more paranoid about messing things up than I was.

"I agree." I smiled encouragingly at him, trying to dissipate his fears. "And you know you would never be able to get rid of me that easily, so let's just forget all about it. It's done. And it will never happen again. So we don't have to give it another thought. Deal?"

"Deal," he said, a slow smile curling his lips. He took a deep breath, the tension evaporating from his shoulders as he released it. "I'm relieved, I was worried that—" He paused, seeming to not want to say the next part out loud.

I finished his sentence for him. "That I would jump on you the second I got you in my apartment?"

"Well, no . . . Yeah, kinda," he admitted.

"You should be so lucky. Didn't you notice that I look like a librarian?" I said, gesturing towards my clothes. "I was worried it would be the other way around. I was trying not to look like I wanted to impress you or something."

He laughed. "Mission accomplished. I thought maybe you didn't care what you wore—I mean, even in public—because you thought we were a couple now."

"Are you serious? Shouldn't we at least be married before you worry I'd *let myself go*, for crying out loud?"

He flushed crimson again and I laughed. We'd both worked ourselves up into such a frenzy, worrying over every little thing.

"I'm just thankful we can go back to making fun of each other and not having to worry that if I hug you or something, you'll think I'm trying to seduce you," I teased, giving him my most seductive look.

He chuckled. "Phew. It looks like your seduction might've been scary."

"Hey!" I yelled, throwing a piece of Turkish bread at him across the table.

He caught it with one hand. "Good, I was going to ask you to pass the bread," he quipped, flashing his lopsided grin.

Jeremy was back. I couldn't stop smiling, the weight had been lifted. My friend was back. I had missed him.

* * *

I spent most of Sunday with Jeremy. Now that all of our cards were on the table and we'd had the most awkward of conversations, we both felt free to completely open up to each other. Without the possibility of sexual tension between us, there was no fear of misinterpretation or analysis of every action. The gray was gone, the shadows of uncertainty vanished. We were completely free to be ourselves.

When he knocked that morning, I answered the door in my yoga pants and tank top, reverting back to the early days of our friendship when I wasn't paranoid about what I looked like in front of him.

He raised his brows as he surveyed my attire and then broke out in a huge grin. "Geez, Is, please don't go to any trouble on my account," he teased.

"You're right," I responded, playing along, "I probably didn't need to bother washing my hair for you. Next time I'll go with a more natural look."

"Any more natural and you might scare the children in the building."

"Shut up!" I yelled as I playfully slapped his arm. "Anyway, if you think this is bad, you should see my new pajamas. You're in for a real treat."

"Sexy."

We spent most of the day teasing each other and laughing hysterically. The kind of laughing fits that make your stomach hurt. I snuggled next to him as we watched a DVD and ate popcorn. He was no longer letting me get away with making him watch any *chick flicks*. Those days were over along with me bothering to put on makeup. We'd settled on a movie that was a favorite for both of us: *Shawshank Redemption*.

But as the movie ended and the evening was fast approaching, my light-hearted mood turned solemn. Jeremy noticed my frown as I looked at my watch.

"Hey, what's wrong?" he asked, throwing a handful of popcorn at me.

I caught some and tossed it back. "It's nothing really. I've got my biannual performance review this week. I have to submit my self-appraisal form tomorrow and I haven't done it yet, so I'm going to have to kick you out now. Sorry, Jez."

"I don't get it. Why do you look worried about it? Surely with the amount of work you put in, it'll be major slaps on the back for you, maybe a ticker tape parade even. I'm sure you deserve it," he said reassuringly.

"I very much doubt that. Let's just say that I've been a little distracted lately. Harrison is going to pull me up on it for sure. He won't sugarcoat it. Plus I have to set my personal objectives and KPIs for the next period. For the first time, I have absolutely no idea what to write."

"Why have you been distracted?" he asked. When I didn't answer immediately—wondering what on earth to tell him—he looked horrified as he jumped to conclusions. "It doesn't have anything to do with what happened between us, does it? I'm so sorry if it affected you that way, Isy, I really am. I know how important your career is to you."

Geez, presumptuous much? "Well, the hours I spent with my therapist did make me miss some important meetings. But it was worth it, she helped me to see that following you to Phoenix was a bad idea." I couldn't help myself—men always seemed to think that women were obsessed with them and they ruled our lives. Although I could admit that I'd been guilty of obsessing over romantic entanglements more than usual lately, I was still able to function. I had bigger problems to consume my days.

Jeremy's face paled, his mouth dropping open. Clearly my sarcasm hadn't filtered through in my voice.

"Relax, Jez, I was just kidding! It had nothing to do with you."

It took a minute to register before he closed his mouth and threw me a look of annoyance to let me know he didn't find me amusing.

"So then, what *was* the problem?"

This was the perfect opportunity to tell him the whole story. As I contemplated my response, the sincerity in his eyes melted me. I trusted Jeremy and I finally felt comfortable enough to share my bare-naked truths with him. But not tonight. Tonight I had to keep focused on the task at hand, and this story would inevitably open up a Pandora's box of questions.

"It's a very long story," I finally answered. "I'll tell you about it another night, I promise. Over a glass—or a bottle—of wine. Right now I better focus on completing this self-appraisal or I'll be up all night. Thanks for coming over. Next time we can have a pajama party." A wry smile curved my lips.

"That might be a problem since I don't wear pajamas," he replied with a mischievous grin.

"Ew, I'd have to plastic wrap the couch. Better stick with jeans, then." I gave him a wink and pushed him out the door.

I stared at a hard copy of my appraisal form questions for half an hour before I even turned on my laptop. I had no idea what I was going to write. I'd never had a problem completing a self-appraisal before. I had always felt confident walking into my reviews. I'd always known what my contributions had been and exactly where I wanted to go.

This time was different. And it wasn't just because I was concerned about being reprimanded for my lack of focus. It was more than that, although that was enough reason to cause my stomach to knot.

I didn't know what I wanted to achieve in the next six to twelve months. Any of the objectives I should set would undoubtedly require complete focus. They would need to be a priority.

For the first time, I didn't want everything to be so black and white in front of me. I didn't want to have my path engraved in stone. I wasn't sure what lay ahead and I needed to take one day at a time. I had other priorities outside of work, whether I'd asked for them or not. Whether I wanted them or not. These pieces also needed to fit into the puzzle that was now my life.

I felt like I was trying to put a thousand-piece puzzle together without having the benefit of seeing the picture on the box. I was clueless about what the final picture should look like. How then, could I work out how the pieces should fit together?

A war was raging inside my head. One part of me was making peace with the unknown. The other part of me—the part that had been dominant for so many years—was angry with myself for questioning the clear path I had been on. After all of my hard work to join the partner fast track, why was I faltering now? I had deviated from the path but it wasn't too late to get back if I proved my commitment to Harrison and stayed focused. It was still within my grasp.

I didn't know if I would even have any more visions to worry about. If I didn't, what would I have if not for my career?

The other part of me considered what would happen if the visions *did* continue. The day would come when I could not cover my tracks, when I would need to be in two places at once.

There could only be one of two outcomes: Either I would fail with my work commitments or I would fail in getting to where a vision told me I needed to be. Both of these outcomes shared one key and horrible word, which was the driving force behind my constant need to work harder and do better. A word that I feared above all else.

Failure.

If the visions continued, it was only a matter of time.

If they continued.

What I needed now was a vision of where I would be in the future pending the decisions that I made now. Didn't I deserve at least that much? Just a little guidance?

With reluctance, I considered that Jules might have been right about looking for a position in a smaller firm. A firm that promoted work/life balance and actually meant it. If I left Barkleys before there were any major incidents, I would have a good reference and leave my reputation intact. But if I waited too long . . .

I opened up my appraisal and started to type. Under the section on future goals, I wrote about my focus on being promoted to senior associate. This is what they would expect to hear. And I wasn't ready to brush aside what was still within my grasp. The idea of telling people that I was moving to a less prestigious firm was still unfathomable to me. After being conditioned for so long that only the best was good enough, it had become part of my very identity. Since I didn't know what lay ahead, I decided not to let go of everything that had laid behind . . . Not yet.

19

DEAD WOMAN WALKING

THE START OF the week passed too quickly for my liking. My review loomed ahead, like the execution day for a prisoner on death row. My movements were sluggish, the invisible shackles emitting a clinking echo that only I could hear. The only thing that made the passing of the days more bearable was the email I received from Matt on Monday afternoon. We scheduled a catch-up after work on Thursday, a day that was now both something to dread and something to look forward to.

By Wednesday evening, the anticipation of my impending slaughter was killing me. I had a sense of foreboding that I attributed to the review, but something was different. My skin burned from the inside, like my blood was boiling. My breathing was shallow and I wondered if the stress had finally exceeded my limits and the dam were about to burst.

My head spun for a moment, and as I closed my eyes to steady myself, a flash of Neil invaded my consciousness—the same images that had recently been haunting my dreams. I sensed the time was drawing near, but instead of tapping into the intuition inside me, instead of centering myself and focusing on it, I brushed it away. I was in the middle of my own anxiety attack. I didn't have room—or energy—for anything else. I knew Rachel would call me when he was arrested. Smugly, I wondered whether she'd want my help as a lawyer. I doubted it. By then Rachel would realize what a douche he was and wash her hands of him.

I turned on the air conditioning and stood in front of it, but it offered no respite from the fire in my blood. I drank a cool glass of water and finally, like a fever breaking, my body temperature dropped.

I flipped on the TV and tried to zone out for a while. I'd just done the washing up—that is, tossed the take-out containers into the trash—when my cell phone sprang to life. I jumped to grab it, wondering if Matt was calling to cancel.

It was Rachel. Was this the call I'd been expecting? *Tonight?* Sheesh, could her repugnant boyfriend have worse timing? I cleared my throat and tried to sound normal, readying myself to feign surprise. I had to resist the urge to be smug. Rachel would be upset and I had to be there for her. That's all that mattered now. Everything else would be put behind us.

"Hi, Rach!"

There was no response, all I could hear were muffled sounds in the background. Ordinarily, I'd chalk it up to a pocket-dial, but I suspected something was going on. I continued to listen and eventually heard her sniffle. She was crying.

"Rachel?" I tried again.

"Isy, Isy . . . something . . . awful happened," she stammered.

"Rachel, what is it? Are you okay? Where are you?"

"I'm okay. I'm at the hospital."

My heart thumped against my chest. If it wasn't Neil's arrest, what else was going on? Who was hurt? "Which hospital? Why?"

"Saint Francis Memorial. It's . . . it's Neil. I think he's hurt real bad. And the police are here asking questions. I . . . I don't know what to do. I thought since you're a lawyer . . ."

"I'm on my way. I'll be there soon. Don't say anything until I get there, okay?"

" 'Kay," she sniffled.

I made it to the hospital on Hyde Street in record time, but the minutes felt like hours. My head was spinning. What happened to Neil? How badly was he injured? Did the police shoot him? *Oh Lord, the police must have shot him.* Then another thought pierced me with fear. *Would he die?* I wanted to bury myself under the covers of my bed and pretend it wasn't happening, pretend I'd never known any of it. How could I have known he'd be critically injured? I didn't like the guy, but I never wanted him to die.

Drop dead, asshole. The words echoed in my head, haunting me like the Ghost of Christmas Past. But I hadn't meant it, it was only a figure of speech! I willed myself to keep it together, I had to be there for Rachel. She needed me now.

When I found her, she was sobbing in the waiting room. My eyes darted to a police officer speaking with one of the nurses. I put my arms around her. "Tell me everything."

"Neil and I had an argument and he wasn't answering his phone, so I drove over there to talk to him. When I got there . . . oh God . . ."

"What? I know it's hard, but you have to tell me, Rach."

"His house was on fire. The fire department and paramedics were there and they were putting him in the back of an ambulance. All they told me was that the neighbors reported an explosion." Her cheeks glistened with tears and she brushed them away.

"It's okay," I soothed. I was slowly putting the pieces together. The fire department, the ambulance. It wasn't police sirens I'd heard at all. I remembered the dreams, the feeling that the sirens were important. But I'd pushed it out of my mind, not wanting to expend the energy. If I had, maybe I would've realized that the sirens I'd heard were the fire department and ambulance, not the police. How could I have been so foolish? I'd jumped to the wrong conclusion and now Neil was in the hospital. I needed to know his condition before I let the guilt overwhelm me.

She choked back a sob. "I stopped for gas, otherwise I would've been there when it happened!"

"What?" I gasped. Oh dear Lord. Rachel. She'd been close to being there. She could have been hurt. Seriously hurt. All the time I'd worried that Neil might hurt her, when the real danger was her proximity to the accident. I wouldn't have been able to bear it if she'd been hurt. A wave of nausea crashed over me and my knees threatened to give way. I took a deep breath.

"Is he . . . Do you know how he is?" I asked tentatively, afraid of the answer.

"They won't let me see him. When I got here they told me that he'd suffered third degree burns and smoke inhalation. A while after that, the police showed up. I didn't understand. They were asking all kinds of strange questions. They said that the explosion happened in the garage and Neil was in there . . . making . . . making methamphetamines." She leaned her head on my shoulder while she sobbed. "But it doesn't make any sense. I would've known something like that." Tensing, she lifted her head. "And then, Isy, they started asking me questions like I knew about it, like I was somehow involved!" Her fearful eyes begged me to help her.

"Don't worry, Rachel, I'll talk to the police. And then I'll go and find a doctor and see what I can find out."

She nodded, wiping at her tears. "Thank you," she whispered.

I think I was even more relieved than Rachel. There was still a chance that he'd be okay. *Please, oh please, don't let him die,* I prayed.

After I spoke with the police, they appeared to be convinced that Rachel had no knowledge of Neil's illegal activities. And even if they weren't one hundred percent convinced, I'd pointed out that they had absolutely no evidence to suggest otherwise. It took me another hour after that to get any updates about his condition from the nursing staff.

Finally, a nurse called us through to speak with a doctor.

She led us down a long corridor awash with the scent of antiseptic and into a small room resonating with the beeping sounds of medical equipment. Neil lay in the hospital bed, hooked up to a heart monitor, with his torso, hands, arms and part of his face—including his left eye—bandaged. He looked like he was sleeping, but for all I knew he was in a coma. *At least he's alive,* I consoled myself. Rachel rushed to his side and gasped. I heard footsteps behind us as someone entered the room.

"Hello, I'm Dr. Austin."

I turned around and my jaw hit the ground. "Matt?"

"Isy! How do you know Mr. Becker?"

"He's my friend's boyfriend. This is Rachel," I gestured.

"Oh. *Oh*," breathed Matt, as he put two and two together. I'd confided in him the circumstances of the vision I'd had of Neil, so he knew better than anyone what this meant.

"You know each other?" sniffled Rachel.

"We met when I was in Florence," I explained quickly. "How is he, Matt?"

Matt's tone instantly transformed into the professional doctor. "He's suffered quite severe burns to his hands, arms, chest and face, but he'll regain full use of his hands. We can't be certain about his left eye, his vision may be impaired. But luckily his right eye appears undamaged. He'll be left with a lot of scarring and may opt to have cosmetic surgery on his face at a later date, but his injuries aren't life threatening, so long as they're treated properly. We'll obviously be keeping a close eye on possible infection."

"Is he in a coma?" I asked.

"No, we've given him something for the pain. The best thing for him right now is to sleep. The pain would be unbearable otherwise. He's going to be okay. He's very lucky that his injuries weren't more serious."

I let his words sink in. "Thanks, Matt," I whispered.

He nodded. "I'll leave you two alone. I'll be just down the hall if you have any questions." He threw me a come-and-find-me-later look and left the room.

"Do you know what the funny thing is?" Rachel whispered after Matt left, keeping her eyes on Neil.

"What's that?" I asked.

"You know how I said we'd argued? We'd actually broken up. I was going over there to collect a few of my things. I had no idea what he was doing. Honestly, Isy. Looks like you were right about him all along. I'm sorry I wouldn't listen. There was more to him than I wanted to see. And I'm sorry I was so harsh and said such awful things. Can you forgive me?"

I stepped over to her and took her hand. "Rach, I don't take any pleasure in things turning out the way they did. I wish he could've been the man you wanted him to be. As for forgiving you—of course. We both could've handled things better."

My cheeks warmed with shame knowing that I had long been looking forward to the day that Neil got busted. Now he was lying in hospital with serious injuries that could easily have been fatal if he'd been engulfed by the fire. There was no pleasure in that. There could never be any pleasure in that. It was true that I didn't know whether I could've actually helped him, didn't know whether there was anything I could've done to help the situation. But it was also true that I'd had no real *interest* in helping him. I'd decided that he wasn't worth my time and walked away. Like I had the right to be judge, jury and executioner. And the worst part was, this wasn't just about Neil. It never was. If not for a few precious minutes, Rachel could have been injured and lying right next to him.

I shivered. All that was left now was Rachel's broken heart, Neil's scars, and my avalanche of regrets.

Rachel sat sobbing in the chair beside him. I left the room to fetch her a glass of water and bumped into Matt in the hallway.

"Isy, how are you?" he asked, keeping his voice low.

"Me? Ah, I'm fine. It's Neil who's in the hospital bed." I couldn't believe that *Matt* was Neil's doctor. I didn't know whether it was fate, or some cosmic joke. The man looked so incredibly hot in his scrubs, on any other day I would have been drooling. But I was too freaked out to appreciate it right now.

I took a deep breath. I had to focus on keeping it together for Rachel. I could fall apart when I got home and allowed myself to think about the only thing I knew to be true: Whatever I was or wasn't supposed to do, *I'd failed.*

"You're feeling guilty, aren't you? I can see it all over your face."

"Wouldn't you?" I whispered. "The whole time I was so smug about knowing what would happen to him—what I *thought* would happen to him. I had no idea how wrong I was, how close he'd come to being killed. And Rachel—she could've been there—" I put my hand over my mouth, covering my quivering lip.

Matt reached out and put his hand on my shoulder, warming my skin under his touch. "Isy, there is nothing you could have done to prevent this. He was doing something extremely dangerous and it literally blew up in his face. What were your options? Tell him not to do it? Firstly, he wouldn't have listened, and secondly, if he felt threatened by you knowing about him, who knows what he may have been capable of? This isn't like the other things you saw—it wasn't about stopping someone from being in a certain place at a certain time. He was in his garage. Unless you were going to trespass onto private property—and what? try to drag him out of there?—what could you have done?"

"I honestly don't know. But the point is: I didn't even care. I didn't *care*, Matt. Worse still, I was glad. Glad! What does that say about me?"

"It says that you can't save the world, Isy. And if you tried to single-handedly stop every person in the world doing something stupid or being injured, you'd get nowhere."

His words consoled me. It was true: I couldn't stop Neil from being in his own garage. Even if I'd been able to prevent it today, what was to stop the same thing from happening tomorrow? Matt was right: I couldn't save the world. Why then, did I feel so awful?

The answer was the unavoidable truth: I only wanted to save the good people. Did I get to decide who was worthy of saving? Who was worth the effort? I had to trust that I saw the visions I did for a reason, even when I didn't understand what that reason was. Everything was connected somehow.

I vowed I would do everything I could to save the next person I saw in a vision, or die trying.

* * *

D-Day arrived on schedule with no regard for my lack of sleep. After the roller coaster of emotion of last night, I didn't know whether I was facing up or down anymore. Nothing was going as planned. I felt like a crash-test dummy careening towards a brick wall.

I sat in the meeting room booked for my discussion with Harrison, my stomach doing somersaults. The small room was on the thirty-eighth floor and overlooked the bay. The breathtaking view was serene and the setting seemed wrong for the inevitable slaughter that was about to take place.

I tried to settle my stomach, telling myself I was being overly pessimistic. My occasional lack of focus over recent weeks had not caused the quality of my work to suffer, nor had I missed a deadline or disappointed a client.

Harrison wore a mask of professionalism as he sat across from me at the small round table and looked down at his file. The last time he sat across from me at a review, he'd been far more jovial. We'd discussed my ambitions for senior associate and he'd been pleased with my enthusiasm.

The Cirque du Soleil routine continued in my stomach. The stale air in the room signaled this meeting would be very different. I found myself squirming uncomfortably in my chair, staring at the bay and wishing I could break the window to let in some fresh air. And perhaps zip-line out of there.

Harrison started the discussion in an official tone. I was right to be anxious, it was the slaughter I'd expected. Although the quality of my work was not in question, the issue of my dedication and apparent change in attitude was quickly the topic of discussion.

"Since your overseas trip nearly two months ago, Isabel, I have seen a change in you. I have to say that it has caught me by surprise. You know how much I have pushed to have you considered for senior associate. I can't help but feel that you no longer have the same level of desire or dedication that you had—and that has made me look foolish in front of the other partners."

There was a long pause. Harrison was staring at me, seemingly waiting for a response even though he hadn't asked a question. This was not uncommon with the partners; they knew if they stared their opposition down, the weak would crack and say more than they may have intended to. It was a mind game, and ordinarily a very effective one.

I had been around long enough to know better. I consciously—and with great effort—calmed myself, knowing that if I let my anxiety take over, I might as well pull the trigger myself. Without allowing the silence to unnerve me, I kept my gaze steady while I thought of an appropriate response.

Finally I spoke, keeping my words brief. It was always better to let the other person show their hand first. "I'm sorry that you feel that way, Harrison. It was certainly not my intention. I have sincerely appreciated your support in me being considered for senior associate."

I returned his gaze and allowed the ensuing silence to fill the room without breaking my resolve. His lack of response was designed to keep me talking. It was amazing how many people completely revealed their hand when they tried to fill the void.

I held my poker face and after considering my best line of attack, I finally added, "I'm completely dedicated to delivering for my clients. I would certainly hope that Parkmores has not been dissatisfied with my work. I have often asked for informal feedback and it has always been very positive. May I ask if there has been any other feedback from them?"

My question was deliberate. The feedback from Parkmores had been glowing. Jonathan certainly wouldn't have offered me a position on his team if he'd had any other opinion of me. Plus, given that Harrison hadn't already mentioned any negative feedback, he obviously didn't have any up his sleeve.

"No, thankfully, Parkmores has not been dissatisfied. I am not worried that you have made critical errors—I am more concerned that you may drop the ball in the future. If your focus is lacking, I cannot be sure that a mistake *won't* happen. I need your full attention."

"You have it," I responded confidently, this time without pause.

"Do I?" he asked with raised eyebrows.

"One hundred and ten percent." I knew I was breaking one of the biggest rules in business—never over-promise and under-deliver. I didn't know what was going to happen tomorrow, let alone next month or next year. But now was not the time to falter. I couldn't tell Harrison anything less and expect to still be respected in the firm.

Another long pause.

"That's good to hear, Isy. I removed your name from consideration for the next round of promotions, given the circumstances. However, if you prove to me that you can give the firm one hundred and ten percent, we'll talk about the possibility of being considered next year."

Again, he waited for a response. I nodded, keeping my expression neutral despite his words vibrating through me like little swords tearing at my flesh. At least he'd stopped using my full name.

"I've been wondering whether your lack of focus since your vacation is because you're considering going to work overseas? If that is the case, we can discuss the possibility of you taking a leave of absence." He eyed me cautiously. He was fishing.

"Thank you, Harrison. I'm not looking to work abroad, certainly not in the foreseeable future."

"Then perhaps you're thinking about taking an in-house role

instead?" He managed to ask the question in the same neutral tone, but his suspicious eyes betrayed him.

I realized that Jonathan might have mentioned the idea of a secondment at Parkmores to Harrison. This shouldn't have ordinarily raised any suspicion. The opportunity to get first-hand experience with a client was encouraged, especially as this made the lawyer—and therefore the firm—more valuable to the client afterwards, given that they acquired a more intimate understanding of the client's business.

"I feel privileged to be part of an incredible firm like Barkleys. I don't believe an in-house role would offer the same opportunities and advantages that I have here." I kept my answer as truthful as possible so my sincerity wouldn't be obscured.

Harrison seemed to evaluate my response and appeared satisfied.

"Well, as you know, Barkleys isn't for everyone. It takes a lot of dedication, which often means that you have to make choices. Sometimes those choices can be difficult. You need to consider the direction in which you would like to take your career. If you still want to fully commit to the firm and take advantage of the opportunities you have here, then we'll discuss your consideration for senior associate next year. If, however, you're thinking about an alternative career path, I would like you to discuss that with me."

He allowed the words to hang in the air, continuing to hold my gaze with lethal force.

"Thank you," is all I said.

Finally, he blinked. "I will review your self-appraisal and complete the review forms based on our discussions today and forward you a copy for your records. Unless you have anything further you'd like to discuss, I have a three o'clock meeting." He was already standing before he'd finished the sentence.

I returned to my office with mixed emotions. On the one hand, I had survived the onslaught, temporarily pardoned by the governor. On the other, I had no idea if and when the house of cards would crumble. I was walking a tightrope and my sense of balance was terrible. There was no safety net. If I fell, I would fall hard.

I had arrived at the crossroads I knew had been ahead of me. But how can you decide which path is the right one when you don't know where to go? Staying where I was seemed like the safest solution for the moment—unless I decided to put away my old dreams and replace them with new ones.

20

SHAKEN, NOT STIRRED

I MET MATT for a drink after work at 7:00 P.M. I was thankful to get out of the office and keen to see him again, eager to get an update on Neil and to discuss everything that had happened. We met at the Spice Market in the Marina District. Matt knew the owner and indicated we'd be able to get a VIP booth for privacy—he knew I was paranoid about anyone overhearing details of my entropic life.

He was waiting out front when I arrived and flashed me a huge smile as soon as he saw me approaching. When I got closer, he embraced me and kissed me on the cheek. He smelled *really* good.

"Hi there," he breathed. "It's good to see you. How are you feeling?"

Not as good as it is to see you, I thought. He looked incredible, without even trying—unlike me who was showing the wear and tear of no sleep. He was wearing black pants and a striped blue shirt that brought out the color of his eyes and hugged his chest just right.

"Okay, thanks, Matt. It's good to see you, too. How are you?"

"Better now that you're here. Shall we go in?"

"Lead the way."

I tried to walk naturally, even though my feet ached from a long day in my four-inch stiletto heels. I told myself that the pain was worth it, I loved the line of the ankle straps and the way the heels elongated my legs. Feeling low that morning, I decided that my favorite shoes would carry me through the day.

The glamorous venue was one of the newest hot spots in town. The lavish ambience was inspired by the exotic spice trade throughout Asia and the Middle East. There were cages hanging from the roof, hard stone floors, rich and colorful fabrics, and antiques from around the world filling the vast space, transporting you to another world. The VIP section was at the back just behind the huge glowing bar. The booths offered complete privacy and, coupled with the noise of the music, I felt confident no one would be able to hear our conversation.

A pretty waitress with long blond hair and porcelain doll-like features came to take our drink order almost as soon as we sat down.

I glanced at the cocktail menu. "I'll have a Turkish Delight Martini, please."

She nodded and turned to Matt for his order.

"A scotch and coke for me, thanks."

She disappeared and Matt turned to face me. He was sitting rather close, but with the loud background noise, he wouldn't hear me otherwise. His scent enveloped me. *Damn it, I wish he didn't smell so good.*

"How is Neil doing?" I asked him.

"As well as can be expected." He quickly continued when he noticed my furrowed brow. "He's going to be fine, Isy, don't worry. He's got bigger problems than his injuries, those will heal. The police were back today. Looks like they're just waiting for him to recover so they can arrest him."

"I suspected as much."

"He'll have to cross that bridge when he gets to it. Frankly, I'm more worried about you. How are you feeling after yesterday?"

"Considering that I'm burn-free and don't have any police at my door, I'd say I'm a lot better than Neil."

"You know what I mean. I hope you're not still blaming yourself."

"No. Well, kinda. No."

"Do you need to buy a vowel?" he teased, bumping his arm against mine.

The corner of my lips lifted, but my attempt at a smile was only half-hearted. My angst over what had happened was too close to the surface to push it back down. "I feel a little guilty that I didn't even try to help him, but I don't think I really could have done anything. It just opened my eyes to a few things, that's all."

"Like what?"

"Like what everything means. Trying to figure out why I see the things I do and how much choice I have in acting on it."

"Isy, you always have a choice. And you have to look after yourself, too. You're not invincible."

There was that word again. "Can we change the subject? So

how was your day?" I asked him.

"Really good actually. We got a new laser at the hospital that I'm really excited about. It's called UltraPulse. The laser uses a very high-energy beam of light to vaporize the scar tissue and stimulate the regeneration of the deeper, healthier skin. It might be something that will be useful for Neil down the track. I used it on my first patient today: a teenager who suffered third degree burns in a house fire. It'll take a while to see the full results, but I'm excited about it."

The passion in his eyes was evident as he spoke. His genuine compassion and desire to heal touched me. And I was glad that it might be something that could help Neil with his scarring.

"That's wonderful, Matt. How many laser treatments will your patient need?"

"Four to six. It's not completely pain-free, but it's nothing compared to surgery."

"Is the patient a boy or girl?"

"Girl. She has a lot of scarring on her arms and she's really self-conscious about wearing short sleeves. It's the emotional pain that's the hardest for her. She's a lovely girl. I'd like to see her smile again."

My heart melted as I listened to him—for this poor girl who had obviously suffered so much and for this wonderful man who cared so deeply.

"She's lucky to have you as her doctor."

He gave me a bashful smile and shifted the topic of conversation. "So, Isy, we didn't really get a chance to talk yesterday. I'm dying to know what's been happening with you in the past couple of weeks—you know, besides . . ." He cleared his throat.

"I've been thinking about our conversation at coffee quite a bit. It seems I can't get you out of my mind. You have me completely riveted."

Those huge ocean-blue eyes gleamed with anticipation of the latest tale of near-death experiences. I was lost in that sea of blue for a moment, nearly drowning in them. I would have launched straight into my tale, but I needed to catch my breath first. The way he was sitting so close to me and looking so deeply into my eyes was making it hard for me to concentrate. I had to look away to break his mesmerizing hold on me. *Just friends,* I reminded myself. *Don't go there.*

I was staring over towards the bar when he put his hand on my knee to get my attention.

"Isy? Don't keep me in suspense. Tell me—what's been going on?"

His hand definitely got my attention. I felt the blood rush to the surface under his fingertips and tensed. He instantly pulled it away.

I was simultaneously disappointed and relieved.

Wanting to avoid eye contact, I turned my attention to the bowl of peanuts on the table, taking one without thinking. I paused, the peanut halfway to my mouth. *Gross*, communal bar nuts—I'd definitely seen the studies on the cesspool of germs festering among its contents. There was a microscopic fiesta going on in that bowl and I could envisage the germs dancing all over the seemingly innocuous peanut in my hand. I swallowed. It was too late, I was committed; the nut was about to take up residence in its new home, accompanied by all of its microscopic friends. Resigned, I popped it into my mouth, ruminating on how I'd given ten times as much thought and hesitation to that nut as I had to jumping in front of a cable car and playing chicken with an out-of-control vehicle. *Therapy, anyone?*

"I wouldn't suggest the nuts," I quipped. I straightened my shoulders and launched into my tale, turning back towards him. I decided that making eye contact wasn't as risky as the cesspool of germs I'd just ingested. "Thankfully, it's not exactly an everyday occurrence, but I actually do have a rather big story to tell. You know how I told you about Jonathan? The one who I'd seen under the scaffolding and also in front of that cable car?"

"Yes. He was the one you'd seen twice and weren't sure if that meant anything."

"Precisely. Well, three times a charm." I tried to observe his reaction without allowing myself to get caught in his web again.

He raised his eyebrows and cocked his head to one side. "Really?" he breathed.

"Aha. It happened last week. It was a bit of a close call with a car. For a second there, I wasn't sure I was going to manage to get Jonathan out of the way in time." Although I was still acutely aware of his presence next to me, I was starting to relax a little and became more animated in my storytelling. It was a good story, after all, and I had so few people to tell it to, I might as well make it good.

He leaned in closer to me as his expression changed from surprise to something else. I couldn't quite decipher it, but his face was serious.

"What do you mean 'get out of the way in time'?" he asked in a tone that matched his expression.

I turned my head away. He was leaning so close to me that I

could feel his breath on my face. Where were those nuts?

"Isy?" he asked when I failed to respond to his question.

At that moment the waitress reappeared with our drinks, rescuing me and providing the interruption I needed. I picked up my glass, happy to have something to busy myself with other than the infected bowl of nut-surprise.

"Isy?" he asked again. He hadn't seemed to move a muscle while he waited for my response. His glass remained untouched on the small table in front of us.

I could hear the concern in his voice. I decided that it was probably best not to give him my Academy-Award-winning narrative of the story, but instead keep it brief and unspectacular. By his reaction to the little I'd said so far, I could tell he wouldn't appreciate all of the added effects and intrigue.

"There was a car that ran off the road onto the sidewalk near my work. All I did was pull Jonathan back out of the way. Like with you. No biggie." I heard him draw in a breath so instantly continued speaking to try and focus his attention on the bigger issue. "But don't you find it interesting that that's *three* times now? I think Jonathan may need a full-time bodyguard. Or the Secret Service." I laughed, but the sound was solitary. He left me hanging, not even cracking a smile. I felt like I'd just waved to someone who didn't wave back and now I was left awkward with my hand in the air. I took a gulp of my drink, disappointed he didn't seem to appreciate my humor. *Geez, tough crowd.*

"You pulled him back, but didn't think that you would have time to get out of the way? You thought that you could've been hit by the car?" he clarified. He was clearly stuck on that point.

"Jonathan," I corrected. "I thought *Jonathan* could have been hit. He was the one in the path of the car, not me. It wasn't as close as it sounded like—I was just exaggerating for effect," I tried to reassure him.

I had to admit, though, I was extremely flattered that he was so worried about me. *Too flattered*, I thought. I tried to fight the blush rising in my cheeks. *Just friends*, I repeated to myself.

He paused for a moment while he looked at me and I felt the blush crawling over my cheeks despite my protest. I averted my gaze back to the drink in my hands. Eventually, he leaned towards me and put his hand on mine.

Just kill me now. My cheeks burned and my heart thumped unevenly against my chest. I could feel his breath like a warm caress on my face and his eyes looking straight into my soul. My entire body trembled. All I had to do was lean forward five inches and I would be able to reach his lips. Was he aware of how close he was to me? Did he realize what kind of affect that had on me? *Too close, buddy, too close. Not helping. Trying to be friends here! A little help?*

Slowly, he withdrew his hand, the rest of him frozen in place. Frozen five inches from me. I froze, too, in fear that I wouldn't be able to resist the temptation to close that tiny space between us. My head told me to move back, but my heart yearned to lean forward. The two opposite forces kept me locked in place. Every cell in my body tingled. *Keep a clear head.*

When he seemed satisfied that he had my full attention and I wasn't going to look away, he spoke. The sound of his voice was like a seductive, hypnotic whisper in my ear. "I don't think so, Isy. I think it really was that close. If Jonathan was in danger, then so were you. I think you could've quite possibly been killed."

I wanted to respond but I was so mesmerized by his voice that all I managed to do was open my mouth, no voice came out.

He continued in that same hypnotic tone. "You can't risk your life like that, Isy. You're not expected to. I'm sure he wouldn't want you to, either."

Somehow, despite the fact that it felt like my erratic heart had just stopped beating, I managed to choke out a few words.

"What would you have me do—watch him die? There was no other way." I tried to look away, but he put his finger under my chin and pulled my face back towards him, his eyes searching mine.

"No. But there must've been another way." He paused for a moment while he seemingly processed alternative options. "Since you know who he is, you could get his cell number—and call him to warn him or something . . ."

I responded in a whisper, barely audible over the thrum of the music. "I do have his number. But what would I have said to him? I couldn't let him think I'm a loon, he's a client."

I saw the surprise in his eyes and realized that I hadn't told him who Jonathan was.

The surprise quickly turned to disapproval. "Who cares if he's a client? You should risk your life because he's a client?"

I stiffened, offended by his disapproving tone and the implication. "You think I saved him *because* he's a client?" I snapped. "That had nothing to do with it. I would hope that you would think better of me than that." The idea that Matt could think I was that hard, that coldly ambitious, hurt me. Did he assume I wouldn't care unless it was someone who could help my own career? Surely he couldn't, given that he'd been a stranger to me once. Although I hadn't been in any actual danger on the street in Florence.

His tone softened as he registered the hurt in my eyes. "Isy, sweethea— Isy, that's not what I meant. I'm sorry. I didn't mean that I thought you only risked your life because he's a client. I meant that you chose not to find a way *not* to risk your life—that you didn't call him because you worried what he might think—just because he's a client. Who cares what he thinks? He should be thanking you and anything less would just make him a jackass—client or not."

His eyes were still searching mine, discerning if the hurt was still there. "You know that I think the world of you, Isy. That's why I'm worried about you. I would be upset—utterly devastated—if anything happened to you."

The hurt melted away. With every fiber of my being, I wanted to throw my arms around him and press my lips to his. I needed to put some distance between us. I shifted awkwardly, fearing my eyes gave away too much.

"Promise me you'll never risk your life like that again," he pleaded.

Once again I was caught in his web, the intensity of his gaze holding me like silken strands. The waitress returned, freeing me from his stranglehold, and Matt ordered two more drinks. The welcome distraction gave me the opportunity to consider his request. I didn't know what would happen from one day to the next and I knew I couldn't promise what I would do given the same situation. After what had happened to Neil because I decided I simply didn't care, after promising myself to not be so careless with the knowledge that I was given—regardless of whether I wanted it or not—I honestly didn't know what I would or wouldn't do anymore.

Even though I felt bad about Neil, I certainly wouldn't throw myself in front of a bus to save him; he probably wouldn't even come to the funeral. A terrifying thought dawned on me and I grimaced: *Dear Lord, please don't let Neil become the new star of my visions.* Given the preponderance of my visions had featured accident-prone Jonathan, anything was possible. I shook my head, deciding I was being overly trepidatious. Surely my path would never cross Neil's again—particularly since he was likely to land himself in prison. I'd been careless with him, but that didn't mean there'd be a do-over; with all the trouble he was in, he had to have learned his lesson. And if he hadn't by now, he probably wasn't going to. If anyone was keeping score, I'd more than made up for that carelessness by managing to save Jonathan. Surely that put me ahead in karma points. *Surely.* I deserved a break—a long one.

The waitress disappeared and I felt Matt's eyes on me. The question remained: What would I do if I were put in another situation requiring a level of risk on my part? There was a big difference between choosing to help someone and willingly swapping their life for yours. I wasn't a martyr and I had no intention of becoming one. That's the only thing I knew for sure.

"Isy?" Matt was looking at me expectantly.

"Um, I promise that I don't have a death wish and I'm not some sort of adrenalin junkie. I certainly won't be looking for it." That was the absolute truth. I wouldn't be looking for danger, I just couldn't help it if danger had been so adept at finding me lately. "Anyway, now that I think *The Jonathan Show* has finally come to an end, I have a feeling I won't be having any more visions for a while. Who knows, maybe I'll be retired for good." I smiled, wanting to lighten the mood.

He wasn't deterred, detecting the omission in my promise. "And if it comes looking for you?" he pressed.

"It can be a split second decision, Matt. I can't know how I'll react until I'm in that moment. All I can promise is that it's not my intention to take any unnecessary risks."

He looked at me for another long moment without responding. Although my response didn't seem to appease him, he couldn't quite argue with it, either.

"I suppose that's the best I'm going to get," he conceded. "I just worry about you."

"I know and I appreciate that." I hesitated, building up the courage to ask what I was thinking. "Why do you worry about me so much?"

The question seemed to take him off guard. He started to say something and then stopped himself. With a sadness in his eyes, he whispered, "I suppose I shouldn't, should I? But whatever I should or shouldn't do doesn't change the fact that I do." He thought for a moment and then asked the question that *he* must have been thinking. "Do you wish that I didn't?"

I didn't hesitate this time. "Of course not. Why would I wish that you didn't care—I mean worry—about me? It only means that you want the best for me. I feel honored that you feel that way. I only want the best for you, too."

For the first time during our conversation, he pulled his eyes away from mine. For the briefest of moments—so brief that I wondered whether I'd just imagined it—his eyes seemed to dart towards my lips.

Then just as quickly, he leaned back from me and shifted his body away slightly.

Maybe it wasn't just in my imagination, this magnetic pull I felt between us, this intense connection. Perhaps he felt it, too. Perhaps he felt the same intense desire to close the distance between us and decided to move away where it was safer.

I was in uncharted territory. Part of me was grateful to have him in my life, he'd given me what I needed to be able to open up and share my secrets with him. He'd offered insights and supported me on a journey that I was finding increasingly difficult to navigate. But the other part of me still wondered whether Julia was wrong, whether I should have kept my distance from the beginning, whether this was a dangerous game we were playing. Then I remembered that I would have run into him at the hospital irrespective of the decisions I'd made. Our paths were connected, I'd been fated to see him again.

His untouched glass on the table finally caught his attention, the ice having all but melted. He leaned across me to reach for it and his arm brushed against my knee, igniting my skin. The waitress returned with our fresh drinks and I took the opportunity to shift away as I reached for my second martini.

"Well," he said after he took a sip, "I think the best thing to do would be to try and figure out whether *The Jonathan Show*—as you called it—is really over, so you don't *have* to put yourself in danger again. What makes you so confident that it is?"

"Well, after the car accid—" I paused, searching for a less dramatic word. "The incident," I corrected, "I met with Jonathan for coffee and we had a good talk. The other things that happened to him didn't seem to affect him much. I mean, he didn't even realize about the cable car, he thought I was the one who nearly got killed . . ." My voice trailed off as I noticed Matt's back stiffen. I remembered I hadn't told him that whole story, either, and I certainly didn't want to retell it now.

"Anyway," I continued, "this last time was different. He realized how close he'd come to a serious accident. And since then, he seems to be reconnecting with his family. He has a whole new perspective on life, like a second chance. Maybe that was why things kept happening to him—like he was in some kind of *Groundhog Day* loop—because he hadn't figured out whatever it was that he was supposed to learn. Your original theory is the only one that seems to make sense, but I'm certainly open to any other explanations if you have any more insights."

He took another sip of his drink while he thought it over. "Actually, I think that fits together. And I certainly hope that's it because it means you won't have to go for a fourth time. I'd worry that the next time would be some kind of parachuting accident and you'd be free-falling two thousand feet in the air to try to catch him." He half cringed at the thought.

"As long as it's not bungee jumping—I prefer to have a parachute." I chuckled to myself that he seemed to share the same thought pattern I'd had.

His lips curled. I was glad to see he had regained his sense of humor.

"So, how do I keep my eye on you then?"

"Two-way earpiece and video camera on a brooch?" I quipped.

"If only I could. How about you promise to call me if and when you have any more visions, before you decide to do anything rash—like jump in front of a train or the newest carrier of disaster?"

"Matt, the last time it happened, I was running out the door immediately. I didn't have time for calls. It wasn't like with you—I was dreaming about you way before I even got on the plane to Florence." I instantly blushed as soon as the words escaped my lips. The way I'd phrased it made me feel self-conscious.

A smile touched the corners of his mouth. "So you run out the door with your cell. Just tell me that you'll try."

I knew it was completely impractical. After all, even if I did manage to call him, what were the chances that he would be available to take the call in that exact moment? And what was he going to do even if he was?

"I promise if I have another vision and get the opportunity, I will tell you about it." I had no intention of running around with my cell phone, waiting for him to tell me what to do. I had to act on instinct. My instinct. The fact was, no one could tell me what to do in those moments, the answer had to be mine. But like the lawyer I was, I'd chosen my words carefully. All I'd promised was to talk to him about it *at some stage* if I had an opportunity. Most likely over coffee.

Nonetheless, my declaration appeased him and subdued his fears a little. He seemed to believe he could be Superman and swoop in and save me from potential danger. Rather presumptuous, given that I wasn't the fair maiden waiting to be rescued in this story. But I knew he was only trying to protect me because he cared. The question was: Who would protect my heart from him? The more time we spent together, the stronger the pull felt between us.

Matt was a kind-hearted person and I trusted his integrity. But I felt like I was in a car traveling too fast. The exhilaration of the ride was euphoric, but it was too easy to lose control and crash. Someone was going to get hurt if we weren't careful, and that someone was likely to be me. Nevertheless, I didn't want to exile him from my life. I couldn't. Who knew what tomorrow held?

It dawned on me that Julia was right: I *was* becoming less risk-averse. I wondered whether that was a good thing or a bad thing, and whether it would eventually catch up with me.

21

FORGOTTEN PASTIMES

MATT'S FEARS WERE UNFOUNDED. The next two and a half months passed without incident, without even a real sighting of Jonathan, let alone a vision of him.

Neil recovered, as Matt had said he would, and the police did indeed come knocking on his door again. Neil apparently decided to delay any cosmetic surgery; he thought the scars would make him look tougher in prison. That, and the judicial system didn't exactly put cosmetic surgery high on the priority list when they sentenced you.

Without any visions to send me running out of important meetings, things happily returned to normal at work. Except for one thing: an obvious change in Jonathan's behavior didn't go unnoticed by Harrison. Although Jonathan was still working long hours to meet tight deadlines, he seemed to make himself less available for anything that wasn't absolutely urgent. After hours and on weekends, emails and calls to Jonathan that could wait, often did.

He took his one-week vacation in August as he'd planned, in addition to a long weekend here and there, taking Harrison completely by surprise. What made Harrison even more concerned was Jonathan's lack of visibility. He had declined a myriad of dinner invitations, including a celebratory dinner at the conclusion of Project Aurora.

This was unlike him and Harrison began to worry that he was being courted by a rival law firm. He also contemplated the possibility that Jonathan was considering leaving Parkmores to take another role.

Harrison was edgy, Parkmores was too large a client for him not to worry. He tried to schedule a lunch with Jonathan to probe him but his futile attempts fell by the wayside.

So Harrison did what any good lawyer would do—he started trying to cement his relationship with other senior members of the Parkmores' team. If Jonathan were going to jump ship, Harrison didn't want to go down with him. Although he would be keen to explore opportunities for the firm with the new vessel Jonathan was sailing away with, if Jonathan were indeed considering leaving Parkmores.

I knew that Harrison's worry was unnecessary. I understood the real reason behind the change in Jonathan and I was pleased to see the affect it had had on him. I couldn't, however, alleviate Harrison's fears by relaying this to him.

When Harrison first asked me if I'd heard any Chinese whispers about anything happening at Parkmores, I tried to downplay his concerns to make him feel better. I instantly noticed the look of disapproval in his eyes when he seemed to perceive my response as nonchalant, proving to him my indifference to the firm.

So I instantly put on my acting shoes, and instead of dissipating his fears, I added fuel to the burgeoning fire and watched as the smoke engulfed him. A little guilt sprang to the surface but I quickly pushed it back down, telling myself that his judgment of me had left me no choice. And so I rallied behind him and joined his defensive attack by promising to spend more time one-on-one with the Parkmores team. I even suggested 'infiltrating' their team in order to get more information—that is, to go on secondment if they still needed the additional resource. This would put me in a position to assure Harrison that no attacks were being planned, while allowing me to get out of the office for a while until the calm returned.

Harrison was pleased with my alliance and considered my suggestion to be useful. He wanted an opportunity to speak with Jonathan face-to-face and managed to lock in a meeting in the third week of October.

I decided to take a leaf out of Jonathan's book and take my own four-day weekend in mid October. It had been over three months since I had promised Mom that I would go to Napa to spend the weekend with her and Dad. I was finally going to fulfill that promise this weekend. I packed a weekend bag and started my drive on Saturday morning, timing my arrival for lunch.

It was a cool day in San Francisco but the weather forecast in Napa Valley was in the seventies and sunny. I was looking forward to letting the sun thaw out all of my past worries, blossoming the new hope within me like a flower bud blooming in the warmth of the sun.

I enjoyed the hour-plus drive, electing to take the scenic route over the Golden Gate Bridge. Driving through the countryside, I marveled at the beauty of the vibrant colors of the changing grape vines, the breathtaking tapestry of the wine country in the fall wrapping around me like a soothing embrace. With my Pete Murray CD humming in the background, I let the serene landscape and calming music revitalize my soul.

I couldn't believe I hadn't made this trip earlier. I had waited for the storm to ease, until I felt that I wasn't consumed by worry to take the weekend to visit my parents. I knew my mom would have been able to see straight through my armor and hadn't wanted to trigger a conversation I didn't know how to begin—or finish.

And yet now as I was sitting in the car, I could feel any lingering stress and anxiety seep out of my pores and evaporate from the vehicle. I was speeding away from all of the doubt and troubles that had been plaguing me.

I wondered if I would've been able to escape all of that nagging stress by making this trip sooner. More likely, I would've driven past the rich tapestry of the landscape and undulating hillsides and not taken any notice of their beauty. Now that the saga of Jonathan seemed to be over, now that he seemed to have a new lease on life, I felt that I had one, too. Beauty was everywhere, if you looked at it, instead of past it.

I took a deep breath and let the appreciation and energy flow through me. I hummed along to the music and tapped my fingers against the steering wheel.

I reached my parents' property far earlier than I'd expected; the drive seemed too short. I turned into their street and traveled down the narrow road until I reached their long drive and parked under the shade of a tree.

I didn't have to announce my arrival, Mom and Dad were in the back and heard my car approaching. Mom ran out first and was at my door before I'd even opened it.

"Isabel! Sweetheart, it's so good to see you!" she cried loudly. Mom always did have a larger-than-life presence about her.

I hopped out of the car and she threw her arms around me. Luckily I'd done all of that deep breathing because she squeezed me so tightly she cut off my airway.

I tried to ease out of her iron grip but gave up when she refused to loosen her hold. It was only when Dad gently pulled her from behind that she let go.

"Okay, okay, let me say hello to my daughter," he told her.

Then he gave me a big hug, but gently enough that I could still breathe. "See what happens when you stay away too long," he whispered in my ear. "Your mom could be a wrestler," he chuckled.

Mom pushed him aside impatiently as she gave me an appraising look up and down.

"You look well, Belle," she complimented me. "I was worried that I would find you all skin and bones."

"Don't worry, Mom, I always manage to eat," I assured her with a laugh.

"Good. Are you hungry, sweetheart? Lunch is ready."

She led me around the back to the barbecue, with Dad close behind. He took my bag and carried it inside for me.

My parents were outdoors kind of people. They had a huge porch that was fully set up with the barbecue, outdoor furniture, plants, a television mounted to the back brick wall of the house and even a spa. Past the porch, they had a swimming pool, huge aviary, rather impressive vegetable patch and large beautiful trees that hugged the fence line.

With the exception of the coolest winter months, they spent more time out here than they did inside.

The barbecue smelled fantastic and my stomach grumbled in anticipation.

"Let's eat."

* * *

I spent the rest of the day being completely fussed over. Having been away so long, it was nice to be looked after, although too much of the star treatment would be overwhelming in large quantities.

As promised, we spent that evening watching Mom's favorite Cary Grant movie, *An Affair to Remember*. It was so relaxing, I felt like I was a child again without a care in the world.

When I went to bed that night, I looked around my old bedroom. Mom had kept it exactly as I'd left it ten years ago. It was clearly a teenager's room, although I'd always kept it very neat and organized. I didn't have any posters of celebrities on the walls or anything that could be considered idealistic or fanciful.

The most frivolous thing in my old room was the large engraved wooden box on the dresser containing hundreds of beads. I walked over to it and peeked inside. I'd forgotten how much time I'd spent searching for the right components at Sunday markets. I lifted the top tray of compartmentalized beads to reveal an array of pendants, chains, wires and earring loops, all organized by size and color. I gently ran my finger over the assortment. The hours I'd spent painstakingly searching for every item in this box was astonishing. I remembered the care I'd taken, the enthusiasm I'd had.

I turned to examine the lampshade beside my bed. My lips curled as I remembered how my handiwork had diversified. I recalled buying the plain white cloth shade and spending a weekend planning my design before carefully stringing, gluing and stitching all of the beads and pieces of silk fabric carefully into place.

The lamp looked rather silly to me now, but I marveled at my creativity. I had long forgotten about this creative outlet; the most creativity I used now was in finding the best legal arguments and twisting the law to suit my client's position.

I was so lost in my own little world that I jumped when Mom came in behind me.

She noticed me looking at the lamp. "Can you believe you made that?" she asked as she sat down on the edge of the bed.

I shook my head. "I'd completely forgotten all about it. It looks kind of silly, doesn't it?"

"No, I think it's beautiful. Whenever anyone comes over, I always tell them that my daughter made it."

She noticed my raised eyebrows and explained. "A few people noticed it on their way to the bathroom and asked me where it came from. It caught their eye. I told them it was an original, there was nowhere they could buy one."

I was surprised to hear that anyone would ask about it, unless it was to make a joke. I looked over at Mom who was staring back at me with pride in her eyes.

"You know, Belle, I always knew you would make a great lawyer. You always won every debate at high school. But I thought you would continue with your jewelry making and designs, too; you just seemed to love it so. I was surprised when you stopped making anything." She lifted her hand to stroke one of the earrings she wore, drawing my attention to it. "I always loved the jewelry you made for me."

Her earrings were a diamond shape encrusted with tiny ruby-colored beads bordered by burnt orange metal. I'd made them over a decade ago and was surprised they had lasted this long.

"I still get compliments on these, you know," she said when she spied me looking at them. "I wear them all the time."

"They must be the best birthday gift I've ever given you, then."

"They're better than anything you could ever buy me," she crooned. "All the effort you put into them—I knew they were made with love. It's the best gift you could've given me."

I grinned. They *had* been made with love. I remembered how proud I was when she unwrapped them on her birthday.

"It's so nice to have you home, Belle," she said as she got up to kiss me good night. "Sweet dreams, sweetheart."

"Good night, Mom. See you in the morning."

I hopped into bed and read for a little while, then leaned over and switched off the beaded lamp, content in my reverie.

I had weird dreams that night. I dreamed that I was making Mom a necklace to match her earrings and I couldn't remember how to do it right. My fingers were bleeding from all of the cuts trying to twist the wires into place. Then Mom brought me a five-foot lamp missing its cover and asked me to design one for her. I stepped back feeling uncomfortable, telling her that it was too big and I couldn't do it. She kept saying, "Yes, you can, you have to" over and over until I finally woke up, squirming.

When I finally got back to sleep I dreamed of Mom again. This time she was crying. As I tried to console her, she looked up at me, tears streaming down her horror-stricken face, and said, "I'm so sorry. So sorry. It was blue. It was blue."

I woke up feeling so anxious I had to stop myself from running into my parents' room to check on her. Her sadness felt so real. But why would anyone be sorry about something being blue? I calmed myself with the knowledge that it made no sense and was unlikely to mean anything.

Even though it was just a silly dream, sleep evaded me and the minutes ticked by. My thoughts wandered. Thinking of the color blue triggered memories of the evening I had spent with Matt. My heart beat faster at the memory of his piercing blue eyes and gentle touch. I tried to imagine him at this very moment, and then instantly tried to wipe that image from my mind when I realized he would be curled up next to his fiancée.

My thoughts drifted to Jeremy—my dear, sweet Jeremy. My Jeremy who loved me even when I looked hideous or was caught up in my own world. I knew I could trust him with my life. It was time to really open up to him about everything. Although if things continued as they had recently, maybe there wouldn't be anything left to tell.

I wasn't sure if that made me extraordinarily relieved, or slightly disappointed. As I came to the surprising revelation that it was both, I let myself drift slowly back to sleep, wondering what the future held.

22

REVELATIONS

THE NEXT MORNING, I awoke to the smell of pancakes. The sweet scent wafted into my room, making my stomach rumble in anticipation.

I was relieved to find Mom smiling as she tossed another pancake onto the plate next to the stove. Dad was sitting at the breakfast bar, shoveling syrup-soaked pancakes into his mouth while he read the Sunday paper.

"Good morning," I greeted. I was feeling a little tired from my restless sleep but was energized by this happy scene in the kitchen. All was well. Dreams were sometimes just dreams.

Dad raised his eyes from the paper but still had a mouthful of pancakes so gave me a nod, his eyes shining.

"Good morning, Belle. You look happy this morning," Mom noted. "Must have been a good night's sleep in your old bed."

I didn't have the heart to tell her I hadn't slept well in the small bed, so I just smiled.

"Fancy some pancakes?" she asked, gesturing towards the massive stack on the plate beside the stove. The morning light danced in her hair, a soft golden halo framing her face.

"Looks delicious, thanks, Mom," I said, pulling two plates out of the cupboard and handing her one. "Let's sit down together."

She hesitated, glancing at the bowl of mixture still to be cooked, but turned off the stove and took the plate to join me. "You know, you never did tell me what happened with your friend, Rachel. Have you spoken with her? What's happening with that boy she likes?"

I didn't want to relive this again, but I saw no way of avoiding it. "Sad story, actually. A couple of months ago, she split up with him and when she went to collect her things from his house, there was a fire." No need to explain the specifics. "Neil was injured but he's made a good recovery, all things considered. A friend of mine was his doctor, believe it or not."

"Oh, that's terrible, honey. I'm glad to hear he's okay. How is Rachel?"

"She's—"

"Wait—I didn't know you have a friend who's a doctor. Male or female?" Mom probed, forgetting all about Neil.

"Male." She opened her mouth to interject, but I pre-empted her question. "No, he's not single."

"Oh. Carry on, then—Rachel?"

I rolled my eyes. My mother was so predictable. "Rachel is much better. She was in shock at first. She helped him while he was recovering, but she no longer sees him now." *Because he's in jail.*

"So it all worked out then? I don't mean the poor boy getting hurt, but Rachel ending the relationship. I knew she was an intelligent girl and would see through him eventually if you gave her time. I'm glad you listened to my advice." She seemed pleased with herself so I didn't correct her.

"Yup. We've planned to have lunch on Tuesday so I'll see her then."

"I'm glad, she's a lovely girl. I would've hated for you to let your friendship be affected by that boy."

I just nodded, my mouth too full to respond.

I ate until I thought I would burst. After breakfast, Dad went out to tend to the yard while Mom and I had a cup of tea to wash down our pancakes.

I told her about the weird dreams I'd had, starting with the giant lamp she was insisting I design.

She took a sip of tea as she listened, the steam rising up like little puffs of smoke. "Hmm."

"Weird, huh. Must be because of our conversation last night," I said.

"Actually, Belle, it might be your subconscious trying to tell you something."

"Like what?" I asked. "That you're really pushy? I already knew that," I quipped.

She gave me a stern look. "Very funny. No—that you're just afraid you won't be good enough at it to give it another try. Everything has to be all or nothing with you, always has been. That's why I think you were so dedicated to it when you were younger."

"What do you mean 'all or nothing'?" I asked defensively. I remembered these had been the exact words Jules had used in Florence and it struck a familiar cord.

"I mean, sweetheart, that unless you think everything will be perfect—that *you* will be perfect—you're not interested. You only pursue what you think you can excel at. You don't like to take chances if you're uncertain about how well you'll do."

She eyed my pout as I crossed my arms. "Now don't be like that. It's only an insult if you think it is. It's that characteristic that's made you the successful lawyer you are. I think it's less interesting that that's the way you are and more interesting that you find that observation to be insulting." She raised her eyebrows, watching me over the rim of her cup, seemingly delighted by her own insight.

As always, Mom didn't hold anything back. It was her usual *'I call a spade a spade'* mantra.

"Thanks, Doctor Phil," I responded sarcastically. "Let's change the subject, please. I didn't tell you about the other weird dream I had. This one was about you, too—maybe we can psychoanalyze *you*," I teased. Although I suspected Mom would find some way of making it about me again—claiming it was caused by the burden of guilt from not visiting enough. Suddenly I didn't want to tell her about the second dream. I was undoubtedly about to open the door to a major guilt session.

"Well?" she asked as she waited.

Too late, I sighed.

"I dreamed that you were really upset and when I asked why you were crying, you kept saying you were sorry and that it was blue. Weird, huh?"

There was a sudden shift in the temperature in the room, taking me completely off guard. Mom became as frozen as a marble statue, her cup halted halfway to her mouth as the blood drained from her face. A shiver went down my spine as I realized that with the exception of the tears, her expression was the same as in my dream last night: completely horrified.

"Mom? What's wrong?" I asked anxiously.

Silence.

"Mom, what's wrong?" I repeated.

She remained unresponsive, apparently selectively deaf. She was staring off into space, the burgeoning tremors in her hand making her cup jiggle before she slowly lowered it to the table. The hairs on the back of my neck stood at attention like little soldiers preparing to face an untold horror.

"Mom!"

She blinked, the statue slowly coming to life. She tried to act normal, but I could tell this was anything but normal.

"Nothing, Belle. Just sounds like a bad dream," she said unconvincingly.

"Then why did you look like you'd seen a ghost?" I probed.

Her eyes darted to mine, indecision flickering across her features.

"Did I? Sorry, I didn't mean to scare you. It was nothing," she tried to assure me.

I wasn't buying it. All of my senses were on high alert and I wanted to know what she wasn't telling me.

I raked my fingers through my hair, expelling a breath. "Mom, it's clearly something. I want you to tell me. I *need* you to tell me."

More silence.

Outside the window, a bird began singing its tune, obviously more talkative than my mother. She glanced down into her nearly empty teacup.

"Mom," I pressed.

"Okay, Belle, okay," she finally conceded. "It's a very long story. I don't even know where to start. The dream is probably just a coincidence, I shouldn't have reacted," she said as she shook her head, clearly wishing she hadn't.

Suddenly, she jerked her head upward to look at me, as if something had just occurred to her. "Have you had strange dreams like that before?" Something shifted in her tone and her eyes were now locked onto mine with laser-sharp focus.

This was definitely a long story and I wasn't about to be deflected from her explanation. "We were talking about you, Mom. Don't try to distract me, it won't work," I responded matter-of-factly.

She examined me for a long moment. "I take it that means you have. Okay, we'll talk about me first—but only on the condition that we then talk about you and any other strange dreams you may have had." She waited for a sign of agreement.

This conversation had taken an unexpected turn. I nodded my head.

"Okay, well, where to start . . . The color blue—it does have a meaning for me."

I raised my eyebrows in surprise. Blue actually meant something? I tried not to make a big deal out of it because I wanted her to keep talking like she was just discussing the weather. Like there was nothing at all to freak out about, despite the fact that I had an inexplicable urge to bring my breakfast back up.

"What?" I asked, in the same tone I would use to inquire about tomorrow's forecast.

"A car . . . and . . . and . . ."

She nervously fiddled with her wedding band, twisting it around her finger. Her discomfort was evident so I tried to ease her into it.

"How about you tell me about the car first, and then you can tell me what else it means," I suggested.

She spoke slowly. She was looking down at her cup, avoiding my eyes. "I never told you this, but when you were very young—too young to remember—I was in a car accident. The car that hit me was blue."

There was another long pause. I tried to help her by filling in the blanks.

"And you said that you were sorry because you felt like somehow the accident was your fault?" I asked gently.

She answered without looking up. "Yes."

I tried to guess how. "Did you run a red light or stop sign, or something like that?"

"No. The other car ran the stop sign."

I wrinkled my brow. "So why do you think it was your fault?"

She didn't answer.

"You can't blame yourself for that," I said soothingly. I knew there was such a thing as survivor's guilt, so I guessed that the other driver must have been badly injured.

Still no response. She shifted uneasily in her chair.

"Was the other driver hurt?" I probed, trying to understand.

"Yes."

"But you were okay."

"No. I lost the baby."

Suddenly I understood the horror on her face. "Oh," I

breathed. I would have had a baby brother or sister. I never knew.

Blue. "A baby boy?" I guessed.

"Yes. David."

"Oh." I searched for the right words to console my mother. How terrible that must have been for her, I couldn't even begin to imagine the trauma—or the guilt.

"But it wasn't your fault, Mom. You can't blame yourself. You couldn't control another driver who ran a stop sign," I said, trying to comfort her.

After a long quiet moment, she finally spoke. "I . . . I could have."

My mind was reeling. "How?"

"I knew the other driver," she said so quietly it was almost a whisper.

I struggled to decipher her guilt. *How could she have stopped it just because she knew the driver?* I wondered. Were they meeting for a secret rendezvous somewhere? Was Mom having an *affair*? I built up the courage to ask—indirectly.

"Were you meeting him somewhere?"

She threw me a disapproving look. "No." Her voice was tight, she had understood the insinuation.

Guilt flooded me. Of course Mom would never do that to Dad. I should've known better.

"Then how could you have stopped him?" I was out of guesses.

"The reason he ran the stop sign is because his brakes failed. I could've told him to check his brakes that morning."

It didn't make sense to me. Her words swam around my head, none of it sinking in.

"But how?" I asked, bewildered.

Then her words suddenly came together. The reason why she had asked me whether I'd had any other strange dreams.

She'd had one of her own.

This realization paralyzed me while I absorbed the enormity of it.

All this time I had hesitated in telling Mom about the visions I'd had, worried about what she would say, and all this time she was the only person who would have truly understood—who had actually experienced it for herself.

I gasped. I was speechless.

Her eyes searched mine, a pleading look swimming in her gaze. I didn't understand why until I realized that she was still wrestling with her guilt and she was worried I would judge her.

I was the last person who would judge her.

A solitary tear slid down her cheek, twisting my heart and making my stomach clench.

"You can't blame yourself," I repeated. "You didn't know. You didn't know it would really happen." I placed my hand on hers, trying to chase away the chill. "How did you . . . see it?" I asked, burning with curiosity.

She didn't pause this time. She knew I understood exactly what she was saying and I wasn't judging her for her inaction.

"The day before, I started experiencing these weird kinds of flashes. I didn't know what they were at first. I could just see blue, a lot of blue." She looked away and closed her eyes for a moment, taking a deep breath. Finally her eyelids fluttered open and she permitted the words to escape her lips. "I didn't know what it was—I thought I was just feeling weird because of the pregnancy. And we had painted the nursery blue, so I thought maybe . . ."

Her voice trailed off before she took another deep breath and continued. "I wanted to think that was it, but I knew it wasn't. When I think about it now, I knew it wasn't," she whispered. "Then that night . . . that night I had a strange dream. All of the flashes came together. I saw Dan in his car, saw him pressing on the brakes but the car not stopping. Then it happened. I saw him hit a white car before plowing into a light post. The sound, that terrible sound . . ." She closed her eyes again, a shiver running through her.

"You didn't see that it was your car he hit into?" I confirmed.

"No."

I shuddered and rubbed my arms, gooseflesh crawling across my skin. I felt for my mother, how incredibly traumatic this experience would have been for her, and the unbearable guilt she had been carrying since that terrible day.

"How did you know Dan?" I didn't want to ask exactly what had happened to him, I didn't want her to have to say the words out loud.

"He lived two streets down from us. Your father sometimes played golf with him."

A scraping noise outside reminded me that Dad was nearby and I turned to see him picking up a shovel and walking back into the yard.

"Did you ever tell Dad about this?" I asked.

"Yes."

"What did he say?"

"He told me it was just a coincidence and it wasn't my fault. That we couldn't have known."

"*We?*" I asked, wide-eyed.

"I told him about what I thought was just a bad dream that morning. Neither of us thought any more of it than that. He was just as horrified as I was that it could've been more."

"Oh." I was still processing this information when the next big question burst into my mind. "So—did you ever experience something like that again? I mean—did you ever have any other strange dreams or flashes?"

"Yes. No. Well, actually I'm not sure."

"What do you mean?"

"I had a strange dream. It was years after that, many years. It was a dream, but it felt real. I was so paranoid, we both were. After the accident, I wasn't able to have any more children, so we were even more paranoid about you."

"About me? What did you dream?" I was completely intrigued.

"I don't really want to talk about the details. I dreamt that someone hurt you, someone near where we lived. That's when your dad and I decided to leave the city and move to Napa. We didn't want to take any chances, we couldn't risk it. At first your dad wanted to go and kill the man I saw hurt you, but I pointed out that it wouldn't be good for our family if he went to prison—and it wouldn't be good for anyone if it was just a dream and the man was innocent."

I could barely take in the gravity of what my mother was telling me. I had behaved like a little monster when I was fifteen and they told me that we were moving to Napa, kicking and screaming until there was no fight left in me. I screamed that they were ruining my life, that I hated them. It had always been a sore spot between my parents and me. When I first moved back to go to college, I only ever went home for the holidays. When my mother had asked why I didn't visit, I petulantly told her that it was their decision to move to Napa and now that I was an adult I didn't have to be anywhere I didn't want to be. It's not that I didn't like Napa, it was beautiful, but I'd wanted to remain in the bustling activity of the city, with my friends.

Learning now that leaving the city was a bigger sacrifice for them than it had been for me, that it was something they had done *for* me and not *to* me, I started to cry. The guilt and sadness completely overwhelmed me, choking me until I couldn't breathe.

Mom instantly put her arms around me. I leaned my face against her shoulder, dirtying her shirt as I heaved uncontrollable sobs against her chest.

"I'm . . . so . . . sorry . . . Mom," I choked out between sobs.

"That's okay, Belle. That's okay," she soothed over and over.

"No, it's not. I was . . . so horrible . . . to you and Dad."

"That's okay, Belle. You were just a teenager rebelling. You couldn't have understood. Hush now, it's all okay."

Eventually my sobs softened to a whimper.

Mom stroked my hair until the tears eventually dried.

I leaned back, seeing the mess I'd left on her shirt. "I'm sorry," I apologized again.

"I know, sweetheart. It's okay. I'm more worried about you and what's going on now, than whatever happened back then. So tell me—what's been happening? What have you seen?"

23

CUE THE DRUM ROLL PLEASE

I STARTED AT THE BEGINNING. I told her about Jeremy and explained the real reason why I ran off to Florence in such a hurry. Hurt flashed in her eyes and I cringed. I'd traveled halfway across the world to see Julia in my time of crisis instead of making the short drive to see her, or even pick up the phone to tell her what was going on.

I tried to gloss over that part because the guilt—particularly given these recent revelations—was still tugging at me.

She didn't vocalize her disappointment, carefully rearranging her features into a mask of contemplation. It was completely against her character not to point out the obvious, but she remained silent. She wouldn't judge me for the way I chose to handle the strange things I had experienced. She knew only too well how discombobulating it was to be plunged into the icy waters of these visions, desperately trying to tread water and resist being swept under by the constant undercurrent of trepidation and uncertainty.

After I'd finished the rest of my story—including all of the sordid details about Neil—her eyes filled with regret.

"I'm sorry you didn't feel you could speak to me about this, Belle. And I'm sorry I never told you about my own experiences. It never occurred to me that you might experience it, too—it should have. It was just so hard to talk about and I tried so hard to forget. I didn't want to tell you it was my fault you didn't have any brothers or sisters." The tears spilled from her eyes, glistening on her cheeks.

"You have nothing to apologize for, Mom. I can only imagine what you went through. I know how hard it was for me. I didn't want to talk about it in the beginning because saying it out loud somehow made it more real. If I hadn't been forced to deal with it, I would've gone on ignoring it. Even after Jeremy, I was still in a state of denial. I thought I was going mad. I'm the last person you have to apologize to. And I'm sorry I didn't talk to you sooner—it never crossed my mind that you might have experienced it, either. I guess like mother, like daughter." I gave her a knowing smile to try to lighten the heavy air of the conversation.

"More than I ever realized," she agreed, mirroring my amused expression. "Thankfully, though, my daughter is a lot smarter than I am. I'm so proud of you for what you've done, Belle. Although I also have to admit that I'm worried about you, too."

"Not smarter, just luckier," I corrected her. "My denial was far stronger, I just had more time to weaken my resistance than you did. Our stories could easily have been reversed." I shuddered at the thought of something bad happening to Jeremy, Matt or Jonathan and my empathy for Mom multiplied knowing the guilt I would have endured.

Mom cringed. Her protective nature made such a thought—for me to have felt even a fraction of the guilt, torment and torture she'd suffered—abhorrent to her.

"And don't forget that I totally struck out with Neil," I reminded her. "He could've been killed. Even though I had so much more time to deal with it than you did, I'm still not infallible. Far from it."

"I wish I'd known what you were dealing with so I could've tried to help you more when I spoke to you about him." I flushed and she put her hand on my arm. "I'm not blaming you, sweetheart. I'm only regretful that I wasn't there for you. So, Julia's the only one you've told then?" she clarified. It was more of an assumption than a real question.

I didn't want to lie, all our cards were on the table now. "Actually, Matt knows, too."

Her eyes opened so wide, I thought her eyeballs might fall out.

"Matthew? The one from Florence?" She'd attempted to keep her voice even, but it raised about two octaves despite her best efforts.

"The one and the same."

"Oh."

I knew what she wasn't saying, I just wasn't used to her not *actually* saying it. This really was a whole new world to me—and a completely new relationship between my mother and me.

Her thoughts were inked into her expression: I had trusted a stranger over my own mother. Julia was my best friend, and extremely open-minded, she could understand that—but Matt was a complete surprise.

A heartbeat later, she edged forward conspiratorially, a knowing gleam in her eye. I repressed a groan as she leaped to an incorrect assumption—well, partially incorrect.

"So, this Matthew fellow, you two are quite close I take it?" she asked, overdoing the innocent act.

"We're not having a love affair, if that's what you're implying," I responded, rolling my eyes at her.

"I didn't say that you were," she retorted. "But you are indeed close—you would have to be to talk to him about this."

She had hit the nail on the head—that was the part that *was* correct: I did feel close to him.

She took my silence as confirmation and nodded her head, impressed once again with her insight.

"He must be a lovely young man, then. Tell me about him."

The boisterous bird outside chirped mockingly, like it knew my secrets and was daring me to confess. I glared at the window, a blush crawling across my cheeks, before I pushed those forbidden thoughts away and turned back to my mother.

"I'm sorry to disappoint you, but there's not much to tell. He sent me some flowers to say thank you when we got back from Italy and he occasionally sends me an email or something. It's nothing."

She wiggled her brows at me. "Somehow, I doubt very much that you told him anything on your computer. I know how paranoid you are about security, especially with something you don't want anyone else to know."

Darn it, she was *good.* She knew me too well. She was eyeing me intently, waiting for me to make some big confession. She wouldn't expect the truth: that I was totally infatuated with a man who was about to be married. *Sorry, no grandchildren here, Mom.*

"You're right," I conceded. "I told him over coffee during my lunch break. He was just appreciative, nothing more. But he's quite perceptive, so he kind of dragged it out of me. I wouldn't have told him otherwise."

An approving smile spread across her face, the thought that he'd been able to outsmart me somehow clearly impressing her. I could see her silently planning our wedding in her mind. I needed to stop her from getting ahead of herself.

"And before you think it's anything else, he's engaged. Matt is the doctor I mentioned earlier. He was in Italy with his fiancée."

As soon as she heard the word 'engaged,' the smile vanished and her shoulders slumped. "That was a coincidence, him being that boy's doctor . . ." Her voice trailed off while she contemplated the significance of that detail. Then she straightened her shoulders and switched her focus. "And what about this Jeremy fellow?"

"No, Mom, we're just friends, too. I love Jeremy, but it's not like that." No need to explain all of the details *there.*

"Well, if you already love him, all good relationships start with friendship, you know," she hinted with a knowing smile.

"Give it up, Mom. Not going to happen."

Disappointment briefly flittered across her face before her expression changed and she opened her mouth to fire off another hopeful question. I cut her off. "Jonathan's married."

That seemed to answer the question she was going to ask. I burst out laughing, flinging back my head and releasing all of the built-up tension. The sound reverberated through the kitchen and I spotted Dad looking over at the window. "This isn't a dating game, you know. I don't think it's called, *Show Me Another Contestant, Please*," I chortled.

"Well, is there anyone else, then?" she asked with the last glimmer of hope in her eyes.

"Sorry, no. It's just me and my crazy dreams to keep me company at night."

She shifted her tone. The hope was still there but it was joined by reassurance and faith. "You never know when the right man will come along. You just have to keep your eyes open and make room for him. I know that you don't *need* a man, but having the right person to love and appreciate you and share your life with can be a wonderful thing. Your dad has been an incredible source of strength and support for me. I only want you to find that, too. And I believe that you will, when the time is right. Until then, enjoy being single." She gave me a big smile.

A whole new world.

I liked it.

I poked her. "Who are you and what have you done with my real mom?" I quipped.

She shot me a stern look. "Maybe if you'd stop assuming you know everything I'll say, you'd actually talk to me more often about things."

I flushed, the residual guilt welcoming me back. She hadn't been abducted, my real mother was still putting me in my place.

"So—back to the part where I worry about you. You said you haven't had any more flashes of Jonathan since the car accident?" she clarified, returning her focus to more serious matters.

"Nope—more than two months clean and sober, so to speak."

"But we don't know if it will happen again. Maybe you should ask him to stay away from any dangerous activities, just in case."

"I can't tell him not to walk down the street. But don't worry, I don't think Jonathan will have any more close calls. Matt seems to think that now he's learned what it was that he was supposed to learn, he'll be fine. I tend to agree. There's been a real change in Jonathan, it's like he's living a second life."

She contemplated that for a moment. Again, I could tell that she was impressed by Matt.

"Perhaps *you* have learned what you were supposed to learn. Perhaps now you can pass the baton onto the next stuntman or woman. I would certainly prefer my daughter not to be jumping in front of any more cable cars or runaway vehicles."

Her words danced around my mind. Is that why I hadn't experienced any more visions lately? As Jules had pointed out, each person had taught me something—even Neil. I had learned from Jonathan's example. He had taught me to re-evaluate what was important to me, had made me feel that *I* had a new lease on life, too. Perhaps I'd graduated from the crash course of Life 101. It felt good. I visualized the imaginary degree framed and hanging on my wall. I wanted to give myself Honors, justifying that Neil was an anomaly and therefore didn't grade me down, but I knew I couldn't. I'd made mistakes. I mused that the important thing was that I'd learned from those mistakes. So, in consideration of my learning, I graded myself back up. I couldn't help but consider myself a high achiever. I mentally straightened my honors degree on the wall.

"You know what? I think you might be right about that. I think my work is done. It's a new chapter." I was smiling from ear to ear. I felt like I'd just run the biggest marathon of my life and finally passed the finish line. The crowd was cheering, I'd made it. Now I could see the masseur and bubble bath waiting for me at the other end.

Life was good.

I looked at Mom, remembering that her marathon hadn't had the same happy ending.

"Do you think that you didn't have any more flashes because you learned whatever you were supposed to?"

Sadness flashed in her eyes and I instantly regretted the question. I couldn't believe how insensitive it was.

She didn't look offended by my thoughtlessness. Instead, she appeared to give the question some consideration. "At the time, I thought it was a one-off premonition to warn me against losing the baby," she explained. "But now that I think about it, it did teach me something quite valuable. I was young back then and I thought it was important to 'keep up with the Joneses.' Your dad was working two jobs so we could do just that. I didn't appreciate the blessings we had.

"I learned that you can't compare yourself to anyone else—regarding what you have or even what you think is 'normal.' The only thing that means anything in this life is what you give back, how you help those around you. The most important gift you can give anyone is love.

"It's also the most important gift you can give yourself. I discovered that the hard way. And in order to do that, I've had to learn to forgive myself. It's harder to forgive yourself than it is to forgive someone else. Have you ever noticed that?"

It was a rhetorical question. She wasn't waiting for a response, she was staring out the window, into the distance.

Her words reverberated through my core. We all have our own journey to make, our own race to run. When you run a marathon, you can't worry about the people around you. What works for them may not work for you. We do our best when we concentrate on setting our own pace, fulfilling our own potential.

I had spent so much energy worrying about not being normal that I hadn't appreciated what Jules called a 'gift.' I'd considered it a burden. And yet, I would not be where I am now if I had not experienced what I'd gone through to get here. I wouldn't have the incredible new friendships I had. I wouldn't have had this eye-opening discussion and bonding experience with my mother. This time with her had enabled me to develop a much deeper appreciation and understanding of her—and also of myself.

24

SAND CASTLES

THAT NIGHT I had more strange dreams.

I dreamed that Jeremy and Rachel were both sitting on the couch in my apartment, arguing about something. I heard my name, but I couldn't make out what they were saying.

I'd been talking about them so much that day that they were obviously on my mind. The dream gave me inspiration: I should introduce them. They'd get along well and undoubtedly become fast friends.

I rolled over, wrapping myself in the covers. When I drifted back to sleep, I dreamed of Jonathan.

He was with his little boy, laughing and playing as they built—or tried to build—a sand castle. His wife and daughter had made a castle of their own and clearly won the competition. The girls were doing a victory dance when the boys jumped up and playfully chased them into the water.

The dream seemed to be in slow motion, like at the end of one of those feel-good movies when they cue the music and show the happily-ever-after scene right before the credits start to roll. I couldn't see myself in the dream but I knew I was there because Jonathan turned around as he was splashing in the water and waved to me, his beaming smile plastered to his face.

I woke up with a feeling of peace and tranquility that I wasn't sure I'd ever felt before. It was exactly how I imagined Jonathan with his family. I was filled with gratitude knowing I'd been able to make a difference in someone else's life, that my being on the planet had made a positive impact.

I fell into a dreamless sleep, feeling so light and joyous that I felt like I was floating.

* * *

I planned to head home the next day after lunch, despite my parents begging me to stay another day.

They got their wish.

Although I was feeling great that morning, by lunch I started to feel unwell. Mom reveled in the opportunity to take care of me, promptly sending me to lie down while she made chicken noodle soup, her ritual when I was sick as a child.

I didn't know if it was a virus or something else. My symptoms were strange, morphing throughout the day. It started with indigestion, before the nausea took hold, making me regret that second helping of pancakes. A feeling of anxiety overwhelmed me, even though I didn't know why, and manifested itself in a shortness of breath, an imaginary weight pressing on my chest.

This was not how I wanted to spend my four-day weekend.

I was too light-headed to drive. I only hoped it was one of those twenty-four-hour bugs and would pass quickly. I'd been looking forward to catching up with Rachel and I needed to get back to San Francisco so I could go to work on Wednesday. After taking a four-day weekend, no one would believe that I was legitimately sick if I didn't show up to work.

As the afternoon rolled on, the shortness of breath and queasiness intensified. Mom suggested taking me to the doctor, but I resisted. I didn't think a doctor would be able to do much for me if it was a virus, and the last thing I wanted to do was get up and go sit in a doctor's clinic.

I moved to the couch under the porch. I felt like I was suffocating inside, I couldn't get enough air.

By 4:00 P.M. the illness peaked, seizing my chest. A terrible chill seeped into my bones. Shivering uncontrollably, I was about to cave in to Mom's pleas to take me to the doctor. As soon as I stood, I had to rush to the yard to throw up.

My stomach felt a lot better after that and my breathing regulated. Whatever it was, the worst of it seemed to be over. Dad helped me to bed and I cocooned myself in the covers, finally able to get warm and drift off to sleep.

When I awoke later that night, I didn't know what time it was but it was dark outside. Mom was there, removing a cold cloth from my forehead.

"Sorry, I didn't mean to wake you, sweetheart. You looked feverish but I think it's passed now," she whispered, the relief clear in her voice.

"That's okay. What time is it?" I asked.

"Eight. How do you feel?"

"Much better. I won't be running any marathons anytime soon, but I feel much better than before," I assured her.

"I'm so glad to hear it. You had me and your dad very worried about you."

"It was just a twenty-four-hour bug or something. I'm better now."

"It was more than that," she argued. "You were white as a ghost and you were hallucinating. You scared us half to death."

I could still detect the residual fear in her voice. I must have sounded out of my mind but I had no memory of it.

"What did I say?" I asked curiously.

"It sounded like you were talking to someone and you were upset. Let's not talk about that now, a lot of it didn't make sense. You need to get some fluids into you. I'll go get you a drink and maybe a dry piece of toast to put something in your stomach. Then hopefully you can get back to sleep and you'll feel like yourself again in the morning."

She left the room to head to the kitchen, her feet softly pattering down the hallway. I was asleep by the time she returned.

When I got up the next morning, I felt a lot better but I was completely drained. I dragged my feet as I forced myself out of bed, my legs feeling too cumbersome to carry me.

Mom and Dad tried to insist that I stay another day to recuperate, but I was adamant that I had to get back home. With chagrin, I called Rachel in the morning to apologize for missing our planned lunch and then rested most of the day until I felt able to drive. They wanted me to stay for dinner, but my appetite still hadn't returned and the idea of food didn't appeal to me.

When I kissed Mom goodbye before getting in the car, she

was still begging me to stay. She finally accepted that her pleas were futile, putting her arms around me and whispering, "Everything will be all right. Call me if you need me and I'll come and stay with you. Look after yourself, sweetheart."

"I'm fine, Mom. Stop worrying so much. Thanks for looking after me. I'm glad I came up to see you and Dad—I'll visit again soon," I promised. I gave her a reassuring smile.

"Whatever you need, I'm here. I love you, Belle."

"I love you, too, Mom."

"Wait—I'll only be a second. I forgot something."

Before I could ask what, she disappeared like a lightning bolt. When she returned, she was carrying my box—the one containing my beads and jewelry-making tools.

"What—"

"Just take it with you," she interrupted, opening the back door of my car and putting it on the floor. "You never know when you might feel inspired."

"But—"

"If you don't want the contents, then I'm sure you'll find another use for it—it's a beautiful box." She smiled. I couldn't quite argue with her logic.

"Okay," I conceded. "Talk to you later."

I hopped in the car and started the long drive home. It wasn't as relaxing as it had been on the way up. I was still feeling off-balance. I opened the window to let in some air and tried taking deep breaths. Instead of admiring the countryside, I kept my eyes on the road.

* * *

The next day, I headed to work feeling much like the day before. A feeling of inexplicable apprehension clouded my mind, making it difficult to focus. I tried to think about something positive to chase away the feeling of foreboding and my mind turned to Jonathan.

Harrison was meeting with him this week. They were going to discuss my secondment and I felt good about the prospect of spending some time working with Jonathan. I looked forward to getting an opportunity to speak with him and find out how he was doing.

A change of scenery was definitely what I needed. My eyes scanned my office, the walls suddenly feeling like they were closing in around me. The air felt thick, making me speculate whether the reason I'd been ill was because I was anxious about returning to work after a few days away. *Was it possible that instead of a virus, I'd suffered some kind of serious anxiety attack?* I wondered. Being back at work didn't feel right. Nothing felt right today. I wanted to get out at lunch—this huge building somehow felt cramped, like it was imprisoning me. I needed more air.

I googled *anxiety attack.* I wanted to find out more about the symptoms. Lately, I was always questioning whether I was having one so it was time to do a little research. My past 'attacks' had been related to premonitions I'd had but this time there was no premonition. This time, it could really be a medical condition relating to stress. All I needed now was to have an anxiety attack in front of Harrison. The secondment could not come fast enough. I wondered how quickly I could start.

Murphy's Law: as soon as you are on the Internet doing something that's not work-related, your boss sneaks up silently behind you.

"Isy, can you please come to my office?" Harrison asked, so quietly that I barely heard the words.

I jumped out of my skin and desperately scrambled to minimize the screen before he read '*anxiety attack*' all over the Google search. *Way to be inconspicuous, Isy*, I scolded myself.

I turned to face him. "Yeah, sure, Harrison," I said too loudly to overcompensate for my jumpiness at having been caught with my hand in the proverbial cookie jar.

I got up to follow him, noticing how extremely pale and fragile he looked. Perhaps there *was* a virus going around and I had googled the wrong thing.

"Harrison, are you okay? You don't look very well. I was ill on the weekend and if you have what I did, it's a quick downward spiral. Perhaps you should head home to bed."

He didn't turn to look at me. "I'm fine," he insisted.

One hundred and ten percent commitment, as always, I thought.

I followed him into his office and took a seat across from him at his discussion table. I cursed under my breath. I'd forgotten to bring a pen and paper.

"Sorry, Harrison, I'll just get my notepad," I apologized as I started to rise.

"No need, Isy. But can you please close the door?" he replied without actually looking at me.

It was probably only because he felt unwell that he was behaving so strangely, but the fact that he called me into his office, I didn't need to take any notes *and* he wanted me to shut the door, made my stomach twist. Perhaps he wasn't going to send me on secondment after all. Perhaps he was unhappy with me about something.

I quickly did a mental recap of events before the weekend. I couldn't think of anything I had done that I should worry about. I tensed, it suddenly dawning that the incessant feeling of foreboding related to the uncomfortable conversation I was about to endure with Harrison.

Slowly, he started to speak. "You're probably wondering why I called you in here."

Freaking out, more like it, I thought.

"I just got off the phone with Jonathan's assistant, Melanie, at Parkmores." He rubbed his chin, hesitating.

His tone and behavior told me that this was *not good.* My heart started racing. The secondment was off. *No, that can't be it,* I thought. Harrison wouldn't look this uncomfortable. He'd question it, certainly—looking for any issues to be resolved or blame to be doled out—and move on with his day. I struggled to think what could disconcert his normally unshakeable composure. Had Barkleys lost the Parkmores account? I dismissed that conjecture just as quickly, concluding that Harrison would be busy telling the partners, not me. I held my breath, out of guesses.

"I don't know how to tell you this . . ." He still wasn't looking at me, keeping his eyes on the table instead.

I wanted to scream at him to just tell me. The torture of having it dragged out like this in tiny bite-size pieces was unbearable. Whatever it was, I'd rather just get it over with.

But I couldn't speak. I was still holding my breath, my apprehension swelling like a tidal wave about to come crashing down.

He continued in the same quiet voice, his gaze finally meeting mine. "Melanie informed me that Jonathan was rushed to hospital on Monday."

My heart thundered in my chest and the rush of air I drew in to fill my burning lungs sounded like a gasp.

Harrison's deflated demeanor was such a contrast to the quietly confident air he usually embodied, I was afraid to ask the next question.

"Is he . . . Is he okay?"

Sadness shrouded his expression. "Unfortunately, Isy, he passed away just after four on Monday afternoon."

Everything stood still. Time froze. I was in a bad dream. This was a bad dream. I had to wake up. I stopped breathing again. *No air, there's no air.*

Traitorous tears trickled down my face, but I refused to believe it.

"No," I said, shaking my head, "*No*."

"I'm sorry to have to tell you this, Isy. I know that you were fond of Jonathan. He certainly always had very kind words to say about you."

"No," I said again.

"I'm sorry."

Harrison remained silent and let me have my breakdown, shifting awkwardly in his chair. The tears gushed down my cheeks, my attempts at wiping them away proving to be futile because more inevitably took their place.

I put my head down on the table and sobbed uncontrollably.

No, no, no, no, no, no, no.

This could not be happening.

It wasn't supposed to happen this way.

Not Jonathan. No!

Why? Why? Why? I screamed it over and over in my head. My world was collapsing around me, pulling me into a black hole. Everything started to fall away until Harrison's hand on my arm tugged me back into the room. He attempted to console me, probably wishing he were anywhere else right now.

I'm not sure how long we stayed like that. When I eventually lifted my head from the table, Harrison's eyes were glistening.

"What happened to him?" I whispered, my throat dry.

Why hadn't I seen it? Why hadn't I saved *him?*

"He had a heart attack. No one could have imagined—he was so young and healthy. He had gone to the beach for a long weekend. They rushed him to the hospital, but the damage to his heart was too severe."

His words were swimming around my head, taunting me.

No one could have imagined. No, I didn't imagine. There were no visions, no warning. *Why?*

He was at the beach. Just like in my dream. But he looked so happy in my dream. *Why didn't I see the rest?*

Heart attack. The pressure I'd felt on my chest. That horrible pressure. *No air.*

He died just after four o'clock. The same time I thought it peaked and the worst was over. *How could I have been so wrong?*

"Are you okay, Isy?"

Harrison's words pulled me back into the room from that faraway place I had drifted to.

I looked at him blankly. How would anything ever be okay again?

"I think perhaps you should go home now, Isy. You don't have to stay at work today. This is a terrible shock to all of us. If you would like to talk to someone about it, remember there is the counseling hotline the firm has available."

I continued to look at him blankly. I could see his mouth moving, I could hear the words, but I couldn't put them together. I couldn't put anything together.

"I've organized a wreath for the funeral on behalf of the firm. I will be attending. I thought that you might like to also pay your respects. It's on Friday. We can meet at the office and go together, if you like."

I was still unresponsive. *No air, no air.*

He eyed me with concern. "We can discuss that later. Go home now, Isy. Get some rest." I could see Harrison's worried expression. I could hear the kindness in his voice. But I had no idea what was happening. I wanted to return to my faraway place.

When I didn't move, he stood and gently assisted me up. "I'll come down with you and get you a cab. Let's go and get your things."

I don't remember the cab ride home. I don't remember putting the key in the lock to my apartment. I don't know how it was that I ended up on the bathroom floor. The cold tiles felt good against my burning skin.

Everything went black.

25

BLACK HOLE

I COULD FEEL someone's hands shaking me. I forced my eyes open, resentful. *Why were they taking me away from my faraway place?* It was safe there. I didn't want to be back here.

"Isy? Isy?" The frantic voice was calling my name over and over.

Slowly, I recognized it. Jeremy.

"What?" I finally snapped, my tone not hiding my resentment. *How did he get in here?*

I opened one of my eyelids partway. He had something in his hands.

"How . . . you get . . . here?" I mumbled. Fatigue clouded my mind and cloaked my muscles. Opening even one eye was a chore.

"The door was slightly open when I got home. I was worried that someone had broken in," he replied dismissively, like the question was unimportant. *Was he speaking in fast-forward?* The words blurred together and I struggled to keep up.

I could barely see him, my eyelid slowly drifting downward.

"Isy!" he cried, shaking me. "Isy, how many of these did you take?" he demanded.

"Wha? Take . . . wha?"

My eyelid fluttered. He was holding a bottle I recognized. It contained Temazepam, a mild sedative the doctor had prescribed me months ago to help me sleep—but I didn't remember taking anything.

"Dunn . . . o," I replied, hoping he'd go away.

I was vaguely aware of him emptying the contents into his hand, counting the tiny pills. I knew the label indicated that there were twenty-five inside.

"There's fifteen here. Did you take all the rest now? Or had you taken some another time?" he probed, his voice frantic.

He was annoying me. Why couldn't he have just left me alone? I wanted to go back to sleep. I wanted to return to the blackness. I closed my eyes.

"Isy! Answer me!"

I groaned. "Be . . . fore," I responded. Hopefully that would appease him and he would leave.

"Before when? Before as in *today* or before as in a long time ago?"

"Long," I replied. I'd taken the pills for a few days when I first filled the prescription.

"Okay." He sounded slightly relieved. "So how many did you take today?" he pressed.

"Dunno," I said with more annoyance. *Why was he still bothering me?*

He released his hold on me. Finally, I could return to the blackness. But it didn't immediately enfold me back into its welcoming arms; I still knew where I was.

I heard him talking again. I could only make out a few words, something about there being ten missing. I wondered to whom he was speaking so I strained to hear the response. When I heard nothing, I presumed he was on the phone.

I let myself drift.

When consciousness once again tore through the blackness of sleep, pinpricks of awareness piercing the delicate fabric of my protection, a soft groan escaped my lips. I had no concept of how much time had passed, but I could no longer feel the hardness of the tiles beneath me. It took a moment to get my bearings, cocooned inthe softness of sheets and pillows. Someone stirred beside me and I realized I wasn't alone. For one brief blissful moment, I couldn't remember how I'd gotten here, or why. Then the floodgates reopened and a tidal wave of despair crushed me with the finality of what I knew. My breath caught and I felt strong arms tighten around me. Reluctantly, I fluttered my eyelids, accepting that the nothingness of dreamless sleep had been ripped from me. Through misty eyes I glanced up at Jeremy, who was eyeing me with concern. He lay beside me on top of the covers, holding me.

"You're awake," he murmured.

"Unfortunately," I grumbled. Outside, rain was whipping against the windows and the wind howled. The windowpane rattled, quivering under the fury of the storm. *Yes,* I thought with satisfaction, *the world should be angry*. Echoing my sentiments, thunder rumbled in the distance.

Jeremy appeared oblivious to the storm outside. Did he realize there was an even more dangerous storm brewing in here?

He brushed the hair out of my eyes, as gently as if he were stroking a kitten. "You gave me quite a scare. I would be very angry with you if I weren't so relieved. How are you feeling?"

"I wasn't trying to O.D., you know. I just wanted to sleep. But thank you for staying with me," I replied. I didn't want to answer his question. There were no words in the English language that could truly articulate the answer to that question right now.

"Of course. I'm here for you. I won't leave you. Will you tell me what's wrong?" he asked hesitantly, looking worried that it might set me off again.

I just shook my head. I couldn't say the words out loud. I couldn't make them real.

He held me as tears spilled down my cheeks, gently wiping them with his thumb from time to time.

"Is there anyone you want me to call?" he asked after a long time.

I shook my head again. Right now I felt safe in Jeremy's arms. He wouldn't make me talk. If anyone else came they would want to know what was wrong.

Where would I start? How would I explain that someone I cared about was dead and it was probably my fault?

Finally, I truly understood the implications of the all-consuming black hole that was the guilt that Mom had carried for all these years.

I remembered what she'd said when I left, about how everything would be all right. It seemed like a strange thing to say at the time since I was feeling better. Did she sense that something bad had happened?

She didn't want to tell me what I'd said when I'd been hallucinating, only saying that I'd been talking to someone and seemed upset. *Did I say something about Jonathan? Could he be the person I was talking to?* I now wondered. Why couldn't I remember?

I only knew one thing for sure: I had failed. I had failed to save Jonathan.

Jonathan who tried to help me. Jonathan who loved his family. The thought of his two young children distraught at the loss of their father propelled me into more uncontrollable sobs.

Jeremy tightened his arms around me. He didn't say a word, he just let me cry until there were no tears left.

Slowly my sadness turned to confusion.

Why had this happened? It made no sense. Jonathan had just started his new life, why was it taken away from him?

Why had I not seen it? Why hadn't I seen the end of that dream? Why hadn't I known that it wasn't a feel-good movie with a happy ending, that it was actually a horror movie instead? Was it because I was too busy gloating about my triumphs that I didn't see the truth? Too busy patting myself on the back? Had I only seen what I wanted to see? Why should Jonathan be punished for my shortcomings?

Each new question was quickly replaced by another as I tried desperately to grab hold of something—anything—that would make sense.

Was he supposed to die that first time under the scaffolding and the universe kept trying to rectify it? I tossed that thought aside. Why would I have seen the things I had if I wasn't supposed to do something about it?

How did it all work? What was its purpose?

Confusion morphed into anger. As the storm continued to rage outside, the fury inside me grew, ravaging my body like poison. The acid in my stomach burned like fire and rose in my throat.

What was the point of saving him over and over *if he was just going to die anyway!* What was the point of risking my life when his was going to end no matter what I did!

What was the point of all of this anxiety, all of the problems it had caused at work, if it was just going to end up like this in the end! What was the point!

Why? *Why!*

Would that be the end now? Now that Jonathan had died, would the visions stop? They seemed to stop after Mom's accident. Was it one strike and you're out?

Good! I screamed inside my head. *I don't want this! I don't want any of this!*

My body stiffened and Jeremy pulled me closer to him.

A horrible thought suddenly occurred to me and I trembled in fear.

If I had saved Jonathan and the universe took him anyway, was Jeremy also on borrowed time? Was Matt?

The fear took complete control of me, overriding my seething anger. I was shaking as I wept hysterically, my whole body turning cold.

"Are you okay, Isy?" Jeremy whispered with fresh panic.

The nausea hit me like a bullet train.

"I'm gonna be sick!" I screamed as I tried to wrestle free of his hold to get to the bathroom in time.

I didn't make it.

I only made it as far as the corridor.

Without saying a word, Jeremy scooped me up and put me back into bed. He returned with a glass of water for me to rinse my mouth. I closed my eyes. I couldn't bear any more. I wanted to return to the blackness.

He lay back down beside me, stroking my hair. "It's okay now," he whispered in my ear. "Go back to sleep. I'm here."

He said something else but I was already gone, the exhaustion returning like a welcome friend. I was far away, lost once more in the sweet nothingness.

* * *

A desperate need for the bathroom woke me some time later. Jeremy wasn't there. I reluctantly tore myself from the safety of my bed and stumbled down the corridor, expecting to have to jump over the mess I'd left there earlier, but to my surprise it was clean.

For a second I wondered if it had been a dream, but then I heard the water running in the bathroom. Jeremy had cleaned up my mess.

I felt terrible that he had to do something so awful. My poor, sweet Jeremy was stuck with a broken, shattered and infected friend like me.

Jeremy smiled at me as he wrung out the towel he was rinsing.

"Hi, there. How are you feeling?"

"Thank you. You didn't have to do that," I told him, jabbing my thumb towards at the towel.

"I wanted to. Friends are supposed to take care of each other, aren't they? Now what do you say to a slice of toast or something? You must be starving, and clearly, your stomach is empty," he joked as he gestured to the towel.

"No, thanks, I'm not hungry." I didn't have any desire to eat but my stomach rumbled loudly and betrayed me.

He looked at me pointedly, eyebrows raised. "I'll go and make some. Do you want me to bring it to you in bed?" he asked.

If there were such a thing as a knight in shining armor, then I had found mine. Jeremy was the best friend anyone could ever ask for. I knew he was the only thing keeping me from completely losing my mind right now and succumbing to the black hole that threatened to swallow me whole.

"I'll come and sit with you at the table. You must be hungry, too," I replied.

After I'd used the bathroom and washed my face, I found him in the kitchen with two plates ready on the table. I sat with him quietly for a few minutes, struggling to get a few bites down. I knew he wouldn't rush me. I knew that I didn't have to talk until I was ready.

"Thank you so much, Jeremy. I don't know what I would do without you."

I burst into tears as soon as the words were out of my mouth. I remembered what had caused me to throw up earlier: the fear that the same fate lay in store for Jeremy and Matt as it had for Jonathan.

Jeremy leaned over the table and put his hand on mine. "You won't ever have to find out," he assured me.

He sounded so sure, so convincing, I wanted to believe him.

"Do you want to talk about it?" he asked gently. "You don't have to until you're ready."

I knew then that I *was* ready. I needed him to know. No more secrets.

"I want to," I told him. "I want to tell you everything."

* * *

Telling Jeremy was easier than I expected. After someone had just cleaned up your vomit, it was unlikely that they would react badly to hearing about some strange dreams and flashes.

He didn't interrupt me. He let me talk, allowing me to burst open my box of secrets and divulge every detail while he continued to hold my hand.

When I finished, I waited for his reaction with my heart in my throat.

"Wow," he breathed, eyes wide. "So, on the roof . . . ?" His voice trailed off while he processed the implications of all that I'd revealed.

I nodded.

"Wow," he repeated.

"I'm sorry I didn't tell you earlier—"

He cut me off with a sharp shake of his head and a squeeze of my hand. He leaned closer, his eyes so soft that it melted my heart. "I always knew that there was something very special about you, Isy."

A fresh tear rolled down my cheek. For the first time in what felt like a very long time, this tear wasn't caused by sadness or pain, this tear was a reflection of the overwhelming love I felt for Jeremy. He made me feel so completely safe, so able to truly be myself, that I didn't know why I'd waited so long to tell him.

As quickly as the tear had escaped, Jeremy's hand was there gently wiping it away. He put his arm around my shoulders.

"Thank you. For that day on the roof. I've never thanked you for being there." He took a deep breath and whispered, "And I can't tell you how much having you in my life has meant to me."

I buried my head in the warmth of his chest, my heart swelling. He was the savior here, not me.

He stroked my hair. "I can't explain how or why any of this has happened, Isy. I wish I could. I wish I could give you the answers you need. But I can promise you three things." He gently pulled away so he could look at me, his gaze intense and resolute.

"Firstly, nothing is going to happen to me. I promise you.

"Secondly, Jonathan's death is not your fault. You can't blame yourself, you did nothing wrong. It was just his time.

"Thirdly, I will come with you to the service on Friday. You won't be alone, I will be by your side. Maybe somehow it will bring you some of the closure you need. But whatever happens"—he cupped my face in his large hands—"I will be here for you. Always."

He leaned his head towards mine and gently kissed me on the forehead.

I didn't know how I would handle the service on Friday, but I needed to be strong, I couldn't break down there. It was his family who suffered the most and I wanted to pay my respects to them. I didn't know how to say goodbye to Jonathan. I didn't know if there were any words to do that. How could I tell him how very sorry I was? I wished that I had the chance to talk to him one more time.

I only knew that Jeremy would be my tower of strength. If I might fall, he would keep me standing.

*   *   *

I didn't go to work on Thursday. It took until Thursday afternoon for me to convince Jeremy that he could leave me to go and shower and check in with his own work. I assured him it would give me time to call my mom, and so he reluctantly left, still looking at me with uncertainty as he closed the door behind him.

It took me half an hour to convince Mom not to drive down to San Francisco. I promised her that I was being taken care of, but after the service tomorrow, I needed some time alone. She unwillingly agreed on the condition that I call her every day to tell her how I was doing.

I didn't ask her about the hallucinations she said I'd had. Everything was so raw to me that I didn't think I could handle anything more right now. I knew if Mom thought it would help me, I wouldn't have to ask, she would have willingly told me. She clearly didn't think I was ready to relive it, and I wasn't.

Somehow she'd known that the burden of that knowledge had been there, lurking in my subconscious, out of reach. I'd had a physical reaction to something that my mind would never accept. Somewhere, in the very fiber of my being, I knew when it happened. But that only hurt me more. If I could only have warned him in time . . .

After I got off the phone with her, I had an overwhelming

desire to check on Matt.

I opened up my laptop and started typing him an email.

> Hi Matt
> Just wanted to say hi and make sure that everything is well with you?
> Isy

I hit SEND and impatiently waited for a response. I prayed he was at his computer and would respond quickly.

My prayer was answered. A reply came through only minutes later.

> Hi Isy
> Great to hear from you. I'm well – how are you?
> Are you free to catch up again soon – maybe drinks tomorrow night?
> Matt

I didn't know what to tell him. I was reluctant to pour out my soul via email, and I needed to explain about Jonathan in person. I suddenly felt a sense of hope; maybe Matt would have some of the answers to the many questions haunting me.

Wishing that I had one last chance to talk to Jonathan and tell him what he meant to me, what he had taught me, I decided to tell Matt how much I appreciated him. This, too, would be better said in person, but being around Matt often rendered me speechless. This was one occasion where I would much prefer not to have to look at him.

I started typing.

> I can't tomorrow – I'm attending a funeral service for a friend.
> Life is far too fleeting – like you said, it's important to tell the ones you care about that you love them, while you have the chance to do it.
> I think you are an incredible person, Matt. I appreciate your friendship and I thank you for all of the support you've given me.
> Your friendship means so much to me.
> I have things to tell you – maybe drinks next week?
> Isy

I waited anxiously for a reply. I had never been so forthcoming with my emotions, so exposed.

My heart beat a little faster wondering what he would reply. Would he tell me that I was special to him as well?

I waited. This time I knew he was at his computer and would've seen my email.

The longer I waited, the more I worried that he was taking too long to respond. Was he concerned about the words he used? Was he worried about giving me the wrong impression? Had I given *him* the wrong impression?

I reread the email I had just sent him. Had I said too much? I'd sent it so quickly that I hadn't carefully edited it like I usually would have with Matt. I caught sight of the word *love—would that freak him out?* I wondered. I hadn't said that I loved him, I only used the word in the general sense. But I did tell him that

I had things to tell him—and maybe he thought that meant a declaration of love was on the horizon.

Maybe he was freaking out.

I certainly was when an hour passed without a response.

If he hasn't responded by now, I thought, *then he won't respond at all.*

What had I done?

I couldn't deal with this right now. It was too much.

Fear turned to anger. He could've at least sent his condolences if nothing else. *It was just plain rude to* completely *ignore me*, I thought.

I closed my laptop. I tried to put him out of my mind. I could only deal with so much pain at any one time and I was already at my quota, my cup runneth over.

If I had made Matt uncomfortable, if he was worried about blurring the lines of our friendship, that was something I would have to think about another time. There would undoubtedly be many hours ahead for me to torture myself about it. Right now I had worse sins to consume me, and more regret than any one person could handle.

26

THE LIGHT AFTER THE STORM

JEREMY STAYED WITH ME again that night. I felt guilty that he had to babysit me but I was relieved he was there.

He escorted me to the service at Grace Cathedral on Nob Hill, the beautiful French Gothic architecture looming over us in its grandeur and making my breath catch. Today the towering cathedral seemed imposing, casting ominous shadows that wrapped around those entering its doors like tendrils. I squinted in the sun. It didn't seem right that the world had stopped being angry. The heavens should be crying, too. Where was the rain?

Jeremy squeezed my hand and pulled me along, sensing my hesitation. He didn't let go of my hand the entire time—not that he could have since I was glued to him. Without his strength, I knew I would shatter into a million pieces.

We met Harrison outside and entered the cathedral together, choosing to stay near the back. The number of people was overwhelming.

His brother, Michael, gave the eulogy. It was so touching, so heartfelt, that it brought the entire congregation to tears. He spoke of the wonderful big brother Jonathan had been, and the incredible father he had become. His wife, Miranda, gave Michael something to read on her behalf, sharing stories of the remarkable life they had together and the overwhelming love he had for his children. She described in detail the happy memories of the family vacations they had just taken together. She praised him for his warmth, his humor, his commitment, and his renewed zest for life.

At the end of the service, they played a slideshow of photos, starting with pictures of Jonathan as a young boy in England through to his teenage and then adult years. I looked at the photos of his graduation, his wedding, the birth of his children. I saw the joy in his eyes. As the pallbearers stood in preparation to lift the coffin, the more recent photos of Jonathan flashed up on the screen.

A steady stream of tears cascaded down my cheeks as I saw the pictures: standing with his children at Disneyland, playing in a pool with his daughter on his shoulders, and pitching a tent in the backyard with his son proudly holding a hammer beside him.

I couldn't contain the flood of tears leaking onto my shirt. Jeremy squeezed me tighter to him and I rested my head on his shoulder, drawing from his strength. Then I saw it: the last picture. The one they left on the screen as the soft music concluded the service and they carried the coffin out of the church.

It was a photo of Jonathan with his family at the beach. The sky was a never-ending blue and the sun shone brightly on them, causing Jonathan to squint as he smiled widely. His son was sitting on his right shoulder with Jonathan's hand securing him in place. I imagined that the little boy must have felt on top of the world. Jonathan's free hand was open, gesturing towards the sand. He was proudly pointing towards the sand castle that he had just made with his son. On the other side of him, his wife and daughter crouched next to their sand castle, beaming.

I froze. It was exactly as I had dreamed.

I wondered if after that photo had been taken, Jonathan and Sammy had playfully chased Miranda and Dalia into the water.

I'd told Jeremy about the dream, so he understood the significance of this photo.

He squeezed my shoulder and whispered in my ear, "You made that happen."

Then he kissed me on the cheek and gently pulled me up, almost carrying me out of the church. I barely felt my feet touch the ground.

Later at the cemetery when my knees buckled as the coffin was slowly lowered into the ground, he clutched me to him, his hold as strong as the pole that secures a flag whipping in the wind.

I couldn't bear the sight of Jonathan's wife and children overcome with grief. Miranda was being strong for her two small children, cradling them both in her arms, with one child on each side of her.

Harrison went to pay his respects to the family, but I declined his offer to join him.

"Don't you want to go, too?" Jeremy asked me after Harrison walked away.

"I . . . I don't think I should," I responded.

"Why not? Stop blaming yourself, Isy. This wasn't your fault.

You're not God and you don't have the power to decide everyone's fate." He said the words quietly so no one would hear them but his uncompromising tone was still audible. He looked at me with determination. "Let's go."

I didn't have the strength to fight him, particularly given that I was glued to his right side. A part of me did want to talk to Jonathan's wife and tell her how deeply sorry I was, so I let him lead me over to her.

As we approached, I desperately tried to think of what to say to her. No words seemed right.

All too quickly, I was standing in front of her, still searching for the words.

I extended my hand to her. "Mrs. Hawkins, I'm so deeply, deeply sorry for your loss. I worked with Jonathan and he often spoke very proudly of you and your beautiful children."

"Thank you, ah . . . ?"

"Isabel. I work at Barkleys," I explained.

Her eyes softened and she released my hand to fold her arms around me. I was stunned.

"Isabel, I'm so very pleased to meet you. Jonathan spoke fondly of you and he told me that you were with him when that car nearly ran you both down. I can't tell you how much I appreciate what you did. He said you saved his life that day."

She released me, her eyes swimming with fresh tears. I hadn't expected her to know me, let alone thank me. Her gratitude gave the burgeoning black hole a greedy feast of newfound guilt and sorrow. I didn't deserve her gratitude. I hadn't saved him. Not when it mattered.

I didn't know how to respond. "I wish that . . . I wish that . . ."

was all that I could mutter.

She seemed to understand what I was alluding to: I wished that he were still here now, that I could have done more.

She nodded her head and took my hand again.

"He called you his guardian angel, you know."

"I'm sorry that I wasn't a better one," I admitted. I couldn't express how truly, deeply sorry I was.

She looked at me with those same warm eyes. Her voice was soft. "Isabel, I don't know if you realize this, but you didn't just save Jonathan from being hurt that day. You saved my marriage. You saved my family.

"The past two and a half months that we had together were magical. He was a different man. Actually, *different* is the wrong word—he was the same man he was when we were first married. The Jonathan I loved that laughed until he cried, that was playful and happy. He found his spark again.

"You gave my children their father. Because of you, they had a chance to really bond with him. Because of you, they have very happy memories of their time with him, and they will always remember how very much he loved them.

"I can't think of a better definition of a guardian angel than that."

My breath caught as a sob escaped my throat and I threw my arms around her. In the midst of her overwhelming loss, it was she who was comforting me. I was supposed to be supporting her, not the other way around. Her amazing strength both astonished and inspired me.

"Thank you," I whispered. "But I think it was Jonathan who was *my* guardian angel. He taught me so much, more than I could ever tell you. It was an honor to know him and I will never forget the wonderful man that he was."

"Thank you, Isabel. That means a lot to me. And thank you for coming today."

I gently squeezed her hand once more before taking Jeremy's hand again and walking back to the car.

He didn't need to wrap himself around me to hold me up now. I was able to feel the earth beneath me as I walked. I squinted as the sun shone on my face and imagined Jonathan squinting back at me, smiling and waving as he had in my dream.

* * *

That night I sent Jeremy home to get a good night's sleep. He offered to stay with me and I almost relented, having gotten used to him being there with me. But I knew that after spending the past two days with me, he had his own life to get back to.

I was feeling a lot better after speaking with Miranda. Jeremy was right—it had helped bring some sense of closure, shrinking the black hole that had threatened to engulf me.

I let go of my anger: at not having seen what was going to happen to Jonathan, at having risked so much only to lose him, and at myself for feeling that I'd failed him somehow. I let it all go.

I finally realized why I hadn't had a premonition of what would happen to Jonathan: I wasn't supposed to.

I wasn't supposed to be there. There was absolutely nothing that I could have done, nothing that anyone could have done.

It happened as it was supposed to happen.

Each vision I had seen of Jonathan had had the same purpose.

It took the incident with the car to finally achieve it: to help Jonathan get to the path that he was meant to follow. It was not to change his destiny, or his destination, merely the path that he traveled to get there.

I finally understood. After all of the confusion, all of the anguish, it seemed so clear to me.

All of those times that I thought I was saving Jonathan, he was really saving me.

It was true that Jonathan was my guardian angel. Just as I had been able to give him the time he needed to find his path, he had shown me the signs to finally walk my own. The signs to help me navigate my own journey and to help me find what would give me back my own spark.

Up until now, I had treated each day as a stepping stone, a means to an end. I was always looking ahead to the next goal to be achieved, the next finish line I saw ahead of me. Galloping like a horse with blinders on, that was what I thought I needed to do in order to be successful.

The sign that Jonathan gave me did not have an arrow pointing north, south, east or west. The sign he gave me had a check mark on it, the kind they have on maps to show you where you are right now: *'You Are Here.'*

Instead of worrying about where I should go next, it was time to plant my feet and look around me. To appreciate the beauty and the opportunities in this very moment. To stop worrying about what might happen in the future and to concentrate on what was happening right now in the present.

I had initially resented the visions I had because I thought they might jeopardize my future; I didn't stop to appreciate the gifts they gave me in the present.

I'd always been afraid of the unknown. As Mom had pointed out, I only pursued that which I knew I would be good at, that which had clearly-defined paths and destinations.

I gazed at the painting hanging in my living room—the painting that Julia had given to me in Florence. *"The white section in the middle is the unknown,"* she had said, *"Find out what's in that space."* I looked at the patch of white now and smiled.

I picked up the phone to call her.

When she heard the fatigue in my voice and asked me what was wrong, I relayed everything that had happened over the past week.

"Oh, Isy, I'm so sorry," she breathed, the heartbreak evident in her voice.

"Me too, Jules. He was such a wonderful person. My heart goes out to his family. I pray they'll be okay."

"You should've called me earlier. It must've been so hard for you, so confusing," she empathized.

"Let's just say that I wasn't in a good place. But Jeremy was incredible and he took excellent care of me. I couldn't ask for a better friend."

"Oh. That's good." Her tone reflected her sadness that she was so far away.

"And, of course, Mom had her turn taking care of me as well. Seems that I've needed a lot of babysitting lately," I admitted.

"What about Matt? Have you checked your email to see if he responded yet?" she encouraged.

"No, Jules, but I have a feeling that he's not going to. I don't want to think about it now."

"Why? Humor me and check now while you're on the phone, would you?" she coaxed. "Please?"

I relented. "Fine, but I'll be telling you the same thing in a minute."

Sighing, I checked my email while she waited. My intuition was correct, there was nothing waiting for me from Matt. There was a horde of work emails glaring at me, though, so I quickly closed my laptop.

"Nothing, like I told you," I reported. "But you know what, Jules? I don't regret sending it. I took the opportunity to tell him how I felt. Life is too short to let those opportunities pass us by. If it made him feel uncomfortable, well if it wasn't now then sometime in the future it would eventually have ended up the same way. Perhaps this is exactly how it's supposed to be. Perhaps this is the patch of white from your painting. And if that's the case, I'm okay with it."

"Are you really? Or are you just saying that?" she challenged.

Now that she'd forced me to think about it, I realized it was true. "No, really. Don't get me wrong, I will definitely miss him, miss his friendship. He was so easy to talk to and it was like he really understood me. We just connected.

"But the fact is that I developed feelings for him that I shouldn't have for a friend. It meant that the friendship was ultimately doomed. At least I know that there is someone like him out there in the world—someone I can feel that bond with who won't judge me, but will support me, even when I'm crazy and insane. He didn't just tolerate my craziness, he seemed to be able to help guide me.

"Maybe that's all he was ever supposed to be—a guide when I

needed one. When the time is right, the right person will come into my life. And until then—as my mom put it—I should enjoy being single." I tried to laugh, but it was half-hearted. Jonathan had put everything into perspective. My infatuation with Matt rated pretty low on the scale right now.

"Well, Is, you have caught me by surprise there. I assumed you would be eating yourself up with regret. I'm so impressed by your positive attitude, I give you a gold star, Ms. Cartier," she teased.

"Gee, thanks," I said sarcastically. "It helps that I know I won't be running into him. I wouldn't be so positive if I had to work with him or anything like that. Then I'd be freaking out like the neurotic Isy you expected and you'd be giving me a time-out in the corner instead."

Jules laughed. "That's my girl. You still don't know that he won't email you, though—the real question is what you'll say if he does," she noted with interest.

"I doubt I'll have to worry about that. I'm not going to spend all of my energy thinking about things that aren't likely to happen—it's all part of my new live-life-in-the-now mantra. I'm not going to worry about '*might*'s. I imagine that'll give me another gold star, hey, Jules?"

There was a brief moment of silence.

"Unless of course you're so surprised by my newfound maturity that your mouth is still on the floor," I said, happy for the distraction from more serious topics.

"I feel like I'm in some weird sci-fi body-snatching movie. I'm sorry—who are you and what have you done with my best friend?" she mocked.

"I got rid of the whiny, obsessive girl. She was annoying me,"

I retorted.

"Well, I suppose one less lawyer in the world . . ." she said playfully.

"Is a better world—yeah, I got it. Well, good night Jules—and beware, the body-snatchers might come for the sarcastic, annoyingly enthusiastic girl giving out gold stars next."

She chuckled. "I'll consider myself warned. Night, Is. Speak soon."

I hung up the phone and called Mom. I knew she would be waiting for my call.

As I was speaking with her, there was a knock at the door. I opened it to find Jeremy.

"Delivery," he smiled, handing me the take-out food he'd bought from the local Chinese restaurant. The delicious smell of prawn dumplings wafted into the apartment, making my stomach growl.

I took the bag and smiled. "I love you," I told him, without any fear of the *L* word.

And I did.

27

PARALLEL UNIVERSE

IT DIDN'T TURN OUT the way I thought it would.

Harrison offered to act as General Counsel for Parkmores until they found a replacement for Jonathan, and organized for me to take a one-month temporary assignment, to start immediately.

So even while I was on secondment to Parkmores, Harrison was still my boss.

The team was lovely but the mood there was, of course, somber. It wasn't easy to go there every day with reminders of Jonathan everywhere. I did enjoy working with people who knew him so well, though; they spoke of him often and it felt good to honor him.

Harrison kept a close eye on me. At times I thought he had eyes in the back of his head. I knew he was taking note of whether I seemed to prefer to work for a corporation in an in-house role rather than at a law firm like Barkleys.

And I did.

This type of role had its own challenges, but the atmosphere was different. Harrison was swamped, as expected, but the role I was in didn't require me to work into the night. Internally at Parkmores, the perception of the legal team was not ideal, they were seen as a necessary evil. But the balance the team seemed to achieve was far greater than I'd experienced working at Barkleys.

I had been there for two weeks when I got a call from Marie, the receptionist at Barkleys.

"I've got a delivery of flowers here for you, Isy. What do you want me to do with them?" she asked.

This took me by surprise. *Who on earth was sending me flowers?* I wondered.

Jeremy. That man was the sweetest man to walk the earth. He must have forgotten to send them to me at Parkmores.

"Do you want me to check the card and tell you who they're from?" Her voice was dripping with curiosity.

"No, thanks, Marie, I know who they're from. Can you please courier them over to me here?" The idea of someone else reading my card before I did wasn't exactly appealing.

"Sure, no problem. So are they from the doctor who sent you the flowers the last time?" she probed.

All credit to Marie, she had the memory of an elephant and she wasn't afraid to pry.

"No. Sorry to disappoint you, Marie, but I don't hear from him anymore. These are from a friend—no juicy story, I'm afraid."

"Oh well, still a lovely gesture," she chirped. "I'll send them straight over."

They arrived within the hour. Harrison raised his brow as he spied me carrying the beautiful arrangement to my desk. Knowing his paranoia, he was probably worried they were from someone at Parkmores trying to entice me to stay. The suspicious look in his eye amused me and I stifled a chuckle. His concerns were unwarranted—the only person from Parkmores who might have sent me flowers was Jonathan. The thought saddened me. I missed him.

I placed the flowers on the corner of my desk and admired their beauty. I picked up the phone to call Jeremy before deciding I should probably read the card first.

When I saw the name at the bottom, the card nearly fell out of my hands.

> *My sincerest sympathy for the loss of your friend.*
> *Thinking of you,*
> *Matt*

Oh. My. Lord.

What? Why?

I hadn't heard from Matt since I sent him that email nearly two weeks ago. Not a single word. Nothing.

He had ignored my invitation to drinks, even though he knew I had something to tell him and it was he who had asked me to talk to him in the first place. Given his lack of response, I'd assumed I would never hear from him again.

I'd resigned myself to that fact. Accepted it. Decided it was probably best. This strange new development was only going to bring me straight back to the same issues with him and I would have to deal with the drama of it all over again.

Mixed emotions whirled inside me. *If he was speaking to me, why had he ignored me for so long?*

I couldn't stay annoyed for long, though, the flowers were too beautiful. Confusion, on the other hand, continued to cloud every thought in my head.

I wasn't sure what to do, whether I should call to thank him.

I laughed to myself as a familiar sense of déjà vu swept over me and I recalled facing this exact same dilemma the first time he sent me flowers. I decided to go with the same solution as before: a short email. This time, though, I didn't agonize over it.

> Matt
>
> Thank you for the lovely flowers.
>
> Isy

That was about all I wanted to say. I hit SEND.

I didn't receive an immediate reply so I returned my focus to work. There was no point obsessing about something that made absolutely no sense to me.

At 6:00 P.M., I started to pack up and head home. As I was about to shut down my computer, a familiar ping announced the arrival of a new email in my Inbox.

> Isy
>
> I'm glad you got the flowers. I'm sorry for the delay in getting them to you.
>
> I hope you've been okay – I'm so sorry I haven't been

> there for you during this difficult time.
> Can we please meet for dinner? I can pick something up and swing by your apartment if you're not up to going out.
> Tonight if you're free?
> Whatever you need – I'm here.
> Love,
> Matt

Oh. My. Lord.

The words jumped off the screen and swirled around me in a blur.

Not a single word for two weeks and now he wants to meet for dinner—tonight. Why?

It didn't escape my attention that he signed it: *Love, Matt.*

That was new.

I was so confused, I sat staring at the screen for a minute, motionless.

I considered telling him that I was busy, but there was only one way for me not to drive myself crazy trying to figure out what was going through his mind.

I hit REPLY and began typing a response when I was interrupted by the buzzing of my cell phone. I welcomed the distraction and picked it up, not recognizing the number.

"Hello. Isabel Cartier."

"Hi, Isy. It's Matt."

I was rendered speechless, my mouth on the floor.

"I'm sorry to disturb you. I thought perhaps it would be better to talk to you rather than email. Did you get a chance to read the last email I sent you?"

There was a pause as I struggled to find my breath. "Ah-ha," I muttered.

"Look, I know that you're probably annoyed with me that I took so long to get back to you and now it's strange that I'm calling you out of the blue and asking you to dinner."

I nodded, knowing he couldn't see me. At least he wasn't ignoring the obvious. He waited for a response and continued when he didn't get one.

"I know you probably don't feel up to going out, but please let me come over."

I was too busy trying to process this to answer him. Good idea? Bad idea? It was just plain weird, I'd fallen into a parallel universe.

"Isy?"

Might as well find out where this was going. "Um, okay."

"Are you free tonight?"

"Oookay . . ." He was clearly determined. It was up to Bizarro-world Isy to deal with this now.

"Eight o'clock?"

"Okay . . ."

"Great. Email me the address and I'll see you then. Thanks, Isy, I look forward to seeing you."

"Okay . . . Bye."

I was at a complete loss for words.

I was on autopilot for the rest of the evening. In a daze, I walked into my apartment and threw myself on the couch. I turned on the television, trying to drown out my thoughts. Ordinarily, I would change out of my work clothes as soon as I walked in the door but I didn't think my sweat pants would be a good look for my visitor. I kicked off my shoes and remained zombie-like on the couch.

Matt arrived on time. I buzzed him into the building and before I knew it, he was knocking at my door.

Keep it together, I muttered quietly to myself.

I opened the door, trying to maintain my composure.

Matt was standing there—looking far too handsome for my liking—smiling and holding two bags in his hands.

"Hi, Isy. I didn't know what you felt like so I got some Japanese and some Italian," he explained as he held up the bags. "Can I come in?" he asked when I didn't move, still in zombie form.

I pulled myself together. "Of course. Sorry," I mumbled and moved aside to let him enter.

He took a quick look around my apartment as he placed the bags on the table.

"Nice place," he complimented.

"Thanks," I replied as I followed behind him. "And thanks for bringing dinner."

I started towards the kitchen to fetch some plates and cutlery, but as soon as he put the bags down and I was close enough, he reached out and hugged me.

The warmth of his embrace took me off guard. He held me closely to him and I could feel the contours of his chest, his spicy scent enveloping me. Despite my best efforts, my heart instantly began to race.

"I'm so sorry about your friend and for not coming sooner," he whispered in my ear. "Tonight's the first chance I had to come."

I felt his warm breath on my neck. I worried that he was

holding me too closely not to feel my reaction so I immediately pulled myself away.

"That's okay," I responded as I broke free. "I'll get some plates." I tried to keep my voice even and nonchalant to compensate for the betrayal of my racing heart and trembling body.

He opened up the containers as I sat down next to him. I went straight for the Japanese food. It looked delicious.

"Oh, good, you like Japanese," he noted, seeming pleased with his selection of food.

"Love it," I confessed.

He smiled. "So, you said that you had something to tell me. What is it?" he probed.

I paused, hesitant. "It was about Jonathan. I don't really want to talk about it now, though, if you don't mind."

"Jonathan? Did something else happen? I hope you didn't face down a runaway train this time," he joked, before turning serious. "Oh, Isy, I'm sorry I wasn't there to help you after I promised you that I would be. I'm really sorry." He leaned over and touched my hand as he spoke, the remorse evident in his eyes.

"It's okay, there was nothing you could do," I assured him.

"Why? What happened?" His expression immediately changed to one of concern. "You're okay, though?" He looked me up and down, appraising my physical condition.

I nodded.

"And Jonathan?"

I shook my head and tears welled in my eyes.

I saw him put the pieces together in his head. He stiffened.

"Your friend? It was *Jonathan*?" he gasped.

I nodded again.

"Oh, Isy! I had no idea! I'm so sorry. How are you? Were you there? Were you in danger?" His words spilled from him in a rush, rippling through the air and shifting the temperature in the room.

"I wasn't there. He was with his family. He had a heart attack," I explained, answering his questions. "Let's not talk about it now—please," I begged as I got up from the table. "I forgot to get some drinks. I'll open a bottle of wine."

I needed the distraction. I wanted to stop the conversation there. I needed to hear what he had come here to tell me and if I got too emotional before he started, I didn't think I would hold up.

I pulled out a bottle of wine and turned to get the glasses when Matt was suddenly in the kitchen beside me.

He wrapped his arms around me again and pulled me tightly to his chest.

"I'm so sorry," he whispered again.

I wriggled free of his hold. If he kept holding me so tightly and I kept thinking about Jonathan, I would surely end up in a flood of tears.

I tried to focus on the task at hand. I pulled two wine glasses from the cupboard and placed them on the kitchen counter.

"Thank you for the lovely email that you sent me. It meant a lot to me," he said as he tried to look into my eyes. He spoke quietly, standing only inches away.

I avoided his gaze, keeping my eyes on the glasses in front of me.

"You mean a lot to me, too," he breathed.

He continued to try to catch my gaze but I resisted. I wasn't sure where this conversation was going.

I heard him sigh as he realized that I wouldn't look at him. He put his finger under my chin and gently turned my head towards him so that he could look into my eyes. I knew that resistance was futile. This time it was me who sighed as I conceded and looked at him.

He was standing so close to me that I could feel his warm breath on my face. I put my left hand on the kitchen counter to steady myself.

"I've never met anyone like you. You never cease to surprise me."

He moved his hand from beneath my chin and gently caressed my cheek as he spoke. He searched my eyes, trying to gage my reaction. My skin burned under his touch.

He cupped my face with both hands. With his mesmerizing eyes still locked on mine, he continued. "I'm completely taken by you."

His piercing blue eyes were magnetic and I got lost swimming in them. *What was happening?* What exactly was he saying?

He moved his left hand to clutch the back of my head and slowly pulled my face towards his, until his lips were on mine.

I'd definitely entered an alternate universe. Every thought was exiled from my mind. Slowly his lips became more forceful, more urgent.

He squeezed me so tightly that he cut off my airway. It didn't matter, I couldn't breathe anyway, my mouth was completely entwined with his.

His hands ran up and down my back leaving warm tingles

across my skin, finally resting at my lower back when he released his lips from mine.

There was something, something I was supposed to remember . . . Coherent thoughts seemed to be on the peripheral, dancing around just slightly out of reach.

He wrapped his arms around me once more. This time I didn't stiffen, I didn't try to escape. My arms encircled his waist and I pressed my face against his chest. I could hear his heart beating. It was racing, just like mine.

"Matt . . ." I started.

His lips found mine once more and I willingly surrendered to him. His hands found their way to the buttons on my blouse.

"Matt, wait," I gasped. I finally remembered what was bothering me and I needed to ask the question before I got lost in the moment again.

"What is it?" he breathed seductively as his lips caressed my cheek, tickling my skin.

"What about . . . your fiancée?" I stuttered.

I wished that I could forget about his fiancée and melt into his arms. Surely him being here was the answer I needed, but I wanted to hear the words. I waited to hear him say that he'd called off the wedding, that he couldn't marry her when he had feelings for me. *Why would he be here otherwise?* This would explain his two-week silence—he'd been busy sorting everything out. It all made sense now. *I should feel guilty about him ending their engagement,* my inner voice whispered. I was too caught in the moment to worry about it, but I knew I'd be agonizing over it later.

His lips moved towards mine again and I put my hand on his

chest, waiting expectantly for the confirmation I needed.

"Don't worry," he reassured me. I unclenched my jaw and started to relax.

"Eliza's in Chicago. We have all night."

I allowed him to momentarily pull me closer as the words replayed in my head, slowly sinking in.

Eliza's in Chicago.

We have all night.

The wedding was *not* off. Was never going to be off.

I stiffened as the words became like the blade of a sword plowing straight into my chest and the realization of his proposition hit me with the full force of a bullet train. The room spun around me.

He was far from my knight in shining armor.

He did not truly care about me.

He would never actually love me.

And he was planning to cheat on his fiancée. Why would I ever want to be with a man who would be capable of that?

Suddenly Jeremy's words came rushing back to me, taunting me: *Be careful of his intentions.* If only I'd listened. If only I'd heeded his advice.

Matt's hands once again wandered to the buttons on my blouse and I slapped them away. After the initial shock had surged through me, anger radiated from my core.

Matt's eyebrows pulled together, the confusion etched on his face. "What's wrong?"

"What's wrong? What's *wrong*!" I roared, my voice like the growl of a tiger reverberating in the room. "Um, how about the fact that I thought you actually cared about me when all you wanted was a one-night-stand!"

He cringed. "I do care about you, Isy. I never lied to you about being engaged. This whole situation is complicated—"

"I think the only person you really care about here, Matt, is you! You're not at all the person I thought you were. You're just a cheating, arrogant asshole."

He flinched, clearly taken aback by my sudden outburst and complete change in temperature. I was gearing up to really launch into him, unleashing all of the adrenalin pumping through my veins.

"Who do you think I am? Who do you think *you* are!" I thundered, about to tear him a new one. "How dare you!"

I raised my hand, itching to slap him, when his words penetrated through the force field of rage enshrouding me. *I never lied to you about being engaged.* It was true: he hadn't lied, he hadn't promised me anything. It was me who had walked straight into this situation, fantasizing about something that was impossible right from the beginning. And suddenly I understood that part of the reason why I'd allowed myself to open up to him was because I always knew that he was unavailable. I never had to worry about being truly vulnerable because he could never leave me if we were never together. The sudden clarity of this realization ushered a tornado of emotion, as anger, guilt and shame all whirled within me.

My misguided feelings didn't make him any less presumptuous to think that I was okay with his proposition. I knew I was worth more than that. I knew his fiancée deserved better than that. I conveniently ignored the fact that I'd been secretly hoping they'd call off their engagement and felt enraged on her behalf about his lack of respect.

I felt like someone had thrown a bucket of ice water over me and I was starting to wake up from a dream, seeing everything for the first time as it really was.

Slowly, I managed to subdue the volcanic eruption that threatened to spill from me, wiping out everything in its path: mainly, Matt. The horror still bubbled under the surface, but I withdrew from myself like an out-of-body experience, before the humiliation and hurt could consume me and I lost all rational thought. I instinctively converted to lawyer mode, taking on the persona of a lawyer standing in a courtroom, making an argument with the requisite emotional distance from the party bringing suit. I spoke matter-of-factly, like counsel representing their client, rather than someone who was just minutes ago all over the opposing party.

"Isy—"

I cut him off. "I appreciate that I hold my share of the blame but you completely took advantage of my vulnerability. And whether you did it intentionally or not, you made me think that this was more than it was, that it meant more than it did. But just so we're clear—this is *never* going to happen and I think you should leave."

"Isy—"

"I don't want to hear it, Matt. I feel stupid enough as it is."

"Isy," he persisted, "regardless of what you think, I *do* care about you. I've been genuine about that. I just don't know what to do. I don't want to hurt you and I don't want to hurt Eliza. I don't know if I can marry her when I have feelings for you. But I've made a commitment and I'm torn in two different directions. I tried not to make whatever's between us more than it should be, I even tried to keep away, but I couldn't stop my feelings for you. I had to come and see you. I had to find out how you felt. And I felt awful about not being there for you when you needed me. I wish things weren't so complicated. Hurting you is tearing me up inside. I love you, Isy—"

"I really, *really* don't want to hear this," I snapped, taking a step back. "You came here to find out how I felt? Why? So you'd know whether it was worth ending your engagement tomorrow, next week, next month? Or whether I'd be okay with being the other woman? The answer is no to both. Regardless of whether you planned to leave your fiancée *afterwards*, cheating is cheating." I took a deep breath. "This was a terrible mistake and I just want to pretend it never happened. Please go."

Lawyer-mode would only take me so far; unwanted tears were en route and I wanted to hold onto whatever dignity I had left, as little as it was. I wanted to cry in private and berate myself alone.

He lifted his hand to touch me, a pained expression shadowing his features, but I threw him a warning look that he'd lose it and he lowered his hand.

He sighed. "I've handled this all wrong. I don't want you to think that I was just looking for a one-night stand or to string you along. That you mean nothing to me. I meant it when I said I love you. I've never been unfaithful to Eliza and that wasn't my intention when I came here—"

"*Please go.*" I straightened my shoulders and staked him with a run-if-you-value-your-life look.

"Okay," he agreed, raising both hands in surrender, "let's erase this whole evening and start over. I'll talk to Eliza. And I'll call you in a couple of weeks."

Somehow I very much doubted that. I walked over to the door and opened it. "I think we both know that whatever this was, it's over. Let's not pretend otherwise. I wish you well, but I want you to leave and I never want you to contact me again. Goodbye, Matt."

He looked like he wanted to say something, but thought better of it. His eyes glistened as he hesitated in the doorway. He took one last look at me, saying very softly, "I'm so sorry, Isy. More than you know," before disappearing into the corridor and walking out of my life.

28

DECLARATIONS

I BURST INTO TEARS the moment I closed the door. How could I have been so foolish? How could I have been so naïve?

All of this time, believing that destiny was bringing us together.

All of this time, playing with fire and fooling myself.

I should have known better.

How could it possibly have ended well? I scolded myself.

Even if he had left his fiancée—*before* declaring his love for me—the guilt of causing that to happen would have always gnawed at me. It was always a lose-lose situation, there never could have been a positive outcome.

Remorseful tears soaked my skin. I always knew it was just a fantasy, but tonight he let me believe for one moment that it could be real, and then pulled that belief right out from under me. I witnessed the foundations ripping and shredding, until I came crashing down with a heart-breaking thud.

I'd lost Jonathan, and now I'd lost Matt, too. His friendship was gone, we could never go back.

I couldn't bear the weight of it.

As I buried my face in a pillow, I remembered that Jules had once made the observation that everyone in my visions had taught me something. I scoffed. What had Matt taught me?

That I'm a big, stupid fool! I thought.

Attempting to revert back to my logical lawyer mode, I reviewed the facts. Why had I clung to a romantic version of him? My earlier insight came back to me. He made me see that I had a propensity to always gravitate toward the safest option: If I knew he was unavailable from the start, then he could never really hurt me, never leave me.

Except that he had.

It wasn't such a safe option after all. I'd walked the most dangerous line I could.

Somewhere in the deepest recesses of my mind I was conscious that I was crying over a version of Matt that I had created, that existed only within the fantasy of him that I had manifested. My Matt understood me completely. He would never have thought it okay to spend the night with me while he was engaged to someone else. *My* Matt was not that selfish and self-absorbed.

The real Matt, on the other hand, was.

I was crying over a fictional character I'd created in the play that I alone had written, and I alone was watching.

I should have paid more attention to the actor playing the character I wanted him to play. He had most of the same characteristics and demeanor, but I couldn't force him to be something other than he was, just like I couldn't force life to turn out the way I wanted.

I should have realized this already by everything that had happened with Jonathan.

Matt had helped me when I was desperate to find someone who would understand. He'd been caring and kind. And despite how things turned out, I was thankful for his friendship during that challenging time.

I once envied his fiancée. Now I just pitied her. I pitied them both.

I remembered the bottle of wine in the kitchen and I decided there was no point in letting it go to waste. As I reluctantly pulled myself out of the fetal position I'd curled into on the couch, there was a knock on the door.

Great. Matt had either left something behind or was coming back to try and make amends. Either way, I couldn't bear him to see me this way: puffy eyes, disheveled hair and Rudolph-the-red-nose-reindeer nose.

"Go away, Matt," I called out, trying not to let my voice shake.

"Isy, it's Jeremy. Are you okay?"

Poor Jez, always catching me at my worst. "Yeah, I'm fine," I called back.

"You don't sound fine. Can I come in?"

Knowing he was going to be persistent, I relented and opened the door. He'd seen me looking far worse than this. Heck, he'd cleaned up my vomit. Puffy eyes, messy hair and a snotty nose surely wouldn't frighten him. There were no illusions of grace and elegance with Jeremy. That ship had well and truly sailed.

When I opened the door, I immediately saw the concern in his eyes. He appraised my condition with a fleeting glance up and down, assessing the damage. "What's wrong, Is?"

I stepped into his arms, seeking the familiar comfort there, and let the tears flow freely. Jeremy enfolded me, gently stroking my hair and letting me cry on his shoulder for as long as I needed.

"You were right," I finally said, my face still buried in his chest.

"About what?"

"About being careful of a man's intentions. Turns out I'm an idiot." I sniffled and wiped my face on his shirt. A very charming gesture that I'm sure he appreciated. But he didn't flinch or complain, he just kept his arms wound tightly around me.

"Do you want to talk about it?"

"No, not really, it's too embarrassing."

"No one hurt you, did they? Because so help me, I'll—"

"No, nothing like that," I interrupted, hearing the trepidation in his voice and wanting to dissipate his fears. "I'm okay, really. Just feeling a little wounded and foolish."

"Tell me what happened," he soothed. I knew he thought he could make it better just by being there. And the truth was: he could.

I sniffled, unwilling to extricate myself from the warmth of his embrace. "I was crazy enough to delude myself into thinking that he truly cared about me. But he wasn't as honorable as I thought, he was hedging his bets."

"This is that guy who sent you those flowers, isn't it?" Jeremy asked, his tone shifting. I'd never really spoken much about Matt in front of Jez; for some reason, it had always felt strange, even though Jeremy and I were just friends.

Jeremy grumbled something low under his breath. I wasn't

sure if he was disapproving of my stupidity or Matt's.

He didn't scold me as I expected. Instead, he tightened his arms around me. "Isy, it's not crazy to think that he cared about you. He probably did in his own way, drawn to you like a moth to a flame. You tend to have that effect on people. I mean, look at you," he said as he pulled me back just far enough to look into my eyes, before pulling me close once more. "Well, maybe not right *now* . . ." I could hear the smile in his voice before he became earnest again.

"You are the most amazing person I have ever met. And not only are you completely charming in all of your neuroses, but you're the bravest and most caring person I know. There's nothing you wouldn't do to help someone, no matter how risky or dangerous it is. You care about people, Is. You really care. Do you know how rare that is?"

I let Jeremy's kindness and gentleness sooth me. Within the safety of his embrace, my tears eventually dried. I could feel my heart knitting back together. He had me in his calming, safe bubble and I never wanted to leave.

Then I realized that Jeremy was always cleaning up my mess, and all too often, I forgot to make sure that *he* was okay. Unwilling to break free of his hold just yet, I muttered, "Sorry you caught me in a crumpled mess—again. Were you stopping by for something? How are you doing?"

"Isy, you never have to apologize for needing comfort every once in a while. I'm glad I'm here for you. I'll always be here for you."

I snuggled closer to him knowing that he genuinely meant it. The soft thrum of his heart beating was the most comforting sound in the world, and I soaked in his musky scent. He smelled like home.

"So did you need something? Or want to talk about something?" I repeated, just to be sure I wasn't hogging all of the limelight again.

He hesitated for just a moment. "Nothing that can't wait."

Now I was curious. There was obviously something on his mind. "Jez, I'm okay. Tell me now," I insisted, reluctantly pulling away just enough to tilt my head back and look up at him.

Indecision briefly flickered across his features.

"Jez," I insisted again, more forcefully this time.

"Isy, it's fine. It's not the right time. We'll talk later. I'd better go now anyway."

So now he was trying to get away from me before I could force it out of him? Not likely.

He started to pull away but I clung to him. "It's exactly the right time. Come and sit down." I grabbed hold of his hand and tugged him to the couch. His eyes darted around the room, looking uneasy.

"It can't be that bad, Jez. Spill it," I encouraged, my hand still in his. I was worried if I let go, he'd do a runner.

"Seriously, Isy. Right now you're feeling vulnerable and your judgment is clouded. I don't want to spring anything on you. We'll talk tomorrow."

"Okay, so now you're starting to freak me out a little. Spring *what* on me? Please, please, *please* tell me that you're not moving away or anything like that?" I held my breath. I was this close to melting down if Jeremy was going to be the trifecta and tell me he was leaving.

He smiled just a little, just enough to touch the corners of his mouth but not enough to reach his eyes.

I was going to kill him if he didn't put me out of my misery. I hated surprises.

"I'm glad you're enjoying my panic attack, Jez," I said sarcastically. "But you and I both know there's no way I'm going to be able to wait until tomorrow. If it's bad, I'd rather know now, and if it's not, I'd rather stop worrying. So. Tell. Me."

The same indecision continued to haunt him. "This is so *not* the way I imagined having this conversation." I threw him a reproachful look and he sighed in defeat. "But I'm smart enough to know that you're not going to let me out of here without incurring your wrath. So—here goes . . ."

He took a deep breath. "I've been thinking about this for a while now but it's never really seemed like the right time to talk to you about it. And just now, hearing you talk about that douchebag asshole, well, I was . . ." He drifted off, averting his gaze.

I gently squeezed his hand. "You were what?"

After an infuriatingly long pause, he finally admitted, "Jealous."

I furrowed my brow. "I don't understand."

He raked a hand through his hair, turning his head to meet my eyes. "No, I suppose you wouldn't."

Ouch. After I'd already been schooled once today, I was feeling particularly sensitive. I narrowed my eyes.

Noticing my offense, he quickly continued. "You're not going to make this easy on me, are you? Let me spell it out. The mere idea of you being with someone else—even if that guy is a total douche—it makes me insanely jealous. Out of my mind kind of jealous."

"Oh." I squeezed his hand. "You know, Jez, no matter what, you will always be a big part of my life," I reassured him. "I'm not going to abandon you just because I'm in a relationship or something. Mind you, I don't think we'll have to worry about that for a long time. I don't see myself being in a relationship anytime in the near future. I mean, who—other than you—is going to put up with me and not think I'm totally nuts?" I joked, lightly punching his arm with my free hand.

He sighed.

"Sheesh, tough crowd. Lighten up."

"Isy, you're not understanding me. I'm not jealous because I don't think we'll be friends anymore. I meant that . . . that I would be jealous because I want to be . . . more than friends . . ." His voice trailed off as he found something on the coffee table supposedly interesting enough to capture his attention.

The real meaning behind his words was finally starting to register. *More than friends.* I was still confused, though. He'd made it abundantly clear that was the last thing he wanted. What had changed?

"But Jez, you told me in no uncertain terms that you didn't feel that way about me, you know, after we . . ."

He finally met my gaze again. "What I actually said is that I couldn't bear to mess things up with you and have you hate me."

I looked at him, expectant.

"That's very different from not having any feelings for you," he finished. "Not that I was ready to admit it at the time, even to myself."

"Oh." I fell silent, the shock of his revelation shooting through me like a zap of electricity.

He misinterpreted my silence for discomfort. "I told you this was not the right time to talk about it." He made a move to stand but I tugged him back down.

"And I told you that it's exactly the right time." I smiled warmly at him, trying to assuage his uneasiness.

He was still a little fidgety, but some of the tension evaporated from his shoulders.

"Jez, you know that I love you . . ." I started.

He flinched. "Why do I sense a *but* coming?"

"No *but*," I assured him. The last thing I wanted was for Jeremy to feel uncomfortable around me. "I love you. I think the world of you. My life is better for having you in it. I don't know what I would've done these past couple of weeks without you. I'd probably still be collapsed on the bathroom floor. I don't know if I've told you how much I appreciate everything you've done. How much I need you in my life. Because I do, Jez, I really do."

"Is this the part where you tell me how much you value my friendship above all else?" he asked, his eyebrows raised.

"But I do, Jez. It's not a line. I really do."

"And you could never bear to lose my friendship, nothing is worth risking that?"

Goodness, if he were going to say it all for me, this would be a very quick conversation. "Absolutely, you're one hundred percent correct there."

"Isy, I know you so well, I knew that was exactly what you would say. The only thing I don't know is whether or not you actually have feelings for me. Whether it's just your fear holding you back, or because you just don't feel that way about me."

"Jez—"

"Let me finish. I've had this whole speech rehearsed and gone over it a thousand times in my head, so at least let me get through it." He angled his body towards mine and straightened his shoulders, taking a deep breath. He spoke with such sincerity, such openness, I could only smile at him. But the tension that had evaporated from his shoulders had found its way into mine.

"Isy, I let fear stop me from exploring something with you before. Fear of it not working out, fear of hurting you, fear of you hurting me.

"And then something terrible happened: your friend, Jonathan, died. And he was in the prime of his life. No warning. Just gone. And I realized that life is so short, so fleeting, we never know when it ends. And nothing—*nothing*—stays the same forever."

He searched my eyes, examining my reaction to his words.

"Don't you see, Isy? Our friendship can't stay the same forever. If either one of us were to become involved with someone else, things would change. It would be inevitable. I know you think that they wouldn't, but trust me, they would. We could never have the type of relationship we have now. And honestly, I don't know if I could watch you be with someone else. I don't think I'd want to."

Oh. My. Lord. His words were starting to sink in: it was all or nothing. He was giving me an ultimatum. I had fought so long to get past my all-or-nothing view of the world, and here Jeremy was, making me make that exact choice. No gray. Just black. Just white. And he was drawing a clear line down the middle.

If I didn't tell Jeremy what he wanted to hear, this would be it: the trifecta. He was going to leave me.

Suddenly, I couldn't breathe. I felt like the walls were closing in around me.

"Isy, are you okay?"

My breathing labored as I struggled to draw air into my lungs. Jeremy was still holding my hand. I pulled it away.

"Please say something," he begged.

"I just . . . Need. A. Moment." I closed my eyes and tried to slow my breathing.

When I reopened them, Jeremy was offering me a glass of water. I gratefully took it and gulped it down.

"I need you to try and relax, Isy. Stop freaking out. Nothing is happening today. I'm talking hypothetically about a future point in time. And if that time comes, it only means that you've fallen for some other guy and you're happy. It won't matter so much that we won't spend as much time together if you're busy with someone else, anyway. So there's nothing to panic about. Just breathe."

His words whirled around me as I tried to make sense of them. He wasn't leaving me, not today anyway. I didn't have to choose right now. We could still be friends.

And I saw the logic in his words: if I met someone and fell in love, I would be happy, wouldn't I?

Except, here was the thing: I couldn't see myself falling in love with some unknown guy. Couldn't see myself loving someone else so much that I would be willing to give up Jeremy. I had grown so close to Jeremy in the past couple of weeks that I would never let him go. If things had been different with Matt and I'd been forced to choose between them, I never would have been able to let go of Jez. The thought had never crossed my mind. What had just happened with Matt made me realize how much the connection I had with Jeremy meant to me. How he was the one I wanted when I was feeling sad, angry, lonely, scared. Whether I was in the depths of despair or experiencing complete and utter joy, Jeremy was the one I wanted to be there. Ever since I had opened up to him about everything, about Jonathan, about the visions, about *everything*, I had closed that last remaining distance between us. He had seen me at my very worst and been the one to help me through it. I trusted him more than I trusted anyone else in the world. I loved him, wholeheartedly. He was the one who I knew would always be there for me. He was my rock. I needed him as much as I needed air.

I couldn't imagine my life without him.

I would never choose a life without him.

No matter who I met. *Ever.*

Then I flipped the situation, trying to imagine Jeremy with another woman. *Him* not having time for *me*. *Her* asking him to choose between us.

Suddenly my breathing labored again and the room was spinning once more. I closed my eyes and tried not to succumb to the dizziness. Not unless I wanted Jeremy to clean up a fresh round of vomit.

Because he would. Jeremy had cleaned up my vomit once before and I knew he would do it again.

He had seen me so overcome with grief that I didn't think I could survive it.

And yet, I had. I had because he had pulled me through it.

He had jumped into the muck and horror with me, held out his hand and pulled me up, into the safety and warmth of his embrace.

And right then, that's the only place I wanted to be: in his arms.

Jeremy took my hand again and I leaned over and rested my head on his shoulder, folding myself into him. Instantly, his arms were around me. And I was home.

29

THE FIRE IGNITED

HOW COULD I have not realized this before?

How could I have been so blind, so stubborn? So desperate to protect myself, I had buried the truth so deeply that not even I could see it? The truth that was so overwhelmingly evident now, it seemed unfathomable I didn't realize it earlier.

I was in love with Jeremy.

I'd been in love with Jeremy for a long time.

I had just been too terrified to admit it.

Without him, nothing in my world made sense. Without him, I never would have been able to survive the death of Jonathan.

Jonathan had taught me to focus on what was truly important in life. Matt had taught me to stop being afraid of letting my guard down, to stop trying to protect myself at the expense of really opening up, really allowing myself to embrace the risk of being hurt. And that fantasies very rarely match reality. And that can be a good thing. My experience with Matt taught me to open my eyes to see the truth of what was right in front of me.

I didn't need a vision to see that it was Jeremy. That it had always been Jeremy. He was the one who taught me that real love started with friendship. And it was worth risking *everything*. Because real love accepted you exactly as you were, picked you up when you were down and lifted you. Real love didn't care when you had a snotty nose. Because it was real love that cleaned your vomit.

Jeremy's hand was rubbing my back in little circles. I soaked in the love of that small motion, letting the warmth slowly spread through every fiber of my being.

Then, without saying a word, I gazed into his eyes, a looking glass into the depths of his soul. The caring and comfort I saw there stirred the desire within me and I closed my eyes again and pressed my lips to his.

At first he seemed hesitant, unsure. But then his lips parted and he kissed me, really kissed me, like it was our first kiss after the longest time apart. Like a soldier returning home from the war. Every cell in my body tingled, every sense was heightened.

When he eventually released me, we were both panting for air. He cupped my face in his hands and stared into my eyes.

"Isy, are you sure?" he asked in a hopeful voice. "I won't disappear if you say no. I won't stop loving you if you tell me you only want to be friends. And let's not forget that it was only a moment ago that you were crying over that super-douche—maybe you're not ready. I don't want to take advantage while you're feeling emotional."

My voice caught in my throat. "Jez, did you—" I stammered, while he waited patiently for me to find my voice, "did you just say that you *loved* me?"

A smile spread over his face. He gently caressed my cheek.

"Did I not make that clear?" he teased playfully. He realized that I'd become putty in his hands and that cheeky smile I loved so much radiated his delight.

He pressed his lips to my forehead, before leaving a trail of gentle, feather-light kisses across my eyelids and down my cheeks. The gentle movement of his lips sent shivers down my spine and melted away every fear, every heartbreak, every worry I'd ever had. There was nothing left but the two of us in that moment.

Heat sparked in his gaze. "I love you, Isabel Cartier. I love your strength, your caring nature, your fearless attitude, and your confidence, which are somehow rolled up with your vulnerability, your occasional neurosis, your complete stubbornness and your tendency to overthink absolutely everything. I love how you make me laugh and"—he gently tapped my nose and gave me a wink—"just how easy it is to tease you. I love that you don't take yourself too seriously, and that when you're sad or hurting, your spirit seems to lift just a little as soon as you feel my arms around you. And I love that whenever I'm near you, my day seems brighter, my life seems happier."

He took my hand in his again. "Does that make things clear enough for you? Or do you need me to continue?" And once again, the undeniable sex appeal of that cheeky smile of his warmed my skin.

He pulled me to him again and his lips found mine once more. His kiss became more passionate, desire emanating from him.

When he finally released me, I was like jello. He quickly grabbed hold of me as I swayed backwards and gave a little chuckle, clearly impressed with himself.

My hands navigated their way under his T-shirt, enjoying the feel of his bare skin under my touch. His body responded and I felt him shiver as he pressed himself against me and roved his hands all over me.

"Jez," I whispered when his mouth briefly parted from mine.

His breath was hot against my ear. "Hmm?"

"Do you know that I love you, too?" I muttered so breathlessly I wasn't sure if he heard me. But I couldn't talk anymore, Jeremy was kissing my neck. I couldn't even think anymore—I didn't want to.

"Mmhmm," he murmured, before moving his lips back to mine.

30

INSPIRATION

AS THE NEXT two weeks passed, I couldn't wipe the smile from my face. My cheeks hurt.

My feelings for Jeremy had been an ember, slowly burning unnoticed until the spark caught and the blaze ignited into a firestorm of passion. Every touch heated my skin, every sensual look stirred my desire.

I couldn't believe that I had just experienced both the lowest and highest points in my life. It wasn't that I had moved from one to the other—it was all wrapped up together. I still felt so much sadness for Jonathan's loss, but I had slowly learned to accept it.

I felt like he was my guardian angel, watching over me.

I continued to dream about him. In the latest dream, he was shaking Jeremy's hand, although I couldn't make out what they were saying. The room was dark. I could only faintly see his smile, his face softly illuminated by the dim glow of the lamp beside them. I couldn't discern the surroundings, it was nowhere I recognized. There was a lot of blue and violet but in the dim light it was difficult to see. In a flash, he was gone. I ran after him, desperate to see him again. When I flung open the door to chase after him, the scene suddenly changed, morphing into a sandy beach. Jonathan was standing in the distance with his feet in the water, waving to me.

I awoke feeling peaceful, knowing Jonathan was okay. But that familiar twinge of sadness still haunted me. I curled up next to Jeremy and he lightly stirred, wrapping himself around me. I went back to sleep, snuggling closer to him and inhaling his comforting scent.

A nightmare ripped me from my peaceful slumber. It was one of those dreams where you're taking an exam you're not prepared for and you can't believe that you haven't studied. I stared at the multiple-choice test, having no idea what the question was, let alone which was the right answer. I looked down at my clothes and caught sight of the flannel pajamas I was wearing. Fabulous.

As my eyes darted frantically around the room, I spotted the examiner sitting at the large front desk, his eyes on me. Jonathan. What was Jonathan doing here? Why was he testing me? In a blink of an eye he was standing beside me with his hand on my shoulder.

I awoke nonplussed. I wasn't panicked about anything so it seemed strange to have a dream like that. For the first time in a very long time, I didn't feel like my life was spinning out of control. I was wondering what was subconsciously troubling me when I considered that I was fast approaching the end of my temporary assignment at Parkmores and I had a lot of decisions to make. *That would explain the multiple-choice test,* I thought.

I felt sad at the prospect of leaving the place that still contained so much of Jonathan's essence. So I was more than pleasantly surprised the following day when Harrison called me into his office to inform me that they'd requested my secondment be extended for another two months.

He seemed to appraise my reaction and I tried to conceal my joy.

"Will you be staying as well?" I asked him.

"Only for another week, as originally planned," he advised. "They'll be making a formal announcement this afternoon about the appointment of a new GC. They have promoted within, so it will be an immediate start. I'll spend the next week with the appointee, as a kind of induction."

"Is it Samantha?" I guessed.

Sam was the unofficial second-in-command in the team. I had an easy camaraderie with her and I could tell why Jonathan had held her in such high esteem. She had been working for him for years, and with him as her mentor, she'd developed a working style and business approach that mirrored his. She was extremely well regarded in the team and her appointment would cause minimal disruption.

Harrison hesitated. He wasn't supposed to tell me who the new appointee was. "Well, yes, but that is not to be repeated before the formal announcement is made," he warned.

"Of course," I assured him. "Sam is a good choice. The team will be happy. And it's good news for the firm, too." An external appointee would have been more difficult to win over.

A sly smile tugged at his lips. It was the kind of smile that said he'd pushed for this outcome for that exact reason. Not that that's the argument he would have given, of course. The benefits for Parkmores and its team—that's what he would have advocated.

I knew what would happen next. Harrison would go above and beyond to be helpful to Sam when he handed the reigns over to her. He would make sure that she knew he was in her corner, ready to assist in any way to see her succeed. He'd ensure that she relied upon him, and knock out any potential future competition in the process.

"You will be my eyes and ears when I'm gone, Isabel. The next couple of months will give you a good opportunity to spend more time with Samantha." Then he added, "You'll be missed at Barkleys. I look forward to you returning to the team in the beginning of February."

Again I could tell he was appraising my response.

"Me too. Two months will go quickly, though, given that it'll be over the holidays."

He merely nodded, then shifted his focus back to the papers on his desk. I knew that was my cue to leave.

* * *

I sat at the table at home, looking at all of the things I had pulled out of my jewelry box. When Mom had insisted I bring it home with me, I'd put it in the closet, not quite knowing what to do with it.

Now I had an idea. And inspiration.

When I was out during lunch, I walked past a jewelry store

and a necklace in the window caught my attention, stopping me in my tracks. My head spun around so quickly that the people walking behind me probably thought they were watching a scene from *The Exorcist.*

I was stunned to see the necklace looked exactly like the matching set to my mother's earrings. Those earrings had been my own design, I hadn't copied it.

When I turned back to look at the necklace again, it looked nothing like it—not even the coloring was the same. I wondered how it was possible that I could have confused this blue necklace with something that would match those earrings. It would be like mistaking Jerry Lewis for Oprah Winfrey—impossible.

But I'd been so sure that I'd seen it, I'd nearly caused a human pileup on the sidewalk.

I pushed it out of my mind until I got home that evening and saw the box in the closet. As I sat at the table, examining its contents, the idea came to me.

Lingering guilt had continued to plague me over everything that had happened with Neil. First ruining Rachel's meet-my-boyfriend dinner party, then arguing with her about him, and finally, the part that she didn't know: me not giving a damn about what I thought would be his ultimate demise.

Even though Neil had brought everything on himself, even though Rachel had finally seen through him and he was now thankfully fully recovered, I knew that I didn't really handle things as well as I should have. I wanted to get her an *I'm-sorry-I-didn't-support-you-even-though-I-was-right-and-your-boyfriend-turned-out-to-be-a-drug-dealer* gift. I just had no idea what would say that appropriately. But something that—as my mom had put it—'was made with love' seemed to fit what I was looking for. Nothing said 'sorry' as much as something that required a lot of thought and effort.

I didn't know if I'd still be able to make earrings that didn't look like they were made by a five-year-old, but I was willing to give it a shot.

Mom had berated me for not trying things. I considered this a relatively low-risk endeavor with the added bonus of proving her wrong. And if they turned out to look ridiculous, then I'd give them to Rachel with a *My-friend-hated-my-boyfriend-and-all-I-got-were-these-lousy-earrings* T-shirt.

I hoped it would be just like riding a bike and it would come back to me, even if I had a wobbly start.

It dawned on me that technically I wasn't trying something new—I was retrying something old—but I ignored the technicality and gave myself an imaginary pat on the back anyway.

Jez knocked just as I was holding up the finished product, examining my handiwork and grinning.

"You know," he said after he gave me a kiss and placed the Japanese take-out on the table, "since we spend so much time at your place, it might be easier if you just gave me a key." He said it casually, but I felt his eyes searching mine.

Give him a key? Wasn't that a little—or *a lot*—soon?

Admittedly, he only lived across the hall and had practically been here every day so I'd stopped asking him *if* he was coming over and just presumed that he was. So I wondered why a key seemed like such a big deal to me. I had nothing left to hide, I had let him in completely. And being with him felt so natural, like we had been together forever. An innocuous little metal object shouldn't have caused me any alarm.

Before I could continue worrying about the whole key thing and analyzing my hesitation, a more scary thought occurred to me: had he moved in without me noticing? How could he have? It had only been *two weeks*.

He must have read my mind, my thoughts etched in my expression.

"Or not. Just an idea, don't freak out. But you know, I'd be more than happy to give you a key to my place. We could stay there, too, sometimes. It's not like you have to travel very far."

He started to empty the contents of the bag when he noticed the mess. He eyed it with curiosity. "What's this?"

"I made some earrings for my friend, Rachel," I explained as I held them up. "I want to invite her out to dinner and give them to her."

He inched closer to inspect my gift. "I'm impressed, Is. You've been hiding this hobby from me, I had no idea that you were so . . . artistic. They're awesome." He pulled me closer to him and kissed me. It was soft, but passionate. The kind of kiss that said, *You're amazing and I can't believe how lucky I am to have you*. The thing was—I couldn't believe how lucky *I* was to have *him*.

"But . . . ?" I prompted.

"But what?" he asked, bemused.

"I don't know, I'm waiting for the rest. Aren't you going to say something like: They're awesome—if they were made by a one-armed prisoner, or a kindergartener with a Barbie jewelry kit, or a contestant on *Minute to Win It?* I'm waiting for the punch line."

He raised his eyebrows. "Why would I say something like

that?"

"Because you enjoy shamelessly teasing me and I'm giving you *a lot* of material with this jewelry thing."

"*We* enjoy teasing each other," he corrected. "I'm just trying to keep up. But the earrings really are great. Stop being paranoid, you know I'd tell you if they sucked. Don't be afraid to believe in yourself."

"When did you become so insightful?"

"When I realized that you didn't come with an instruction manual and I had to assemble you all by myself," he retaliated with a cheeky grin.

"Now there's the Jeremy I know and love. I'll conveniently ignore the Frankenstein comparison."

"Actually, I was thinking more like Ikea. But I'm not anti calling you Frankie." A mischievous grin continued to play on his lips, his eyes dancing with amusement.

"Be careful, I think he turned against the mad scientist in the end. See what happens when you become too cocky?"

"Yup, you have to pull the plug on Frankie. But don't worry, I think I'll keep you," he said, kissing me once more.

He was such a smartass. But he was my smartass. Despite my knee-jerk reaction to the whole key thing, I knew that I was completely and irrevocably in love with him. I knew that I loved seeing him every day. I knew that two weeks was long enough for me to already have become accustomed to having him hold me at night and it would be strange now to sleep on my own.

How can I be so happy and so freaked out all at the same time? I wondered.

Although it was the most natural thing in the world to be

with him, he still made my heart race when he kissed me. After being just friends for so long, it sort of felt like we were doing something we weren't supposed to—not in a bad way, more in an *I'm-getting-away-with-something-naughty* kind of way that made it that little bit more exciting.

When he unlocked his lips from mine, he kept his arms wound tightly around me. My mind eventually wandered back to the task at hand. I held up the earrings for closer inspection.

"I don't want them to look handmade. I want them to look good enough to buy," I confided, voicing that part of my brain that continued to worry about things needing to be perfect.

He gently stroked my cheek, his eyes sparkling with sincerity. "No joking, Isy, they're awesome."

He kissed me again and I forgot what we were talking about.

"How do you make me feel like I'm a school girl kissing her hot teacher?" I whispered when I came up for air, panting.

He chuckled. "Probably because I'm so wise. But I think out of the two of us, you're the one who fits the book-loving, rule-abiding teacher profile. You know, if you want to role-play . . ." He quirked an eyebrow, a suggestive look in his eyes.

"Are you worried that we'll eventually end up feeling like an old married couple?" I asked, ignoring his suggestion but mentally banking it for later.

"No. Eventually we *will* be an old married couple. But even old married couples can still be passionate about each other—it's just more deep-seated. Look at those old couples you see still walking hand-in-hand. I think it's cute."

I noted his reference to our future nuptials. Again, this both thrilled and surprised me. He was so sure and so sincere, he made my heart swell. All of my innate fears of growing old—and I had many of them—seemed to fade away.

I was so happy, I wanted to share it. Thinking about relationships incited an inspired idea, one I thought ingenious and just sneaky enough to work.

"I have a suggestion," I enthused. "Who's your buddy that you shoot hoops with? Brad something? You've been friends forever, right? He's obviously a good guy . . ."

He suddenly looked dubious. "Yeah . . ." he confirmed reluctantly. "Why?"

"He's single, isn't he?"

His suspicious expression morphed into one of horror.

"Hear me out. What about if instead of inviting Rachel out to dinner, I invite her here for a bite instead and you invite Brad?"

He gave me his *you're-playing-with-fire* look. "First of all, I think it's a little presumptuous, and I don't know how kindly Brad will take to it. Plus, I mean, no offense, but what exactly does Rachel look like?"

I wanted to assure him that Rach was very attractive, and it was me who should be interrogating him more about Brad's looks, but he made it clear he wasn't finished with his objections.

"And second—and please don't take this the wrong way—but food poisoning isn't exactly a conduit for romance."

I rolled my eyes. "Can I respond now?"

He nodded, but the tension remained in his jaw.

"First of all, Rachel is *very* good-looking. I have no doubt Brad will find her attractive. If anything, it's whether Rachel finds *him* attractive that is yet to be determined. And second, Mr. Smarty Pants, I was actually planning to be devious and order in and just put it into the dishes. I might even dirty a pot or two for that authentic look," I said conspiratorially.

He was still hesitant so I gave him my best puppy-dog eyes until he relented. After the horrifying ordeal Rachel had been through with Drug Dealer Neil (as I'd renamed him), I wanted her to meet some good guys and be reminded that there were still decent guys out there.

"Okay, I'll ask Brad if he's willing . . ."

"No, don't do that, then it'll be awkward. Just tell him that we're having a couple of friends over and I'd love to meet him."

He scoffed. "Yeah, because him figuring out it's a set-up when he gets here won't be awkward at all."

"Fine, invite two of your friends then. Then it won't be as obvious. Besides," I argued, appealing to his own self-interest, "the alternative is that it's just Rachel, you and me, and you'll be subjected to an evening of girl talk. This way you'll be able to bring in reinforcements and balance the onslaught of estrogen with testosterone."

He considered that. "I suppose I could also invite Ammon from work. I'm sure he wouldn't say no to a free feed."

I flashed him a reassuring smile. "Then it's a plan."

"Okay, but I want to be on the record that this could be a total disaster. I don't know if Brad wants a serious relationship. I think he prefers playing the field to be honest. So if they hook up and Rachel ends up angry or whatever, don't blame me. Or Brad. You have to agree not to hold any grudges, he's a good buddy. Agreed?"

"Agreed. They're two adults and what they do is up to them. So long as Brad doesn't lie and try to manipulate her, I don't have a problem."

"Nope, Brad's straight up. Besides, he doesn't need to lie, women fall all over him."

"Oh, okay, then," I said, nodding in mock agreement. "But I might hold the applause until I judge for myself." For Rachel's sake, I hoped he wasn't one of those guys who worked out at the gym while making love to himself in the mirror.

Jeremy shook his head, clearly exasperated. "So, since you insist on trying to play cupid, and since this is the first time we're having friends over for dinner, we should probably do it right. I'll cook."

His offer made me feel inadequate. Since when could Jez cook? And, more importantly, why hadn't he dazzled me with his culinary prowess before?

"You cook? Since when?"

"I actually used to cook for Becca all the time. I just haven't cooked much lately. Just because *you're* oblivious in the kitchen, don't just assume that I don't have any cooking skills. I guess there're still a few things you don't know about me, after all," he said, crossing his arms over his chest and looking smug. My eyes drifted to his chest, noticing how good he looked in the shirt he was wearing.

I quirked an eyebrow. "What other things don't I know about you?"

"I haven't told you about the year I spent in Australia yet." His voice shifted into a near-perfect Australian accent and I had to stop myself from instinctively looking around the room to find the mysterious stranger. "That's where I picked up my nickname."

"That accent is freaky—and awesome." I paused, drinking him in while I banked this with his role-playing suggestion. "Hmm, what other secret talents do I not know about?" I asked coyly.

"Wait until tonight and I'll show you . . ." he teased in a low voice.

"Maybe you should show me now," I challenged, eager for the demonstration to begin.

His eyes were scorching, the heat in the apartment suddenly skyrocketing. So quickly that I barely had time to realize what he was doing, he scooped me up in his arms and carried me to the couch, his warm breath caressing my neck.

"Wait—are you sure? About the cooking, I mean. I'm certainly not questioning your other talents."

"Yeah, yeah. You just take care of dessert," he breathed, his voice husky.

He leaned in to kiss me and noticed my furrowed brow. "I don't expect you to make it, just pick up something on your lunch break."

Ah, that I could do. I may not have been a world-renowned chef—or someone who could make anything more complicated than toast for that matter—but I practically had a black belt in shopping.

"You've got a deal," I agreed, sealing it with a kiss.

Frustration flittered across his face when I pulled away, and a groan escaped his throat.

"I'll find out if Rach is free this Saturday and you speak to the guys."

"Yeah, yeah, yeah," he muttered, the beckoning heat in his eyes indicating he was clearly uninterested in talking any further.

Jeremy was a well of surprises. Not only was he wonderful, kind and understanding, but he could cook, and he loved me exactly as I was—someone who couldn't. He understood all of my obsessive tendencies and idiosyncrasies, my fears, my struggles, my strengths and my weaknesses, and he loved me for—or *in spite of*—all of them.

And I loved him, even though he didn't have the decency to be as obviously flawed as I was.

31

INTRODUCTIONS

THAT NIGHT, I had the same multiple-choice test dream again. The same feelings of uncertainty, inadequacy, regret and dread rippled through me. This time, when Jonathan put his hand on my shoulder, I was able to talk to him.

"Jonathan," I whispered, afraid that the other students around me would hear, "I don't know this. Tell me which one is the right answer."

Jonathan leaned down and murmured in my ear, "Only you know, Isabel. Only you know."

The last thing I remembered before I woke up was the warmth of his breath on my ear. *Could that be more cryptic?* I thought. Clearly he didn't understand the way cheating worked. At least this time, I wasn't wearing the pajamas. That had to be progress.

My hand instinctively touched my ear. It still felt warm from his breath.

* * *

As luck would have it, everyone was free on Saturday.

We went to the Ferry Plaza Farmers' Market that morning to buy some fresh produce. There was a sea of people roaming through the stalls, acquiring family-sized bags of goods along the way. Inside the Ferry Building, the smell of seafood, cheese and coffee hung in the air, the clamor of bustling activity rumbling through the market.

Jeremy walked the aisles like a pro, pausing here and there to collect his list of goods before we stopped for lunch at MarketBar. I started roaming through the marketplace, entranced by everything on offer, but Jez pulled me back. "Another day," he promised.

We unpacked our purchases back at my apartment. It looked like a truck had just backed up at my door and unloaded.

"So what can I do to help?" I asked rather reluctantly.

"You can put the flowers we bought into a vase and then you can get out of my kitchen," he ordered, a smile playing on his lips.

"Yes, Sergeant," I said, giving him a mock salute and breathing a sigh of relief.

So while Jeremy slaved in the kitchen, I turned my attention back to my jewelry box. *Perhaps a matching bracelet*, I thought.

* * *

Rachel arrived first, carrying a bottle of wine.

I gave her a big hug. "So great to see you, Rach. Come in."

Jeremy walked up behind me and extended his hand. "Hi, Rachel, I'm Jeremy. It's nice to finally put a face to the name."

"It's a pleasure to meet the man who has finally stolen Isy's heart," she told him as she shook his hand. "You must be a magician."

I rolled my eyes at her, flashing back to her comment about no one being able to live up to my expectations. Jeremy surpassed any expectations long ago, and still never ceased to amaze me. I pushed thoughts of previous arguments with Rachel out of my mind. She had returned to her normal self again and past discussions during that tumultuous period with Neil should stay there—in the past.

"Rachel and I went to college together," I explained to Jeremy. "You'll love her. Rach is the opposite of me—she's easy-going, trusting, positive about *everything*. An act-before-you-think type of person. She got me into a lot of trouble in our college days. Oh, and she's an excellent cook. Probably the only thing we have in common is our excellent choice of friends." I gave her a wink.

"Opposite, huh? Are you calling me stupid?" she quipped.

Jeremy laughed, the rich, warm sound sending shivers of pleasure through me. I knew the two of them would hit it off.

Rachel's eyes darted towards the table, raising her eyebrows at the sight of the five-place table setting.

"I hope you don't mind, Rach, but I've invited a couple of Jeremy's friends to join us. I figured since we—I mean Jeremy—was going to the trouble of cooking, we might as well make it the more the merrier."

Jeremy cleared his throat. "I've been slaving in the kitchen all day, girlfriend," he announced in a girly tone, adding to the effect with a feminine hand gesture.

Rachel laughed. I could see that she was warming to Jez

immediately. Although I couldn't imagine anyone *not* warming to him, charisma practically oozed from his pores when he wanted it to.

Right on time, there was another knock at the door. "That'll be one of the guys," Jez said. "I'll get it."

A tall and rather handsome guy was smiling and carrying a six-pack of beer. His flawless skin was a shade lighter than chocolate.

"You didn't have to bring that, dude," Jez told him. "Come in."

"*You* don't have to drink it," he responded with just a hint of an accent. His smile was dazzling, revealing perfect white teeth.

Jeremy took it from him and carried it in. "Ammon, this is Isy and her friend, Rachel."

"So this is the girl you're always talking about—and why you walk around all day at work with that stupid grin on your face," Ammon said to Jez as he extended his hand to me.

"Nice to meet you, Ammon. And *I* love the grin," I responded. My gaze briefly landed on Jeremy, whose eyes were sparkling. The knowing look he gave me heated my skin.

I turned my attention back to Ammon, who smiled warmly at me before extending his hand to Rach. "Now I see why he's always grinning. He's hanging out with beautiful women all the time."

Rachel giggled. *Giggled.* I hadn't heard her giggle in a long time.

"So, Ammon, do you work in IT with Jeremy?" I inquired.

"Excuse me for a sec," Jeremy apologized while pulling his phone out of his pocket. I looked at him curiously. "It's on vibrate," he explained, before leaving the room.

"No, I'm in Finance. I'm the one who has to give the okay when Jeremy wants to spend ridiculous amounts of money on upgrades. That's why I'm on his good side—I've been signing a lot of checks lately. That guy likes spending other people's money," he said light-heartedly.

"Well then, you and Rachel have something in common. Rachel works in recruitment and she specializes in the finance area," I explained to Ammon.

"Yes, and we have a number of senior finance positions at the moment. If you're interested, I'd be happy to look at your CV," Rachel offered. She was always looking for good candidates and apparently couldn't resist the urge to try to poach one of Jeremy's colleagues. Lucky Jez wasn't in the room.

Right on cue, he returned. "Sorry about that, guys. That was Brad. He rolled his ankle at the gym and can't make it."

My shoulders slumped. I was looking forward to Rachel meeting him in hopes of them being a good match. "That's a shame. Another time then."

Ammon seemed unfazed and turned back to Rachel. "I'm not actively looking, but I suppose it couldn't hurt." I noticed the way he looked at her and wondered whether he was more interested in having an excuse to see her again. *Hmm, there may be hope for this evening yet*, I thought with a smile. Funny that I hadn't considered Ammon earlier, but things popped up where you least expected them. Sometimes when we try to go in one direction, life circumvents our plans and takes us on a completely different course.

We sat down to dinner at Jeremy's request. He didn't want everything to get cold and I couldn't blame him after all of the effort he'd put into preparing everything. As he'd suggested, he indeed had many secret talents. The lemongrass oysters, green curry and steamed dumplings were all delicious. I was almost completely preoccupied by how good the food was, if something else hadn't ensnared my attention. The chemistry flying between Rachel and Ammon practically sizzled. I noticed Rachel reach out and flirtatiously touch Ammon's arm when he said something she found clever. I threw Jeremy a conspiratorial look. He eyed me suspiciously.

I was dying to get confirmation from Rachel.

After dinner, we were sitting on the couch when I asked Rach if she wanted more wine. Of course, I needed her to assist me in getting it.

With an open-plan apartment, the kitchen wasn't exactly far from the living area—and it most certainly wasn't soundproof. But I couldn't control myself.

In a hushed voice, I cornered her. "So, you and Ammon seem to be getting along really well."

She narrowed her eyes. "Yes . . ."

"He seems like a really great guy."

"Yes . . ." she responded in the same cautious tone. She could clearly see where I was going with this.

"I'm just saying." I didn't need to probe any further. If Rachel were turned off by the idea, she would've said so.

Rachel rejoined the guys in the living area, while I tended to dessert. As I headed back over with the plates, I heard my name. I suddenly had a feeling of déjà vu. *Why did this feel so familiar?* A shiver slid down my spine and gooseflesh covered my arms. *This was the scene from the dream I had where Jeremy and Rachel were arguing on the couch.*

I missed what they'd said, but curiosity got the better of me. "Did I hear my name? What are you two talking about?"

Rachel looked guilty. I knew it couldn't have been anything complimentary. Of course, this only made me more curious. I tapped my foot. "Well?"

Jeremy laughed. "Rachel was talking about goldfish and I told her that anything that came into this apartment would be flushed in a week. We started debating how long it would take you to kill them if I didn't feed them. Rachel had more faith in you than I did. I stuck with a week."

"Gee, thanks for your faith in me, Jez. Good to see you guys amusing yourself at my expense." I tried to sound indignant. Just when Rachel looked *really* guilty, hanging her head and flushing scarlet, I threw in, "I'd put five bucks on four days."

Rachel's normal color returned and her lips curled. I was pleased that Jez and Rachel appeared to have an easy camaraderie, although it occurred to me that they were likely to join forces in their jokes at my expense. I would need to up my game and try to recruit Ammon. Although I was guessing that he'd side with Rachel no matter what.

That reminded me of the gift I had for her. I brought her back over to the kitchen.

"I have something for you, Rach."

"Really?" she asked, her eyes wide.

"Don't get too excited until you see it," I warned. "It's handmade."

Her expression was imprinted with intrigue. I handed her the earrings, wrapped in pink tissue paper tied with a silver ribbon.

"Why are you giving me a gift?"

"It's just a little thought to say I'm sorry about how everything turned out with Neil."

"It's not your fault that he was a drug dealer. It's not like you knew."

I cringed.

"And even if you'd told me, I probably wouldn't have believed you."

Hearing that straight from the horse's mouth, I relaxed again.

"I mean, you tried to warn me about him and I wouldn't listen. I really hate that you were annoyingly right, you know. I'm sorry I was so angry with you, especially when you were the one who was really there for me when it all turned to shit. But I had to work things out for myself, and I wanted you to support me even if you didn't agree with me."

"I totally understand that now. That's why there's the gift," I said, holding it up and smiling. "Just open it. I'm dying to see if you like it or not."

She unwrapped it and held up one of the earrings, examining it. "Did you say that you made these?" she asked in wonder.

"Yes. Do you like them? Be honest."

"You—you made these?" she repeated.

"Yes."

"All by yourself?"

"Rach, you make it sound like the concept is unfathomable. I'm not without talents you know. But if you don't like them, you don't have to wear them."

"Like them? I love them! I just can't believe that you took the time to make them. And they're so pretty!" She immediately took off the earrings she was wearing and put on her new ones.

They looked lovely on her and I beamed with pride.

"Have you made anything else?"

"Actually, I just made a bracelet today. Do you wanna see?" I grabbed it from the box sitting on a side table.

"It's lovely," she remarked as she inspected it. "You know, Isy, if you like making jewelry, I'm pretty sure that I could sell some of it to the girls at work. If you're interested."

I hadn't considered selling it and the idea intrigued me. "That's an interesting thought," I mused.

"I'm sure you could get a few sales going at your work, too. Once people see your stuff, they'll want it for sure."

"Do you really think so?"

"Absolutely. It's unique. Who doesn't love something that's one-of-a-kind?"

I rubbed my chin. "Well, technically, I'd have to set it up as a business if I were to sell anything."

"Don't be such a lawyer. Just try it out with a couple of pieces—low key—and see what happens."

She got me thinking. "My firm has a 'market day' every few months for staff, which runs during the lunch period. There's everything from bags, shoes, jewelry, clothes, Tupperware—you name it, I've seen it. Staff organize it. I could probably ask to join in if it's not too late. We have one coming up in a couple of weeks in time for Christmas shopping."

"That sounds like a great idea," she encouraged.

"Definitely something to think about, anyway."

Smiling, she leaned in and whispered, "I really like Jeremy, Isy. I think he must be really good for you. I can see a lot of changes in you. You seem more . . . relaxed, happy. And these earrings—you're full of surprises."

"I *am* more relaxed and happy. Partly due to Jeremy, and partly due to . . . other things. I've had a lot of ups and downs lately and I've met some wonderful people who've been inspirational to me. I guess I've just learned to appreciate the good things in life and not worry so much about the rest."

"I'm so happy that you're happy," she said as she hugged me. "You deserve it."

"So do you. So, let's talk about Ammon."

32

SANCTUARY

I SLEPT PEACEFULLY in Jeremy's arms that night. Nothing could ever hurt me when he was there. When I awoke during the night, the quiet humming of his breathing was so soothing, I drifted straight back to sleep.

I could see Jonathan ahead of me on the crowded street. I ran to try to catch up to him but the faster I ran, the faster he seemed to go, never looking at me. I chased him until he reached a storefront. Standing in the doorway to enter, he turned back and looked straight at me and smiled.

He disappeared inside. I frantically ran in after him, gasping for breath.

It was dim inside. The sight of him bathed in the soft glow of a lamp talking to Jeremy triggered a fleeting sense of recognition. The setting looked familiar, dancing along the fringes of my memory. There was something about the colors—blue and violet.

Jonathan turned to me and gestured behind him, the soft light giving him an almost angelic glow. A display cabinet stretched along the wall, empty except for an item on the middle shelf: the matching necklace to Mom's earrings.

Stunned, my eyes darted back to Jonathan. He met my gaze, a beaming smile warming his features.

I woke up, furrowing my brow. The pieces were slowly starting to come together but there were still too many missing for me to understand the whole picture.

The feeling of familiarity kept gnawing at me. Jonathan persisted in showing me this place. I previously thought it was a room, but now I realized it was a store. The necklace was the same one I thought I'd seen in a storefront, which proved to be nothing more than a figment of my imagination. Now I wasn't so sure . . .

Was I supposed to locate this jewelry store? There didn't seem to be anything happening there that I needed to worry about.

Then the jigsaw pieces gradually rearranged themselves in my mind as I looked at it from a different angle. I considered the possibility that perhaps Jonathan wasn't showing me something that needed to be prevented, but something that should be *pursued.* If I could find this store, perhaps I could one day talk to the owner about providing a jewelry line to sell in the shop.

Could I? I wondered.

I tossed in the bed, careful not to wake Jeremy. I wasn't anywhere near that standard yet, but it was something I could aspire to. Maybe it wasn't outside the realm of possibility that my work could one day be showcased in a real jewelry store. Maybe—just maybe—*anything* was possible.

I didn't have the time to do anything on a large scale, though. I didn't want my new hobby to become so time intensive or overwhelming that it became a burden.

Nonetheless, the idea of working towards having my jewelry showcased in a store thrilled me. I remembered Jules's advice the last time I was getting pieces of a puzzle shown to me in stages: *Try to pay attention to other clues in the surroundings.*

I needed to see the name of the store. I'd been vaguely aware of the front window as I ran in, but I hadn't paid any attention. My eyes were only searching for Jonathan.

Jonathan. His memory filled me with longing and gratitude. I didn't want to forget any of the things he'd taught me.

Suddenly my reoccurring dream began to crystallize. Jonathan was still trying to teach me something. He said that only I knew the answer.

I would try to wait patiently and have confidence that I would see the missing pieces of the dream when I should.

In the meantime, I decided that it was time to see my accountant and set up a business name. Anything worth doing was worth doing properly.

I needed to think of a name. As I lay awake, buzzing with excitement, I mulled over some options that came to mind, but *Jewel of the Nile* got stuck in my head. Good movie, but no help.

My thoughts swirled from the Nile to the sea. Something seemed to fit there. The sea. It reminded me of Jonathan and the image of him at the beach. I liked the idea of the name being a tribute to him.

This triggered the inspiration of using part of his name, sparking the idea of *Jona's Jewels*. It felt right. He had taught me so much about figuring out where I wanted to be and taking the time to enjoy what I loved. That each day was a blessing, a jewel.

Jona's Jewels didn't just seem to fit—it was perfect.

* * *

I spent nearly every waking minute over the following week and a half madly trying to get a respectable range of jewelry ready for the market day that I had managed to join.

This would be my test-market. If there were a positive response, I would continue to organize future stalls and let Rachel talk to her colleagues to gage their interest. If I were completely snubbed—or worse still, laughed out—I would confine myself to making a few pieces for family and friends.

The process of designing and creating the jewelry actually relaxed me. All of my thought and energy went into it, allowing my everyday worries and stress to melt away. While that creative part of my brain was activated, the part that was used for my usual incessant worry had the switch turned off. My usually noisy mind became quiet, still.

I now remembered why I had spent so many of my teenage years poured over my box: I had found my sanctuary.

When the worry trickled in over the limited time I had to prepare my little collection, I reminded myself that there was no performance appraisal to be completed, no boxes to be ticked. And once again, I would eagerly open my box and let everything else wash away. I visualized the designs and let my hands move rhythmically to create them. It felt like a soulful dance and I allowed myself to surrender to the music within.

* * *

Jeremy was particularly supportive. It was his encouragement during my initial reluctance about taking part in the market day at such short notice that helped cement my decision.

During that week and a half, he didn't complain when I only half heard what he was telling me as I continued to wire a charm into place. He didn't complain that I spent all of my free time either out searching for supplies or at home sketching designs incorporating my newfound treasures.

I had no sense of time when I was entranced by my creative outlet. When Jeremy returned from drinks out with Brad one evening, I asked him why he was back so soon because it seemed no more than half an hour had passed.

He laughed at me. "You seem to go into this trance-like state when you're doing the jewelry thing—you barely hear a thing. If only I'd known that was the secret to getting you to be quiet."

I crossed my arms, a charm still in my hand.

He snorted. "You know I'm kidding. If I didn't miss you, I wouldn't be here every day."

Jeremy allowed me to showcase the day's creations at the end of each evening. To his credit, he managed to show interest while he examined the pieces, although I'm sure he wished my hobby had more to do with sports or cars than jewelry.

He spent more time at his own place that weekend. Although I enjoyed having the time to myself to lesson my guilt about directing all of my energy towards preparations for the stall, I missed him.

I was startled when I hopped into bed and there was a knock at the door.

"Hey," said Jeremy, "I know it's late. I didn't wake you, did I?"

"No, you have perfect timing, I'm just going to bed now. And I was just thinking about you," I admitted.

"I was thinking about you, too. How did you go tonight?"

"Good, I have a new necklace, bracelet and earrings set to add to the collection. I used the silver pendant I showed you last night. I'm pretty happy with it. How was your evening?"

"All right. Brad and I just went to the local pub for a couple of drinks."

"I'm glad. I've been monopolizing a lot of your time lately, haven't I? Well, until this week, anyway."

"I've wanted you to *monopolize* me," he said in a low voice, his salacious grin adding heat to his eyes.

I felt my cheeks warm as I took his hand to lead him in. "Are you staying tonight?"

"I thought you'd never ask."

"Do you have plans tomorrow night?"

"What do you have in mind?" he asked in the same suggestive tone.

"Whatever you want," I played along.

"Really? Well that could be dangerous," he breathed mischievously. "Do you need to do some work for your stall? What time will you make yourself available to do *whatever* I want?"

I giggled at his devilish grin. "Eight?"

"Eight is perfect."

"So what exactly do you have in mind?" I asked coyly.

"I think you should venture across the hall to my place. I mean, I know it's a little far, so I'll pick you up if you want."

"I'll try not to get lost."

"Be there at eight. The rest of the evening will be a surprise."

He paused, cocking his head. "Anything goes," he teased, a dangerous glint in his eye.

"Okay. I'm looking forward to it. I think."

"Not as much as I am, my slave girl," he chuckled, his brows dancing.

"Slave girl? You're starting to make me nervous . . . I don't want to re-enact *Fifty Shades of Grey*, if that's what you're thinking?"

His laugh didn't subdue my nerves—there was something devious in it.

I knew I wasn't getting any more out of him; whatever he had planned, he wasn't giving it away. Given I'd only just discovered his cooking skills, I hoped he'd be flaunting his domestic capabilities again. But the heat in his eyes led me to believe it was something else he had in mind. I was a little nervous, but flushed with eager anticipation. Whatever was on the evening agenda, I knew I was in good hands. Warm, masterful hands . . .

I snuggled closer to him and breathed in his familiar scent.

"I might give you a preview," he murmured in my ear, his voice deepening as he tugged me to the bedroom and pulled me onto the bed. A wave of heat immediately ignited within me and my hands found their way under his clothes. The feel of his skin against mine, his body moving with mine, took my breath away.

Later, I fell asleep in his arms, my last thoughts of the unbridled anticipation of whatever he had in store for the following evening.

It started as it usually did. Me looking down at the multiple-choice test with Jonathan's hand on my shoulder. Then the scene shifted and I was no longer in the exam room looking at a piece of paper. A piece of paper couldn't physically hurt me, what was now in front of me could.

Absolutely terrified, I dared to take a glimpse at the man holding the gun. He was dressed all in black, wearing a riding jacket over a T-shirt and jeans. His face was completely obscured by the black helmet he wore. I glanced behind him and saw my terror reflected back at me in the eyes of the woman behind the teller.

There were four other people in the bank, besides the three tellers. A woman, with a young girl who appeared to be between ten and twelve, and two men. One of the men looked to be in his forties and wore a navy suit with a gold tie. The other was in a black suit with his back to me. When he slowly turned, I was surprised to see it was Jonathan. He nodded in acknowledgement. His expression was solemn.

The young girl began screaming, a scream that made your blood run cold. Her mother instantly tried to placate her, eventually smothering her mouth when those attempts failed. That only intensified the screaming, agitating the girl more.

The gunman flew into a rage, demanding the girl be silenced before *he* silenced her. His hand twitched in fury. *Could he honestly harm a child?* I wondered, as fear crashed over me. The interminable screaming shrilled through the bank as the girl thrashed in her mother's arms. My skin tingled, the air electrified with trepidation.

The gunman pointed the weapon directly at the child, narrowing his eyes. Time slowed down, like someone hit pause. I frantically searched for Jonathan. Again, he merely nodded. "Tell me what to do," I pleaded desperately.

He shook his head almost imperceptibly. A feeling of complete and utter helplessness reverberated through me as I realized that he would not help me, would not give me the answer. I was alone in this and completely powerless.

A number suddenly flickered in my vision, flashing like a number on a screen: 12.19. I blinked, the light as momentarily blinding as the flash of a camera. Then I noticed the calendar. All I saw was Thursday before the scene began to move once more, still in slow motion. My attention instantly returned to the gunman. His finger inched towards the trigger. His whole body was shaking.

Panic crippled me. "Please!" I called to Jonathan.

His sad eyes pierced my soul. Everything suddenly clicked together. *This* was the multiple-choice test he was giving me. He'd said only I knew the answer. He couldn't help me.

A growl erupted from the gunman's throat as his feeble control shattered and his finger pulled back the trigger.

There was no time left to decide, to think. There was only time to act. Instinctively, I jumped in front of the young girl as I heard the deafening crack of the gun being fired.

I jumped so violently that I awoke, drenched in sweat.

* * *

Jeremy jolted beside me. "Are you okay? Bad dream?" he asked, his voice groggy. "Isy, you're shivering." He wrapped his arms around me. I was shaking uncontrollably.

He rubbed my arms as he held me. "Tell me what's wrong," he coaxed. "This wasn't just a bad dream, was it? This was something more. Tell me what happened."

Concern peppered his voice. I desperately wanted to tell him all about it, to share the weight of it and work through it together. I wanted to tell him more than I wanted to tell anyone anything in my entire life. I needed him to help me, to make sense of the unimaginable. *What did it mean?*

But I knew what it meant. I heard the gun fire. I saw myself fall.

I knew exactly what it meant.

And as much as I wanted to share the burden of that knowledge with Jeremy, I knew that was the most selfish thing I could do. I knew the vehemence of his fear for me would be unbearable to him.

I couldn't do it to him. Not when I hadn't figured out what I could do to prevent the outcome of the premonition. Perhaps if I just avoided that bank altogether, none of it would eventuate. I immediately dismissed that thought, sensing that the same scene would take place, just without me there. The young girl could potentially be killed.

These horrifying thoughts swirled in my head, making me dizzy.

There had to be something I could do that didn't involve the child *or* me being harmed. Surely. *Surely.*

A sad smile touched my lips as I recalled the promise I'd made in the hospital after Neil had been injured. I'd sworn to save the person in my next vision, or die trying.

I couldn't believe the irony. The universe apparently had taken me literally and decided to cash in that chip, testing my resolve.

I shook my head. It couldn't be that black and white. I decided that gray was my new favorite color. There had to be more choices than I could initially see. There had to be.

There just had to be.

I shivered once more and a sudden wave of nausea rolled over me. I pushed it down. I knew I had to pull it together for Jeremy.

"Isy, tell me."

"It's nothing, Jez, really. I jumped because I was falling in my dream. I had that reoccurring dream when I'm taking a test and I don't know the answers. It's just silly." If I ignored the more serious parts I'd carefully omitted, the rest was true, I convinced myself. I hated lying to Jeremy.

"Are you sure? You seem pretty wound up, it's like—"

He stopped himself from saying it but I knew what he was thinking. The last time he held me while I shook uncontrollably was when Jonathan died. If I was reacting this badly, it had to be bad.

"I just felt really out of control, like I had the weight of the world of my shoulders and everything was crashing down on me. Like the test was a life-and-death situation. You know me, I hate to fail a test," I tried to joke, keeping my voice light-hearted. "I'm just being melodramatic. Don't worry so much." I cuddled him, trying to show him that I was okay.

"But maybe if it felt like a big deal, maybe there's something more to it we should consider—"

I interrupted his thoughts. I didn't want him to go there.

"Now who's the one who takes everything too seriously? Maybe *you* will be the teacher in the role-play after all . . ." I hoped my playful tone would appease him, circumventing his concern.

He snorted. "Hardly."

The tension in his muscles didn't dissipate. He knew me better than that. But I was determined to protect him.

"We'd better get back to sleep. Something tells me I'd better rest now while I can, I may need my energy for your big night of secrecy." I kissed his neck and rolled over, pretending to relax even though I knew I had slept about as much as I was going to that night.

He chuckled, but this time there was no humor in it.

33

DOOR OF HOPE

I WALKED AROUND the next day on autopilot, completely in a daze.

I was a swirling vortex of emotions: confusion, fear, foreboding, anxiety, uncertainty, frustration, anger, denial, and most strange of all—hope.

Hope that this was not what it seemed. It couldn't be (that was the denial). It was too much—I wasn't law enforcement and I wasn't the girl's mother (hello, Frustration). How could such a burden possibly fall to me? It just wasn't fair.

Of all the visions I'd had so far, a lot had been asked of me. Usually it predicated the need for faith—a lot of it—and the willingness to risk my carefully attained reputation at work. I'd believed that potentially damaging my career had been a lot to ask. Until now.

Never in my wildest dreams did I ever imagine that *more* could be asked of me—*so* much more.

Everything.

There was no justice in that. My reward for all of my sacrifices up until now could not possibly be this. If others were worth saving, was I not worth the same?

Was it selfish of me to not want to recklessly endanger my own life?

Surely I wasn't responsible for the actions of a crazed gunman? Surely it wasn't *me* who was expected to pay the price of his actions? How could it be?

But how could I ignore the screams of a terrified child? If anything happened to her, those screams would haunt me for the rest of my life.

This was when the anger flared.

It wasn't right that I should be expected to choose! It wasn't right that I had this burden to bear!

This was too much! I never signed up for this! No one ever asked!

Just when things were really going well, the rug was being pulled out from under me. What was the point of showing me the possibilities of pursuing my own jewelry line if that wasn't destined for my future? That was just twisted. A mocking, flaunting, cruel joke. *Here, Isy—here are all your dreams and the perfect guy to boot. He loves you unconditionally. Now kiss it all goodbye.*

Was the point of all that to make it that much harder to choose? To have more to lose? I felt like an insignificant pawn in a sadistic game.

If I allowed that scene to play out, if I jumped in front of the child, what would happen? Would I be seriously injured? Or would I be killed? Either one was a distinct possibility.

Jeremy. I couldn't do it to Jeremy. I couldn't leave him. Especially after everything he'd been through this year. What would this do to him? It would completely devastate him. And who would pick up the pieces? Who would comfort him at night? Who would love him the way that I loved him?

And it would anger him. Sizzling, seething rage. Directed at the world—and at me. He would never understand. Would the scorching flames of his fury engulf him? Would he ever be okay again?

Just the thought of leaving him made my chest clench and my breathing uneven. I couldn't do this. I couldn't even handle the pressure of *thinking* about it, let alone actually acting on it.

They had the wrong girl.

This girl deserved a break.

This girl deserved the happiness she'd found.

If life was precious, then mine was, too.

And then a crushing thought suddenly made my blood run cold and nearly brought me to my knees. *What if I were exactly like Jonathan?* What if my time was up? What if my time was always going to be up and this was about making the most of the time I had left? *What if I were going to die no matter what I did?*

I ran to the bathroom and threw up.

No. No. No. It couldn't be. If this were a multiple-choice test, there had to be options. There had to be more than one way that this could go. It couldn't be predetermined. My fate couldn't be sealed. Not yet. Fate could not be that cruelly twisted. *Could it?*

I tried to think logically. If this were a multiple-choice test, what were the options?

A: Do nothing to prevent the death of an innocent child.

B: Willingly sacrifice myself to save the child and in doing so kill the man I loved.

Neither of those options appealed to me.

I consoled myself with the knowledge that multiple-choice tests always had more than two options. In fact, I knew the statistics showed that the majority of correct answers sat at option C.

C. I liked option C. I had no idea what it was yet, but it was definitely the one I wanted to go with. The one that didn't involve A or B.

Option C *had* to be the get-out-of-jail-free card. Option C had to be something that would protect both the child *and* me. It just had to be.

And so I completed the circle and arrived back at the door of hope.

*   *   *

I was determined to forget about the crushing burden that had been unjustly thrust upon me so I could enjoy that evening with Jeremy. I didn't want him to see me visibly shaken. Tonight, I was going to stick with shameless denial. He clearly had something mysterious planned for the evening and I intended to show him that I appreciated it.

I knocked on his door promptly at 8:00 P.M., brimming with curiosity.

He gave me a huge smile as he opened the door, but my eyes only caught a glimpse of him before being drawn towards the interior of the apartment, which was completely bathed in firelight. He grinned at the astonished look on my face and gently pulled me inside.

My mouth was open as I surveyed my surroundings. The entrance opened into the living room, with a hallway to the right. The hallway was lined with dozens of candles, the shimmering flames glowing brightly and casting swaying shadows on the wall. The living room was also aglow in soft candlelight. Soothing jazz music filled the room, the flames dancing along to the melody.

I noticed that the coffee table had been moved up against the wall. In front of the couch, a sheet was laid out on the rug and bordered by rose petals and more candles, with pillows and a folded towel at one end. A small box lay nearby.

I was transported to another world: a serene and romantic sanctuary where nothing bad could ever reach you, where you were completely cocooned from everything in the outside world. In that moment, there were only two people in the entire universe, and we were both in this room. Everything else ceased to exist. It was exactly what I needed to allow the air to slowly filter back into my lungs. In this sanctuary, I could breathe again.

My heart fluttered as I gazed up at Jeremy who'd been watching me intently and seemed pleased by my reaction.

We were silent for another moment as I took it all in. "Is that Miles Davis playing?" I finally breathed.

"Yes. You have a good ear," he murmured.

"I can't believe you did all of this," I told him, incredulous. "For me."

He wrapped his arms around me and pulled me tightly to his chest. "I would do anything for you, don't you know that?" He lifted a hand to the nape of my neck and brought my lips to his, his kiss like a soft caress. "It's not what I originally had in mind,

I have to admit, but you seemed a little tense this morning and I wanted to do something special."

"Thank you, Jez. Really, this is too much. You've taken my breath away."

He beamed proudly before his voice turned husky. "I plan to—later." He gave me another kiss before unlocking his arms. "Are you hungry? Let's have dinner." He took my hand and led me into the open kitchen and dining room.

He pulled a chair out from the table for me before taking his seat next to mine. There were candles in the middle of the table but they didn't adorn the rest of the room. Instead, a lamp stood in the corner, the gentle light enhancing the serene atmosphere. An arrangement of beautiful long stemmed red roses completed the table centerpiece.

"I wish I'd had time to make dinner, but I picked up some Japanese," Jeremy apologized as he lifted the lids off the serving dishes.

"Are you kidding? This is perfect. And with the amount of time it would have taken to set all of this up, I'm surprised you even had time to pick up dinner. This is absolutely amazing, Jez, and a wonderful surprise." I leaned into him. "A little different to what I was expecting, I have to say. Okay, a lot different to what I was expecting."

His eyes gleamed with pleasure. "There's more to come. Just wait." Then he brushed his lips against my neck, adding in a low voice, "I'll take a raincheck on my original plans."

The tone of his voice instantly made my heart race. "Why wait?"

His breath was hot against my ear. "All good things are worth waiting for."

Clearing his throat, he turned his attention back to the table while I tried to compose myself. He dished out a feast of all my favorites: salmon sashimi, miso soup, chicken yakitori, osinko and gyoza. It looked delicious.

"So how has your day been?" I asked him, shifting my attention. "I mean, before you performed this little miracle here."

"Not bad. We started rolling out a new software upgrade at work, so it was pretty hectic. There're always bugs that have to be ironed out in the beginning, and a lot of frustrated campers to deal with. So I wasn't exactly Mr. Popular today. Well, except with Ammon. I grabbed a bite with him at lunch. You'll be happy to know that he's totally into Rachel. They've been talking a lot and he met with her to 'talk about his CV'"—he air-quoted the words and gave me a wink—"I think they're going out for dinner one night this week."

"Really? That's great news! Rachel hasn't said anything." I snorted at him. "And you told me it would be a total disaster." I treated him to my best I-told-you-so look, basking in the glory of being right.

"Ah-hem," he cleared his throat. "If I do recall, you tried to set up *Brad* with Rachel. The Ammon thing was a lucky coincidence. And it's early days so let's not put any expectations on it. Or take any credit."

"Still, the dinner was a success. I'll take a win where I can get it."

He gave me a troubled look and I briefly wondered if he thought that was a reference to the premonition last night, but he didn't probe me. I changed the subject back to his workday.

After we'd finished dinner, I started to clear the table.

"Leave that," Jez ordered. "Now it's time for your surprise," he announced as he took my hand. He led me back into the living room and I eagerly followed.

He lowered me down onto the sheet and pulled off my shoes. Then he reached over and opened the box next to the sheet, revealing an assortment of essential oils.

"What's this?" I asked.

"Like I said, it hasn't gone unnoticed that you've been tense. I thought I'd try to help you relax. Maybe if you can let go of some of the stress, you'll be able to talk about it." He gave me a knowing look, indicating that he *definitely* wasn't fooled by my nonchalance last night. "So I'm going to give you a massage. I have a choice of lavender, rose or sandalwood. The sales lady told me that all three are quite popular. Which would you prefer, ma'am?"

"You must be tired, you don't have to do that. Why don't I give you a massage instead? After all, I thought I was supposed to be the slave this evening, not the other way around." I felt so guilty that he had gone to so much trouble already today and must be exhausted. Jeremy was always looking after me.

He shook his head. "Nope. This is the deluxe service for our VIP guests here at the Plaza. We aim to please."

I smiled, he was just so sweet. "Seriously—"

"Don't argue with me. This is my hidden ploy to get you to disrobe," he said, a teasing smile playing on his lips. "I want to spoil you tonight. To make sure that all the tension and stress are completely gone and you can relax for a change." He handed me the towel. "Now please remove your top, ma'am," he instructed, a glint in his eye.

I opened my mouth to protest, but he cut me off again. "Indulge me."

I dutifully obeyed, laying down and resting my head on the pillow. Jeremy's hands were magical, first gently rubbing my shoulders and back and then slowly applying more pressure. He seemed to find the knots in my back and massage all of the tension out of my body. I closed my eyes and let the relaxing music soothe me as his strong hands extinguished the sense of foreboding that had been swelling inside me.

I mentally added masterful masseur to his long list of many talents. I was wondering what other secret talents lay waiting when I began to worry whether I'd be around to find out. I quickly banished the thought from my mind, that was a problem for another day. If I had to stay away from the bank, that was what I'd do. There was no way I could give this up, give Jeremy up.

Jeremy didn't talk as he ran his warm hands over my skin. The sensation of his touch sent tingles down my spine. He always made me feel so treasured, enveloped in such a tender bubble of pure love. I could only faintly hear the melody of his steady, deep breathing. Eventually, the sound became louder and I realized that the deep breathing I heard was mine. I was so deeply relaxed that I could feel myself drifting off to sleep.

I didn't know how much time passed before I felt a towel being wrapped around me. My eyes fluttered as I tried to remember where I was.

"Jez?"

"Shh," he whispered. "Go back to sleep. I'm taking you to bed."

I was vaguely aware of him lifting me and carrying me down the hallway, with the flames of the candles still dancing.

34

OPTION C

AFTER HAVING A PREMONITION involving my own impending death, funnily enough, the market stall didn't seem like such a big deal anymore.

I continued to go though the motions. Until I had more information about the bank robbery, I knew that it wouldn't take place yet. And sitting in a dark corner numbly rocking myself back and forth wouldn't suddenly reveal the miraculous Option-C to me, no matter how much I wished it would.

I burned to share my burden, but I came up empty. I knew I couldn't tell my mom, she'd *freak*. She'd speed down to San Francisco like she'd just robbed a bank (yes, I saw the irony) with ten police cars in pursuit, then—if she managed to make it in one piece—she'd chain me to a wall and probably go to the bank herself. Nope. No way I could tell her.

I considered calling Jules but I resisted telling her as well. I didn't want to worry her, either. She was so far away, I knew the anxiety would practically kill her. And this time, I didn't think she could really help me. This time, I had to wrestle with it alone. My decisions had to be my own, no one could tell me what was in my heart or in my future.

In any case, I wasn't really sure if I was ready to say the words out loud. I knew they would get caught in my throat, like a rising scream choked off by terror. And so the words remained tightly locked in my own mind, tormenting only me.

And life went on. Despite the fact that I only half paid attention to it.

By the time I arrived home on the day of my market stall, I was exhausted.

Harrison was now back at Barkleys, so I'd cleared it with Sam to get an extended lunch break to run the stall. She was very encouraging and even asked to see my collection. She eagerly snapped up a pair of silver earrings before two more girls in the team overheard the commotion and wandered over, providing me with sales numbers two and three.

All three girls had been particularly complimentary—no laughter or snickers like I'd feared in a previous life (BCG—Before Crazed Gunman) where ridicule seemed like such a big deal to me. Sam suggested showing the collection to a few other girls within the company, but I initially resisted. I only had a small collection to begin with and I needed to preserve some of my favorite pieces for the stall. I promised that I'd bring back any remaining stock.

To my surprise, the enthusiasm for the collection trickled over at Barkleys and I returned to Parkmores empty-handed. Everything had been sold and I even had orders for more. Had it been a week earlier, I would've been able to bask in the glory, knowing that my creations had been a hit. I would've been practically bouncing off the walls with excitement.

But as the days passed, everything I felt was numbed. Like I had a protective, almost impenetrable shield around me that only the barest of emotion could filter through. I was in a bubble. It was the only way I could keep putting one foot in front of the other. Numbing the fear and anguish unfortunately meant numbing any happiness as well.

I couldn't believe the popularity of my collection, though. Somewhere in the deepest recesses of my mind, a thought trickled through: It was good enough. *I* was good enough.

Too bad the universe was out to kill me. Freaking murderous bastard.

I shook my head and dismissed the thought before it could embed itself into my consciousness. There was more that I could not see. There had to be.

I turned back to thoughts of the market stall and tried to allow myself to enjoy the success. I briefly wondered whether I'd priced it correctly. I pushed back my obsessive fixation on always making things better, *being* better, being *more*. That just reminded me of the bank and the excruciating pressure I was under. I refused to allow my normal compulsive tendencies to ruin this one thing that I knew I'd done right. Refused to look for possible weaknesses and shortcomings like I did every day in legal arguments, like I was doing with the impending choice that I would soon face.

Jeremy was at my door before I'd barely had enough time to change out of my work clothes. I knew I had to feign enthusiasm—he'd expect nothing less.

"Hi, Jez. Come in." I plastered a smile to my face like I'd just stepped in front of a group of paparazzi.

"Hey, Is. So how'd you go today? I take it the smile is a good sign?" He kissed me and perched himself on the back of the couch.

I took a deep breath, knowing I was about to talk fast. Show time. "Better than I'd expected. I completely sold out and I've got orders for more—can you believe it? Who would've thought?" I didn't need to fabricate the surprise in my voice, the success of the day hadn't completely sunk in yet.

"I did. I knew it would go well, I've never known you to suck at anything—well, except cooking. But even then, it's like you decided that if you were going to be bad at something, you'd be the *best* at being bad at it." Jez started laughing but cleared his throat when he noticed that I wasn't joining in. "Are you okay, Is? I'm worried about you."

"Yeah, I'm fine, I—"

It was difficult to lie convincingly when the room started spinning around you.

I blinked and I was no longer standing in the apartment. I was standing in the bank.

Oh good, I can't wait to experience this again. Right now in front of Jez. That's just perfect. Kick a girl when she's down.

The scene played out exactly as before, except now I could smell the overpowering scent emanating from the gunman: a mix of smoke, alcohol and sweat.

The young girl's high-pitched screams made me want to cover my ears. The same sense of terror and anxiety flooded my senses. Jonathan was there again. This time he looked at me and then turned towards a sign on the wall, trying to draw my attention to it. I now recognized the bank and knew exactly where it was, situated halfway between Barkleys and Parkmores. I'd been in there less than two weeks earlier and seen that sign.

Everything was happening in slow motion again.

"Jonathan, what's option C?" I pleaded. "There has to be another way!"

His sad eyes briefly focused on mine before turning to the gunman. I looked over as I saw the gunman's finger inch towards the trigger, and once again I was falling . . .

* * *

When I opened my eyes, I was back in my apartment and in Jeremy's arms. He'd caught me before I hit the ground.

"Jez—" I started, not knowing what I could say this time but desperately wanting to assuage the anxiousness in his eyes.

"No, Isy, don't tell me it was nothing this time," he warned, his voice thick. "I know it's something. I know it's something so big that you don't want to tell me. Which makes me think you don't want to worry me, which makes me think that I should be *very* worried."

I fought back the tears at seeing his distress and knowing I was the cause of it. The fierce determination etched on his face told me that no quip could brush this under the carpet. "What happened?" I asked him.

"You said Jonathan's name and something about some kind of option, and then you were falling. I just caught you in the nick of time. Where were you?" His voice was edged with apprehension.

I started fidgeting. "I— I—"

He raked a hand through his hair, letting out a long breath. "I tried to give you time, hoping you'd tell me on your own. But I'm done waiting for you to figure out that you need to let me in."

"Jez—"

"No, I don't want to hear any more bullshit. I'm done pretending that everything is fine and playing along when you're clearly hiding something from me." He eyed me with a fierceness in his eyes that dared me to deny it.

"You know, when you took so long to tell me everything that was going on with you, I wasn't upset because I knew how hard it was for you to open up, and I knew it was something that you didn't tell anyone"—he paused briefly when I cringed at his words—"but now, it's different. I tried to be patient, I even tried to help you relax, but this is ridiculous. You have to—" A frown shadowed his features, his brows drawing together. The fierceness in his eyes morphed into suspicion. "Wait. When I said you didn't tell anyone about your visions, you had a funny look on your face. Who else did you tell?"

I sucked in a breath. This conversation had just moved in an unexpected direction. "I never said that I hadn't told anyone. You just assumed."

"Who?"

"The trip to Florence, it's why I went. To talk to Julia."

"Who else?"

"My mom."

"Who else?"

"Why is this an issue all of a sudden?"

"Why are you dodging the question?"

"Because I don't understand why it's important."

"Because you're making it important."

I eyed him with a look of incredulity. "Me? You're the one doing the interrogating!"

He crossed his arms over his chest. "The fact that you think it's an interrogation and behave like you have something to hide is the exact reason why you're the one who's making this a big deal. If it's not, then just tell me who else."

My gaze darted to the floor. His scrutiny felt like a thousand-watt light bulb in my face.

"Isy," he said more forcefully this time. "Who else?"

I squirmed under the intensity of his gaze. I should've just said from the beginning. He was right, now I'd put more emphasis on it. I swallowed.

"Matt. Matt knew." I dared a peek at him and quickly returned to inspecting the carpet when I saw his face flush.

"Who's Matt?" He said his name like it was a swear word. "You have got to be freaking kidding me. Do *not* tell me he's the douche."

My inspection of the carpet didn't waver. Maybe if I stared at it long enough, I'd disappear into it.

"Do not tell me that you confided in that douchebag, that you trusted *him* but not me."

Given his dislike for Matt, I expected him to be unimpressed, but I hadn't expected his words to be edged with pain. Finally, I stopped cowering, lifting my gaze and putting my hand on his arm.

"Jez, it wasn't like that—"

"Tell me honestly, Isy"—his voice was barely a whisper and I had to strain to hear him—"am I the consolation prize?"

My mouth dropped. The pain in his eyes felt like a knife twisting in my heart.

"If he'd left his fiancée for you, would you be with him right now? Is he the one you really wanted?"

"God, no!" Did he think so little of what we had? Did he think I didn't love him as much as I did?

I lifted my other hand to his face and a tear spilled down my cheek. "How could you think that for even a second?"

"How could I not? You seemed to have no problem trusting him, letting him in. But me—you're still hiding things from me. What else am I supposed to think?"

I cupped his face in both hands, a desperate pleading in my eyes. "Listen to me. I love you, Jez. More than anyone or anything. I'd die for you. Just the thought of not being with you tears my heart out. There's no one, *no one,* that I trust more than you." I pressed my lips to his, needing to feel him, but he was still and didn't mold to my touch.

I sighed. "Telling Matt wasn't a deliberate decision. I didn't actually *want* to tell him. He saw me do something that gave me away and he guessed. I swear it. I don't think it's fair that you'd hold it against me, or imply that it somehow means I don't trust you or love you. I haven't told you about the premonition I had because I love you *so* much, don't you see? I didn't want to worry you. You're the only one I want, the only one I need."

He took my hands in his, his eyes solemn.

"It's hard to feel needed when you won't open up to me, Isy. Are you always going to keep me in the dark? Or are you going to open up to me? Because I can't be in this relationship by myself.

And you can't keep things from me because you don't want me to worry, or burden me. Your problems *are* my problems. Can't you see that all I want is to help you? All I want to do is protect you, but you won't give me the chance."

"All I want is to protect you, too."

"Well, don't. The only thing I want to be protected from is being kept in the dark. No more secrets."

He kissed me, this time with the intensity and passion that was lacking before. I reached for his shirt but he caught my hands and pulled them away, the fierceness in his eyes blazing again.

"So tell me. Now."

And so I did. I explained about the bank, about Jonathan being there, the gunman, the terrified cries of the young girl. I omitted the gunshot, there had to be something I could spare him. But he knew me too well. He knew I was holding back.

"Is that it?" he asked.

"Yes." My voice was barely a whisper.

"Then why were you falling?"

"I—"

"Why?" he pressed, resolute.

"The young girl . . . He was going to hurt the young girl."

That's when the tears started. And wouldn't stop.

* * *

"Okay," Jeremy said as he handed me the glass of water, like it wasn't up for discussion, "I don't want you going anywhere near that bank." He took a seat beside me on the couch, angling his body to face me.

"Jez, believe me when I say that I don't want to. It's just not as clear as that. I'm not sure what to do. I can't do *nothing*. There's got to be a way to save her."

"I'll go. I think I've figured out when it is. You said—"

I cut him off right there. "You will *not* go."

He was just as stubborn as I was. "*You* will not go. I know you'll somehow end up there even if you don't want to. So I'll go. End of story."

"Don't *end-of-story* me. You don't get to order me. And you don't get to just risk your life. No way."

"Oh, but you do?"

"Who had the vision?" I asked petulantly.

"And who's the stubborn idiot who won't accept help?" he snapped.

Emotions were running high and our voices were getting louder. I knew we should take a breath before this got out of hand, but all of the built-up emotions came spilling out of me and it was too late to stop it.

"Oh—so what? You think I'm the damsel-in-distress? Don't be so condescending. You can't magically fix it any more than I can."

I'd never seen Jeremy so furious before. He jumped off the couch, erupting like a volcano. The anger rolled off him, so tangible it seemed to fill every space in the room. "Since when have I *ever* treated you that way? Not everything is about you! You think you can control everything—and everything has to be *your* way. You're too blind to see when you're in over your head. And too arrogant to think that maybe—*God forbid*—I may be able to work out something you can't!"

His words cut me like a knife and pierced my heart. I wrapped my arms around myself and blinked away the impending tears.

I didn't want to fight with Jeremy. Oh, how I didn't want to fight. And yet, that's all we seemed to be doing tonight. How did we get here?

"Is . . . Is that what you really think?" I choked out in a small voice, feeling more vulnerable than I ever had in my life.

I instantly saw the remorse in his eyes. He sat back down next to me and extended his hand to touch me, before slowly pulling it back like he was afraid it would be unwelcome.

"No, Isy. God, no. I'm . . . I'm so sorry. I didn't mean to yell at you."

I could see that he desperately wanted to rewind the last few minutes. He didn't want to hurt me.

"I didn't mean what I said. I know this is not about you. This is anything but. You're more worried about a kid you don't even know than yourself. I know you. I know you want to do the best you can. I know you need to find a way to help that kid. I know you're confused. And I know you need me. I'm sorry for attacking you. I'm just so terrified of losing you. And I was still upset that you tried to keep this from me. We're a team. We're going to work this out together, okay?" He reached forward and gently laid his hand on mine.

"Okay," I responded, trying to mask the residual hurt in my voice. I knew I was far from perfect, and trying to keep this from him had hurt him more than I'd known. "And I'm sorry, Jez, for dragging you into all of this. I know it's not easy being with me. This is more than you should have to deal with."

"Isy, no. Don't say that. I don't want you to think for one second that I feel that way. I'd go to the moon and back with you. I would run into a hundred burning buildings to protect you. Can't you see how terrified I am of losing you?" His voice cracked, his eyes glistening. "I couldn't bear it, I just couldn't bear it."

I lifted my free hand to his cheek. "I couldn't bear to lose you, either."

His tender gaze flashed with love.

"Okay," I continued. "For now, let's assume that neither one of us is going."

"Okay . . ." he agreed, but trepidation flickered across his features. He looked worried I was just waiting for him to turn his head while I made a run for the door.

"You said you think you've figured out when it is. How?"

"Oh no. I love you but I'm not telling you squat until you *promise* me that you're not going into that bank."

"Jez."

He crossed his arms. "You heard me. Promise me that you will not—*under any circumstances*—go into that bank and I'll tell you."

"Jez, you know I can't do that. I'm ashamed to admit that I'm cowardly enough that it's highly unlikely I'll go in, but I can't promise you."

"Then I guess we're at an impasse." His arms remained fixed in place, his resolve unwavering.

I sighed. "So according to you, what am I supposed to do?"

"Okay, this is my plan." He uncrossed his arms and leaned forward. "*We* go there together and stay outside a few doors down. As soon as we spot the guy in question, we call the police. For a bank robbery, they'd be there in a heartbeat."

"Jez, I don't think they'll get there that quickly."

"Well, we know the day. As soon as you get a better sense of the time, we'll call it in. We won't wait for the guy to show."

"Then maybe the police will show up too early."

"That's even better. I should've thought of that. Then the crazy guy won't go in at all, will he? Not if there're cops roaming around. Crisis averted."

"That just means he'll go back another time, or to another bank," I pointed out, revealing the flaw in his plan.

"And?"

"What do you mean—and?"

"As far as I'm concerned, you're worried about the kid. I don't think you'd be jumping in front of a loaded gun for some random guy." He raised an eyebrow, daring me to contradict him. "It's the kid. The kid won't be in the bank if he goes back another time."

"So it doesn't matter if he shoots someone else?"

He snorted. "Forgive me for caring more that he doesn't shoot *you* and not finding it in my heart to put some stranger's safety above yours. Besides, it's because the kid is screaming and disrupts his plans that he freaks. If there're other people in the next bank he tries to hit, then those people should be—and hopefully will be—smart enough to just do what he says. Either way, not our problem. Sorry, that's the cold, hard truth. We can't save the world."

It was a little harsh, and I wasn't entirely convinced it worked that way, but I was desperate. Rightly or wrongly, I could see the wisdom in his plan. If the police showed before the gunman, he would never go in. The police would be infuriated and try to find the source of the presumed hoax, but the gunman would never go in. The young girl would be safe. I would be safe. It was neither A or B.

I think we just found Option C.

*   *   *

After I promised not to go in the bank and to stick with Jeremy's plan, he explained his theory of when this would all take place. He believed the numbers 12.19 referred to the date: December 19. It was so obvious I couldn't believe that I hadn't thought of it. I'd just presumed the numbers referred to the time, not the date. But Jeremy checked the calendar and it was a Thursday. It all fit.

The nineteenth was in nine days. And so we played the waiting game. Together.

35

PATCH OF WHITE

WHEN SAM CALLED ME into her office the next day, I was delighted to see her wearing my earrings.

"Are you going to be making more jewelry?" she asked, after we'd discussed the upcoming office Christmas party.

"Yes, I think so. I'm just not sure about the time commitment," I admitted. She believed I was referring to the amount of time required to make it, not comprehending the real meaning of the word *time* to me now.

"Well, make sure you bring it in when you get some more stuff together. I'd love to see it."

"I will," I agreed. "Thank you."

She shifted in her seat, straightening her posture. "I asked you to come in here because I wanted to talk to you informally about something. Just run it past you."

"Sure. What is it?"

"Jonathan thought very highly of you." She swallowed, her

eyes clouding. Jonathan's absence continued to haunt the team and a silent sadness momentarily fell over the room before Sam cleared her throat and smiled. "And you really fit in well with our team here. Your expertise and experience is exactly what we're looking for. I know Harrison would absolutely *kill* me, but I'll deal with that later." She paused, assessing my reaction before verbalizing her proposition. "I was wondering whether you would ever consider making this arrangement more permanent?"

I sat motionless, contemplating what she'd just asked. It wasn't something that I would have ever considered six months ago, but now . . . If I had a second chance after next Thursday, I didn't really intend to squander it by going back to my old life at Barkleys.

She saw a small window of opportunity and moved in quickly. "I mean, I know you have a distinct career path at Barkleys so it would be a big decision to join our team full-time. We'd be looking to sweeten the deal to make it worth your while." She flashed me a gleaming smile.

She definitely had my attention. Again, I sat quietly, but my eyes betrayed me.

"I know in the long-term, we could never compete on salary. What we offer is time. You just mentioned that you wanted time for your jewelry-making endeavors, and you'd certainly have more time for those kinds of outside interests here than you would at Barkleys." She'd seen the window of opportunity widen slightly and was sending in the marching band. "If you would consider it, just tell me what it would take to entice you and I'll see what I can do."

It wasn't that often that I was given the opportunity to sit in the driver's seat—when they were asking me what *I* wanted, instead of the other way around.

"Tell you anything I want?" I confirmed, enjoying the moment.

"Shoot," she encouraged.

I decided to start big so we could negotiate something smaller. "Well then, speaking of time, I don't suppose you'd consider letting me work from home on occasion, or making the role four days a week instead?"

"Would you really want to work four days?"

"Would you seriously consider that?" I was stunned. I'd assumed she'd tell me to forget it. I knew she wanted another full-time resource.

"It's not my preference, I admit, but if that's what it'd take, then I'd consider it."

Oh. My. Lord. The possibilities were enormous. I'd never considered such an option before. There was no way it would ever be considered at Barkleys, only a few people were given the allowance and all were mothers with very young children.

Being able to reduce my hours would mean that I could still spend time making jewelry but also have time in the evenings and on the weekends to spend with Jeremy and friends. I would have loads of time to fill my orders and prepare for the next market stall . . .

I hoped.

Unless, of course, I was dead.

Again, I forced myself to stay positive. Option C was going to work, I reassured myself. Then my train of thought was interrupted by a sudden realization: I wouldn't be at the next market day (dead *or* alive) if I wasn't working at Barkleys. That was when it hit me that I would be walking away from the firm I'd known for the past three years.

Was I really ready to do that?

Sing it from the rooftops, I couldn't be more certain. The idea had frightened me up until now. It would mean letting go of the dreams I'd had for so long, the dreams I'd worked so hard for.

A feeling of certainty flooded me and washed those thoughts away. I wasn't letting go of my dreams, I had just replaced them with new ones. The dreams I'd had no longer held the same desire for me. What I wanted in the past was not what I wanted in the present. Nothing reinforced that more than my current predicament. Life was short, far too short, to waste any of it. I was still galloping, but I'd finally taken off the horse blinders. My line of vision was no longer linear.

Come next week, after the nightmare was—hopefully—behind me, things would be different. I was ready to take a leap forward. Up until now, I'd been reluctant to leave Barkleys because I thought that my position there was entwined with my very identity. But now I fully appreciated that it was the piece of the puzzle that no longer fit. I had been trying to squeeze all of the other pieces around it, thinking it was the central piece—the epicenter. Instead, it was the piece that was out of place when all of the others joined together.

I was ready to let go of everything that was holding me down and embrace what lay ahead.

I had enjoyed my time at Parkmores. I liked the culture of the team. I liked that no one eyed me suspiciously if I left the office while there was still daylight to enjoy. I particularly appreciated not having to bill for every six minutes of time. I respected Sam and her management style—especially now that she was offering me a world of possibilities.

Everything pointed to yes, even after the left side of my brain screamed the words: pay *cut.* Reducing my hours would result in a sizeable pay cut, compounded by the salary reduction in leaving Barkleys.

Surprisingly, that didn't bother me as much as I would have expected. Time had new meaning for me now. And it was worth so much more than monetary currency.

"I'm definitely interested," I told Sam.

"Great," she beamed. "Let's talk again later in the week."

* * *

"What do you think?" I asked Jeremy as we sat on the couch that evening. I was doing my best to mask my residual fears about the following Thursday and act like there was no doubt at all that it was just another stepping-stone.

"I think if that's what you want, you should do it."

"There'll obviously be financial ramifications," I pointed out. "I'm not used to having to watch my pennies, but I'll get used to it."

He seemed to fight back a smile. "Well, you know, I have an easy solution," he said conspiratorially.

"Okay, let's hear it." I rolled my eyes. I was waiting for him to start preaching about eating out all the time, or spending too much money on shoes—neither of which I would find particularly amusing.

"There's an obvious way to *not* worry about watching your pennies." He tried to sound casual but the corners of his mouth were turned up in a grin.

The fact that he was dragging it out only irritated me more. I raised my eyebrows at him, urging him to get to the point.

He shook his head, sighing. "You honestly don't know where I'm going with this, do you?"

"So are you going to enlighten me or drag it out all night?" I retorted.

He raked a hand through his hair. "We spend most of our time together. I'm usually here and my apartment is empty. Just across the hall. Empty." He paused while he studied me.

I didn't move. I was still processing what he was saying.

"So," he continued, "wouldn't it make sense if we made it official and I moved in here?"

My mouth dropped open. I was speechless.

"Why do you look so surprised? I'm here all the time, anyway. Does the idea of living together really freak you out that much?"

Still no words.

"Is, come on."

I tried to choose my words carefully, but it just came rushing out. "I don't think you should ask me to live together just because you think I want to save money."

"Hang on, Is," he interrupted. "That's not the reason I'm asking. Although financially it would make sense and I thought I'd appeal to the logical side of you. I'm asking because I know what I want. I want to be with you. I want to see you every night and wake up with you every morning." Then he added with so much conviction it surprised me, "And I want my own damn key to get in."

I didn't know what to say. My instinctual reaction was to laugh it off. Was he crazy? Things had moved so quickly. I planned to tell him all of the reasons why it was a bad idea but the words never materialized. Nothing in recent times was as I'd expected, nothing followed the rules of logic I'd always counted on.

He was still looking at me, expectant. I got up quietly and left the room.

"Isy," he called out after me, the frustration clearly audible in his voice.

I didn't reply, but returned moments later.

"Hold out your hand," I instructed.

He furrowed his brow but reluctantly did as I requested. I dropped the spare key I'd retrieved from my dresser drawer onto his palm.

It wasn't the first time he'd mentioned a key; I should have given it to him sooner. I was so accustomed to being on my own, so accustomed to being in control of everything, that I didn't know how to let go. Releasing that control terrified me. But it was that same fear that had kept me from moving forward. The same fear that had caused me to shut him out when I needed him most.

"I'm sorry," I apologized. "I should've given you that already. You're right. You keeping a separate apartment across the hall is rather profligate. I know what I want, Jez."

A smile burst across his face, making his warm eyes sparkle. He knew what that key represented to me.

He enfolded me in his arms. His kiss was like a torrid love

letter, making every inch of my skin burn as my passion for him bubbled to the surface.

* * *

The next day I stepped out early to get lunch. With only seven more days till D-Day, nerves were really creeping in. Any time I allowed my thoughts to wander, the anxiety threatened to take hold of me. I extended my walk, hoping the fresh air and exercise would help release some of the tension in my muscles. The sun warmed my skin and I willed it to chase away my dark thoughts.

The street noise rippled through the air, humming in my ear. A car blared its horn at another driver while three men engaged in a heated discussion over some kind of stock trade and two nearby lovers embraced, murmuring to each other. As I averted my eyes from the intimacy of the couple, I caught sight of the bank: *the* bank.

I realized I'd unconsciously ventured to the scene of the crime, pulled along like a puppet on a string. Sometimes the more you wanted to avoid something, the more it drew you in, just like a sore tooth that you felt compelled to touch. This sore tooth was made of bricks and glass, and it was daring me to venture closer.

I can do this, I reassured myself. *Jeremy will be with me. I won't be alone.*

I took a couple of deep breaths and tried to focus on something menial to distract myself, like what I should pick up for dinner.

That's when the nausea suddenly overcame me. A fire burned in my stomach and my vision blurred. I lifted my hand to my head, closing my eyes for a second. *Not again, not here in the middle of the street,* I thought, groaning. I needed to sit before I face-planted onto the sidewalk. *Why now?*

When I reopened my eyes, I thought I saw Jonathan. I blinked and he was gone, replaced by a woman. I gaped at her and the answer came like a whisper into my nervous system.

We had the wrong Thursday. *This was it.* Today. Now. The time had come.

She grabbed her daughter's sleeve tightly as the young girl tried to shake her off. Even in just that moment, I could see that the girl had a mind of her own.

My knees went weak with the realization that I didn't have time to call the police. The mother was leaning down to reason with her daughter and, by the direction she was pointing, it was evident that she was about to enter the bank.

Every muscle in my body tensed. I shook my head. *No, no, no.* It wasn't the nineteenth. This could *not* be happening. Then understanding dawned. I looked at my watch. 12:17 P.M. I had two minutes. It wasn't the date. It was the time all along.

In exactly two minutes, there would be a gunshot.

In exactly two minutes, everything would change.

In exactly two minutes, someone could die.

Terror crashed over me and froze me in place. *I wasn't ready.* Jeremy wasn't here. I couldn't do this alone.

What should I do? *Someone please help me, I don't know what to do!*

Should I turn and run? Or should I enter the bank? Should I try to call Jeremy? I was completely panicked by indecision. To stand here and watch that child be killed . . . it was unimaginable.

To consider the possibility of my own life coming to an end, it was unfathomable.

This was the moment that would define everything. With trembling hands, I wiped the beads of sweat that moistened my forehead. Precious seconds were ticking by. I had no time to think, to plan. I only had time to act.

I looked wildly around me to locate the gunman. I couldn't see him. Maybe he hadn't arrived yet.

I had to act fast. Holding on to hope, I unglued my feet from the ground and charged forward. Allowing instinct to take over, I was saddened by the idea that Jeremy would think I'd broken my promise. *I'm sorry, Jez.*

But it wasn't too late. If I could stop them from entering the bank and get them away from here, I could save her. Save us both.

The woman was in front of the doors when I grabbed her arm.

"Excuse me!" she cried in a huff, taken aback.

"I'm sorry, I don't have time to explain. You have to get your daughter away from here!" I exclaimed. "Now!"

"Get your hands off me!" she yelled.

Exasperated, I tried again. "You don't understand, in there—" I paused as I shot a glance into the bank and went cold, catching a glimpse of a black helmet. He was already in the bank.

He was already in the bank!

I started to hyperventilate. He could pull out his gun at any moment. Heck, he could burst through those doors with us still standing there arguing about it.

There was no time for pleasantries, or subtleties. "Look, lady, there's a gunman in the bank and you need to get your daughter out of here *right now!*"

Her eyes darted towards the interior of the bank. I sensed she wasn't convinced that I wasn't completely insane, or a potential accomplice, but who bothered to challenge someone who was screaming about a gunman in a bank? She instinctively pulled her daughter away from the doors, keeping her eyes locked on mine.

I glanced at my watch—12:18 P.M. The lady pulled her daughter a few more steps back when time simultaneously seemed to slow down and speed up. Everything happened so quickly, but I observed every detail like I was holding a remote control with a freeze frame button.

The gunman burst out of the doors, his back to the street as he kept his gun pointed towards the people in the bank.

He bolted out so hastily that neither he, nor the pedestrian walking on the sidewalk, had time to avoid the collision.

The impact caught him off guard and I heard the sound of metal hitting the pavement. The pedestrian heard it, too. He spotted the gun and, either because he didn't realize what he was doing or because he was afraid of it being used against him, he reached for it. The gunman hit him, hard, and the two men struggled to grab hold of the weapon.

Their brawl caught the attention of those nearby, but no one had time to process what was really going on. No one screamed, no one ran. They didn't have time.

The struggle became more desperate. Neither man had a firm grasp on the weapon.

The first blast rang out, causing passersby to scream. I didn't think the first shot hit anyone.

That was the moment I would have expected to be paralyzed with fear. Instead, all of my confusion, anxiety and uncertainty were washed away. A feeling of calm swept through me and slowed my erratic heart. I knew Jonathan was there, watching. I knew I wasn't alone, after all.

Suddenly I understood everything, like the universe was revealing all of its secrets to me.

When you change one variable, another enters the equation. The gunman would've remained in the bank those few moments longer if he had been distracted by the young girl. He never would have exited at that exact moment and plowed into the pedestrian. There never would have been a struggle for the gun in the street.

And yet, even though the variables had changed, *nothing* had changed.

The options on the test remained the same.

And it couldn't be left blank. I had to choose which way I was going to go. And only I could decide the answer.

I couldn't cheat. Couldn't try to outmaneuver the universe. Couldn't control the test by creating an option C that never really existed. There were only ever two options.

Everything crystallized at once. I knew what was about to happen before I heard it. I knew it in every fiber of my being.

And surprisingly, incredibly, a sense of peace reverberated through every cell of my body. There was no fear. No anger. No regret. I put my fate completely in the hands of the universe.

The amazing thing about relinquishing control is the freedom it brings. I used to think that freedom meant having a strong hold on the reigns. My hold had been so strong that my hands had cramped. I had always planned out everything for myself. I had followed only the paths with a clear and certain destination ahead. Where I could control the outcome.

Then I started to see things that weren't there. And I couldn't control it.

And I met Jez—amazing, endearing, surprising Jeremy. I realized that taking a leap of faith with him was more exciting and more frightening and more wonderful than anything I'd ever known.

I had finally summoned the courage to shift the direction of my career despite years of careful planning. If my visions had taught me anything, it was that we never knew what lay ahead; sometimes the most challenging and frightening things were also the most rewarding. They helped us achieve our purpose.

And I knew now what my purpose was. I knew now what I had to do.

I leapt.

The second shot rang out but I was already in the air, already in position to block the young girl.

My last thought was that I did indeed keep my promise. I never went inside the bank. I hoped Jeremy would understand.

I felt the burning sensation of the bullet entering my flesh. Then everything went black.

36

THE OTHER SIDE

WHEN I OPENED MY EYES, I was no longer on the pavement.

I was lying in a meadow.

I had no idea how I'd gotten there, but I wasn't afraid. A sense of peace enshrouded me; I felt like my entire being was filled with light and love and serenity. I felt like I was home, like this was where I was always meant to be. Nothing could hurt me, nothing could take away the pure, unfiltered joy that warmed my soul.

"Hello, Isabel," a familiar voice greeted.

I looked up towards my visitor. He was bathed in golden light.

I smiled. "Hello, Jonathan."

He knelt beside me and extended his hand to me. "I've been waiting for you."

Taking his hand, I sat up and tilted my head back, letting the warm sunlight dance across my skin.

He seated himself beside me on the soft grass, the most brilliant shade of green it almost glowed. The air was scented with the fragrance of freshly cut grass. The undulating hills surrounding us were bursting with color, boasting a thousand different flowers in full bloom. I felt a light breeze on my skin, and it felt like a caress.

"How are you?" It was a silly question, I realized. I knew that in a place like this there was nothing but pure love and happiness, a weightlessness unencumbered by problems or worries or fears.

"That's true." Jonathan smiled warmly at me and I was surprised that he could sense my thoughts.

I should've been asking him a million questions about what happened, panicked about having obviously left everything behind and crossed over to the other side. But it felt like time didn't exist here. There was no rush to do anything but enjoy the present moment. And it was impossible to feel panicked when you were tapping into the bright, all-encompassing purity of love.

We sat together quietly for a few moments, content to just sit in each other's company. I thought back to the last time we spoke, and then remembered I wasn't completely sure when that was. "Was it you I was talking to when I was hallucinating?" I asked him, glad to finally solve the puzzle.

"Yes."

"I don't remember it."

"Once I understood everything you had done for me, I wanted to thank you and say goodbye. I came to see you, but you weren't ready to accept it yet. The mind is a powerful thing. You blocked it from your memory."

"I saw you making the sand castles, though."

He smiled, undoubtedly recalling the memory. "That's all you needed to see. It was a perfect last day, wouldn't you say?"

I nodded, remembering how happy he looked. "I've missed you."

"I've never been far from you," he assured me.

"I know. You were there for me the whole time. I'm sorry I was angry for a while."

"I understood. You wanted more than guidance, you wanted to be told what to do. But that would have taken away your choice, and it doesn't work that way."

"I see that now. So, did I pass the test? Did I choose correctly?"

"There was no right or wrong answer, Isabel. Each choice we make leads us down a different path. The real question is: Are *you* happy with the choices you made and the path you took?"

I contemplated that for a moment. I'd only had one choice, really. Not because I couldn't have chosen differently, but because any other choice would not have been right—for *me*.

I nodded.

"Then you have your answer."

"I am sorry about Neil, though." A twinge of guilt had always stayed with me, long after the accident.

"You were not responsible for his actions, Isabel. He alone was responsible for them. When we hurt others, eventually it catches up with us. It is inevitable. What we put out, we always get back. Your visions were not about transferring responsibility to you, or holding you accountable for other people's choices."

So what were they? This time I didn't bother to voice the words aloud, I knew he could hear them.

"Look around you," he instructed. "What do you think the universe is really about? What do you think is the true meaning of life?"

I answered without hesitation, without any trace of uncertainty. It was impossible to be here, completely bathed in it, and *not* know the answer.

"Love."

"Exactly. But people seem to lose sight of that, to lose sight of each other. How easy it is for them to disconnect from one another. How do you really make a difference in someone's life? Help them to feel connected.

"You helped the people in the visions you had, including me, not just by avoiding danger but by helping us to connect again. You have a magnetic force that people are drawn to, a light all of your own. The further you deviated from your path, the more you focused on all the wrong things, the more that light started to dim. But as soon as you started experiencing the touch of sight, you started connecting with people again, and your light has shone brightly ever since."

He gave me a moment to absorb the full extent of his words.

Jules had been right. The people I thought I had been saving had really been saving me.

"You made a difference in a lot of people's lives, Isabel. You should feel very honored by that. And it wasn't just the people you tried to protect. The things you did in your everyday life held just as much importance. Simple gestures like smiling at a stranger on the street or having a kind word to share, you'd be surprised by the impact they have."

A soft breeze ruffled my hair, and the scent of jasmine permeated the air. Somewhere in the distance, I heard the soothing sound of a trickling brook. I closed my eyes, allowing my other senses to drink in the beauty of my surrounds, and considered everything that had happened since that very first vision.

"I messed up with Matt, though. For a while, I thought that maybe we were destined to be together, and I put myself in a bad situation," I confessed. There was no point denying it since Jonathan knew anyway, and it felt cleansing to release it.

"You were both guilty of not respecting the parameters of what your relationship should have been, and you were both hurt because of that."

I raised my brow. *Matt was hurt?*

"Yes. He deeply regretted his poor choices. It torments him, still. More than you can imagine. But he learned from it, too. He finally built the courage to speak to his fiancée. They were not together for the right reasons and they needed to be honest with each other. When the time is right, he will be united with the one he is meant to be with. That time is not now. He has his own journey."

My eyes were wide. "They called off the wedding?"

He nodded.

I ran my hand over the soft grass, the blades tickling my skin. So much had happened and I still didn't fully grasp it all. Every thread was tied to another, an intricate maze forming an awe-inspiring tapestry beyond my wildest imagination.

"It is simple, really," Jonathan explained, again sensing my thoughts. "If not for your gift, you would never have reached out to Jeremy, and you both needed each other. Although he is the one who eventually pulled down your wall, it was Matthew who started to slowly tear down the bricks. Matthew was able to see something in you that you hadn't yet seen in yourself, and he proved to you that you could be accepted exactly as you are. He hurt you, but he never deliberately intended to do so, and the pain he caused himself was far greater. Although you don't yet realize it, you saved each other."

I turned this over in my mind, trying to link all of the pieces together. *What about Neil?* I wondered.

"Neil tested you. It is easy to do the right thing when we care about the person we are helping, but it's more difficult when that person is not close to us. It is then that we must decide who we want to be, who we want to become. The choice is a more conscious one.

"But Neil also showed you that everyone has their own journey and you can't control their choices."

Rachel.

"Yes. She had to see for herself. She had to learn.

"Her experience with Neil changed her, just as it changed you, too. You wouldn't be who you are now if not for that experience. You may have made different choices, chosen a different path. In the end, you learned the true value of life. And that is the greatest gift you could have ever been given."

We sat quietly for a few moments drinking in the sun while I reflected on the life I'd led and all of the choices I'd made. I felt so peaceful and yet so energized all at the same time, my spirit was humming.

"It's funny, you know. I feel so alive—more alive than before. It's hard to fully grasp that I'm dead," I mused.

"That's because you're not dead. You're just in a different place.

Life is a circle, we are continually learning and evolving.

"I know that you think a huge sacrifice was asked of you, that you were asked to sacrifice your life. But sometimes when you think you're making the biggest sacrifices, it's really you who is gaining the most.

"All the people you helped, they taught you so much about yourself, about your courage, your strength, your ability to love. They've shown you what's really important, helped to tear down your walls, and taught you things that most people never learn in a lifetime. They taught you to open your heart, and the more you opened it, the more it was filled.

"You haven't sacrificed your life, Isabel. That's something that can never be taken."

The faint echo of another voice gently brushed against my consciousness and Jonathan nodded. Noticing my expression, he answered my unasked question. "You have many guides, Isabel. I was given the privilege of greeting you because Gabriel thought that you might like to see me first."

He stood and extended his hand to me, his beaming smile magnetic. "I have so many wondrous things to show you. But before that, you have one more choice to make."

* * *

My whole body hurt. Even the hairs on my head seemed to ache. Blinding pain seared through my chest; it felt like part of my body was on fire. Sadly, I realized this was what Jonathan had meant by pain. But the words didn't seem to do it justice.

He'd brought me to the hospital. We'd watched on in the

operating room as my heart stopped and the doctors frantically tried to revive me. It was a surreal experience to be looking at your own body lying on an operating table, blood seeping into the cloth beneath it and dripping onto the floor. Oddly, I found myself wanting to comfort the doctors and tell them how to stop the bleeding. Not because it was my body that they were working on, but because I merely wanted to help them and ease their burden.

Jonathan had explained the choice to me. Explained that my body was still alive and I had the choice to return to it. It would be a long and painful recovery process, but the choice was mine to make.

It would sound odd to anyone who had not experienced the pure and unbridled joy of the glorious light I had just felt—still felt—that I did not make my choice instantly.

I felt so at home in that meadow that I didn't want to leave. *This is where my true essence belongs,* I thought. And I'm home.

But then I thought of Jeremy and the promise I'd made him. The idea of leaving him seemed so selfish, so thoughtless.

Jeremy. The thought of him echoed through me.

It was like he pulled me to him. One moment I was in the operating room and the next I was in the waiting room, watching Jeremy pacing so anxiously I thought he'd end up needing a doctor himself. His face revealed such intense fear that I yearned to comfort him, to wrap my arms around him and kiss his forehead. Eventually he slumped into a chair and began sobbing so uncontrollably his breath became ragged.

I'd never seen Jeremy cry before. Even in his darkest hour, I had never seen him like this.

I could sense his thoughts and was surprised to find that the anger I detected was directed inward. Not at the gunman, not at me, but at himself. Rage and guilt blasted through him, transforming his sobs into unrelenting shivers of anguish. He blamed himself. Blamed himself for getting the date wrong. Blamed himself for thinking that I wouldn't do what I did and for not camping outside the bank himself. Blamed himself for letting me out of his sight for even one second. Blamed himself for not protecting me.

He couldn't see that the events that had transpired were not in his control. That they were never meant to *be* in his control. I knew this would haunt him until his last breath. I couldn't bear to see his agonizing pain.

I turned my attention to the mother of the young girl sitting in the corner of the room, absentmindedly running her thumb over her key chain, which contained a photo of her daughter. I could sense traces of guilt—being so relieved it was me in the operating room and not her daughter—but that was overshadowed by the overwhelming sense of gratitude that pooled around her.

I did something good, I whispered to Jonathan.

You did something extraordinary, *Isabel. You didn't just save one girl. You healed a family. Your selfless act has caused a ripple that will help more people than you realize.*

Jonathan's response was more than just words, it was a funnel of clarity. Every single person I'd seen in my visions was somehow tied to me. The girl was connected to me, too, and we had more in common than I'd guessed.

She's important, isn't she?

Yes. Gemma is special—like you.

Jonathan didn't elaborate but I knew what he wasn't saying. She, too, had gifts that would be difficult to understand. She would need to navigate the confusion and uncertainty to find her way. She had the ability to help people. She also had the ability to hurt people. It depended on her choices.

She's so young, I thought.

Yes, but she is strong. Her gifts will develop more fully over time, but they will start to manifest soon, so that she may learn how to manage them slowly. We are never given anything we can't handle, Isabel. You should understand that.

I desperately wanted to help guide this child, offer her the kind of support she would undoubtedly need. If I had struggled as an adult, how much more difficult and confronting would it be for her as she entered her teenage years?

I looked at her grateful mother and wondered if she, too, had had her own experiences, like my own mother.

No, Jonathan responded. *It will be difficult for her to understand.*

Then why . . . ? I didn't finish my question but Jonathan understood what I was asking.

Nothing is by chance, Isabel. This is something you have learned. Just because the mother cannot teach her daughter how to manage her gifts, it does not mean that she does not have a great deal to teach her. She will teach her that it is not her gifts that make her special, just as those without these gifts are no less special than she. And in turn, the daughter will teach her mother about acceptance. They have a tumultuous path ahead, but they will bring each other to where they need to be. Love is stronger than fear, anger and pain.

Yes, I agreed. *Love is stronger than anything.*

I turned my attention back to Jeremy. His fury had subsided and all that was left was the constant stream of tears flowing down his face. I tried to wipe them away, instinctively reaching out my hand. I could almost *feel* him. His eyes widened briefly and he absentmindedly touched his cheek. *I'm here*, I tried to tell him. He wiped his tear-streaked face with the back of his sleeve and reached for my purse. It was the first time I'd noticed it at his feet. The hospital must have found his name on the emergency card and given it to him.

What is he doing? I asked Jonathan.

He's looking for your parents' number in your phone.

Oh.

Oh . . . My parents. I was their only child. This would kill them, too.

He hung up the phone without saying a word.

I turned to Jonathan. *I've made my choice.*

* * *

I was vaguely aware of someone holding my hand. A low groan escaped my lips.

"Isy? Isy?" cried the frantic voice.

I willed my eyelids to open. They felt so heavy.

"Jeremy." I tried to smile. The relief was evident in his bloodshot eyes.

"Oh, thank God," he murmured. He dropped his head into his hands briefly, letting it sink in that the worst appeared to be over. When his eyes met mine again, they were brimming with tears. "How are you feeling?"

"Like I've been shot."

He smiled meekly. "You scared me half to death. Don't ever do that to me again, okay?"

"Where am I?"

Concern flittered across his face. "In hospital."

"I know that. I meant, where?"

Relief immediately washed away his apparent fear that I'd lost some of my marbles. "San Francisco General."

"How long have I been out?"

"A few hours. The worst hours of my entire life. They rushed you into surgery. The doctors said they'd managed to remove the bullet and finally stop the bleeding. It missed your heart by less than an inch and it punctured your lung. It's a miracle you survived, you could've drowned in your own blood. You hit your head pretty hard when you fell and they were concerned about swelling. They told me the first few hours would be critical. I was out of my mind with worry. If I had lost you . . ." He buried his head in his hands again.

I tugged his hand back, squeezing it. The small motion caused a ripple of pain through my chest but I swallowed it down. "It's okay, Jez. Everything is going to be okay now," I reassured him. "Have you eaten anything?"

"You've just woken up after life-threatening surgery—I mean, you nearly *died*—and you're worried about whether I've *eaten*?"

"You look pale. You probably haven't eaten all day and you've been through a traumatic experience. You need to eat."

"Isy, food is the last thing on my mind right now. I'm not leaving you for one second." He gave me his and-that's-final look, before his features transmuted into suspicion. "Why are you so calm? Do you remember what happened?"

"As strange as it may sound—although with me, you're certainly used to that—I feel more peaceful than I have in a long time, I think than I ever have." I paused a moment while I debated whether or not I should drop anything on him just yet.

He raised his eyebrows at me.

"I—I saw Jonathan," I stammered.

His eyes widened.

"I'll tell you all about it later. But he opened my eyes and I finally understand everything. And Jez, it was so amazing, so beautiful, beyond my wildest dreams."

His hand tightened around mine, like he was afraid I'd disappear.

"I'm not going to worry about anything anymore. Not everything has to be planned out. I'm going to try to appreciate each day and enjoy each moment. Each moment with you."

This time when he smiled, it reached his warm eyes.

I had no idea what was in store for me. I was finally prepared to willingly venture into the unknown—and allow myself to appreciate the beauty of the journey, rather than solely focus on the destination—and welcome a fate so miraculous and surprising, I could never have planned it.

"I love you, Isy. So, so much."

"I love you, too, Jez. I'm so sorry that you had to go through that," I apologized, remembering all too vividly the tsunami of pain and fear he'd endured.

"Just promise me that you'll never do that again. No more heroics. My heart can't take it."

"I don't know what life has in store for us, Jez. But I can

promise you one thing: No matter what happens, I'll always come back to you. You're stuck with me forever."

"I'm counting on it." Jeremy caressed my hand with his thumb and brushed something on my wrist. I looked down to discover that I was wearing the bracelet I'd made, and he explained, "I put it back on you, I don't know, for luck or something."

I smiled and then realized I'd forgotten to ask about my parents. "Why didn't you speak with my parents when you called?" I inquired.

"Because it went straight to voicemail—" he started to reply, before his jaw dropped and he looked at me curiously. "How did you— How did you know that?"

"Because I was there with you," I told him, knowing it would probably unnerve him a little.

"When . . . when I felt . . . my cheek . . ."

"Yup. Kinda cool, huh?"

He didn't appear to appreciate the cool factor as much as I did. "The doc said he gave you CPR before the ambulance arrived and he drained the blood from your lung. I didn't want to believe that your heart could've stopped. Now to learn that your spirit could've moved on, that you really were that close to—" He couldn't bring himself to say the *D* word. "That close to leaving me . . ."

I didn't understand why he was so agitated. He'd known how seriously I'd been injured. "Don't you see, Jeremy, that I could never leave you? You've given me so much love, and I never really knew what that was until I met you. You are my little slice of Heaven, and I intend to grow very, very old with you before we go there together someday."

He let my words settle over him for a moment, unclenching his jaw before the corner of his mouth turned up in that sexy grin I'd missed. "We better be talking geriatrics kind of old."

I chuckled and it vibrated through my head, which felt like someone had recently taken a sledgehammer to it. I closed my eyes briefly, trying not to let the pain show on my face. "So old we'll be putting our teeth in a jar."

"Mmm, I'm looking forward to drinking my food," he murmured, licking his lips.

"Speaking of which, I'm thirsty. Would you mind fetching me some water?"

"Of course, I'll be right back," he said, standing. "I need to let the nurses know you're awake, too. You just missed the doc. He was waiting here with me until he got called away." He cocked his head to the side, as if just remembering something. "He said he knew you. I was too freaked out to bother to ask how."

A shiver ran up my spine. I knew the answer without asking. "What was his name?"

"Ah, Austin, I think. They said if he hadn't arrived when he did, it would've been too late by the time the ambulance got there. He saved your life. Thank God he was there. He's definitely my favorite person in the whole world—after you, of course." He flashed me another lopsided sexy smile and some of the color returned to his cheeks.

I couldn't speak, shock rendering me mute.

Matt had saved me.

His words from an old email came flooding back: *One of these days you may need rescuing yourself, you know. I'm always at your service.*

It was too much to process right now, but I knew Jonathan was right—everything was connected. His words from the meadow replayed in my mind: *You both saved each other.*

I finally understood what he'd meant by that. Our fates had been entwined. If I hadn't helped Matt in Florence, he may not have been there today. Jonathan had meant it in more than just the physical sense, though. We both had things to learn from each other, and we both had left our mark on each other's lives.

I briefly wondered whether to tell Jez but I figured he'd had enough shocks for one day. I'd save that revelation for another time. I could barely wrap my head around it myself.

"Jez," I called after him as he left the room.

"Something else?" he asked, turning back.

"Yeah. Don't come back without getting yourself something to eat. I mean it." This time I gave him my don't-even-try-to-argue-with-me look.

He sighed and disappeared around the corner.

Alone in my room, my thoughts wandered back to Jonathan. I knew he wouldn't be too far away. I was amazed by how much had changed in a few short hours. Just that morning I was a mess of anxiety and doubt, worrying incessantly about the future. And now everything had changed. *I* had changed. Everything that I thought was important had been washed away by a storm, leaving the ground beneath me fertile and lush, ready to sprout more love and happiness than I'd ever known.

I absent-mindedly fiddled with my bracelet as I remembered my time with Jules in Florence, and the constant need I had to try to turn every element of my life into a neat piece that would all fit together as planned.

Although I didn't know exactly what lay ahead, I finally knew what the image on that puzzle box was supposed to be: a blank canvas. A blank canvas of endless possibilities.

Jonathan's words echoed in my mind and wrapped around me like a warm blanket. *You did something extraordinary, Isabel.* The only thing I knew for sure was that there was a young girl who would need my help. Possibly soon. I felt a responsibility to be there for her when that day came.

I knew I wouldn't be alone. I would never be alone.

Jeremy returned a few minutes later with water and a couple of muesli bars he must have liberated from the nearest vending machine. He wasn't gone long enough to go anywhere else.

"Happy?" he asked as he jiggled his purchases in the air. He gave me the water, which I gratefully drank before he sat down and took my hand again. His hand was so warm, so strong, I never wanted to let it go.

"More than words can say," I replied.

And I was. As long as I had Jeremy, I could weather any storm. I welcomed whatever lay ahead, content to enjoy every moment with him.

He smiled and gently pressed his soft lips to mine.

I was home.

NEXT BOOK IN THE GIFTED SERIES

DANGEROUS GAMES

Being gifted can be dangerous when the wrong people discover your secret.

Isabel learned that the young girl she saved was 'special,' and destined to manifest her own gifts. Isabel will soon discover how Gemma's gifts will impact all those around her, and delve her into a world more dangerous than she imagined. When Gemma goes missing, Isabel must race against the clock to find her—before someone else does.

For more information, please visit:
www.LauraAnile.com

OTHER WORKS

UNMASKED SECRETS

How BIG is your secret?

Each story in the anthology reveals characters hiding a secret with devastating consequences.

Will their secret be uncovered before it's too late?

Will the secrets destroy them, or can they be saved?

Unmasked Secrets (Anthology) is available as a free ebook as a gift to readers.

OTHER WORKS

TIME SHIFTERS
Book One: Beyond Time

When you wake up in the wrong body within a futuristic world, being yourself can get you killed.

Seventeen-year-old Ryder is hiding a secret... He's not who he says he is. After waking up in a futuristic world, trapped in a body that isn't his, he is forced to conceal his true identity. Now his life depends on him being able to convince everyone that he is Ziron, the boy that swapped places with him. He is involuntarily pulled into a battle that isn't his fight, and his only refuge is a guy who can't stand him. If that wasn't bad enough, he feels an undeniable pull towards a girl who refuses to stay away. But how can he be with her when she thinks he's someone else?

To view the *Time Shifters* book trailers, please go to:
www.LauraAnile.com

OTHER WORKS

LET'S GO, FABIO!

(Florence)

Join Rosalie and Fabio on an adventure to Florence!

With the story in both **English and Italian**, readers will immerse themselves in Italian culture. Translations are provided for both beginners and advanced levels of comprehension.

Comprising photographs of Florence, this children's book appeals to young and old.

ACKNOWLEDGMENTS

First of all, I have to thank my wonderful family for their endless support and enthusiasm. They are, without a doubt, the greatest blessing I could ever receive. And without them, this book may never have been published. Thank you for listening to my endless chatter about the characters, and discussing them like they are real people. You rock! Much love.

To my review team: Sylvia Pastore, for your enthusiasm for the story and willingly sacrificing your time. And thank you to Adam Mannix, who confirmed my sentiments about where the weak spots were in the first draft. I appreciated your constructive criticism. Having the opportunity to discuss the story and bounce ideas was invaluable.

I would also like to extend my sincerest appreciation to Bronwyn Murphy, gorgeous cover model, PR agent and all round supporter, and Sean Quinn, IT guru, who both continue to go the extra mile without being asked. Without your incredible generosity, this journey would have been a lot more arduous. Big hugs to you both. And a special mention for Dan Mangan, cover model!

A shout-out to fellow authors, Danielle Bannister and Darrell Pitt, who generously offer support during the journey down the rabbit hole. I am thankful to know you both and share this experience with you. Check out their books!

Finally, thank you to all of the readers who take a chance on a new author. Thank you for affording me the privilege of entertaining you. I hope you've enjoyed Isabel's story, and will continue to take this amazing journey with me.

Laura has had a lifelong love of writing, which she explored in a successful marketing career before penning her first novel. She is fascinated by the ideas of fate and interconnectedness, central themes in her story. She loves all things humorous, laughs too loudly and finds her own jokes amusing. She has a passion for traveling and exploring the world but has a phobia of suspect hotel rooms with questionable hygiene. And, oh yeah, she isn't clairvoyant and doesn't own any crystal balls.

Visions is her debut novel. She has also written *Time Shifters*, a YA dystopian series; a children's book, *Let's Go, Fabio! (Florence)*, written in both English and Italian; and a collection of short stories, entitled *Unmasked Secrets*, which is available as an ebook.

For more information about her books, please visit:
www.LauraAnile.com

You can also connect with Laura via:
Facebook Page: Laura N. Anile, Author
Twitter: @LauraAnile
YouTube Channel: www.youtube.com/laurananile

www.ingramcontent.com/pod-product-compliance
Lightning Source LLC
La Vergne TN
LVHW050912080826
845145LV00001B/65